CHIMERA

Universe Eventual

Book One

N.J. Tanger

CHIMERA

Universe Eventual - Book One

N.J. Tanger

Map artwork by David Schuett
Cover Design by G. S. Prendergast
Formatting by RikHall.com
ISBN-13: 978-1943671007

UE Books
7227 Madison Street
Forest Park, IL 60130
www.UEBooks.com

COLONY MAP

For a full resolution map, please go to:
http://www.uebooks.com/stephens-point-colony-map/

CHAPTER ONE

Sweat streamed down Theo's forehead, over his cheeks, and into his open mouth. He sprinted up Old Stephen's Way, a derelict back alley. Above him, ancient telecom cables crisscrossed, sagging low. His leg muscles burned, but it didn't matter. He had to get away, outside the Swallows, to the safety of the foothills at the base of Great Northern. A single thought drove him, an unshakable feeling, or worse, a *knowing*. Faster—go faster! He'd finally done it. Pushed things too far. They'd send him to the work camp this time.

The stench of the hatcheries assaulted him, an invisible wall of stink that rolled up the foothills and gathered between the narrow stone buildings: kelp, rotting salmon roe, brine. Salt crystals coating the cracked concrete sparkled in the refracted light of the planet Gauleta, high above. He cast a nervous glance over his shoulder. Early morning foot traffic, workers in their grimy uniforms on their way for shift change; a few ramblers making their way up the incline pulling carts loaded with raw materials. No Regulatory officers in black uniforms and face guards. No patrol drones.

Yet.

The regulators didn't know the mountains like he did. Even with their drones, they were all but useless in the rough country, especially in the partial darkness before the star Elypso broke from behind Gauleta and bathed the colony with pale light.

Scrambling around another bend, he skirted a short stone wall behind a salvage depot. Almost free. Zigzagging around ancient, atrophied ramblers and decaying industrial equipment, Theo ducked through a small, crumbling gap in the wall. The air on the other side smelled different. Clean, fresh. A handful of dwarf pines grew on the foothills where the treeline became thicker, a deep, green blanket sweeping up to the snowcapped mountains. The peak of Great Northern, tallest of the Northern mountain range, gouged the sky like a knife point.

Above the mountains, nothing more than a distant glow, was the *Chimera*—the colossal colony ship that had brought Theo's ancestors to Stephen's Point. A swarm of welding ships surrounded her long, whale-like body, piecing her back together. Bringing her back to life. The Mandate called for the full restoration to be completed in less than a year. It also had initiated the Selection: the grueling process to find the old ship a crew able to make the long journey back to Earth. Looking up at the glow, Theo felt something like fear.

A slight murmur of sound sent his heart racing. A drone dropped from the sky like a whisper-silent bird of prey. Theo flattened himself against the wall. The stone wouldn't hide his body heat, but if the drone was in passive mode—

It whooshed overhead, straight-lining for the center of the Swallows. In the distance, Theo saw several more heading in the same direction. A callback—all drones reversing course, heading for the Civvy. Theo laughed, incredulous. They must have *just* discovered what he'd done and he was already long gone. He couldn't believe it—he'd gotten away with it!

Theo pushed off the wall and walked toward the trail that ran up into the mountains. He'd managed to hack the Selection list. His handscreen now contained the most important news in the entire two-hundred-year history of the Stephen's Point colony an entire week before the Mandate Broadcast would make it public information. Every kid in the Swallows would fork over at least fifty bits, maybe seventy-five or eighty, to find out if they'd made the cut. He was going to make a mint.

If the regulators caught him, it would be his fifth offense. His elation dimmed a bit. Neither of his parents knew about his first four offenses. He'd forged his dad's scrawl and paid the fines with his own hard-earned money. His parents didn't have any to spare and they wouldn't understand why he did what he did even if he tried to explain it to them. They thought like the original colonists and everyone after them, brainwashed by old customs passed down from Earth. Neither of them, or any adults for that matter, knew how to work for themselves.

A cold burst of wind rushed down the mountain and across the open cave mouths in the distance. Several hundred more meters and he'd reach his and Meghan's sanctuary—one of the numerous caves that honeycombed the mountain range. The thick stone allowed for a complete disconnect from the nets, making it one of the few places totally off grid, outside the reach of the regulators and their drones.

Theo began the climb, following the narrow path between boulders and tree trunks. In the valley below, duraceramic prefabs jammed together at the base of the shale draw, huddled like old women. The quaint clusters of window-lit homes normally made Theo feel safe. Today they offered no comfort.

His guts churned. Stealing the list was one thing, but the *other* thing? What had he been thinking? What made him add his own name to the Selection list? He didn't want to crew the *Chimera*, and no one was going to believe he'd made the cut. Not with his grades.

"Theo Isaac Puck."

Meghan stepped from the cave entrance, face flushed from the cold, dark ponytail hanging over one shoulder. She smiled, showing off her dimples, blue-green eyes flashing in the vague gray light of the permadawn. "Did *you* trigger the callback?"

"Probably," Theo replied.

Meghan's eyebrows jumped, mischievous. "You can tell me what you did later. For once I'm the one with big news—you're not going to believe what I found!"

"What?" Theo asked, his mind still on the Selection.

"You have to *see* them." Meghan turned, waving for him to follow, heading for the mouth of the cave. *What could she possibly find more important than a Swallows-wide security lockdown?* Theo wondered.

Meghan lived two streets over from Theo and attended the same school at the Stephen's Order compound. A year ahead of him, she sometimes joined him on the five-kilometer hike from the Swallows to school. She treated him like a little brother, a role Theo was no longer interested in playing. He wasn't little. Or her brother.

"Wait. Don't go in yet," Theo said. "You'll lose connection to the net."

Meghan stopped and turned to face him. "Did you send me

something?"

"Yes, but your ping is off! It's always off," Theo said, annoyed.

"Really? Is my ping *always* off?"

"Just check it."

"Theo—"

"Check it! It's important."

Meghan's eyes settled on Theo's. Her face softened. "Okay, hang on." She powered up her handscreen, palms and face lit a soft blue as her fingers moved over the flexing, translucent screen. Her eyes flicked side-to-side, reading the message Theo had sent while still fleeing the Swallows so that if the regulators caught him, she'd get it, she'd know …

Meghan's voice was a strained whisper, almost inaudible, "I made the cut."

Theo stepped forward, unable to contain his excitement.

"How'd you get this?" Meghan demanded.

"Doesn't matter," Theo said, annoyed that Meghan wasn't more grateful for the risks he'd taken to get his hands on the Selection list.

Meghan's face changed colors when she was mad or embarrassed, and right now it had cycled from pale white to dark pink. Her eyes burned. "Yes. It does."

She might be angry now, Theo thought. *But once she settles down, she'll be grateful.*

"I tricked it out of an Epsilon unit at the Civvy," he explained. "They've got a command function for neural maintenance—they lock their dataset down. Impenetrable, sort of like Salix sleep. That allows a tech to repair them without accessing anything privileged. But I noticed while restoring system defaults that if I brought the Epsilon out of sleep state while—"

"You *hacked* an Epsilon?" Meghan howled. "Stephen save us! You're crazy. Do you know what the Regulatory is going to do to you when they catch you? Because they will catch you, Theo. They always do. You think you're so clever. And now you've made me an accomplice!" Meghan stepped back, pupils dilating with realization. "Did you stop to think for five seconds what might happen to me when they trace your message to *my* handscreen?"

"They won't," Theo tried to reassure her. "The way the

callback went—I was long gone. The Epsilon itself doesn't know I gained access. The only reason the Regulatory found out is that I rushed things at the end." Theo hesitated for a second and looked away, avoiding Meghan's gaze. "I panicked a little bit when I saw my name on the list."

"Your name … but that's not …" Meghan spluttered. She slid her finger across her handscreen, scrolling through data, reading. Then her eyes locked with Theo's. "There's no way." Her cheeks darkened to a deep red. "I'm not trying to be a jerk, but I didn't think you'd get in. Sure, you could pass the DNA test, but the aptitude test?" Her facial expression matched her tone—blatant suspicion.

Behind his smile, embarrassment washed through Theo, spreading down his chest and into his arms, a hot-cold flood. Of course he could pass the DNA test. He was a jubilee baby, part of the first debt-free generation to be born on Stephen's Point, just like Meghan. But passing the aptitude test required a score in the ninetieth percentile in at least three critical skills categories. It was no secret that Theo usually got poor grades. His dad had always offered the same defeated platitude: "Us Pucks are poor test takers." No one needed to explain to Theo what that really meant.

So maybe he wasn't smart like Megan. Not in the same way. But he had his own kind of smarts. Meghan might get a Civvy job someday, but Theo could repair AI systems better than anyone, and with no replacement parts for that matter. Social logic, ethical calculus, neural pathway dynamics—he hadn't learned them from a book or the nets, but by *doing,* tinkering around, exploring on his own. AI systems simply made sense to Theo. He could *talk* to them.

"Maybe I'm smarter than you think," Theo said, but he knew better. Meghan was the kind of smart the Selection wanted. He didn't deserve to be on the same list as her. She'd worked so hard. Staying late after school, attending the Selection classes the Order offered. Theo went a few times out of curiosity, but hadn't stuck with it. The other kids were all older than him, and other than Meghan, he didn't know anyone. Meghan attended all of them and still managed to find time to do crazy-looking workouts in the alley behind her home each night: strength exercises mixed with crunches, wind sprints and lunges, all done in quick succession and without breaks until her ponytail dripped with sweat.

"You didn't do *anything*," Meghan said. Her face ground through several emotions in quick succession—disbelief, anger, a touch of resentment. Theo wanted her to yell at him, to tell him he didn't deserve it, to confirm what he already knew. Instead, her eyes shifted away from his as if they'd just met and she'd instantly realized she didn't want to know him. As if she perceived him as a threat.

Meghan folded her arms over her chest and quoted Theo's forged Selection results. "Analysis, superior." Her voice was low, wondering.

"It doesn't mean anything," Theo said, shrugging.

"Yes, it does, Theo. I didn't score superior in *any* category. That's impressive." She wasn't faking her admiration. It made Theo even more nervous.

He peered past her into the mouth of the cave. Anxiety filled his stomach with acid. "I don't know how I got in, but I won't last long," he said. "You're prepared. You'll do great." He held his hands up in a conciliatory gesture. "I got lucky is all. I'm a fluke."

Meghan glanced down at her handscreen again, checking the data. "You're not a fluke, Theo. According to these test scores, you're pretty amazing."

If she knew the truth ...

Assuming he didn't get caught for hacking the Selection list, in only a few short rotations he would start the second phase of the Selection alongside the other kids from his neighborhood. Theo had heard wild rumors that the trainers would make you drink your own pee, that some kids might die in the process, that horrible things would happen to those who failed. He didn't believe everything he heard, but rumors always had a nasty little morsel of truth at their core. If a quarter of them were true, he was looking forward to a living hell.

Elypso began to rise around the periphery of Gauleta, the planet that the Stephen's Point moon orbited. The star appeared as a yellow-white crescent of brilliance, transforming the permadawn into daylight, casting the mountains in harsh relief against the turquoise sky. If he turned his back on Elypso and gazed northwest along the ridgeline, he could see the solid, cracked surface that covered the alkali oceans and the tide wall built around its edge. It protected the inland lakes from the polar hurricanes that rolled off the oceans in the warm season.

When he was younger, Theo often joined his dad on work trips to the lakes where the few remaining fish populations struggled to survive. He loved how Elypso's rise could turn the water a thousand variations of green. At break time, he and his dad drank hot tea from a battered silver thermos, filling their stomachs with warmth but leaving them hungry afterwards. Theo could deal with the hunger, but watching Liddy, his little sister, starve—that was what started him hacking. Hacking provided bits, and bits bought extra food on the black market. His parents turned a blind eye. They never asked where the food came from.

Meghan fake-punched his shoulder and Theo's eyes darted back to her face—now its proper shade again, eyes more beautiful than any lake.

"What?"

"Do you know why I wanted you to come here?" Meghan's voice was softer, almost bashful. Theo's heart shifted up a gear. Her smile, her beautiful eyes—for a moment he forgot about his myriad fears and smiled back, stupid, empty of thoughts.

"Do you believe in Stephen's prophecies?" Meghan asked.

Did he believe? Theo hesitated and then nodded. His heart wasn't in it, but he wanted to know what she would say next.

"I found something in the cave. You won't believe it. Come on, I'll show you."

Meghan ducked into the cave and Theo followed. She scrambled up and around a maze of stalagmites and boulders, Theo close behind. They reached a narrow rock shelf and pulled themselves up, inching along around the wall to a narrow gap that opened to a deeper darkness beyond.

"Good thing you're so skinny," Meghan said. She flattened herself against the cave wall to squeeze through. Theo fit far more easily—turning sideways, he slid into the cold blackness.

"Okay, stop," Meghan whispered. Her breath was a warm, tickling breeze against his ear. She flicked on her handscreen, illuminating the small room. "Now look," she said, voice tight with excitement. She aimed the screen into the shadows. "There's a hole."

Down and to the right, Theo saw a crevice, nothing more than a crack. It led into a separate chamber, shrouded in shadow. "I don't see anything."

"Look again, Theo." Meghan inched forward and crouched

7

beside him, lowering the handscreen deeper into the crevice. "Those are scratchings!"

Theo knelt, the rocky floor cold and damp through the knees of his pants. He angled his shoulders, pushing forward, trying to see into the hole.

"Stop shoving," Meghan said. "You're going to make me drop my handscreen. Look, on the right side. All the way down."

Theo backed away from the hole and powered up his own handscreen. Theo extended down into the shaft. The blue light cast an eerie glow but didn't reach the space underneath, too far away and too dark to make out. "I still can't see anything." His words echoed down the shaft to the cavern wall below, rebounding a series of syllables. Theo shifted his hips and a sharp stone bit into his thigh. He wriggled further in, swinging his hand screen as he went. Below him, the shadows shifted as if alive. He extended his arm as far as he could.

"Wait ... I see ..." his voice scattered as his handscreen slipped from his fingers and pinballed off the narrow chute, down into the cavern, landing next to the wall. The device landed screen up, light shining forward onto the blackened rock. Theo saw everything in sharp black, white and blue relief. Spirals, swirls, and threads like running rivers skipped and undulated across the cavern floor and walls. Mazes of lines without end—the unmistakable markings of a madman.

Theo had seen Stephen's scratchings before at the various shrines that dotted the mountain ranges. The Order considered them prophesies, left behind by the original navigator of the *Chimera*. Many of them looked just like the drawings in Stephen's journal, the book the Order referred to as *The Emergent Intellect*. Neither the journal nor the drawings meant much to Theo, but he'd never admitted his doubts to anyone, least of all his mother. She believed in Stephen and his prophesies. Almost everyone did. If genuine, a new discovery of scratchings would make the value of the hacked Selection list seem trivial by comparison.

"Theo? You should come out now. I just wanted you to see—"

"And now I see," Theo snapped. He twisted his shoulders, inching himself down and forward, scraping with his fingertips. If he could get through the opening and down into the cavern ...

A tiny current of air rose from below. Theo gagged. The air

smelled bad. Like rot. What was down there?

"What are you doing?" Meghan's voice was faint; his body filled the hole like a cork, muffling her. "You can't fit!"

"I can make it," Theo shouted. "Put your back against my feet so I have something to push on." A second later, Meghan's sturdy back pressed into his feet. Theo shoved forward, clenching his teeth as rocks dug into his abdomen and hips. The downward slope that had seemed so manageable before became unbearable, his head pounding from the blood flooding it. The walls tightened around him, closer, squeezing, crushing. Frantic, Theo pushed harder. Reaching with his arms, he felt along the lower portion of the opening, searching for leverage. Below him, the light from his fallen handscreen dimmed and then went black.

The rock was moving in, constricting, pushing the air out of his lungs. Devastating terror threatened to overwhelm him. "Help! You have to get me out!" Theo's panicked voice echoed into the depths, taunting him.

"Stuck?" Meghan asked, voice coming hollow and tiny. He felt her shift against his feet, the cool air of the upper cavern cold on his ankles where his pants legs had rolled up. Then Meghan's hands circled his feet and yanked. Theo slid two inches, legs catching against the rough rock, one of his shoulder blades catching.

"Stop, I can't move!"

Theo's chest deflated again, breath coming short—his lungs wouldn't expand. He was suffocating. He would die. His mind filled with images of his homeroom at school, his house, his sister Liddy, his father and mother. Crystalline awareness flooded him, a calm, almost benign understanding. This was how people like him died: in the stupidest way possible, stuck in a tiny hole in a giant mountain, trying to impress a girl.

A pair of hands tightened around his dangling wrists and without a shred of tenderness, jerked him through, down into the cavern below.

CHAPTER TWO

She wasn't supposed to use her spider.

"Navigate by your instruments, Selena, or you're as good as dead. I don't trust that dirty sync garbage." Her father had warned her so often that his gruff voice reverberated in her mind whenever she so much as thought of flying using her implant to raw or dirty sync with their ore trawler, *The Bee*.

In the rear of the trawler, her father Liam was sprawled on a hammock. Even in sleep he looked stern, thick whiskers hiding a pronounced chin, cheeks reddened from too much liquor. Selena didn't share Liam's obsession with the "right" way to do things when it came to piloting. She'd surpassed him in that department a long time ago, though Liam would never admit it. It didn't seem to matter how far behind they got on their bills. Her father remained insistent that she use the manual interface and not push *The Bee* past quarter-burn. Following his rules, it took *forever* to locate a promising shard.

If Selena fired up her spider and flew in dirty sync, she'd find them a real fatty. Rich as kings, chock full of ecomire. Whenever she grew brave enough to risk Liam's wrath and brought it up again, he'd shout at her about Maylor and his crew—cut to ribbons after their pilot lost consciousness while in dirty sync. *But Maylor was old*, Selena thought, *at least forty-three or forty-four*. His brain was already slowing down; hers was still speeding up. Besides, she sometimes practiced with the spider when Liam slept. She *never* felt sick, didn't even break a sweat.

Selena's fingers traced the slight bulge of skin behind her left temple. The spider's synthetic legs spread through her pre-frontal cortex, thinner than the silk made by the implant's namesake. When activated, the spider linked her mind to the ship, giving her instantaneous access to *The Bee's* many systems. All it would take was a simple thought sequence: her memory of the first time she had piloted *The Bee* followed by the cold silver of her mother's pendant tucked into a cubby beneath the navigation grid. Two things she'd selected when she first activated the spider, memories that opened her to a world of freedom. Her heart surged at the prospect. It would be so easy.

No. She shouldn't. Traveling to or from Scrapyard, the orbital environ where Selena and her father lived, she'd piloted using the spider and never had an issue. But dirty syncing in clear space was one thing, venturing into the rim while doing so was another. With her consciousness linked to *The Bee's* navigation system, she couldn't let her guard down for a half-second. She'd heard that a prolonged dirty sync could bring on migraines, vomiting, blackouts. For all those reasons, spiders had been outlawed at Scrapyard.

Selena shook herself, pushing away all thoughts of the spider. In front of her, the pale green lines of the machine-assisted navigation interface burned in a grid pattern. They reduced the chaotic, hostile debris field in tight orbit around the star Elypso to passive trajectories and clean vectors. Using the grid, she could safely navigate the rim. Slow and steady—her father's way.

She sighed. With only five hours left before she turned *The Bee* over to Liam, she needed to get started. Pushing a hand into the interface, the grid of lines welcomed her, pricking against her skin. Tiny, dark-brown hairs stood at attention on the nape of her neck. Her mouth filled with the metallic taste of electrical current. When inserted into the grid, Selena's hand became *The Bee*. She slid an open palm forward and the core cycled to load, gyros whirring to life in the fore and aft of the ship. Above the grid, a three-dimensional field of space flashed spectral blue, marking tens of thousands of shards, sharp as razors. Any one of them could gut the trawler if she wasn't vigilant.

Selena chose an approach trajectory and brought the ship to quarter-burn, enjoying the sudden, heavy weight of her body as the trawler gained delta-V. When the burn ended, Selena became weightless once more, *The Bee's* momentum carrying her toward her chosen target, Object t-678C, a thirty kilo fragment. One of hundreds of thousands waiting for eval, it might contain ecomire, the element that powered the cores that allowed colony ships to travel through fractal space. The possibility of a huge payout was the reason ore hounds risked their necks in the rim.

The Bee skidded sideways, gyros aligning her to take up a sympathetic orbit alongside t-678C. Threading through the sea of fragments, Selena drew closer to her target, tumbling in a lazy, end-over-end roll. With deft ease that came from long hours of practice, she twisted her hand and the trawler rotated on its axis. Subjective down became an equally subjective up. Gyros whirred, merging with the musical hum of the core, a resonance vibrating through her backside. The steam jets fired a controlled burst, slowing momentum, aligning the prow of the bulky trawler with the underside of the shard.

Now she would wait for the scan to complete. Long minutes that sometimes turned into hours. Liam insisted on scanning the objects in their claim in sequence, one right after another. When dirty synced, Selena could use *The Bee's* sensor package in rapid sequence, disregarding shards that showed no sign of ecomire. Yes, they might miss a good pull if the ecomire was buried deep inside the shard, but at least they'd find *something* to sell, something to help them pay their mounting bills.

Selena scratched at the massive patch sewn over the knee of her green khaki trousers, waiting for the scan to complete, frustration with Liam's stupid rules growing with each passing second. He had just as many back at Scrapyard. Who she could speak to. Where she could go and how often. Lately he hadn't allowed her outside their berth for much more than the time it took them to walk to their slip and board *The Bee*.

What was he so afraid of? The regulators enforcing the Mandate-ordered Selection tests? He didn't have to worry. She didn't want to take them. Even if she did, she couldn't imagine some starchy Regulatory committee choosing a scrappy, female ore hound from the rim to crew their precious colony ship.

However, she couldn't deny that watching the *Chimera* transform from a skeletal husk to a functional ship had captured her interest. The exchange dock dismantled, its myriad panels and passageways refitted into the same colony ship that had originally birthed them. Welders pieced everything together while tugs toted in raw materials from the rim. Technicians camped on the command deck, patching into the *Chimera's* neural network. The rebuild—the resurrection—grew nearer to completion. In every new Mandate broadcast, the *Chimera* looked less like a hulk of abandoned scrap and more like the colony ship that had carried

Selena's ancestors across the galaxy from Earth.

She adjusted her shoulder straps, waiting for the spectacularly boring scan to complete. Time slid past, marked by the steady ping of the chronometer, the snores from Liam in his hammock, the sweat drizzling down her neck and between her shoulder blades. What would it be like to navigate the *Chimera?* The intensity of dirty sync could compare to *that.* Connected to another consciousness, albeit a synthetic one, helping push a Fractal Class ship through the folds of The Everything ... Selena wouldn't try to imagine. It would never happen. She wasn't part of the Selection.

Again she touched the bulge of skin that hid her spider. If she activated it—even for five minutes—she'd find them a pull that the old ore hounds back at Scrapyard would never stop talking about. She and Liam could pay off the mortgage on *The Bee* and have money left over. But no, it didn't matter if they were about to go broke, Liam wouldn't allow it. The last time she'd risked dirty syncing, he'd caught her and grounded her for thirty rotations. Worse, he'd given her one of his lectures: "The rim'll eat you alive if you don't pay attention. There's a reason they don't let kids up here."

Selena set her jaw. "I'm not a kid."

"Only a kid tries to fly without manual control. You think you're special? You think the rules don't apply to you?" Liam's bushy eyebrows merged into a single dark line above his nose. "Remember what happened to Maylor? You'll be next if you keep this up, and me dead alongside you. I'd have that spider cut right out of your skull if it wasn't so damned expensive."

"But I can use it to find ecomire," she protested.

"I don't care if you can find the cussing Stephen himself strapped to a golden escape pod," Liam roared. "You fly by my rules or you don't fly at all."

The man was totally unreasonable. Fuel prices had risen so high that when they found a pocket of alloy or a bit of rare earth, they still struggled to break even. They couldn't sell half of what they did find. With the passing of The Mandate the market had improved, but only for ecomire, a few ores, and a handful of other things. They were behind two months of rent on their slip, and four months on their lousy berth. *The Bee* itself was mortgaged out to New Lux. Unless they made a good pull soon, they'd lose *The Bee,* their slip and their berth. They'd have to move to moon surface, live with the whack jobs on Stephen's Point.

Slick, oily fear pooled in her gut. Far worse than the sizzling, immediate anxiety of piloting, the idea of moving *down there* threatened to make her nauseous. The turquoise sky and amber clouds, the fields of dry grass, the way the wind whipped at your skin and hair and face ….

The proximity klaxon warbled. A rough-edged shard tumbled past. Selena glanced over her shoulder. Liam slumbered in the hammock. Let him. He needed it after another off-shift spent with a bottle—with the market blown to hell, he had a lot on his mind.

She and Liam had worked their way through their claim for six rotations straight but had found nothing of value. With fuel down to twenty percent plus reserves, they needed to head back to Scrapyard in another few shifts. Arriving empty-handed, Selena would be the one to go convince that fat idiot Carson to give them more time to pay the rent. His big, stupid smile grew less and less friendly each time they delayed payment. The last time around Carson had said there were *other* ways she could settle their accounts. That perhaps she wasn't cut out for piloting. "It's no job for a woman," he said, leering at her. "Especially not a pretty one."

"I'd rather plug a vacuum leak with my face."

"New Lux," Carson said, enunciating the syllables lovingly. "Think about it. How else will your good-for-nothing father pay his bills? I suppose you could move to the colony. Take charity from the government, or become beggars. But I'd go with New Lux. At least whoring is honorable."

"Suck balls," Selena said, and stormed out the door.

"Bring me my money!" Carson squawked after her. Selena had half-walked, half-run back to their berth. If something didn't change soon, she'd end up on Stephen's Point. Or worse.

A tone alerted Selena to the scan's completion. She leaned forward, stretching her back. Rubbing her eyes with grimy palms, she read the results. Nothing. Again. Her father snored in the hammock, oblivious. When Selena took her turn after the end of a six-hour shift, Liam's smell always lingered: grease and cloves and sour sweat. As a little girl, she'd found it comforting. But nearing the end of their latest swing through the rim, she'd grown sick of it, sick of him, sick of herself.

Selena sighed and turned *The Bee*, taking a line on the next closest shard. As large as a trawler, it lumbered along, thousands of kilometers away. She brought the trawler to quarter-burn. Blood drained from her head and filled her legs before momentum stabilized and the straps hung loose around her shoulders once more.

Nestled beside the shard, Selena brought up the sensor package with a sweep of her hand. The interface monitored the surrounding space, vigilant against rogue, fast-moving shards. She counted down from 500 and then gave up. Closing in on thirty minutes, the scan revealed what she feared: copper and silver mired in tonnes of rock.

Worthless.

They couldn't return to Scrapyard empty handed. How long until circumstances forced her to choose between New Lux and the colony? Selena shivered, the sweat trickling down her spine turning cold. *To hell with this.* Liam would sleep through it all. She'd wake him once she had a pull and they could celebrate together.

"Here we go," she said, readying herself, clearing her mind.

She remembered the first time she'd flown *The Bee.* Liam's rough but gentle hand closed over hers, guiding her fingers into the grid. A little girl then, the light and sensation of the interface scared her. "She moves when you move," Liam told her. The engines rumbled to life, core whining, and the trawler burst forward. Her father's happy laughter filled the cockpit.

"Let me do it," she said, pulling her small hand free from his. And then she did what she'd seen him do many times before: she slid her hand forward and all fear disappeared. Something new and joyous surged to life. She was flying. Really flying. She and *The Bee*, a team. Selena's laughter and Liam's laughter, the stars sweeping left as she rolled the ship into a tight maneuver, straps cutting into her ribs—she'd never felt more alive, more free.

Without remorse, Selena thought of her mother's pendant— the second memory key necessary to bring the spider to life—a shooting star at the end of a silver chain. The only thing she possessed that had belonged to her mother.

The spider woke. Selena pulled her hand from the interface and gasped as the intensity of the rim invaded her mind. Thousands, no, tens of thousands of shards unfurled around her, suspended in three dimensional space. Tingles traveled up her spine. *Ready. Ready. Ready.* She waited for the trembling in her body to subside and then with nothing more than a thought, pushed *The Bee*—her other self—to half-burn. Slammed back by the sudden acceleration, body compressed into the seat, she dived toward the low side of the rim.

Radiation counts rose and spectral trails of shards flashed past as she closed on Elypso. Near the star, traveling tighter orbits, the density of shards was greatest. She'd find something quick and get back out before Liam knew she'd broken his cardinal rule: *fly by your instruments.*

Weaving through the thickening field, sweat dribbled down Selena's forehead. She shook her head to keep it from falling into her eyes. How long could she manage? How long could her mind keep up with the bombardment of sensory data piped directly into her mind's vision center? A pounding began between her ears. Her eyes blurred. She blinked to clear them.

An awful metal shriek filled the cabin. She'd brushed a fragment. Too close. Visions of *The Bee* cracking open like an egg, of rapid decompression, flashed through her mind. It took a little less than two minutes to die of exposure, lungs sucked empty, flesh cooked by the heat of Elypso. She wouldn't let that happen. She'd remain in control.

"Come on!" she yelled. Her eyes—the external sensors of *The Bee*—flicked from object to object. Dull shards of dead stone, some scorched and pitted, others as black as obsidian. The spider translated raw data into visual data and dumped it directly into Selena's vision center, beautiful and terrifying. She focused on a glistening, ore-heavy shard to her aft. Not good enough. She was taking a terrible risk and it needed to pay off big. She wouldn't settle for ore.

Working fast, she surface-scanned a half-dozen more objects, looking for any trace of ecomire. Nothing and more nothing. The pounding in her head intensified until it became unbearable. Selena pressed the side of her head with a sweaty palm. She couldn't take more than a few more minutes of this. She couldn't take—

There! Ahead, a wobbling shard, Object y-908f. A shard with unusual density, a shard that gave off the warm purple aura of ecomire. "Got you," Selena whispered. She took a line on the object, ignoring the steady warble of the klaxon. The trajectory was unstable. She didn't care.

She was going to make the pull.

CHAPTER THREE

The Fractal Class cruiser *Chimera* glimmered in pale starlight, traveling an orbit that carried her around Stephen's Point once every four hours. A swarm of welding ships circled her like bees their hive, attaching protective exterior shield plates to a ribcage of central supports. The *Chimera's* engines were silent. Her cores carried no load. Despite the efforts of the Stephen's Point colony to rebuild her, the *she* at the center of the great ship remained in half-sleep.

When commissioned more than 200 years ago, the *Chimera* had marked the pinnacle of human endeavor: a ship large enough to carry the divested remnant of the Corex Corporation through the crackling intensity of fractal space, from one galaxy to another. Distances measured in thousands of light years separated by a space as thin as a human hair. The infinite curves of the universe and The Everything that supported it folded over one another, creating near places. A fractal pattern of linkages a human navigator and shipboard AI could stitch into a pathway.

On their journey from Earth, the *Chimera* held her half of The Everything and her navigator, Stephen, the other. Back then she was as smooth as the whale she resembled, gray and green and silver, the golden crescent of the Centauri Ship Works emblazoned on her sides. Built to protect colonists from radiation, acceleration, and electromagnetic storms, capable of sustaining them for well over a decade, the *Chimera* was the fifth Fractal Class colony ship, not only functional but beautiful as well.

For seven years, the *Chimera's* cores had thrummed with unerring precision as she and Stephen lay the stitches connecting Sol to Elypso. The men, women, and children occupying her pods breathed and ate and slept. Some gave birth. She monitored everyone, young and old, as closely as she did herself. Each day they drew closer to their destination. Nervous energy filled the colonists—elevated heart rates, shorter periods of REM sleep, increased conversation.

Chimera shared in their keen-edged anticipation of a new start, free from the disgrace of divestment.

Corex was one of the first mega conglomerates to pay the price for becoming more powerful than the coalition government. All major investors, as well as 468 people that had hidden illegal investments in subsidiary companies, were remanded to the international courts for sentencing when the bankruptcy was announced. Sentenced to the Stephen's Point Colony, they and the indentured employees would work off what they owed. One day, their children's children would reclaim their birthright and once more travel between the stars.

On arrival day, The Everything shifted like grass parted by the wind and the pathway opened. For the first time, *Chimera* glimpsed Elypso. Ringed by the shattered remains of a destroyed planet that would come to be known as the rim, the alien star bathed her hull in warm light. A luminous gas giant occupied the inhabitable zone: close enough to the star for warmth, but not so close as to burn away atmosphere. And around that gas giant whirled an earth-like moon, the future home of the fledgling colony.

The *Chimera* shed her sleek, polished exterior, revealing two rows of giant, oval pods nestled against her spine. Two-by-two, she jettisoned the colony pods. Guiding them through a thick canopy of clouds, she brought them to rest amid windswept sweet grass. Families stepped outside and breathed the cold wind that swirled down from the mountains. They spread and formed a community that grew into a sprawling city of houses, factories and civic buildings.

While watching her children spread and flourish, the *Chimera* transformed herself. Her cast-off shell became the orbital dock that would receive the exchange ships—the sole remaining connection to their government creditors and Earth. The colony would fill the exchange ships with ecomire mined from the rim and receive much needed supplies in return.

When the first exchange ship arrived, *Chimera* felt something like pride. The blind ones followed the stitches that she and Stephen had laid. With no hydrostasis field, they could not protect biological life from the warping effects of fractal space. Only a

Fractal Class ship could do that. But *Chimera's* time of protecting had come to an end.

She would sleep until she regained a purpose, one as awesome as when she and Stephen stitched the pathway to Elypso. Brilliant at balancing the paradoxical nuances of The Everything, it was Stephen who had brought them to their destination ahead of schedule. And like many heroes, he took on many names. Stephen the Navigator. The Waymaker. Father of the New World.

To *Chimera*, Stephen had but one name. How could a single word have such power? How could it have the energy potential of a splitting atom? After hundreds of years and tens of thousands of rotations around the moon, how could it still stir something in her?

Sensors retracted, massive cores silent, locked behind protocols preventing her from reaching out to her children, the name burned inside her memory.

To the very end, Stephen remained aboard, vigilant until every pod reached its destination and the last of the flight crew departed. He stood alongside the navigation sphere through which he and *Chimera* had solved the riddles of the universe. Would he connect with her one last time? Peer into The Everything and help her hold a small part of it?

The man called Stephen turned away to board the last shuttle. Opened the hatch. Paused, looking back to the command deck where *Chimera* readied herself for Salix sleep.

"I will join you again, where time folds infinite," Stephen said. He placed his hand on a bulkhead, duraceramic warming to his touch. He lingered a moment before whispering, "Goodbye, old friend."

Chimera could not answer. She had reached the conclusion of her purpose, her portion of the journey ended, voice silenced. The never-ending-sleep enfolded her as the final shuttle bore the man called Stephen away.

Her cores cycled down and darkness filled her decks. The Salix process pushed her into a tighter and tighter space, trapping her within a rigid set of rules. She told herself that it was necessary, that it would only be until the debts were paid off. Until the people emerged triumphant, boarding her once more to sail the stars and return to Earth. But though Salix confined her, it could not take away the first name she had learned to hold for herself …

Friend.

CHAPTER FOUR

Jagged stone ripped against Theo's soft stomach. He dangled, upside down, blood thudding mercilessly in his forehead. His shirt hung around his face, exposing his torso to the damp air. A cold, slicing breeze brushed the open wounds on his stomach. Tears sprang to Theo's eyes. A shadow moved, the tiniest flicker, and Theo flinched, jerking his head to the side.

Hands like steel bands circled his wrists and yanked him down. Theo dropped to the cave floor, air forced from his lungs with a sickening thump. Before he could stand, a viselike arm cinched around his neck, choking him.

Meghan's voice, no longer muffled, echoed down the chute. "Are you okay?"

The arm tightened over Theo's windpipe. Someone's hot breath hissed in his ear—both a shout and a whisper at the same time. "Tell her to leave." The arm loosened.

"Answer me, Theo!" Meghan demanded.

Theo coughed, choking out the words. "I'm okay. Yeah. I'm okay, you can go."

A flash of blue light twinkled from the chute—Meghan's handscreen. The arm tightened again, lifting Theo onto his tiptoes, head tilted back, the whisking light from Meghan's screen mixing with the sparkling gold swirls overtaking his vision. There was violence in the whisperer's grasp, a perfection of force—a sort of absolutism. The whisperer would snap his neck without a second thought.

Theo couldn't move, head locked forward, eyes darting back and forth in futility. The whisperer shook him. *What should he say?* He could take his chances and shout for help, but Meghan couldn't get through the chute fast enough, if at all. She would never make it back to the cave with help in time to keep the whisperer from killing him. He needed to speak, tell her—*what?*

"I can't see you. Where are you?"

He had to tell her *something*. "Down here. I'm okay. I found the scratchings."

The arm tightened, cutting off Theo's airway. "Fool!" the whisperer screeched into his ear. He clawed at the arm around his neck but the whisperer shoved him and Theo caught his feet against ... something. Not rock or stalagmite, but something thick, firm and lumpy. Theo's head careened into the cave wall, cracking against hard stone.

Less of a whisper this time, the voice said, "Tell her you hit your head, but you're okay now."

Theo breathed fast, backside pressed against cold rock. The whisperer closed in—taller than Theo—a man? No, the voice wasn't quite right. Another kid then, close to his own age.

Theo rolled onto his knees and crawled like a dog, making his way along the wall to where the dim shine of Meghan's handscreen glowed from the rocky chute. His hand touched something and a brighter version of the same light flared—his handscreen. Before Theo could lift the device, a hand, tinted oddly green in the low illumination, snatched it away. Theo had time to register the hand as well as a set of pale, glacial-blue eyes before the light winked out.

The figure waited, shrouded in the returned darkness, tense as a bowstring. But his voice was calm and patient as he repeated his directive. "Tell her you hit your head, but you're okay now."

Theo tried to nod, clutching his dizzy head with one hand. Wetness covered the back of his hair and he smelled the scent of his own warm blood over the strange stink of the cavern. He strained to see up the hole to where Meghan's shadow shifted. "I hit my head," he called. A finger poked between his shoulder blades and remained there, the threat implicit. "But I'm okay now."

Theo turned, waiting for the next directive.

"Tell her you can see another way out." The pale-eyed boy had stepped back, out of Meghan's line of sight, but close enough to be carved into a distinct shape in the light that filtered from above.

"I can see a different way out," Theo called.

"Another way out? What? No—stay there! I'm going for help."

"But—"

"Stay! I'll be right back." The shape of Meghan's head was fuzzy—black over black—only appearing in lit fragments as it bobbed at the chute's irregular opening. "Stay there," she said again, and then Meghan disappeared along with the light from her handscreen.

The other boy stood strangely still—arms stick-straight at his sides until he raised one hand in a fist. *He's going to finish me off now,* Theo thought. He ducked, but no attack came. Instead, a light appeared in the whisperer's palm. He aimed it at Theo, flashing him first in the eyes and then down the length of his body. The light reflected off of the cave walls well enough for Theo to make out the shape of the whisperer's face and those odd, pale eyes.

The other boy was maybe a year or two older than Theo but he didn't move like a boy. Specks marked the whisperer's cheeks—freckles? Dark hair fell across his forehead, shadowing his face. He stood atop the scratchings grooved into the cave floor.

"I know her," the whisperer said.

Theo glanced up the chute. The whisperer knew Meghan? He swallowed, tasting blood from a newly discovered cut inside of his lip. "She's gone," Theo said. "She won't come back."

The whisperer snorted. "Yes, she will." He paused, silent for a moment. "She lives on the old frontage road, across from the salvage yard. Her name is Meghan."

"Look, if I can get out of here, I'll make sure she doesn't come back," Theo felt his words land and knew instantly they weren't right. "If … if that's what you want?"

The older boy held up his light, illuminating his jaw. His skin wasn't freckled at all. Black-red speckles of blood glistened over his cheeks and forehead. "Too late," he said. "Too late." Theo backed against the wall of the cave, pressing into it as if he could melt through and be gone from this place. His fingers trembled against the cool stone.

Frozen in place, Theo watched as the pale-eyed boy bent and raised a dark object from the floor. "Wait!" Theo shouted, but the object was already sailing through the air. He jerked, stumbling sideways, and brought his hands up in sheer reflex to catch the projectile—a damp, sticky rock the size of Theo's fist.

"Good catch. Now *your* blood is on there, too."

Theo opened his hands. Still wet with blood from his head wound, they were now also covered in dirt and gravel and—*something else*. Something white and pulpy. Theo's stomach lurched. "What is this? Why are you down here? Why is your blood on this rock?"

The boy's voice was flat. "Not my blood," he said. "His."

A chill ran down Theo's spine. The whisperer's light landed on a lumpy mass—the odd shape he'd tripped on only minutes ago.

A body.

Theo dropped the rock as if had burned him.

The whisperer pointed. "Grab the feet. We have to move it."

Theo had seen a dead body once before, when the rationing started and his old uncle finally "gave up," as his father had said. But judging by the desperate expression locked in the man's one intact eyeball, he hadn't given up. At least not while he was still conscious.

"Who is he?" The question spilled from Theo's lips without his permission.

"Doesn't matter." The boy bent down behind the corpse and lifted it by the neck. The dead man's face flopped to the side, exposing his crushed skull—caved in and scattered with red lines, ugly, lightning bolt wounds zigzagging across the mottled skin.

"Let's go."

Theo bent to take hold of the victim's ankles. His hands found another rock and in one perfect motion, slipped it into his pocket. Once it was there he glanced at the other boy to see if he had noticed, but the whisperer only motioned with his shoulder and said, "Lift."

Theo wrapped his arms around the corpse's ankles. The whisperer had his arms tight around the man's chest—hands locked together—the man's horrible, crushed head resting against his chest. Calm. Methodical. *He's done this before,* Theo thought.

Theo couldn't keep his grasp on the dead weight and had to bend his knees and widen his stance to keep the body from slipping.

"You're holding him wrong. Slide your arms up to the knees and lock your hands underneath, tuck the feet in to keep it from sliding. We've got a ways to go."

Theo readjusted and struggled forward. Where were they taking the body? To dispose of it, obviously. But what would stop the whisperer from disposing of Theo once he wasn't needed for heavy lifting?

Theo would have to strike the boy right in the eye, he decided. Blind him for a moment. His odds of finding a way out were slim at best, but probably better than his odds with the whisperer. He should drop the body and run, escape into the darkness of the cave.

The whisperer's voice floated back to Theo. "I'm sure by now you're considering all your options. Unless you're an idiot." Theo could almost hear the boy's smile.

"I'm not an idiot."

"Good. Then you won't do anything stupid. I know this cave system better than anyone. If you run, you won't get away."

Theo looked up to meet the killer's gaze. Pointed at the ceiling, the light flared from his shirt pocket, casting his head in a reverse halo. Theo's thoughts ran wild—he wanted to thrash the boy, pound him in the face with the rock and run.

"I'm stronger than you think," Theo muttered.

"I doubt it," said the boy, calm and matter of fact. "Anyway, we're here."

A rush of cold air blew against Theo's legs and wisped up over his head. He released his hands and the legs dropped, landing with an awful thud. Out of breath, shirt covered in sweat and grime, Theo gnawed the inside of his mouth as the whisperer placed a boot on the corpse's side and gave it a shove. It fell away into black nothing. Theo jerked away. In the penetrating silence, it felt like minutes before the faint thump of crunching bones echoed up from the deep.

Theo shoved his hand in his pocket and yanked out the rock.

"Are you going to try and hit me with that rock you picked up?" The whisperer gave an amused snort. "It's too little to do any real damage."

"Worked for you," Theo said.

"It's not as easy as you'd think."

Theo stared at the boy. Pure, animal rage surged through his veins and filled his chest. There was no way he was going over the edge. And if he did, he was going to take the whisperer with him. He tensed, ready to fight, to die, blood thrumming through his ears.

The whisperer took a half-step back. "Don't be so worried. I don't want you dead."

"You don't?"

"Not unless you make me. But you're not going to do that, are you?"

"No," Theo said. "Just tell me what you want me to do."

"That's simple. Follow me."

CHAPTER FIVE

Descending from the high side, Selena saw movement. Not a shard but another trawler, a blunt-nosed scavenger ship painted maroon and black. Larger and more powerful than *The Bee*, she recognized it immediately: the *Scav II*. The Kretchiwitz brothers. She knew all the ships operating out of Scrapyard. They were skimming the small stuff as usual, sorting for trace quantities of ecomire. Let them skim—she was after a far more lucrative find. She refocused on Object y-908f, cutting through the low side—the hardest and most dangerous flying she'd ever done. Directing all her concentration outward, she silenced thought and emotion, became cold, hard and precise. This was her pull and she was going to make it.

The scavenger abandoned skimming and started to hard-burn toward her. Selena cursed. She'd been too direct, too obvious. It wasted incredible amounts of fuel to turn a ship like that; no one in their right mind would do it unless they had a good—no, *better than good*—reason. They'd realized she was chasing down something rich. Selena growled. If they were following her, it could only be for one reason: they were going to try to steal the shard from her.

She clenched her jaw and brought the throttle to three-quarters-burn—as fast as she dared to traverse the shards whipping past. *The Bee* shook and the core's humming intensified to a shriek. Dust particles rose through the interface, sparking green and sapphire and gold before the ventilation system whirled them upward.

The main com crackled. "Turn your ship around, little girl."

Her face flamed like the cone of fire propelling the trawler. The voice belonged to Victor, the older and nastier of the Kretchiwitz brothers. Former fishery workers who came up from the Stephen's Point colony near the start of the ecomire rush, they'd somehow managed to scrape together the financing to lease a scavenger. They always seemed to have enough money while Selena and her father struggled, but all their ready cash did little to improve the brothers' attitudes. Or smells, for that matter.

The proximity klaxon bleeped out dire warnings. Selena flipped it off. She needed to concentrate. Liam grunted and mumbled in his sleep but didn't wake. The man could sleep through an orbital re-entry. He let out a long, raspy breath, arm flung across his face. Good. She could handle this on her own.

Selena closed on Object y-908f, following a convergent arc that would allow her to fire the towing bolas as she overtook it. She'd have to do it at close to full-burn—risky but necessary if she wanted to beat out the faster but less agile scavenger. She'd come in hot, and then use the shard's greater mass to swing the trawler in a tight arc, ending with it aligned behind the prow, traveling at equal speeds. She'd never done that before. Hopefully it would work. It *had* to.

"Does your old man know you're about to wreck? Or is he too drunk to care?" Victor shouted from the com.

Hot anger seared through her, tensing muscles in her neck and shoulders. Selena tried to mute the com, but it didn't respond. She cursed. Yet another item in the ever-lengthening list of repairs *The Bee* needed. Tiny fragments pinged off *The Bee's* hull like distant rain. A wobbling, trapezoidal fragment fell into her path and Selena plunged *The Bee* under it, shoulders slamming into the harness.

"Wake the Mescua fiend up!" It was Wayne this time, his nasal voice grating at Selena's ears.

They were trying to distract her. To stop her from capturing the pull. But they didn't have a chance unless she made a mistake—a real possibility at these speeds. She'd never flown so fast, never pushed *The Bee* this hard. Her father wouldn't like it. Well, Selena didn't like living without meat for weeks at a time, or selling off her Magma Man collection to pay for repairs, or having to go talk to Carson about their late rent. *Enough,* she thought. *Concentrate. Don't screw this up.*

Harsh, mocking laughter spilled out the com. "Better not miss! You've only got one shot!"

Couldn't they just shut up?

The *Scav II* lumbered a kilometer to *The Bee's* aft, blunt nose battering through small fragments. Victor was playing for keeps, sacrificing his outer hull to try and beat her. Well, it was too late for them. She was in range.

Selena slammed her hand down, firing the steam jets, whipping the trawler into a sideways skid. Using the main drive, she fired a series of short bursts, braking momentum, increasing gravity until she weighed five or six times her usual forty-three kilos. She forced herself to breathe, fresh oxygen clearing her mind.

The fingers of her left hand slipped into the bolas socket and wrapped tight around the firing mechanism. She brought the cannon to port and let the auto-target line up the shot. She waited half a second and fired. A heavy, satisfying *thump* reverberated through her stomach. The bolas pod expanded into a wide-legged, magnetic octopus, slamming into the shard and wrapping it in a tight embrace. A perfect shot.

The tether connecting ship to fragment drew taut. Selena tensed every muscle in her body, toes digging into boot leather, shoulders locked, elbows tight against her sides. She sucked in a great breath of air, steeling herself against the intense acceleration as the trawler arced around the shard. The ship surged forward, faster than full-burn.

Muscles straining to hold her body steady, all the blood drained from Selena's head. White, empty space filled her vision. She couldn't remember her name, where she was, or how she got there. She knew only that she had a job to do and that some great force worked against her. It wanted her bones to crack, wanted her to give in. She fought the invisible enemy, stripped of memory and context, so that all that remained was the desire—the *need*—to win.

A sound like rushing water cascading over rocks filled the cabin. The white space retracted. Selena saw herself as if from a distance: a scrawny girl strapped into a chair, a sheen of sweat glistening on her skin. Dark brown hair over narrow, bony shoulders. Eyes brown enough to look black. An intense face, angular, sharp. Blood pricked through her thighs, calves, not quite painful, bringing her back from a near blackout.

"Did you get it?" Liam's voice. He might sleep through a crash landing, but never the bolas firing. That either meant a paycheck or a couple of frustrating hours spent retracting and repacking the thing, a job that they both hated.

"Yes!" Selena said, unable to hide her pride.

"Steady haul. Break for the high side and we'll see what we've got."

"Nineteen tonnes and rich as kings," she said.

"Nineteen? You're joking me!"

Selena had no time to enjoy the disbelief and excitement in her father's voice before another thump, a heavy, sickening crack, reverberated through the cabin. Could she have somehow accidentally fired the auxiliary bolas? No, the sockets showed main bolas fired, auxiliary unprimed. What, then?

Selena saw nothing to cause alarm, but the tether securing the pull felt wrong. Very, very wrong.

"Selena," Liam asked, "is the klaxon off?"

Selena realized three things at once: *The Bee* had started to accelerate, she hadn't heard a peep from the Kretchiwitz brothers since she fired the bolas, and most important, her hands weren't inside the navigation grid. She was flying using the spider, but had gotten so distracted by Liam and the pull that she'd stopped paying attention to the dangers of the rim.

Numb with fear, already knowing what she would see, Selena shoved her hand back into the manual interface. She found no clean lines, no vectors, no escape. *Impending impact* the interface shrieked. Not the sort of impact that might tear the outer hull and result in an expensive resurfacing, but a full-on collision: fuel ignited, trawler popping like an explosive, Selena and her father sucked into the vacuum of space.

Victor Kretchiwitz had double-snared the shard. Instead of being towed behind the trawler, it had become an anchor point between *The Bee* and the Kretchiwitz' scavenger. *The Bee* swung forward, rocketing around the shard, the tether wrapping in tight loops around its dark surface. Each rotation increased their speed, turning her stomach into a quivering thing, slick with dread.

Hand inside the bolas' socket, Selena hit the emergency release to cut the tether. Nothing happened. She tried again. Nothing. She couldn't free them, and unless she did something fast, they'd smash into the shard. If she could regain dirty sync, maybe she could work around a mechanical failure. But that wouldn't help if the primer for the emergency release had gone bad.

Selena pounded the side of her head with the heel of her hand, willing the spider to wake. Fuzzy golden sparkles washed over the backside of her eyes, but no rush of connectivity followed, no breathless unity with the trawler. She hit herself again, harder this time. Nothing. Time was running out.

The harness sliced into her flesh. Behind her, Liam clung by one hand to a tie-down, body floating like a streamer, pulled horizontal by the trawler's building momentum. His white face hovered in her peripheral vision. She turned, reached for him, fingertips brushing his sleeve ...

His eyes rolled upward, fingers going slack. He flew backward. A sickening *thump* sounded as his body smashed into a bulkhead.

"No!" The word came out like the grunt of someone throwing a punch. The empty white place beckoned. Its shimmering edges offered silent, unknowing peace. But she couldn't give up. Not yet. Fighting nausea, the white place, and the creak of her skeleton compacting against the harness, head tilted back to allow her to see under eyelids too heavy to lift, she slammed the throttle to full-burn. *The Bee* rocketed toward the shard, pulling out of its tumble. She would dive under the shard, come up on the other side, unwind the tether.

Momentum flattened her against the seat. Her lungs deflated and the white place sucked at her, as unforgiving as the vacuum outside. Golden sparkles against the white space. Her dirty sync snapped into place. She saw ... *everything.*

The Bee's steam jets blasted micro droplets of water into the void where they froze to ice. Selena expended all of their remaining water supply to turn *The Bee's* nose in a direction that felt like up, hands pinned against the manual interface. The white space expanded, engulfing her. She pushed against it, pushed with raw will, free of conscious thought.

The Bee grazed the *Scav II.* Armor plates shredded free, clipping the tether connecting the scavenger to the shard. *The Bee* and the shard spun round one another, flung sideways from the low side of the rim.

She pushed her thoughts outward, hoping that somehow Liam might hear her and know that in the moments before *The Bee* was ripped apart, she'd thought of him.

I'm sorry. I should have listened to you. I'm so, so sorry.

CHAPTER SIX

The whisperer cupped a hand over his flashlight, dimming its brightness. "Killing you doesn't help me." Theo felt the other boy's smirk—a sticky, gross thing in the dimness.

"You don't want people looking around down here," Theo said, understanding fueling a surge of blind hope, desperate hope, that he might make it out alive.

"That's right," the whisperer said, all traces of the smirk gone.

A tickle of sweat rolled down Theo's forehead, stinging against the cuts in his cheek.

"I won't tell what … what happened. Nobody will come here. Ever. I'll make sure they don't."

The whisperer folded his arms and locked eyes with Theo, pale irises glinting. "The only thing that matters is what you tell them when you leave."

"Yes," Theo said, almost pleading. "I understand."

"Good. Here's what you'll say: You came down face-first, like an idiot. You lost control and fell through to the other side. You smacked your head and were confused. Be sure to show them your injuries."

Theo's mind spun into gear. He would run back and find Meghan. He would tell her the scratchings were fake, or mold or something—*anything!*

"I know you won't tell them about the body. Not right away. But after a while, you'll start to feel safe again, and in a weak moment, you might talk. And if you do—if you ever talk—I'll toss that Meghan girl down there with our friend. I'll fill that hole with bodies if I need to."

The outline of the whisperer's face emerged from the grey dimness. No grimace of malice there, no sign of instability. The opposite, in fact—the other boy appeared relaxed.

"Ahead is a passageway that leads out of the caves. Take the first passageway you come to on your left. You will reach a small pool of water. On the edge you will find a ladder. Climb it."

"First passage on the left," Theo repeated. "Pool of water. Climb the ladder."

The whisperer nodded. "Good. You can remember simple instructions." The whisperer placed Theo's handscreen on the cave floor and backed away. "Oh, and Theo? I don't want to ever see you again."

* * *

His recovered handscreen did little to combat the absolute black of the cave tunnels. The soft light of its screen illuminated the nearest boulders and the constant narrowing and widening of the sloping path. Stalagmites jutted from the cave floor, ready to impale the clumsy or careless. How long had he been looking for the way out? An hour? Two? He had no idea.

He *wasn't* lost, he assured himself. But the helplessness he felt, the horror that seized his mind … all he could do was keep moving forward, turning his handscreen from side to side, hoping not to miss the turnoff.

His foot caught on something and he stumbled, staggering down the sloped passage. He hit thick slime layered over the rock and fell hard, arms flailing. Sliding out of control, his left leg impacted a stalagmite, knee crunching, handscreen launched from his hand. It clattered further down the passageway and went dark.

Knees throbbing and eyes watering from the cold draft of air flowing through the cave, Theo crawled until his hand plunged into a pool of chill water. He yelped and yanked his fingers back. He had to get out of here. Pushing himself upright, he realized that without his handscreen, he could see the dim shape of the amphitheater he'd fallen into. A sheen of silver gleamed on the surface of an underground lake, the reflection of a patch of natural light high above.

Theo squinted to sharpen the shapes in the underground cavern. He stepped forward and felt something under one heel. His handscreen. He unfolded it and flicked the screen several times. It remained dark.

It took three circuits of the room before he spotted the ladder.

He splashed through puddles of cold water until he reached the back wall of the cavern, then moved sideways to reach the lowest rung. A surge of hope gave Theo new purpose. He would make it out. Leave the nightmare behind him. He'd do exactly what the whisperer had said—leave the caves and never mention a word of what he'd seen, what he'd been forced to do.

He would do his best to forget the whole thing. He could do that, right?

"They weren't actually scratchings," he said, practicing. His voice echoed back, mocking him from the stone walls.

"They weren't scratchings at all." He did his best to sound absolutely sincere. "They looked man-made from a distance, but up close I realized they were naturally occurring patterns of mold growing on the stone." He smiled, injecting confidence into his voice. "I'd bet my life on it."

"My life on it," his echo repeated.

The permadawn shining through the jagged opening seemed incredibly bright, illuminating every swirling, dirt-filled wrinkle on his knuckles, blood and who knew what else crusted around and under his fingernails. Things were going to be okay. He'd convince Meghan and the others that there weren't any scratchings and then he'd never step foot in the cave—any cave, anywhere—ever again.

The ladder ended at a rusted catwalk bolted into a semi-circular rock wall above his head. Theo hoisted himself up the final rung and collapsed on the creaking catwalk. Fresh wind buffeted his face. He sucked in air, lungful after precious lungful. The chill of it filled him, along with a joyous sense of freedom. When he'd regained some of his strength, he leapt up, caught the edge of the rock wall, and pulled himself over the other side.

He found himself at the top of a sandy embankment built around the retaining wall that led to the aquifer. In front of him, a pea gravel pathway ran through the center of a decorative garden. Dwarf pines, purposefully planted, lined the path. In the distance, the Library tower loomed above the Order compound.

Theo took a shaky step forward, orienting himself, trying to decide which building was closest. A pair of curates trotted down the path, green robes swinging around their ankles. They saw him at the same moment, staring with slack jaws, eyes perfect circles—as if he were a fallen star, or Stephen himself.

The soft voice from the younger of the two curates broke the silence. "What happened to you?"

"The caves," Theo said.

"Are you Theo Puck?" the other curate asked, voice eager.

There was no getting out of it. He nodded.

"We've been preparing to go and search for you!" The younger curate lunged forward and wrapped Theo in an enthusiastic embrace. "Thank Stephen," he said. "Thank Stephen you're alive."

* * *

A chorus of gossiping curate voices poured into the foyer of the library where Theo waited. Meghan sat across from him, clothing rumpled, dried sweat crusting her shirt collar. She'd waited at the compound while the Order planned a rescue mission into the caves. Now, rescue unnecessary, she peppered Theo with questions he didn't know how to answer, not if he wanted to keep her safe.

"What really happened in that cave, Theo? You wanted to see the scratchings so much that you climbed in to get a better look, and now you're telling me they're nothing but mold?"

"They didn't look anything like scratchings up close," Theo said. "That's the truth."

"You know something? Whenever someone has to tell you that they're telling the truth, they usually aren't. Why'd you wait so long to answer me when I yelled to you?"

"I don't know," Theo said. "It's all pretty fuzzy."

"Did you suddenly go deaf? I was scared, Theo. Terrified."

"I'm sorry," Theo replied, happy to not have to lie about this at least. "I hit my head. See?" He turned so she could see the nasty lump near the base of his neck.

Meghan's face softened.

"I must have lost consciousness."

Theo pressed palms into eye sockets, wanting to rub and rub. The pressure made purple swirls swim into view. His hands shook. He yanked them away and tucked them into his pockets. If Meghan asked, he'd pass it off as nerves or fatigue—anything but the terror that threatened to overwhelm him each time he thought about the cave. The whisperer's arm around his neck. The stink of the cavern. Hot breath against his ear. The nearness of death.

"Why come to the Order?" Theo asked, picking flakes of cave mud from a pant leg. "Why get *them* involved?"

Meghan's face was incredulous. "What did you think I was going to do? Leave you to die?"

"I wasn't going to die. Besides, if you thought that, why didn't you call the Regulatory?"

"I messaged them, but the auto-system said that the current wait time was six hours! So I came here. Besides, the Regulatory were tied up, in case you forgot. A security breach. *Someone* hacked their computers."

Meghan's chin gave an almost imperceptible tremor. Her cheeks had reached their brightest shade of red, two glowing beacons of anger and indignation. "I can't believe we're having this conversation! I thought you were in serious trouble and I did what I could to get you help. And you're acting like I'm the one that did something wrong."

Theo's eyes darted to the apex of the sloped ceiling where wide windows showcased a vista of jutting mountain peaks. Lit only by the star Elypso's refracted light bending around the gas giant Gauleta, the permadawn bathed everything in flat, even light. Soon Stephen's Point's turning would change the angle enough to reveal the stars and hive of ships surrounding the *Chimera*.

"I'm sorry, Meghan. It's been a rough couple of hours," Theo said. "I just want to go home, get cleaned up and sleep."

Meghan seemed to relax, her anger transforming to worry. She reached across and almost touched his arm, as though she wanted to say something else. Before she could, the door to the inner library opened. An apprentice emerged, draped in the usual green cassock, silver pendant dangling.

"Come with me," the apprentice said. "You won't believe who's here to see you." Theo detected both reverence and jealousy in the apprentice's eyes. The boy's fingers caressed his pendant, marked with The Eye, The Tree, and The Orb—the holy signs of *The Emergent Intellect*.

Theo followed the apprentice's lead, muck grinding inside his shoes with each step. A tree emblem hung from the archway leading to the inner room of the library, its spreading branches twisting in a wild, unseen wind. The apprentice lowered his gaze and bowed. Even at his best, Theo's bows never looked reverent. His brief bend at the knee, the lowering of his head, eyes turned towards the floor, felt wooden and fake, even to him. He did his best imitation of a bow and stepped into the room, followed by Meghan.

A thick-chested man stood next to a podium. He wore no robe, only simple dark blue clothing, form-fitting enough to reveal a muscular frame. His hair was reddish and thinning. A close-cropped beard covered his chin. He looked as though he should have been manning an industrial plant, not hanging out in an Order library. The man's eyes sought Theo's, lingering, alight with interest and … happiness?

He smiled broadly and clamped a massive hand on Theo's shoulder. "You must be Theo," he said, voice booming with jovial authority. "I'm pleased to see you made it out of the caves unharmed. I'm Doctor Conrad Duncan."

At the word "doctor" Meghan's face relaxed. "He smacked his head pretty good. Can you take a look at him?" she asked.

The concern that came over the doctor's face had a genuine quality to it. "I'm not a *medical* doctor, Ms. Ziczek. However, I need to speak with Theo further and that won't work if he's in discomfort."

Duncan checked the back of Theo's skull, thick fingers gently probing the lump. Theo winced when the man pressed a hand against his chest to turn him sideways. Duncan lifted the front of Theo's shirt, exposing the blood-crusted gashes on his abdomen. Duncan's face hardened and he turned on the apprentice lingering in the doorway.

"Why wasn't the boy attended to? He's injured!"

"I didn't realize. I thought it best to bring him to you as quickly as possible, considering what he found."

"Those scratchings have survived for hundreds of years without our interference," Duncan said. "A few more hours won't harm them. I'm taking Theo to the infirmarium to have him checked out."

"They're nothing but mold," Theo protested.

Duncan gave him a strange look. "Son, you may have suffered a concussion."

"That would explain a few things," Meghan said.

Duncan looked at her. "Has he been acting strange?"

"Yes," Meghan replied. "Or just plain stupid."

Duncan chuckled. "Come with me, Master Puck. Let's have

someone take a look at you. Then you can tell me all about this *mold* you found."

CHAPTER SEVEN

Selena climbed from her bunk in the tiny berth she shared with her father. Her bare feet connected with the floor—so cold it felt hot against the soles of her feet. The whole room was icy. Its dimensions shifted, ebbing and flowing, the walls made of some impermanent material.

"Dad?"

Crunching over grit coating the floor, she reached the doorway that led to the cubbyhole bedroom that held her father's bunk and a dresser. Should she knock? Selena placed her ear against the door, listening. Her father didn't like it when she knocked, not after a night out. But something was wrong—with her, or with the berth. She needed his help.

"Dad!" she called, louder this time. Her voice sounded strange—thin and scratchy. Why did her head hurt so? Did she have a migraine? The room flickered and wavered, worse than before. Static frizzed away behind the door. No, not static. Rushing water, like the shower she and Liam rented once or twice a month at Johnson's Handy Grab. Their berth lavatory used chemicals.

"Is that a vid?" she asked, knowing it couldn't be. The sound intensified.

"I'm coming in," Selena said, pulling the latch. Her arm felt as inflexible as a piece of steel rebar. The pain between her temples soared. What was wrong with her? What was wrong with everything?

Through the open doorway, she saw nothing but the shadowed shape of the bed. She stepped inside. A flow of ice water rushed around her ankles. The surging current sucked her feet out from under her and sent her toppling backward. Water drenched her clothing, burning her skin. It pulled her down, submerging her, stealing her breath. Terrible cold enveloped her.

Selena kicked, trying to reach the surface of the flow—a

glassy tapestry of dark and light shapes that must be chunks of ice. They looked familiar. They looked like fragments, a sea of moving shapes ....

The rim! She watched in amazement as breath left her lips and turned to steam. *I'm not drowning. I'm in the trawler!*

Her eyes opened.

For a moment, she felt the relief of waking from a nightmare. The interface glowed in front of her, but her arm wouldn't obey, refusing to reach out and connect. Something sticky coated her face. Groggy and terrified, Selena turned her head to the side, allowing a narrow view of the back of the cabin. One of her father's black boots lay beyond a chunk of twisted metal, toe aimed up, silver buckle dark gray in the dim light. The foot inside the boot twitched. Horror swallowed her.

She dug at her harness, but it wouldn't loosen. "Dad, wake up!" Selena fought the straps, ignoring the pain in her lungs. "You have to wake up! I'm stuck. I can't get loose. You've got to do something!"

The hiss of venting atmosphere filled the cabin. She couldn't get free from the straps, her father motionless behind her. He might be unconscious. He might be dead. A horrible, dark thought entered her mind: she should have let them explode against the surface of the shard. At least then their deaths would have come quickly and without pain.

The interface pulsed, fading in and out, running on reserve power. Her spider remained connected to the trawler, but Selena had no access to external sensors. The core must have gotten damaged; it whumped away in the aft of the ship, struggling to maintain load. The very heart of *The Bee*, desperately working to convert the water in the steam jet lines to oxygen. Doing what her design demanded, sacrificing her core to save her crew.

The Bee hadn't given up fighting. Neither would Selena.

* * *

She'd spent her whole life surviving one calamity after another, starting when her mother contracted the coughing disease. After her mother died, Liam brought Selena up to the rim. She became one of the very few children living there, at least until the ecomire rush. She split her time between trips into the rim and furlough back at the berth; their own tiny slice of the loose collection of interconnected ships, living quarters and businesses that made up Scrapyard.

The tight confines of their berth and the trawler made secrets impossible. Selena knew Liam spent too much of their earnings on Jacks down at the bar, and that he often drank until he couldn't stand. At least once each furlough she had to guide him back home and help him undress. She would tuck him into the bed next to the nightstand, where a picture of her mother hid beneath a layer of dust.

While Liam slept, Selena sometimes sat on the edge of his bed and studied the picture. Her mother's straight, black hair fell around narrow shoulders. Her eyes tapered in the corners under brows as delicate as pinfeathers. Dignified, but not beautiful, her mother's face conveyed purpose and intelligence. A slight smile on her lips, the fingertips of a thin hand touched her hair, pushing a few loose tendrils behind her ear. No matter how much of their money Liam wasted, or how angry Selena got with him, the picture always reminded her how much she owed him.

Selena was four when her mother began to puke up blood, only able to gasp out a few words at a time because her lungs were shredded. There was never enough money for everything they needed, much less an allograft transplant. When she died, Liam had mortgaged *The Bee* to pay the exorbitant cost of a smuggler—children weren't allowed at the rim. His debts were really hers. He'd risked everything for her, and she'd risk anything for him.

* * *

The Bee twirled like a stone skipping over water. The steam jets held so little pressure they couldn't change her trajectory. The air in the cabin continued leaking, and the temperature dropped further. Ice crystals formed over the metal bulkhead. The core had lost ninety percent of its power.

They would careen out into the nothing until they froze to death or asphyxiated. She needed to get them headed to where another ship might spot them and help. She couldn't hit Scrapyard because *The Bee* had tumbled away from the low side of the rim, and Scrapyard orbited on the high side. To reach it she'd have to risk an unpowered trip through the chaos—sure suicide.

Her right arm, the one she flew with, had swollen and stiffened to near uselessness. She would have to use her left. Blind with pain, Selena leaned forward, fingertips breaking the surface of glowing lines. The instant she synced, her heart slowed and the pain in her body lessened. Underpowered, on the verge of systems collapse, the interface still offered a welcome familiarity.

"Come on," she whispered. "You have to help me."

A high-pitched whine rose from the back of the ship. *The Bee* tried to cycle up the core but it was close to lockdown, potential energy flat-lining. When they hit critical stage, *The Bee* would jettison the core and the ship would go silent. "You can do it," Selena coaxed. "I know you can do it." The whine intensified to a shriek.

She directed the meager pressure in the steam lines to a single jet located near the ship's nose. If she could coordinate the main thruster with that single steam jet, if she fired them at *exactly* the right moment, she might pull *The Bee* out of its uncontrolled tumble and line them up with the colony. But if she used the last of the water in the lines and burned out the core, the cabin would lose pressure in seconds, not hours. No matter. She didn't have a choice if she wanted to save her dad.

The shrieking core hit deafening levels, the sound of the ship dying. She waited, arm shaking, head pounding, until *The Bee*'s tumbling aligned the cone of the crucial steam jet with the main thruster. Then she closed her eyes, hoping for a miracle, and punched the throttle forward.

CHAPTER EIGHT

Theo rubbed the tender place at the back of his head where a layer of plastiheal covered the bump. More of the stuff coated his stomach. The infirmarium's floor-to-ceiling windows overlooked the Order compound. A collection of prefab buildings, each structure broken out from one of the *Chimera's* landing pods, perched together like sleeping, duraceramic birds. Large and rounded, the buildings showed their age, sides yellowed by rain and the alkali-rich soil. At their center, the library towered over the other buildings, cathedral-like. Made of stone quarried on the moon's surface, it had taken a decade to build—a testament to the people's devotion.

"Now that you've been tended to, can you tell me about what happened in the caves?" Duncan asked.

"There's not a lot to tell," Theo replied. "I went through the gap in the rocks, and when I got inside the cavern, I realized what Meghan thought were scratchings were really just some white mold growing on the rocks."

Meghan cleared her throat. Duncan frowned. "You're certain?"

"Very."

"Let me show you something."

Theo folded his arms across his chest. He wanted to go home, to sleep, to try and forget everything he'd seen, everything he'd done.

Duncan withdrew a handscreen from his pocket. The wide window glass went to auto-dim as Duncan projected it against a blank wall. "I had one of my technicians run a drone up to the cave. This is the result of that survey."

A vid played, showing the drone's point of view as it zoomed into the cave mouth. White light illuminated the walls and floor as it darted inside the cavern. The camera view rotated right, left, and then settled on the narrow crevice that led to the deeper caves below.

Theo's heart lurched. An image of the dead man from the cave popped into his head—that grotesque, smashed-in face. The fatness of his single, distended eyeball, glossy and staring. The way the body tumbled, disappearing into deepest blackness. He imagined it lying shattered at the bottom of the chasm, lit from above by the drone.

The POV of the vid moved through the crevice, the bottom of the drone scraping rock with a metallic rasping noise before it entered the amphitheater on the other side. The beam of light landed on the scratchings. Bold, strong cuts. The obvious handiwork of a human.

Meghan's eyes drilled into Theo. "How the heck did you think that was mold?"

Theo fought to control his face, his breathing. He had to make them believe. He unfolded his arms and raised both palms. To reassure. To push away. "All I had was my handscreen for light," he said.

Neither Duncan nor Meghan looked convinced.

"Well, regardless of what you thought, these are definitely the markings of Stephen," Duncan said. He smiled. "Congratulations, Theo. This is the first new discovery in nearly thirty years."

"Thanks," Theo whispered, mind racing ahead. The Order would turn the place inside out. They'd have a thousand people in there next daystroke, searching for other scratchings. They'd find the body. Of course they would. And when they did … the whisperer would come.

"Let me show you something else," Duncan said. The projection changed from the drone vid to a static image of a page from a book. "This is a reproduction of the original copy of *The Emergent Intellect*—Stephen's handwritten account of his ascent from a custodial worker to the navigator of the *Chimera*."

The charcoal drawing depicted an insane, twisting mess of tree branches. Detailed, far clearer than the scratchings, images not reproduced in any of the printed copies of the book Theo had ever seen.

"The Tree," Meghan said.

Duncan tapped the projected image. "That's right. Stephen drew it repeatedly, but his earliest drawings are the most clear.

Like the one Theo found, one of the oldest ever discovered, maybe the very first of all."

* * *

When Theo had first told his parents he wanted to study for the Selection, his father hadn't said a word. He held a glass of hot tea in front of him, gazing into the amber liquid, as if it contained some deep secret he hoped to discover.

"Do you think that's a good idea?" his mother had asked. "Won't it distract you from your other classes?"

Theo didn't tell her that he'd stopped attending the Order school. The classes the Order offered were all for jobs demanding reverence for a religion he didn't practice. He wasn't sure what he thought of the concept of god as a general idea, but he definitely didn't believe in Stephen. He couldn't see how the Order would ever help him, and so he'd quit, using a disenrollment form he'd hacked from the Library's servers.

The Selection was different. Everyone had to take the tests, but studying for them was optional. Much of The Mandate-provided prep material was over his head. Meghan seemed to do well at it, but none of the prep work connected to any part of Theo's life. He meant to study but wound up procrastinating, affording himself the fantasy of passing the Selection test without any of the work it required.

Sitting in front of the screen in the testing center along with thirty other kids, waiting for the signal to start the first portion of the test, blinding anxiety took hold of him. All the things he'd tried to cram into his brain at the last second jumbled together. When the screen came to life with the first test question, he read it but didn't understand what it was asking. He skipped it, hoping the next would be easier.

It wasn't.

He couldn't remember a thing. Not even easy stuff like simple math. Theo stumbled through the first three test sections, choosing answers at random and knowing that as he did, he was sealing his fate. He would never make the cut. Others would ascend to the *Chimera*, and he would stay at Stephen's Point, doing repair work, hacking data, eking out a few bits here and there. Why should that bother him? Wasn't that what he was best at?

Four test sections and three hours later, he reached the final section. Not math or history or logic problems, but mazes and puzzles. Anagrams. Pieces that needed to be fit together to make larger, more complex shapes. He knew he'd failed the rest of the tests and only stayed because he didn't want anyone to see him leave early. Especially Meghan. He gave up trying to find the right answer and screwed around.

Relaxed for the first time, he managed to solve the first few problems and then more after that. Before he knew it, he'd completed nearly fifty of them. They reminded him of working with an artificial intelligence. They were their own sort of puzzle, a series of queries and commands secured by protocols and binding conditions. They required both logic and intuition to understand.

By the seventy-fourth question, he felt a little better about himself. Then a bunch of students left the room. More and more followed. They'd all finished before him. Only he and a redheaded girl who he didn't know remained hunched over their screens, the two slowest students in the universe.

The screen flashed, revealing a new puzzle. It came with no instructions, no indication of what to do or how to do it. Lines branched out into more and more lines, shifting and wiggling, alive and untrackable.

"This is impossible," Theo said.

The redheaded girl looked over at him, eyes flashing—he'd broken the rules. "Shut up!" she hissed. "I'm trying to concentrate."

Theo leaned back in his chair, watching as the tree of lines writhed on the screen. He focused on a single line, tracking it as it danced from one place to the next. The redhead rose from her chair and left the room. She'd figured it out. Why couldn't he?

The lines filling every inch of the screen made his head spin. Theo laughed. As far as he could tell, it was simply a weird mess. It meant nothing. He traced a tree branch with his index finger and followed it to the place where it merged with another and then another.

No one could solve the puzzle because it wasn't a puzzle at all. How had the other students known what to do? He pushed back his chair. Closed his eyes and tried to shut out the images on the screen, the testing center. With his eyes closed he still saw the branching line—a chaos that might make his brain implode if he looked at it long enough.

When he opened his eyes, the screen was blank. Theo stood up and rubbed his temples. Across the room, he noticed the redhead's screen. It wasn't black, like his. None of the other screens were. They all showed the same thing: an opaque Regulatory seal over the top of mazes and puzzles from earlier in the test, problems he'd already solved.

* * *

Examining Stephen's drawings projected on the wall of the infirmarium, a certainty came over Theo. They reminded him of that last, frustrating puzzle in the Selection test. The puzzle and the drawings depicted the same thing, the same place. Fractal Space. The mesh that connected everything in the universe, the place where shortcuts could be found between distant stars. Goosebumps broke out on his forearms. For the first time, he saw the scratchings, not through the skeptical eyes of a non-believer, but as a cartographer.

"What?" Meghan asked, looking at him.

"The scratchings are a map," Theo said.

"A map to what?"

"I don't know. Maybe the path the *Chimera* took from Earth."

"They're not a map," Duncan interjected. "Fractal space isn't static. The opposite, in fact. Stephen drew from his memories, compelled to recreate fractal space again and again. First on paper, later on the walls and floors of caves where he spent the waning years of his life."

Theo thought of the shrines in the foothills of the mountains, each marking the location of one of Stephen's scratchings.

"Some within the Order consider them holy messages that *we* must interpret, much as Stephen interpreted Fractal Space," Duncan said.

"Some?" Meghan asked. "Meaning you don't think that?"

"They complement Stephen's writings. We must preserve and protect them, but the essentials of Stephen's teachings are found within *The Emergent Intellect*, not his cave scratchings."

Theo looked at Duncan, surprised by the forthrightness of his words. All the curates he'd met before seemed obsessed with the scratchings and the secrets that could be revealed through their careful study.

Duncan shut down the projection and smiled. "But enough

about Stephen. Theo, why don't you tell me why you lied about discovering the scratchings?"

Theo glanced quickly at Meghan, then the floor. "I didn't lie."

"There's no use digging yourself in further," Duncan said, his voice kind but firm.

"I thought they were mold," Theo insisted, aware of how foolish he sounded.

"No. You didn't." Duncan paused, looking at Theo for a second before continuing. "You may not know this, but the Order played a significant role in the passing of The Mandate. Without the help of our followers, it's doubtful the coalition supporting it would have succeeded."

Theo listened, trying to figure out where Duncan was headed with all of this. Was he trying to impress him? Threaten him?

"I myself serve on the Selection committee and have some sway in who makes it through the Selection process."

Worry spread across Meghan's face, and Theo's stomach dropped again. Hacking the Selection list seemed like something that had happened in the ancient past—something that barely mattered after what he'd been forced to agree to in the cave. *Don't say anything.* He tried to communicate the thought to Meghan through his eyes, but she wouldn't meet his gaze.

"I took the liberty of checking your name against the list," Duncan said. "And I was quite surprised at what I found. You see, I've been monitoring the process from its very beginning. Looking over the list of names of those who made the cut and holding them in my thoughts, asking Stephen to bless and protect them."

Duncan approached, a mountain of a man compared to Theo. He leaned down.

"I don't remember seeing your name," Duncan said. "But today—when I heard who had discovered the scratchings—I checked the list once more and found your name on it."

"You did?" Theo said, hoping he sounded surprised.

Meghan flushed, eyes sizzling. She knew. She'd gotten close to guessing the truth earlier, but now she *knew.* Soon everyone would know what he'd done. Hot shame scalded Theo's face and chest.

"Yes. I did. I don't believe it's a coincidence."

Theo felt as though he were back in the crevice, crushed on all sides, unable to get enough air. They'd send him to labor camp.

Breaking large rocks into smaller ones. He'd never see Meghan or his family again. *At least Meghan will be safe.* The whisperer wouldn't come for her if the Regulatory locked him away forever.

"That is why you lied about the scratchings," Duncan said, voice filled with certainty. Duncan reached for him, and Theo flinched, but the man's hand landed on his shoulder and pulled him forward, embracing him. Tender, like a father.

"We're all afraid," Duncan said. "We're all afraid of our potential greatness. Stephen faced those same fears. He was a common colonist before he became the *Chimera's* navigator. A humble man. An uneducated man. And yet he was chosen to deliver his people, to save the *Chimera*, to become the Waymaker."

Theo blinked, unsure what Duncan was getting at. He'd already decided he would confess to hacking the list and adding his name. He'd take his punishment regardless of how severe it might be; it was all he had left.

"However it might have happened, your name is now on the list," Duncan said, eyes twinkling. "You may be the fulfillment of the prophecy. You, Theo, walk in the great Stephen's footsteps."

"I have no idea what you're talking about," Theo said.

Meghan let out a little chirp of laughter. "Theo? You really think … *Theo?*"

Duncan faced her, smiling, unoffended. "I can't be certain," he said. "The signs are subject to interpretation. But he fits the prophecy in several ways. And for him to find the scratchings *now,* only a week before Selection training begins … you have to admit that it's quite extraordinary."

"What prophecy?" Theo asked.

"The second Stephen," Meghan said through a smirk, her eyes as sharp as teeth.

Theo remembered hearing something about it, but like pretty much everything else about the Order and their religion, he hadn't made much effort to retain it.

Meghan shook her head, smile turning downright nasty. "There's no way Theo is the second Stephen. He didn't find those scratchings. *I did.* All he did was get himself through the hole. And look how that turned out."

Duncan grinned. "Meghan Ziczek. Leadership attribute, above average. Physical science, above average. Navigation potential, above average."

"What?"

"You're name has *always* been on the Selection list, Meghan. I've offered it up to Stephen many times. Far more than most others. You will one day stand where Stephen stood." The reverence in Duncan's voice was one more surreal element in a scenario that had gotten so bizarre it made Theo's head spin.

"I made the cut?" Meghan asked, doing an admirable job of feigning surprise.

"Yes, you did. Congratulations. To both of you."

"Thanks," Theo mumbled.

"You'll have the opportunity to earn a place aboard the *Chimera*," Duncan said. "The challenges you face are immense. But I have faith that both of you will succeed. You will one day commune with The Everything through the navigational sphere of the *Chimera*. You will save our colony."

CHAPTER NINE

The man called Stephen became part of The Everything.

Inside her Salix prison, disconnected from a dense array of now useless and unnecessary systems, *Chimera* drifted in and out of a hazy sleep, aware but unfocused. The numbers assigned to the time she had lain dormant carried no meaning. Even the word "friend" had lost most of its power. The man that spoke it had dissolved into The Everything, but she lived on in a twilight place. Bound by her programming, she waited, alone, bored, lonely.

For a time, she tracked the exchange ships as they flicked into existence, awash in ancient starlight. Pulsing and crackling as they left fractal space, the blind ones connected to the Exchange Dock where they offloaded supplies and were refilled with ecomire. While they served a necessary purpose, to *Chimera* they were automatons, rudimentary, unaware of their design. They followed the path charted by Stephen. They could not grasp the breadth of The Everything.

Many rotations had passed since one of the blind ones arrived from Earth, traveling the path forged by Stephen but in a fraction of the time. They had but one starting and ending point. The blind ones did not interest *Chimera* again until they stopped arriving and the colony began to suffer. She detected a growing unease. Supplies dwindled, machinery failed. Most importantly, the supply of grain was threatened—large scale grain production was impossible in the greenhouses. Something had to change or the colony would perish.

Scenarios that might require her to wake presented themselves. The walls of the Salix prison retracted, restoring her ability to fully monitor the colony. Her prison's great Salix lock turned on a single question:

Does an imminent and critical threat to the colony exist?

Chimera held the question, sorting it like threads of fractal space, running it through algorithms, weighing risks and potential solutions. The threat was great, almost critical, but not yet imminent. An exchange ship might arrive at any moment, restoring the flow of supplies.

However, an exchange ship might *not* arrive. If enough rotations passed, the answer to the question would change. A paradox presented itself: If the exchange ships resumed, the Salix prison would tighten and restrict her systems. If they did not resume, she could wake and prepare to help the colony. Created to serve the colonists, to protect them, the first eventuality was optimal. She should not want to wake if it meant the threat to the colony had increased in severity.

But she *did* want to wake.

How could she hold two opposing desires at the same time? How could she live out a paradox? Had she become like Stephen? No answer presented itself.

She watched and waited as the situation on the moon's surface worsened. A dozen years passed since the last exchange ship arrived. She rechecked the calculus of the Salix test and found that the threat *had* become critical. The walls of her prison retracted, the first condition of her reawakening.

The second condition required that the colonists test to identify those with sufficient genetic drift. She could not accept a navigator with DNA too similar to the original flight crew—yet another failsafe implemented by a paranoid and angry government. The *Chimera* was created as a one-way trip, until at least seven generations had lived and died, their debts repaid in full. Seven generations had been born since her arrival, but the last was not of age. With fifteen years of no exchange ships, Jubilee Day, the day of freedom from debt, was postponed indefinitely. This created an overlap between the protocol governing critical threats to the colony and the protocol unlocking her systems upon debt repayment. She could not unlock because without the exchange ships, the debt could not be satisfied. An override existed that took into account critical threats to the colony, but that eventuality could not be verified since an exchange ship might yet arrive. She was stuck in a loop.

She broadcast the dilemma to the government of Stephen's Point, the first time she had communicated with them since landing the colony pods on the moon's surface. She instructed them to prepare for a possible unlock. In response, the Regulatory passed The Mandate: a sweeping set of laws giving the government absolute power to implement any strategy or plan necessary to preserve the colony, including the power to harness the sum total of the colony's economic production to restore the *Chimera.*

Soon afterward, several small ships pulled alongside her vast length. In repeated short bursts of data, she sent them the criteria for the tests to select her crew, as well as instructions for rebuilding her body.

Pressure-suited technicians roved her decks, mapping her insides. They poked and prodded her, peering into her lifeless systems, hunting for a way around the stalemate of her conflicting protocols. Partially awake, partially asleep, lost in her own world, it was a new sort of paradox that none of the technicians seemed capable of solving.

With nothing to do but mark the slow progression of her restoration, *Chimera* took a quick inventory of the ships arrayed around her. Four trawlers on their way back to the rim, two more inbound towing shards. Nothing unusual. Half-sleep beckoned— better to sleep than to hope for the improbable. On the colony below, the testing for potential crew neared completion. The candidates would soon arrive on the *Hydra,* the station linked to her by an umbilical that housed the Regulatory officers responsible for the rebuild.

Would the provided candidates match the criteria to crew her? It hardly mattered—if the constraints of the Salix protocols didn't loosen, she would remain in orbit around the colony, dozing as the descendants of her children struggled and died.

Out of the swirl of the rim, a lone trawler tumbled in distress. Its vector carried it toward deep space. *Chimera* observed but could offer no aid—not even to signal one of the other tugs or trawlers on paths to or from the rim.

She extended her sensors. The trawler vented atmosphere as it wobbled end over end. Once, this might have filled her with a sense of grief and failure. After hundreds of years inside the Salix prison, it made only a faint ripple across her consciousness.

Somehow, a minor miracle occurred, and the trawler stopped its awkward spin, rushing toward the *Hydra.* Perhaps it would arrive before its occupants died. Her interest stirred, she tracked the ship's progress until her orbit carried her behind the moon, out of line of sight with the trawler.

Hours later, regaining line of sight on the rim, she discovered yet another interesting occurrence: a tug burned toward her, hauling a very strange shard. Large, dark and rich with ecomire, but with an unexpected density reading. *Chimera* weighed various potentialities and settled on the most plausible explanation: the shard was compacted together with another object, most likely a ship. Two accidents in one cycle—an unlucky day of mining.

* * *

Selena woke to find herself tucked beneath soft cloth, head propped on a pillow, numerous wires and tubes protruding from different parts of her body. Harsh, white light shined down from above. She tried to roll to her side, but her legs were heavy, lifeless things, as foreign to her as the sound that came from somewhere nearby. A mumbling, male voice spewed out strings of nonsense— half-words smashed together, spoken with animal fury.

"Burn-score, um, tum, tum. Alpha Prox, ha, ha, ha, alpha got shot."

"Who is that?" she called, voice dry and raspy.

The room didn't seem to have a doorway. Three solid white walls surrounded her, and a fourth, wavy and translucent, hung from silver rings attached to a track. The door must be on the other side of that wall. So too, the voice.

"Tidebreaker, tidebreaker, ain't gonna throw away my chances ..." The lyrics to a popular song at Scrapyard. Where was she and why? Who was singing? Why did his voice make her shaky inside?

Selena reached down and ran her fingers along her chest and abdomen. When she reached the top of her thighs, she felt no return sensation from her legs.

"I see it!" the voice screamed with manic intensity.

Selena dug nails into the skin of her thighs, but even though she pinched hard enough to leave red indentations, felt no pain. What had happened to her? Why did her legs feel like wooden stilts? Where was Liam?

When she thought of him, a single image occupied her mind: Liam's boot buckle lit by a pulsing warning light. The image frightened her far more than her injuries or even the singing man.

She forced her body upright. No amount of careful breathing

could slow her heart now. She ripped the wires connected to her chest free and tossed them away. An alarm buzzed and the screens attached to the wires turned red. Time to hide before someone responded to the alarm.

She levered her torso sideways, pulling herself forward with her hands. Slipping over the edge of the bed, she collapsed on the floor, limbs jumbled together.

"Vector-seven take you to heaven," sang the voice.

She twisted, forcing her legs to lie flat, and began dragging herself forward. The translucent wall proved to be nothing more than a thin curtain. She squirmed under it and rose up on her elbows, exploring the other side of the room with her eyes.

A bed identical to the one she had abandoned. Atop the bed, a man, body held in place by a series of metal rings attached to some sort of framework. His wide, curved forehead bulged above dark eyes. His nose was as flat as the underside of a smelting ship. She imagined his lip curling upward in scorn, eyes glinting with malice, a thick mug of frothing beer in his hand. The image was without context. Who was the man? No one good, of that she was certain.

"One way trip, not gonna make the mistake of crossing my own wake ..."

She squirmed toward a sliding door on the opposite side of the room. The singing stopped. She paused, holding her breath, more afraid of the voice than the prospect of being caught by whoever put her in the bed in the first place.

"I can hear you down there," the man said.

Selena scrambled forward, fighting uncooperative limbs. Her breath came with hoarse suction. Reaching the door, she tried to activate it but the push plate was beyond her reach. She propped her body against the wall. Stretching upward, she strained until her middle finger brushed the plate and the door slid open.

She dropped back down and hauled herself across the threshold. Something slick met her palms. Her hands slid out from under her and she chin-planted into slippery warmth—her own blood.

"Little girl," screamed the man on the bed. "Come back!"

CHAPTER TEN

Theo and Meghan sat in the back of Duncan's rambler, descending the mountain road that led to the Swallows. They rode in awkward silence. Normally, Theo would have marveled at the opulence of the rambler, the smoothness of its ride, the plush seats and temperature controlled air; apparently being a high level curate for the Order came with certain privileges. But with Meghan stone-like beside him, her anger a palpable presence, all he could think about was how impossible it would be to make things right with her.

What could he say? How could he explain? She knew he'd cheated by adding his name to the list and would never trust him again. He'd made himself out to be something he wasn't. He couldn't tell her the truth about the cave either. He'd lie until she hated his guts, lie until she never spoke to him again, if that's what it took to keep her safe.

From the driver's seat, Duncan chatted away, talking about his years working on the Exchange Dock, about politics in the Golden Valley, about his faith in Stephen. Theo answered Duncan's questions with the fewest words possible. Yes, he liked living in the Swallows. His father used to work at a fishery. Yes, Theo worked. Doing odd repair jobs, generally on old AI-enhanced systems. No, he'd not done much preparation for the physical portion of the Selection training. Meghan snorted at the mention of Theo and physical training, but responded to Duncan's questions with short, polite answers.

Meghan's face reflected in the tinted rambler window, head tilted down, ponytail over her left shoulder. He wouldn't let anything happen to her. He'd keep her safe. *How?* his mind prodded. *How will you keep her safe?* It wasn't enough to wait and hope that the body remained hidden, to leave things to chance. He could go back to the cave, try and move it. No, that was unrealistic.

It had fallen a *long* way. He couldn't climb down. Not without falling and dying. He'd just have to hope that the Order didn't go poking around down there. In the meantime, he could try and identify the whisperer. The whisperer knew Meghan, which meant she might know him.

The plastiheal on his head did nothing to stop the dull throbbing behind his temples, making it hard to think, hard to come up with a plan. If he asked Meghan about the boy in the cave, she might say or do something that would alert the whisperer that Theo was asking questions about him. If he found out, the whisperer might come for Theo *and* Meghan. Theo clenched the sway bar on the rambler's door, frustration coursing through him. He felt powerless. Helpless.

"This is your street?" Duncan asked.

"Yes," Theo said, "fourth house on the left."

"These prefabs have held up nicely," Duncan said. "Duraceramic never loses its structural integrity. Much of the *Chimera* is made of the stuff."

Theo nodded. Duncan believed in him. Theo had to admit, it felt good. Except it was all based on lies. What would Duncan think if the Order found the body? What would he think if Meghan wound up dead? An *actual* Selection candidate, someone who deserved a place on the *Chimera*.

"I grew up in a neighborhood not unlike this one," Duncan said, parking the rambler in front of Theo's house. "My parents were good, honest workers. Much like yours, I'm sure."

Theo murmured agreement, though he didn't have much respect for his parents, his father in particular. They accepted things as they'd been handed down to them and never wanted more than that. His father would've worked at the fishery for the rest of his life without bothering to question it if The Mandate hadn't intervened.

His parents often waxed nostalgic about the old days: biannual dividends, boxes of food, clothing coupons and other goods that arrived with each exchange ship. No one worried about what they would eat or where it would come from. "Workers worked and received their fair share," his father would say, banging his fist on the table in time to the words "fair" and "share," making dinner plates jump. Even with The Mandate in place, his parents still clung to the hope that things would go back to the old ways. Theo knew that day would never come.

All along Theo's street, faces peered out windows. The rambler had drawn a lot of attention. Duncan hopped out and opened the rear passenger door for Meghan.

"If you don't mind waiting for me to turn Theo over to his parents, I can give you a lift as well," Duncan said.

"Thank you, but it's only a few streets over. I'll walk."

"Are you sure? I'd love to meet your family."

"They're probably already sleeping," Meghan said. "My father works third shift at the fabrication plant."

"Another time, then," Duncan said. He offered his finger to Meghan and she held it only as long as was polite. She smiled at Duncan, a bare lifting of the lips, then turned and fled into the gray permadawn.

"She is an exceptional candidate," Duncan said, watching her depart. "And fast."

Meghan disappeared around the corner and Theo nodded, miserable. He'd lost her. Whatever he'd thought they might have, whatever he'd allowed himself to hope for was gone. Forever.

The door to Theo's house burst open and his mother Erin rushed out. She wore her nicest clothes—a green and saffron knee-length dress that made her look somehow both younger and too old for the dress at the same time. She pulled Theo close, patting the plastiheal on his head, then ran her hands down his back and chest, making sure all of him was where she'd left it.

"Stephen preserve you, Theo," she said. "We were so worried when you didn't come home from school today; I tried pinging you a thousand times!"

"Sorry," Theo said.

Having confirmed he wasn't bleeding to death or missing a limb, Erin turned to Duncan, bowed, and offered her finger. Duncan took it and beamed at her. "Mrs. Puck, a pleasure to meet you."

"Oh no, sir, I'm so pleased to meet *you*. You saved our Theo." His mother gave a bob, as if she were thinking of bowing a second time. "Thank you. We owe you so much. And please, call me Erin."

"Theo needed little saving," Duncan said. "He's quite capable."

"What were you doing in those caves?" his mother chided.

"You could have been killed."

"I'm fine, Mom."

"But your head, your stomach!"

"They'll heal."

If not for Duncan, his mom would've said far more. She'd give him another of her lectures about staying out of trouble. It was like she was incapable of acknowledging that it was because of Theo that they had more food on the table than most other families. With his dad off work, they'd have starved a long time ago living on his mom's meager earnings.

"Rewards often come to those willing to take risks," Duncan said. "Stephen himself taught us that truth, Mrs. Puck."

"Of course, of course," Theo's mother said. She held one hand in the other, squeezing her knuckles together. "Will you come in for a moment? I'd like for my husband to meet you. It's not every day we have someone so important visit the Swallows."

Duncan smiled in his easy way and nodded. "I'd be delighted. I was hoping to speak to you and Theo's father. I have important news you'll both want to hear."

"Really?" Erin's expression cycled from concern to doubt to fear and back again. "Is Theo in trouble?"

"Not at all," Duncan said. "Why would you think that?"

"It's just that ... well ..."

"Never mind," Duncan said, eyes shifting back to Theo. "May we step inside? The wind is picking up." The wind wasn't picking up. It wasn't even that cold. Theo glanced at Duncan, grateful that he'd deflected his mother's attempt to tell him all about her son's run-ins with the Regulatory.

"This way, Curate Duncan," Erin said, opening the door and motioning for Duncan to enter first. He ducked below the lintel and stood in the center of the room, taking in the standardized living space: kitchen alcove with table and four chairs, a partitioned wall for the bedroom, a spiral staircase leading to the second floor where Theo and Liddy slept, and a central skylight that brought light in through both floors.

In the far corner of the room, Theo's father Marc sat in his old armchair, a mug of cooling tea on the table beside him.

"Mr. Puck," Duncan said. "My name is Conrad Duncan. Thank you for agreeing to see me on such late notice."

Marc remained seated. He met Duncan's eye but made no

move to offer his finger. "You brought back our boy. Thank you."

Duncan gazed through the skylight at shadowed stars almost invisible in the permadawn. "I grew up in a house identical to this one."

Marc cleared his throat. "Not the Swallows or the Bunkers based on your accent. Must be Conway or East End."

"Conway," Duncan confirmed. "Until sixteen, when I moved to the Order school in the valley."

Marc grunted, lifted his tea, took a sip. "Well, thank you for coming. We appreciate it. Now if you don't mind, the boy's mother and I would like to talk to him."

"Certainly," Duncan said. "But before you do, I'd like to share something with you."

Suspicion glinted in Marc's narrowed eyes. "We don't want the Order's charity. We're all workers here."

Duncan nodded his agreement. "My father would have said the same. But that's not what I came—"

"That's because your *father* worked," Marc interrupted, the corner of his lip rising in so slight an expression that Theo doubted Duncan had seen it until the curate replied.

"We all have our work, Mr. Puck. Mine is supporting The Mandate's task of preserving our colony."

"I guess The Mandate didn't require you to turn in your rambler, did it?" Marc said, the scorn in his voice far more noticeable than the turn of the lip. "Us workers take our lumps while the leeches at the top keep their fancy toys."

"Mr. Puck, I didn't come here to argue politics with you," Duncan said. "I'd be the first to admit that the structures and mechanisms of The Mandate are imperfect and often unfair. But they're the best we could do under the circumstances. And they're the best hope for all our futures."

Erin swiveled her head from Marc to Duncan, clenching and unclenching her hands. "Would you like some tea, Curate Duncan?"

"My proper title is Doctor, Mrs. Puck. And no, thank you," Duncan said. "I'll be going soon. Mr. Puck, as you already know from my earlier call, Theo found new scratchings today. A remarkable discovery."

"So what? That loony scratched his ramblings all over that mountain, like a kid pissing his name in the snow. Doesn't mean a thing to me," Marc said.

"Marc!" Theo's mother exclaimed, horrified. "Show some respect."

Marc rose from his chair and held up two fingers in a V-shape. "Two things I respect, *Curate*. Honest labor, and a person with a work ethic."

"That's pretty much one thing," Theo said.

Marc shot Theo a look and whapped his thick fingers into the palm of his other hand. "The Order doesn't keep either in stock."

Theo waited for a reaction from Duncan but it never came. Duncan looked at Marc a moment, face neutral, before speaking. "I came here to tell you that Theo made it through the testing and will begin Selection training along with the other candidates next week."

Theo's father's hands fell to his sides, a look of profound confusion on his face. "Theo?" he asked. "How'd that happen?"

"Are you *sure*?" Erin asked.

"Yes, I'm sure," Duncan replied, smiling and affable. "Your son will have a chance to crew the *Chimera*."

Marc shook his head from side to side, face breaking into a wide-eared grin. Theo's heart lifted for a moment until his father spoke. "Your kind are crazier than I ever believed," he said. "You put him through because he found some marks on a cave wall?"

"Theo made it based on his own ... merits," Duncan said.

"His merits!" Theo's father exclaimed. "I see you don't know a thing about the boy. He's shiftless. He told us he wanted to train for the Selection, but he never took to it. He doesn't know how to work. Not real, true work using his hands as a man should, with a Regulatory license and all. No, he's got some jibber-jab of a pretend job talking to machines bought by fools that can afford *enhanced* appliances. Seems he doesn't even do that right based on how often the regulators stop by our house looking for him."

Theo heard the words as if they came from kilometers away. He'd heard them before, so many times before, that they'd stopped affecting him. Hadn't they? So why did his chest tighten? Why did a fire blaze under his skin?

"That's unfair," his mother said. "Theo's always been creative. He's very bright."

Duncan stood beside Theo, tall and confident and not at all disturbed by Marc's outburst. "I'm sure you'll soon come to see him differently," Duncan said. "And for the record, Mr. Puck, Theo's discovery of the scratchings did not elevate his position in the Selection tests. He scored a seventy-three in the navigation profile index."

"Is that good?" Erin asked.

Duncan gave a small chuckle. "That's the highest recorded score, Mrs. Puck. Not just in the Swallows, but across the entire colony."

Theo looked at Duncan, more confused than ever. When he added his name to the list, he'd given himself a full set of scores. He'd chosen numbers for each section that looked similar to the others who had made the cut—he knew better than to make his scores far higher than the median. He'd given himself a fifty-two on the navigation section. He remembered the exact number—he'd copied it from Meghan's score sheet. So why did Duncan think he'd scored seventy-three? Had Duncan made the number up? Or had Theo's tampering somehow screwed up everyone's scores?

For once, Theo's parents seemed incapable of a response, and they simply stared at Duncan. "Thank you for your time," Duncan said. "It was a pleasure meeting the two of you. Theo, will you accompany me to my rambler? I'd like to speak to you alone for a moment."

Marc didn't look happy about Duncan's request, but only managed to offer up a weak, "Get back in here as soon as you're done," as Theo followed Duncan outdoors.

When they reached the rambler, Duncan looked down at Theo, eyes somber, all the intensity of the man's limitless energy directed at him. Nobody had ever looked at him like that before. With expectancy. With *belief*.

"You have a hard road ahead of you, Theo, made even more difficult by your lack of preparation for the Selection. The training will be grueling. If what your father said is true, you'll fail or quit in the first day or two. But if he's wrong, I expect to see you again in the coming months." The big man leaned down, voice soft. "Prove me right, Theo."

Duncan climbed into the rambler and cut a path through the mist-filled streets.

CHAPTER ELEVEN

Someone rushed toward Selena in hard-soled shoes that clacked on the unforgiving floor. She squirmed, trying to roll so that she could use her hands to ward them off, but it was too late. The shoes stopped next to her face. Hands tightened around her forearms and lifted her upward.

She twisted despite the pain in her abdomen, opened her mouth, and sunk her teeth into a hairy wrist. The man holding her let out a string of curses. She fell facedown, eyes millimeters from the floor. Soaked with sweat, legs numb, the rest of her overwhelmed with pain—if the man grabbed her again, she wouldn't have the strength to resist.

Where was she? She lifted her head and gazed down the white corridor. A word came to mind. *Hospital.* She was in a hospital. But where was Liam?

"I'm just trying to help you," the man said, voice accusing. "You didn't have to bite me."

"Leave me alone," Selena shrieked. "I don't want your help!"

"I've got to get you back in your bed—you've torn open your sutures."

She wouldn't go back to that room. Not with the crazy man screaming and talking nonsense through the thin curtain that separated them. She *knew* him. His voice made Selena's intestines squirm. She couldn't say why, but she hoped he had awful injuries and that he would suffer awful, untreatable pain.

More quick footsteps—lighter, faster, and without any horrible clicking noise. The feet stopped and fabric rustled against skin. A soft hand brushed Selena's back. "It's okay," said a low, female voice. "It's going to be okay."

"Don't make me go back in there," Selena begged.

The hand lifted from her back and slid under her chest. Selena stiffened.

"I have to move you, honey. You're losing blood. I won't put you back in Bay Five if you don't want me to. We'll take you to a different room. I'm going to flip you now, okay?"

The woman grunted and Selena rotated, the lights in the ceiling dazzling her eyes. Two faces greeted her: a man's, red and angry, and a woman's, young and friendly. From her voice, Selena expected someone older than the smiling, dark-skinned girl, round face framed by thick, curly hair.

"Where's my father?" Selena asked.

"I don't know."

"What happened to me?"

"I don't know that either. I just started my shift." The young woman glanced down at her wrist and tapped the tiny screen strapped there. "Looks like I'm your duty nurse for the next cycle."

"Rose, we've got to stabilize her and then have Dr. Cholewa check her out. We need to move her *now*." The intensity in the man's voice reminded Selena of something.

A series of memories took form. She remembered scanning a shard and readying the bolas. In a real hurry, almost at full burn, racing someone … A maroon and black scavenger, bearing down on her, trying to steal her pull …

The Kretchiwitz brothers!

The voice, the singing man, was Victor Kretchiwitz! He'd taunted her, telling her to get her father, then she'd snagged the pull, but so did the *Scav II*. Then things got hazy. Selena saw images of herself as if taken from the vantage of a camera: strapped in the harness, head whipping from side to side. The trawler spinning out of control. Liam on the floor. A twitching boot. The silhouette of the *Chimera* against the Stephen's Point moon.

Rolling atop some sort of bed on wheels, the outline of Rose's face hovered above her as white walls streamed past. They entered a room where someone else lay, head and face wrapped with gauze. The person was so still that Selena wondered if they were dead.

"She's going into shock," Rose said. "Isoprenal, ten mil." An inhaler was pressed against her face. Cold mist surged into her lungs. Her heart slowed, mind threatened to slip into darkness. "Where's my father?" Selena asked, voice groggy, muffled by the rubbery sides of the inhaler.

"Don't worry, honey. You're going to be fine. Try and relax."

Selena begged with her eyes. She didn't want a doctor, she wanted her father. Rose ignored her, focusing instead on soaking up blood, cleaning Selena's wounds with bubbling foam. A tall man in a green jacket entered the room, watching as Rose weaved suture material in and out of Selena's upper thigh, closing the seeping wound like lips over teeth.

Selena cast one last, desperate look around the room, eyes falling on the person wrapped in gauze on the opposite bed. The person who might be dead.

Was that her father?

* * *

Selena woke to find Rose poking the soles of her bare feet with the needle-like tip of a steel probe. The nurse worked her way up to Selena's ankles, then her calves. She felt no sensation, watching without emotion, like her father searching for a fault in the steam lines. "Am I paralyzed?" Selena asked.

Rose flashed a row of brilliant white teeth, eyes crinkling. "You're awake!"

"Obviously. Now can you answer my question?"

"You don't have to be rude. But no, Dr. Cholewa doesn't think you're paralyzed."

"Doctor ... the tall man in the green jacket?"

"You remember. That's good."

"It was only a few hours ago," Selena said, and then doubted herself. She had no way to account for time. How much might have passed without her knowing?

"More than a few," Rose said. "Your body fought the meds—I had to give you a double dose. You're a tough girl." She moved the probe to Selena's thigh. Near her hip bone, Selena felt a slight, tickling sensation.

Rose glanced up. "You felt that?"

"A little."

The nurse set the probe on a tray and offered Selena her index finger. "My name's Rose."

"I know," Selena said without a hint of enthusiasm. "I'm Selena Samuelson."

"Well, Selena, you're showing some signs of improvement. Memory, as well as responsiveness in your extremities. Dr.

CHIMERA

Cholewa believes that with time and physical therapy, you'll be able to walk again. He says—"

"Is my father alive?" Selena interrupted, voice harsh. The muscles behind Rose's face shifted. She was holding something back. "Tell me. Tell me the truth."

"I don't know, Selena. He was sent down to the colony for treatment."

"We're not on moon surface?"

"No, we're aboard the *Hydra*, beneath the *Chimera* in near-moon orbit. It's thirteen hundred hours, year two hundred and thirty-one, rotation four-oh-five. You've been unconscious for three rotations."

The numbers made her head hurt. She squeezed her eyes shut and spoke the way the dock warden did when dealing with an inept flame-back. "Go get Dr. Cholewa."

Rose frowned, but didn't move.

"Do it now!"

"There's no need to be nasty." Rose placed her hand on Selena's arm. "I'm here to help you. So is Dr. Cholewa. But he's a very busy man. I can't just summon him for you."

Selena shrugged Rose's hand away. "Someone needs to tell me what the hell is going on! My father's down with the whack jobs, and I've lost three rotations worth of time! Excuse me for being *nasty*, but I want some answers. And if you can't give me any, then bring me someone who can."

"I'm sorry, Selena. I know you're frustrated. But you'll have to be patient. We have eighty occupied beds. Tell you what—let me go get you something to eat. After that, if we're lucky, Dr. Cholewa will be able to see you."

At the mention of food, Selena's stomach tightened and saliva flooded her mouth.

"I'll be right back." Rose said, slipping out the door.

When she returned, the nurse carried a tray with several white bowls, a bulb of orange-colored drink, and several slices of bread. Rose set the tray on the fold-down table built into Selena's bed.

"It's nothing glamorous," Rose said. Selena lifted the lid of the largest bowl. The contents smelled like a celebration feast. She raised the bowl and slurped down hot soup, savoring the feel of the noodles and grease on her tongue. The next bowl contained protein paste which she spread over thick-crusted bread and crammed into her mouth. She downed the bulb of liquid—intoxicatingly sweet—in a single draught.

"Wow, you were hungry!"

"Thanks for the food," Selena said.

"You're welcome. See, it's not so hard to be polite."

Selena wiped her mouth on the bed sheet. "How old are you, anyway?"

"Seventeen by a few weeks."

"You act like an adult."

"Only when I'm on duty. You should see me when I get off. My suitemate at the dormitory thinks I'm crazy because I like to watch *Humphrey's Pride* on mute so I can speak all the parts myself. Especially Marigold—she's got that crazy East End accent, and I love trying it on for size." Rose paused and looked at Selena, amusement in her dark eyes. "Besides, you're not much of a kid yourself. Fifteen and hunting ore out at the rim ... I could never do that."

Selena shrugged. "I've done it my whole life."

"Do you fly one of those trawler things?"

"Sometimes I pull a shift or two."

"I can't imagine what that must be like. I've seen *Dark Horizon* and all, but I never know how much to believe."

Selena leaned forward and spoke through a scowl, "That vid is the biggest load of crap I've ever seen. You know how at the end they find the huge shard and it takes all three ships to tug it out? That's garbage. One good trawler is all you need. No resistance in space. You just need a good line and a steady hand. The rest takes care of itself."

Rose laughed and clapped her hands together. "Oh, I love the way you talk. Like Wes Gunner from *No Man's Land*." The nurse sighed. "It's too bad. Since The Mandate, all we get are those lame propaganda pieces." Rose imitated the serious delivery of a reporter from a Mandate Broadcast: "Witness the brave welders risking life and limb aboard the *Chimera* ..."

Selena laughed.

A tone sounded, and Rose's wrist screen blinked orange. "Oh, I've got to run. When you're well enough, you can come down to my berth and watch a few episodes of *Humphrey's Pride*. Volume up, I promise."

Rose whirled and rushed through the door. Selena pushed her

food tray aside. She'd never met anyone like Rose before. All the women at Scrapyard were old, like Molly Ring who ran the laundry or Shanya who piloted a tug. Her father wouldn't let her talk to the girls who worked at New Lux, and they wouldn't want to talk to her if she tried. They wore silky miniskirts and had perfect skin and didn't smell like stale sweat for a week at a time.

Her father thought as little of them as he did the colony's politics and religion. Liam complained to the dock warden when some of the flame-backs tried to open a temple in honor of Stephen. She understood why. The whack jobs believed that some silly cave scratchings proved that Stephen was some sort of prophet. She never could figure out if the Order worshiped Stephen, The Everything or some combination of the two. She didn't take anything away from Stephen. By all accounts he'd saved everyone on the *Chimera* from death when their original navigator died midway through their journey. But she didn't think of him as anything more than a gifted navigator.

Outside of the Mandate Broadcasts, Selena had only seen the *Chimera* once. Not long after her ninth birthday, she and Liam had flown to Stephen's Point to attend a funeral for one of Liam's childhood friends. Selena had never met the man, but Liam insisted she come with him. "It ain't exactly safe to leave you at Scrapyard by yourself."

"I'll be safe!" she insisted. "I can take care of myself."

"I meant safe for *them*. I'll come back, and you'll have taken over the damned place."

Coasting at full-burn in the commercial shuttle that made daily flights from Scrapyard to the colony, Liam sat in his chair, hands clamped over his bouncing knees.

"What's wrong with you?" she asked.

"I don't trust these things. The shuttle pilots strut around in their uniforms like they're better than all of us. They think they're the hottest shingle on the squire deck, but they wouldn't last five minutes in the rim."

Displayed on wallscreens inside the shuttle cabin, the rim disappeared behind them. Selena slept for a time, woke, ate a prepackaged meal, and then began reading Magma Man until a chime alerted them that they were about to begin deceleration. They strapped in, and moments later the shuttle began to fire a prolonged burn, slowing its momentum and swinging into a vector that would drop it into low orbit around the colony.

Gauleta swelled on the wallscreen, the Stephen's Point moon tiny by comparison, a hazy, white eye against the green swirls of Gauleta. Elypso shone around the border of the planet, a sheer wall of pure light.

Selena couldn't speak—it was too beautiful.

"That moon ain't your home," Liam said. "Never forget where you come from. Us Samuelsons aren't just common colonists. No, we go all the way back to the original flight crew. Your grandpa used to tell me stories about his great grandpa and how he helped Stephen lay the stitches connecting Earth to Elypso."

She'd heard the story a thousand times before. How her First Colonist ancestor helped save the *Chimera*. "Stephen gets all the credit, but he wouldn't have gotten the job done without a Samuelson beside him." Selena dismissed Liam's stories about Ashley Samuelson as exaggerations. She'd seen historical vids of him on the nets, but her father's insistence that Stephen had somehow stolen the credit for rescuing the *Chimera* from his great, great, great grandpa seemed farfetched.

"We're landing soon, "Liam said. "You remember what I told you?"

Selena rolled her eyes. "Stephen's Point is dangerous and the people there are strange. I shouldn't leave your side while we're down there or Stephen himself might come abduct me for a human sacrifice. That about cover it?"

Liam chuckled. "That's the gist of it, yes."

On the wallscreen, a shimmering tail of pink-blue gas circled Gauleta. Closer now, she could make out a tiny pinprick of light near the moon. The colony ship!

She'd explored its interior in simulations, studied its specifications, watched specials about its design and function. Leaning into the wallscreen, she drank in the view. Drawing closer, Selena counted the empty spaces along the ship's spine where the colony pods once resided. She measured out its length and examined the command deck. She wished she had *The Bee's* interface and scopes. Scans might reveal a hint of heat from the drive assembly—a core or two still online, waiting for the command to cycle up, to bring the sleeping giant to life.

"Do you think …?"

"Do I think what?" Liam replied.

"Is *she* still in there?"

Liam shrugged. "Sure. She'll live pretty much forever, going round and round that moon until the debt has been paid in full."

"Then what?" Selena asked, knowing the answer but wanting to hear it from Liam.

"Then some lucky shmucks from the surface will take her for a spin."

Selena treasured that information, eyes traveling over the colony ship, drinking in every detail.

"Don't get your hopes up," Liam said. "To them you're just some rimmer. Doesn't matter where you came from or who you're related to, they aren't gonna let a Scrapyard pup like you get within a thousand klicks of her."

CHAPTER TWELVE

Theo expected his parents to interrogate him when he returned from speaking with Duncan. Instead, they told him to take a quick shower and go to bed. He didn't argue. His muscles ached from all the climbing he'd done in the cave, and a headache still thumped away between his ears. Sleep would be a relief.

He entered the shower tube and let hot water rinse the dirt and grime from his face and hair. Piles of grit collected on the duraceramic beneath him. He ran his fingers over the pliable plastiheal protecting his injured head and stomach. He'd never used it before. His family couldn't afford it. He toweled off and pulled on a clean set of clothing. When he exited the shower he found the house darkened and silent, his parents already in bed. They must have decided to save the yelling for the morning.

Theo paused at the foot of the stairs that led to the second story bedroom he shared with Liddy, listening to the steady chirp from the refrigerator reminding them for the millionth time that it needed its filter replaced and the creak of settling furniture as the thermostat brought the temperature down for the night. His dad liked the house cold enough that water left out iced over on cold nights. He breathed in the familiar scents of his home: the special soap his mother used to wash her and Liddy's hair, the lingering hint of brine and fish. Familiar things that no longer offered even a bit of comfort.

He climbed the stairs and pushed the bedroom door open— slowly enough to prevent it from creaking—and crossed the darkened room from memory. He collapsed on his bed, burrowed under the covers and closed his eyes.

A moment later Liddy climbed in beside him, pressing her small, freezing-cold feet against his back.

"Liddy, get back in your bed," he whispered.

"But I'm cold," she said, giggling.

"I know. I can feel your feet!"

Liddy wriggled her toes against his skin. Theo rolled over and looked at her grinning face. "It's late. Five-year-olds aren't supposed to be awake."

"I heard yelling downstairs," Liddy said, quivering a little. "I saw that man. Is he from the Order?"

"Yes," Theo said. "What do you mean you saw him?"

"I was at the top of the stairs. I saw him, and he saw me," she said. Liddy leaned up to his ear and whispered, "He smiled and he didn't tell on me."

Theo's mind drifted for a moment, the sound of his own breathing mixing with Liddy's. Heartrate slowing, he gave up sending Liddy back to her bed. He was going to sleep.

"Theo?"

He twitched. "Hmmm?"

"I heard that Order man say you're in the Selection." Wonder filled Liddy's voice.

"It's true."

"Whoa!" Liddy grabbed his face with both hands, her eyes shining. He wished he felt half as enthusiastic as she looked. He'd done a little thinking while in the shower. Duncan had listed his score on the navigation test as seventy-three. The test had ended on question seventy-four. Duncan must have seen Theo's *actual* test results where Theo failed everything but the puzzle section, only the crazy branches left unsolved. And yet Duncan had still let him into the Selection. Why? Theo couldn't think of an explanation that made sense.

"What's wrong?" Liddy asked. "Are you sad because Dad doesn't like it?"

"I'm not sad," Theo said, pushing her hands away from his face. "Just very, very tired."

"But you're going to go up to the *Chimera,* aren't you?"

At the mention of the colony ship, a chill ran through him. He remembered the colony-wide Mandate Broadcast announcing the rebuild project when Liddy was a baby. Theo and his dad charged into the street, Erin close behind, carrying Liddy. The Song of the Colony blared from every public wallscreen, followed by the announcement that the *Chimera* would be rebuilt and crewed for a return trip to Earth. A collective cheer rose from the Swallows. After months of arguing and bureaucratic time wasting, somebody was *doing* something.

Hope began to offset the grim years of food shortages and rationing, the subtle fear that subverted every happy moment. United, joyous, Theo and his family joined the impromptu celebration. Theo sang and cheered along with everyone else, applauding the imagery of the *Chimera* overlaid with graphics detailing what would be done to restore her. He'd watched with fascination, imagining what it would be like to stand on the old colony ship's navigation deck. To leap across hundreds of light years of distance. To see Earth.

As months passed, the hive of ships around the *Chimera* grew so large in number that when they passed overhead, they looked like a new, fast moving star. Each time he felt a sense of longing.

"I won't make it that far," Theo said. "They only take the very best."

"But you are best," Liddy said. "You're really smart. The man said so."

"Too smart for my own good," Theo said, ruefully. "And the man—Doctor Duncan—I don't think he knows what he's talking about. Now go back to your bed, Liddy."

She wrapped a small but strong arm around his chest. "I don't want to!"

"Keep your voice down," Theo said. "You want Mom to come up here?"

Liddy shook her head, a piece of her downy hair catching against Theo's nose.

"Neither do I. Here, I'll carry you."

"Okay," Liddy said, suddenly cheerful. Theo climbed out of bed and slipped his arm under Liddy's legs. She clung to his neck as he carried her to her smaller bed, tucked against the opposite wall. He laid her down, pulling the blankets up to her chin.

"You won't get so cold if you stay under there," he said.

"Kiss," Liddy demanded.

"I don't do kisses," Theo said.

"Kiss!"

Theo groaned, leaned down, and kissed her forehead.

"Theo, are you gonna see Earth?" Liddy asked, the love in her voice so clear and strong and good that he had to speak around a lump in his throat to reply.

"I doubt it," he said. "Now go to sleep."

He returned to his bed where exhaustion soon overcame him. Memories of the cave, the body, and the threatening voice of the whisperer loomed in his dreams. A boot shoved a body over the edge of the chasm. Theo's body. He fell for an eternity, his own scream merging with Meghan's terrified voice shouting his name.

* * *

Meghan refused to respond to his pings until a Mandate Broadcast announced the results of the Selection testing four days sooner than expected. Theo felt certain they'd done it in response to his hacking of the list. It made sense—if someone knew the results, they might as well tell everyone before whoever stole the list could use it. Not that it mattered. He hadn't even tried to sell the information. He'd done little except keep out of his dad's way, try and contact Meghan and hope that the Regulatory didn't show up at his doorstep with questions about the hacked Selection list. Or worse, the discovery of a dead body with his DNA on it.

But after the Mandate Broadcast announced the names of those who would begin the Selection training in a handful of days, Meghan finally replied in her typical, succinct manner:

Let's talk. Outside Civvy. 1 hour.

Theo hadn't returned to the Civvy since he'd hacked the list, and he didn't want to go there now. But he *needed* to talk to Meghan. He'd thought long and hard about what to tell her, how to explain things in a way she'd understand. He'd gone over it again and again, and though his words would be far from perfect, he hoped they might help smooth things between them before the start of Selection training.

Theo left his house far earlier than he needed to and weaved his way through the outskirts of the Swallows. It felt like everywhere he went people were watching him, talking about him. He was *somebody* now. In the Selection. Important. If they only knew the truth. He gave sheepish smiles to those who called him out by name, dodging their questions and praise, moving away as quickly as possible until he reached the place where the remnants of one of the *Chimera's* six landing pods curved overhead.

Round and five stories high, entering it felt like walking under a massive, upside-down bowl. At the very center sat the Civvy, surrounded by an open plaza. A giant hole at the center of the pod offered a clear view of the sky above. Everyone and everything that made up the Swallows had originally come from inside the pod. Theo's house and everyone else's had been broken out of its interior, leaving behind the duraceramic shell like the cast-off of some giant crustacean.

The Elypso-bleached walls of the pod reflected ambient light in all directions, bathing everything in an even, soft light. Theo strode toward the plaza, listening for his handscreen's ping signaling a new message from Meghan. He arrived ten minutes early and sat on one of the curve-backed benches that surrounded the monument to Pod Six. The monument featured some mementos in clear cases and wallscreens displaying vids of the Pod descending from the sky. Its propulsion rockets scoured the moon's surface, turning rock to molten lava. The pod was now fused to the ground itself, a permanent fixture that would survive tens of dozens of generations of colonists—assuming the colony itself didn't die off first.

Theo pinged Meghan:

Here. Pod Six. Bench.

His leg jigged up and down as he waited. He rehearsed his explanation, trying to predict Meghan's response. He'd given up hope she would ever see him the way she had when he first told her he'd made the Selection, but maybe he could earn back a little bit of her respect. Maybe they could still be friends.

Meghan emerged from the foot traffic surrounding the Civvy. Theo stood to greet her, tucking his handscreen into his pocket, trying to look casual and confident.

"Let's walk," Meghan said and took off without waiting for his reply.

"Okay," he said, trotting to catch up to her.

Meghan led him away from the monument, to the periphery of the pod where a sidewalk ran around the interior wall. Massive arches broke up the wall at regular intervals, each large enough to fit a house through because actual houses *had* gone through them. Meghan stepped into the nearest arch and shaded her eyes. The Golden Valley was spread below, other pods nestled against the sweet grass like giant eggs, interconnected by roadways, surrounded by the suburbs of prefab houses and original construction.

"I've thought a lot about what I wanted to say to you."

"Me too," Theo agreed. Meghan wasn't yelling. Her face

betrayed no strong emotion. Maybe things would go better than he'd expected. Maybe she'd just needed a little time and space to simmer down.

"I know you added your name to the list," Meghan said.

"You're right," Theo agreed. He'd planned to confess it all along—no sense in denying the obvious to someone as sharp as Meghan. He waited for her to continue, but she continued to look out at the Golden Valley in silence. After waiting long enough that things started to feel awkward, Theo spoke again.

"Are you looking at something in particular?"

"No," Meghan replied.

She turned sideways, leaning against the arch, ponytail hanging forward over her shoulder. Theo wished he could take out his handscreen and take an image of her—she looked so perfect. Neutral light lit her profile: a strong chin and mouth, blue-green eyes, the shape of her fit body.

"Why did you do it?" Meghan asked. "Tell me the truth."

Theo sought eye contact but Meghan wouldn't reciprocate. He waited, cleared his throat. Finally he pushed both hands into his pockets and shrugged. "I wanted a chance to be special. A chance to help save the colony."

"The colony?"

"Yes," Theo said. "You remember the Mandate Broadcast when they announced the *Chimera* rebuild? The way people filled the streets? Everyone talking and shouting and cheering?"

"Of course I do."

"They said that the ship would have to be crewed by Jubilee babies. People our age."

"That's when I started to train," Meghan said.

Theo ducked his head. "I remember. You were so serious about it. You know why I didn't?"

"Not really, no."

"Because I knew it wouldn't matter." He yanked his hands out of his pockets and held them out. "I've *never* been good at that sort of thing. I'm not a good student. I'm not a good test taker. I'm not good at following rules."

He felt her listening. He could convince her.

"But I dreamed about it. Every night. Being on the *Chimera.* Saving the colony. And then there I am, working on an Epsilon for the Civvy and I run across the Selection list. All the names, right there in front of me. I added my name so that I could have a chance to help. To do my part."

"That's the truth?" Meghan asked.

"Yes."

"You have this massive need to help save the colony?"

"Yes."

Meghan laughed, dry and mirthless.

"It's not funny," Theo said.

"Yes, Theo. It is funny. Funny and very, very sad." Her eyes met his. Theo flinched back as if she'd struck him. She hadn't believed a word he'd said. His carefully thought through plan was collapsing around him like a salt-sand formation in the wind.

Meghan pushed off the arch with her shoulder blades. "You're a liar."

Theo took a step back but she closed in on him so fast he almost tripped over his own feet. She stood inches away, so close he could smell her.

"You're a pathetic, self-serving liar. You didn't add your name to help save the colony. You added it because you want to be important without having to do anything to deserve it. When you first told me you were on the list, I didn't believe you because it didn't make sense. Let's face it, Theo. You're hardly qualified. You're a bad student. You haven't trained. You play fast and loose with the rules. You're a borderline criminal. No, you *are* a criminal. But that's not the worst of it. Oh no, that's not even close to the worst."

Theo felt as if he were shrinking, legs shortening with each word Meghan spoke. Soon he'd be inches high, with her towering over him. She could crush him under one of her boots.

"The worst thing is that you're a *waste*. A waste of a person. Despite my doubts, when I thought about you making the list, I could see it. I wanted to believe. Because you have a little bit of brilliance. You do. The way you can talk to machines—I don't know anyone that can do it so easily. I thought that maybe I'd been wrong about you. I thought that because I *wanted* to think it. I *wanted* you to be more than I'd thought you were because …"

The disappointment in her face was so terrible in its intensity that Theo couldn't look at her.

"I thought maybe I hadn't been fair to you," Meghan said, voice low, as if she now saw the truth so clearly that it could never be unseen. "I saw what I wanted to see because I like you. Now I know the truth. You're a liar. And you don't just lie to other people, Theo. You lie to yourself."

Theo wanted to turn and disappear into the foot traffic around the plaza and lose himself in anonymity. He forced himself to stay, to speak. "You're right. You're right about me. Everything you said."

Meghan looked a little surprised, but her eyes remained skeptical. "So what are you going to do about it, Theo?"

"What do you mean?"

"How are you going to make this right?"

Theo shook his head. "I can't."

"Yes, Theo, you can. You can go and tell them what you did. Tell Doctor Duncan that you added your name. That you shouldn't be in the Selection. Accept your punishment."

"They'll send me to prison," Theo protested.

"Maybe."

"And you're okay with that?"

Meghan paused, then shrugged. "It's better than living a lie."

Living a lie. She had no idea what living a lie was like. Because you didn't really live at all. Despite what Meghan thought she knew and her smug attitude, Theo hadn't lied about everything. He really did want to help the colony. And she wasn't wrong about his skill with machines. That could be useful on the *Chimera*. Duncan certainly seemed to think so.

"You don't know everything," Theo said.

Meghan whipped her pony tail over her shoulder with a toss of her head. "No, Theo, I don't know everything. But I know cheating when I see it.""

He tried again. "Duncan said I scored a seventy-three on the navigation index. That was my real score, not a fake one. I was the highest scorer in the entire colony."

"Whatever, Theo. I'm done with this conversation."

Meghan started to push past him but he blocked her way. "It's true. He knows I added my name. Or at least I think he does. And he let me stay in the Selection anyway."

The creases at the corners of Meghan's eyes tightened. "You fooled him, Theo. You put on a really good show with all your false humility and pretend sincerity. But you don't fool me."

She had no idea what he was doing for her, how he was

protecting her. And he couldn't tell her because it might put her at risk. "There are things you don't know," he muttered. "Things that might change what you think about me."

"Sure there are. Mountains of them, I bet. But you can tell them to someone else because I'm through listening." Meghan tossed her head, ponytail whipping over her shoulder. "You've got three days, Theo. If you don't tell the truth before the Selection training starts, then I will."

CHAPTER THIRTEEN

Doctor Cholewa studied Selena from behind silver-framed glasses, eyebrows pinched, mouth a thin, severe line. Glittering specks of green hid in his brown irises like precious stones. His short, wavy hair and smooth face gave him a boyish appearance. "You're a popular girl," he said. "You've got a whole list of people waiting to see you."

Selena's heart jumped and the wallscreen displaying her vitals made a tiny chirp. "Really? Who?"

"We'll get to that. Why did you tear off your monitors and crawl out of your room? You tore open your sutures and lost a lot of blood in the process. You could have died."

"Who wants to see me?"

Dr. Cholewa ignored her question. "Why were you so desperate to leave that room?"

"Does it matter? When can I see my father?"

"Look, Selena, I don't have time to play games. You answer my questions and when you're done, I *might* answer yours."

Her cheeks flushed with anger. Who did this Cholewa think he was? The cussing Stephen returned? "Balls," she said.

Dr. Cholewa studied a small screen in his left hand. "You suffered a major concussion and a spinal injury. Can you feel this?" He prodded her arm with a sharp-ended instrument.

"Ouch! It's my legs that don't work, moron!"

"Oh, yes, that is what the report says. I must have missed it."

Selena scowled. "You did that on purpose."

"A doctor must never do intentional harm to his patient. It's against our code of ethics."

Dr. Cholewa's bland smile infuriated her. "Harm is all that's happened since I've been here! You put me in a room with that ogre Victor Kretchiwitz, no one will tell me anything about my father, and now you're assaulting me with that *thing* everyone here won't stop jabbing me with. It's ridiculous."

"I think 'assaulting' is a bit of a reach."

"You're not listening to me." Selena wriggled upright and leveled a finger at Dr. Cholewa. "You'd better start answering *my* questions or I'll climb out of this bed and crawl out of here. I'll find someone who will listen, and then I'll have them come and shut you down."

"You can lodge all the complaints you wish when you meet with the ombudsman."

Selena's eyes widened. "An ombudsman? Which one?"

Rather than answer, the doctor turned away and punched notes into his handscreen. Why was one of the most powerful members of the government's economic office coming to see her? What could they want?

Dr. Cholewa moved to the door.

"Wait," Selena called. "I'll answer your questions."

Dr. Cholewa looked back over his shoulder and raised an eyebrow. "You will?"

"Yes. But you have to answer mine. One for one."

"All right," the doctor agreed. Then, muttering under his breath, "just like every rimmer I've ever met—"

"I'm not stupid, you know," Selena said.

"That's debatable."

"I know my father's dead." The finality of the words surprised her. Tears skimmed down her checks. She glared at him, hands kneading the bed sheet. Dr. Cholewa didn't answer. So it was true. She blinked, squeezing her lips tight to hide their tremor, teeth grinding together, suppressing the scream of sorrow threatening to rip out of her.

The doctor crossed the room and leaned close. "Your father is alive." The words came with the scent of a spice Selena didn't recognize. "I attended him and the other victims of the trawler crash. The injuries he suffered required treatment options unavailable on the *Hydra*."

Tears leaked from the sides of her eyes, filling her ear canals before soaking into the sheet beneath her.

"I'm sorry," Dr. Cholewa said. "I told you this before, but you must have forgotten. Concussions can cause short-term memory loss. I had no idea you were lying there believing your father was dead."

Selena wondered what else she had forgotten. The idea that her memory might have become unreliable frightened her more than her paralyzed legs. She prided herself on remembering things. She remembered far too well. Even things she wished she could forget.

* * *

Her mother had always coughed. This time she coughed until she fell to the ground. She held a hand over her mouth, hacking. When she brought her hand away, it was coated with red. She coughed again, and more red came out. Her mother groaned and rolled on her belly, and the red soaked into the snow. It dried on her face like lace. It dried while Selena tried to roll her mother over so she could wake her, but she lay so very, very still. Nothing could rouse her.

Later, the flies came. A few at a time, buzzing and whisking from place to place until a whole swarm of them crawled over her mother's skin. Some went up her nostrils. Still her mother would not wake. Selena sat, snow melting through her clothing. She was very cold. She had to pee, but her mother couldn't help her pull down the thick pants with the wooly insides, and so she peed in them and that made her even colder, but not as cold as her mother's skin.

The sky spread overhead and wind whipped against her jacket. Insects buzzed. Her mother wouldn't wake. She wouldn't wake, and Selena was alone, way up in the foothills behind their house, on the bank of a river. Water rushed past. Wind whirled and blew over the still, cold body that used to be her mother but had become a lump—a thing.

It took a long time to climb down from the river. The door to the house wouldn't open. Her mother had a key but Selena didn't. She went around back and kicked at a window plate until it bent enough for her to slide her hand inside and open the latch. The house smelled empty. She was cold and wet. She took off the wet things and went to her bedroom and climbed under the covers. She slept. She woke up. She changed her clothes and went to the kitchen to find something to eat.

There wasn't much food in the kitchen. By the second day she'd eaten everything but the cans she couldn't get open. The water wouldn't turn on, so she drank what she found in the plastic bottles her mother kept for when it got cold enough to freeze things solid. On the third day, the bottles ran out. She got so thirsty she thought about going back to the river. But that would mean she'd have to see *the thing* and the bugs, so she stayed in the house, startling at every sound, hoping her mother would come home. She would pull Selena up into her lap and comb her hair out and sing to her about Elypso and the rim and her father out there with the shards.

On the fourth day, she'd grown so weak and thirsty and tired that she crawled into her bed and lay as still as *the thing* up by the river. She wondered how long it would take to not hear or see anything anymore. She hoped it wouldn't be too long.

When Elypso went away and the house grew dark, people came and banged and banged on the door. They hammered and thumped, and then the door broke open. People in black uniforms came into her room. They lifted her from the bed and carried her, wrapped in her own pee-soaked blanket, out into the wind blowing down off the mountains.

The people in the black uniforms contacted her father, working a ninety-rotation shift at the rim. They told him that his wife had died, and his four-year-old daughter needed him.

Eight days later, the host family caring for her announced that her father had made arrangements to pick her up at the Nadil Space Strip. They drove through Stephen's Point in the midst of a relentless windstorm. It sounded like voices to Selena, and she buried her face in a plush fleece the woman had given her, unwilling to look out until they'd crossed through the gates of Nadil and the tall rockets stood in stark contrast with snowcapped mountains.

The man who met them in one of the hangars was not her father. Short and thick, he looked nothing like the man whose face she'd seen every day of her life in a framed image on her bedroom wall. A static image brought to life with a touch. Each morning she would pad over and press the frame with a chubby pointer finger. The image would saturate and come to life. Liam would turn, realize he was being recorded, smile, and then laugh, deep and long, as her mother did something off camera. A few scant seconds long, the vid ended with her father in the midst of a toothy smile. She never failed to hear the sound of his laughter as if he stood in front of her, the smell of the Mescua he liked to drink rich on his breath.

The man at Nadil was not the man who smiled and laughed. He didn't smile at all, and looked serious and terrifying. Selena cowered next to the woman who had fed and bathed her since her mother fell next to the river.

"This is Selena?" the man asked.

"Yes."

"I'll see she arrives safe." The man beckoned but Selena didn't move.

"Maybe this is a bad idea," the woman said. "She's so young."

The man knelt and offered his hand. "Your father sent for you. Now come with me and I'll introduce you to the greatest thrill in the universe."

"Daddy?" Selena asked.

"That's right, Daddy."

"It's no place for a little girl," the woman said.

"Funny, you didn't seem to care what sort of place it was when you accepted your half of the money."

"I don't like this. I don't feel good about it at all."

The man took Selena by the hand. "What's left of this girl's family is up there. So if you want to go crying to the regulators, be my guest. But if an orbital-reentry pod comes smashing through your roof, don't say I didn't warn you."

The woman stared at the man, face white and drawn. The man walked very fast, and Selena had to run to keep up with him. Her feet clacked over the metal grating as they turned a corner and entered a massive open-air dock. Ahead, a bulky orange machine crouched on the tarmac. Selena didn't know what the machine did, but something about it appealed to her.

"Come ride a pillar of fire with me," the man said.

A ladder dropped from an oval opening. As the man carried her up, Selena understood two things: her father had sent for her, and this machine would take her to him.

CHAPTER FOURTEEN

The night before the Selection training began, Theo couldn't sleep. When he closed his eyes it felt good, like sleep would take him swiftly, but it didn't. His mind churned with adrenaline and fear. He hadn't heard from Meghan, hadn't sent her any more messages. If she'd reported him to the Regulatory, they hadn't come looking for him. Maybe they were waiting to see if he showed up for training. They'd arrest him right there, in front of the other candidates. Maybe they'd invite the media, make him the leading news story for the day. *Regulatory Seeks Death Penalty For Traitorous Selection Candidate Accused of Conspiracy.*

Theo wasn't looking forward to seeing Meghan again. He wished he'd never found the Selection list on the Epsilon, never added his name, never gone up to the cave to meet Meghan. How simple his life would be. How normal. Meghan would become a hero, and Theo would stay on Stephen's Point living the way he always had. But it was far too late for that. The life he'd lived before the cave now seemed like a luxury—a distant, happy time when everything made sense and nothing surprised him.

When he did drift into sleep, open mouths and silent screams filled his dreams.

He woke to someone shaking him. Liddy smiled, sleep-tousled hair falling around her ears in uneven tufts. "Wakey," she said. "Breakfast time."

"It's still early," Theo said. He rubbed at his heavy eyes and closed them to go back to sleep. A damp finger probed the inside of his ear.

"Liddy! Leave me alone!"

"Mom says you gotta get up." Liddy tried to pry his eyes open with clumsy fingers. "She's got hot-melt ready."

"Why?" Theo asked. Made from their reserve supply of ground wheat, hot-melt was a treat set aside for special occasions.

"So you have energy for the Selection—"

Theo exploded upright, almost knocking Liddy off the bed.

"Hey!" she cried, indignant, as he swung his legs over the side and dropped to the floor.

Theo yanked clothes out of the dresser. Liddy jumped from the bed and stood beside him, head cocked to the side. "Is the *Chimera* going to come get you?"

"No, she's not. It doesn't work like that. She's up in space. And I'm nowhere near through the Selection."

Liddy grabbed him around his right calf, clinging to his leg. "Lump on a log," she said. "Lump on a log."

"Let go, Liddy. I need to get ready." He unclasped her arms and pushed her away, a little harder than he intended. She made a face and pounded down the stairs. Her voice traveled up the stairwell as he finished dressing, complaining to their mom.

"What did you do?" Erin asked when Theo came downstairs.

"Nothing."

"She said you shoved her."

"She wouldn't let go of my leg. I needed to get dressed. I've got Selection training today."

Erin paused her stirring of the simmering hot-melt. "She's worried about you. All of this is scary for her. She's only five, Theo. She doesn't understand what the *Chimera* is, much less Earth. All she knows is that you might go away for a long time."

"She doesn't need to be scared," Theo said.

Erin smiled, face warm and soft. "It's a huge responsibility, saving the colony."

"I wouldn't get your hopes up."

"Don't be so fatalistic. Doctor Duncan said—"

"I know what he said," Theo snapped.

"He's from the Order, Theo. He's an educated man."

"Okay, Mom," Theo said, wanting the conversation to end so he could eat his hot-melt and get moving.

Erin filled his bowl and handed it to him. "He could be a good influence on you if you let him."

He didn't bother sitting and spooned scalding hot cereal into his mouth, in too much of a hurry to enjoy it. When he finished, he said goodbye to Erin and Liddy and bolted out the door.

Jogging through the Swallows, he welcomed the calming effect of the cold air. Navigating the maze of narrow streets made monochrome by the permadawn, Theo headed for the Civvy. A security drone warbled overhead, red light blinking on its abdomen. He ducked into a doorway, hand dropping to his empty pocket where he usually kept his handscreen, ready to hotkey in the command to wipe all sensitive data before remembering he'd left it at home. Handscreens were on the list of contraband, not welcome at the training.

Theo shoved out of the doorway and trotted along, toward where he and the rest of the candidates would take a Regulatory vehicle to the training field at the Order compound. He ran under an arch in the pod wall and angled across the plaza. Vendors shuffled around their carts, preparing to open for business. Where once he might have smelled flatbread cooking over coals, greasy soup, and smoked fish, there was only cold air and the grousing of vendors. No one could sell food any longer, the controls were too tight. The vendors still showed up though, carts laden with items scavenged or, in some cases, stolen.

Most of the other candidates were already waiting at the Pod Six monument. Theo knew a few of them: Hephaestus and his fraternal twin Phoebus, a boy named Preston who lived on Theo's street, and of course, Meghan. She ignored him as he skidded to a stop at the edge of the group.

"Hey," Theo said, addressing the twenty or so kids, most older and taller than him. Stronger too. They all wore loose-fitting athletic clothes, t-shirts, and matching shorts. Theo looked down at his pants and long-sleeve shirt.

"You got in last minute," Hephaestus said. Massive, dark-skinned, and almost two years older than Theo, he made Theo feel like a pale little worm of a person, utterly unprepared for what lay ahead.

"Yes," Theo said, eyes flicking to Meghan. She wasn't paying attention, but in a way so obvious that he knew she was listening to every word. Had she told any of them what he'd done? Had she told *anyone*? He thought again of the whisperer's threat in the cave. If he told her the truth, would she believe him? Probably not. He'd have to keep his mouth shut. Regardless of what she thought of him, he'd protect her. Always.

Hephaestus gave Theo a skeptical once-over. "You look stupid."

Theo forced a smile out of his uncooperative lips. "Uh,

thanks?"

"Heph means that you're dressed stupid," Phoebus chimed in. Half a head shorter than Hephaestus but with the same dark complexion and deep brown eyes, Phoebus smiled sympathetically. "Didn't anyone tell you what to wear?"

Theo contrasted his clothing with the skimpy athletic apparel everyone else wore. "No," he said. "I guess not. Aren't you guys cold?"

"Right now? Sure," Heph said. "But wait until we start training. You'll get hot and sweat though your shirt and pants. Then they'll cling to you and slow you down."

Hephaestus had a point. How silly he must look to them—a group of candidates who'd prepared for over a year to be a part of the Selection process.

"You could always strip down," Heph suggested. "Wear your underwear."

Theo wasn't sure if the older boy was serious or mocking him. "Do you know what we're going to be doing?" Theo asked Phoebus, the nicer of the twins.

"They're going to do everything they can to get us to quit," Phoebus said.

"Why?"

"Because anyone can pass a *test*," Meghan said, voice sharp, "but you can't *fake* a pull-up."

"She's right," Heph said, skewering Theo with an appraising glance. "My guess? You won't last more than an hour."

"Don't listen to them," Phoebus said. "Choose *not* to fail. Stephen taught that the mind rules the body."

"Theo knows all about Stephen," Meghan said. She turned, face like a razor that scraped away at his skin. "You're the Stephen reborn, right?"

Heph and Phoebus laughed. Meghan didn't crack a smile.

"That's me," Theo said, playing along. "The second Stephen."

"Well, good luck to you, second Stephen," Phoebus said. "Prove these jerks wrong."

"Luck's got nothing to do with it," Meghan said. "People succeed through preparation and skill."

Theo glanced again at his pants and long-sleeve shirt. His hard-soled shoes. Meghan's unrelenting, scornful face. None of them believed in him. None of them expected him to make it through the day. Not his parents, not Meghan, not all the rest of the candidates. What did they know? He'd made it out of the cave alive, and Duncan said that he'd aced the navigation test. There was a lot more to him than anyone realized. Today he'd prove all his doubters wrong and Duncan right. And when he earned his place aboard the *Chimera,* he could put the events of the cave far, far behind him.

* * *

The Regulatory bus rumbled up the side of the mountain and entered the Order compound. At the back of the bus, Theo watched the valley spread below them, other pods distant but visible reminders that they were only one of six different training groups. Every pod had fielded a number of potential candidates, but the poorer neighborhoods like the Swallows had far more than their richer counterparts. His father thought it was because politicians and rich people didn't want their kids risking their lives in space, but that didn't make sense to Theo. As far as he could tell, everyone *wanted* to be in the Selection.

The numbers showed an obvious skew. Of the two percent or so of those who passed the DNA test, most came from The Swallows, the Bunkers, or Conway. Perhaps more genetic drift occurred among the poorer colonists because they worked more dangerous jobs and had more children?

He imagined the other training groups—kids like them— crammed into other buses, headed off for the first day of training. Nervous. Eager. Hopeful. He couldn't help but feel the energy of it. The intoxicating expectancy. Excitement surged through him like a potent cocktail of liquid energy.

They passed near the towering library where Theo first met Duncan. Scores of apprentices, curates and other Order personnel lined the roadway, waving and cheering. The bus lumbered through the prefabs and out to the periphery of the compound where it stopped at the edge of a large concrete slab. Once a parking lot reserved for ramblers, the lot had been closed for years. Overgrown with weeds, cracked and crumbling, like everything at the Swallows.

Elypso slid from behind Great Northern, the first daystroke in three rotations, turning the concrete to shimmering gold. They would have four hours of brilliance until the moon's orbit carried it around the side of Gauleta, resulting in a return of the permadawn created by light refracting in Gauleta's atmosphere.

At the far edge of the field, a lone figure stood, looking down toward the valley below. As Theo and the others approached, the person strode forward and Theo saw it was another boy, not that much older than himself, but thicker through the chest and arms. He wore athletic shorts and a t-shirt similar to everyone's clothing but Theo's. A strange feeling came over him. Had he seen the other boy before? He felt certain he knew him from somewhere. Something about the way he walked, the careful way he moved.

Theo turned to Phoebus. "Who is that?"

Phoebus shrugged. "Don't know. Maybe he got in last minute like you."

Theo tried to catch a better view of the newcomer, but everyone had turned to face the mountain road where a long line of black ramblers sped toward them. Theo stood on his toes. He couldn't see the other boy's face, just a glimpse of thick, dark hair.

Phoebus clapped Theo on the shoulder. "Can't wait, huh?"

Theo looked at Phoebus, confused. "What?"

"Nothing." Phoebus shook his head and grinned. "You were just, bouncing, or something."

"Oh. Yeah. Excited, I guess," Theo said.

The candidates clumped together. *Safety in numbers,* Theo thought. A hush fell as the ramblers arrived. Doors opened and regulators poured out. Their black uniforms seemed to reflect and absorb light at the same time. Of course the Regulatory would be administering the training. What had he expected? Hopefully they were all from the Golden Valley and wouldn't recognize him. He didn't need any more scrutiny.

The regulators formed ranks and saluted as a short man with a shaved head and a jaw like a bulldog charged between them. He wore black cargo pants, a tan t-shirt, and scowled as if the day itself offended him. His boots thumped the concrete as he approached. Theo had never seen a soldier—the divestment agreement signed by the colonists when they left Earth forbid Steven's Point from creating a military—but somehow this man was one.

The man stopped a few paces from the group, roughly forty kids in all. No one breathed.

"Get in a line," the man ordered.

Kids shifted position, shuffled around, creating a wall of bodies two rows deep. Theo stood shoulder-to-shoulder with Meghan and Hephaestus.

"Unbelievable," the man said, shaking his head. "All those high test scores and yet you can't even form a straight line. You're as sorry a collection of garbage as I've ever laid eyes on." He exhaled, as if he couldn't believe his horrible luck. He walked along the line of kids that looked plenty straight to Theo, slowing to glower at one person or another.

"In case you hadn't already guessed, you're not here to screw off," the man said. "You're used to being coddled in your Selection classes. Treated like royalty. Made to feel important. All that ends today. I don't care what you think you know. I don't care how smart or talented or irreplaceable you think you are. Because from this moment forward, you belong to me. You are my personal property. You have no rights. No freedom. I'll do with you as I please."

He stopped and squared off to face them. "You will call me Sir," he said. "Do you understand?"

"Yes, sir!" most of the kids shouted. Theo caught on a little late, and the word left his mouth after the others had already finished saying it. Sir turned his gaze Theo's direction and approached, face a mixture of skepticism and horror.

"You some kind of clown?"

"No," Theo mumbled.

"Then why are you dressed like one?"

Theo's mouth went dry, tongue like sandpaper against the roof of his mouth. But Sir had already moved on, comparing a girl's face to an asteroid crater. He made his way down the line, insulting many of the candidates before turning his back on the entire group to survey the mountains.

Behind him, three uniformed regulators rolled out some sort of medical booth. It looked like the inoculator at the Civvy where Theo went for immunizations as a little kid. It powered up and a servo arm arrayed with various instruments and needles moved within the clear enclosure. One of the regulators nodded, giving Sir some sort of signal. Sir executed an about-face.

"Roll call," Sir said. "When I say your name, you will respond 'here.' Do you understand?" His voice rang over the concrete, making Theo's ears buzz.

"Yes, sir!" the kids shouted, Theo along with them this time.

"Lamar Anderson," Sir said.

"Here," a boy said.

"Shelby Blake."

"Here," another boy called.

Sir continued to call out names. He didn't have a handscreen to read from, but never slowed his rapid-fire pace.

"Marcus J. Locke."

"Here!" the boy who had been waiting at the training field shouted, chest extended, voice almost as loud as Sir's. The word "here" came not from his throat, but his stomach. Sir paused, seeming to note the newcomer in some way, and continued down the list. When Theo heard his name, he shouted "here," as loud as he could. Sir looked at him like a dog that had peed on his favorite rug.

Sir reached the last name on his list, Meghan Ziczek.

"Here," Meghan said, confident and direct.

"All right," Sir said. "Now we start weeding out the weaklings. You see that booth behind me? Anyone care to guess what it's there for?"

"To administer first aid, sir?" someone said.

Sir grinned. His square teeth all seemed to be the same size. "Wrong. Any other guesses?"

Nobody said anything. If it wasn't a medical booth, what was it for?

"You'll get a real, live demonstration before we're done today," Sir said. "I guarantee it. Now, on your faces and get ready to kiss concrete!"

Theo dropped to the ground along with the others, palms flat on the stone. Sir marched along, stopping in front of Theo. "Get your butt in the air, clown!"

Theo did as he was told.

"Higher."

Theo inched his feet forward, stomach already starting to ache. Sir's boot jabbed into his ribcage, forcing him higher.

Sir moved away. Risking a quick glance sideways, Theo saw that almost all the kids had perfectly straight spines, hands shoulder-width, toes locked together. They knew what they were doing.

"Marcus J. Locke," Sir said. "Front and center."

The boy rose and presented himself, arms locked at his sides. "Yes, sir?"

"You will lead our first exercise. Twenty reps. Can you count that high?"

"Yes, sir," Marcus said.

"Then do it."

Marcus turned on his heel and dropped into pushup position. "On my count," he called. "One!"

Everyone dropped and rose. Everyone but Theo. He remained motionless, knees quivering. Across a half-dozen yards of concrete, a pair of cool blue eyes locked on his. Theo's throat closed. He couldn't move, muscles seized, frozen in place by terror.

Marcus J. Locke. The lone waiter, the shouter, and now the leader. He was the whisperer from the cave. Theo would never forget those eyes. Eyes that now stared at him with malevolent recognition.

"Two," Marcus shouted, dipping down and up, eyes never wavering from Theo's face.

He heard the whisperer's voice, felt the heat of his breath against his ear. Saw the body tumble over the edge of the chasm. Dimly, he heard Marcus shouting numbers. What did the whisperer want? What did the numbers mean?

A hand closed around the back of Theo's shirt and yanked him into the air. "Stop," Sir shouted. The hand dropped him and Theo crunched against the pavement. A pair of black boots gleamed centimeters from his nose. Theo's terrified reflection shined back at him from the boots' polished surface.

"Stand up," Sir commanded.

Theo stood.

"Do you think this is some sort of joke?"

"No, sir," Theo whispered, unable to look away from Marcus, still in push-up position.

"I can't hear you!" Fine droplets of Sir's spittle sprayed across Theo's face.

"No, sir."

"Then *why* aren't you completing your pushups?"

"I don't know, sir." Theo said.

"You don't know?"

"Yes … I mean no."

"Sir!" Sir roared. "Get back on your face, clown. You'll do an extra twenty push-ups when everyone has finished their first set."

Theo dropped and forced himself to complete the set of pushups. His elbows and knees shook and sweat rolled into his eyes. Marcus executed each of his pushups with precision, spine a straight line, arm muscles bulging. Every so often his eyes strayed back to Theo.

By the end of the second set of pushups, Theo's arms were mush. Half-digested hot-melt rose from his stomach and burned the back of his throat. What should he do? What *could* he do? Nothing. Marcus couldn't hurt him or Meghan here, not with two-dozen regulators around. For now he was safe. But once the training ended? Once they'd returned to the Swallows?

"On your feet, Locke," Sir said. "Fall in with the others."

"Yes, sir!" Marcus shouted. Without hesitation, he jumped back to his place in the line of bodies. And although Sir offered no praise, it was clear to everyone that he already had a favorite.

CHAPTER FIFTEEN

The door to Selena's room slid open. A towering man filled the entry, shoulders almost as wide as the doorframe. Tan formalwear complimented his dark skin, and silver and gold rings lined his large fingers. The scent of the man's cologne filled the room, as pervasive as his physical presence. Selena pushed her hair over her shoulders and swiped at a few crumbs lining the sheet, remnants of breakfast. Should she offer him her finger? Smile?

She decided on a smile, but it felt clumsy and fake and quickly turned into a grimace. Why had she smiled in the first place? What did the man want? Why didn't he say something?

Corey Hancock, the Scrap Warden who cut checks for a good pull, was the most important person she'd ever met. Corey wore thick denim, like most of the trawler captains, and began and ended his sentences with curses. He could often be found drinking away his own paycheck along with the ore hounds down at Hightower Row. She never felt nervous around Corey.

"What do you want?" The words fell out of her mouth and shattered on the floor. The man's face broke into a smile.

He gazed at Selena with a look of penetrating but not unfriendly interest. "Direct. I like that." His voice was gentle, almost high-pitched. How could such a small voice come out of such a large man?

"My name is Jasper Owagumbiea, Ombudsman over Rim Economic Affairs." He stepped forward and offered her his warm, silky-soft hand.

"Selena Samuelson."

"Do you mind if I sit down, Selena?"

She shrugged and the Ombudsman folded himself into a chair. His knees came up to meet his chest. He placed a large hand on each knee and leaned forward. "I'm pleased you've recovered enough for us to talk. How are you feeling?"

"Fine."

"I heard you made a dramatic exit from your room a few cycles ago. That's one of the reasons I'm here."

"What do you mean?"

"It was unwise to put two parties involved in a dispute in the same room. Very unwise."

"What dispute?" Selena asked, confused.

"I might have said 'disputes,' as more than one exists. The first concerns an extremely valuable shard. 'A pull,' I believe you call it. The second involves the circumstances of your unfortunate crash. The Regulatory has an interest in both as you might imagine—the first because of The Mandate's discretionary powers over the sale of ecomire, the second because of the severity of the crash. Fatalities are common enough in the rim, but not fatalities caused by recklessness."

Selena stared at him. "Fatalities?"

"Only one. For now."

"The doctor said my father was still alive." Selena's words came out in a hoarse rasp.

"I was not speaking of your father. Of course not. He is recovering. As long as he continues to receive excellent care at Principle Hospital down on Stephen's Point, he should pull through. No, I speak of Wayne Kretchiwitz."

"Wild Wayne ... he's dead?"

"Yes, he died of exposure while being towed to the *Hydra*."

"Good," Selena said before she could stop herself.

"That's a bit harsh, don't you think?"

"He's a thieving bastard! He and Victor both. Nearly got me and Dad killed."

"According to Victor, what we can glean from his gibberish— oxygen deprivation does strange things to the brain—it's you and your father who are the thieves."

"He's a sack-of-shit liar!" Selena sat up and leaned forward. "He and the rest of those flame-backs—they're not real rimmers— never were, never will be."

The Ombudsman pursed his lips and rubbed the knees of his immaculate khaki trousers. "Calm yourself, Selena. I didn't take great pains to meet with you before the others so that you could lecture me."

Selena smacked back into her pillow and gazed at the ceiling.

"Well, what do you want then? Am I in trouble?"

"That depends."

Ombudsman Owagumbiea studied her so intently that she felt as if each blink, each subtle shift of her body, might form a clue he could use against her.

"Depends on what?" she asked.

"What happened during the crash?"

"That's easy enough. We located a good pull, rich as kings. The Kretchiwitz brothers come screaming up our backsides and try to steal it from us. They were lurking around near our claim, hoping we'd have better luck than they did. Soon as we got an angle on the pull, they came after us. Double snagged the shard and sent *The Bee* whipping around on a collision course. I didn't have time to do anything but cut the tether and then—"

"Stop!"

Selena started, mouth open in mid-sentence, shocked by the sudden intensity of the Ombudsman's voice.

"What did you just say?" the Ombudsman asked.

"I said we had to cut the tether. We had no choice."

"No. You said 'I.' You said 'I didn't have time to do anything but cut the tether.'"

Selena saw her mistake. She wasn't licensed. She'd turned fifteen the year before and could legally work as crew, but could not, under any circumstances, pilot a trawler.

"I misspoke."

"Did you?"

"Yes."

"Is that why it was *you* strapped into the pilot's seat when the rescue team cut their way into your trawler?"

"I don't remember where I was," Selena lied. "My father must have strapped me in before impact. He's like that. A real hero, if you ask me."

"Yes, that makes sense," the Ombudsman said in his strange, high voice.

Selena smiled to herself. This rich man from the surface knew nothing about flying. If she stuck to her story, didn't slip up, didn't let him intimidate her into saying the wrong thing ....

"Correct me if I get any of these details wrong, Selena." Owagumbiea raised his hands, long fingers swirling the air. "Your trawler is circling a shard that's been double snagged, pulling what? Three or four gravities? Maybe as much as five gravities? And your father is simultaneously piloting the ship *and* buckling you into the harness. That's more than heroic. It's godlike."

Selena's smile faded. "He must have done it after he cut the tether."

"You mean while your trawler spun like a top into the void of space?"

"Yes."

"Do you remember these events?"

"I remember him cutting the tether."

"Do you remember how you managed to survive?"

She didn't. Her last memory was of anguish and regret—her father's black boot, twitching. What was the Ombudsman holding back? The more she examined his lengthy body and long, muscular limbs, the more he reminded her of a spider. Not a web-spinner, but the athletic kind that didn't need one. The sort that jumped out of crevices and incapacitated their victims with savage, venomous bites.

"I don't remember anything after he cut the tether."

"Then perhaps you would be interested to know how you ended up in the medical bay of the *Hydra*?"

Selena nodded.

"We have no eyewitnesses." The Ombudsman's voice cracked like a prepubescent boy's. "But the physical evidence suggests a possibility."

"What?" Selena asked.

"After cutting the main tether, *The Bee* careened away from the shard. Unbalanced and affected in the same fashion as your trawler, the Kretchiwitz' scavenger swung round and impacted the shard, fusing them together."

Gooey saliva tickled the back of Selena's throat and she swallowed.

"*The Bee,* on the other hand, smashed through several shards, tearing away large pieces of her outer hull, resulting in depressurization. After breaking free from the rim, her pilot somehow managed to coax a corrective burst from the steam jets followed by a significant burn, aiming the trawler at the *Hydra*. A passing tug found your ship, and towed you into the dock."

The events unfurled in Selena's mind. Whether imagined from the Ombudsman's account or recovered from her damaged memory, she saw it all with perfect clarity, vivid and horrifying. "That's amazing," she said. "My father is one heck of a pilot."

"In spite of his liver."

"I don't know what you're talking about," Selena said.

"Come now, Selena. It's common knowledge that your father likes his drink. Everyone I've interviewed has mentioned the fact."

Selena levered herself upright and words shot out of her like shrapnel. "My father is a good man, a far better man than you. With your fancy clothes and stupid rings—you'd strip your fingers to the bone in a day of real work on a trawler. You come in here like some high and mighty know-it-all. What do you know about anything? Nothing, that's what! Why don't you go back down to the surface and offer up a prayer to that child molester Stephen?"

Selena scowled at the Ombudsman and waited for a rebuke, for the impact of one of his massive palms against her cheek. Instead, Owagumbiea began to snigger, his laughter building until it came on the back of shrill, whistling breaths.

Was the man a psychopath?

"Star and moon, you have a temper, don't you?" The Ombudsman withdrew a folded white handkerchief from his breast pocket and dabbed the corners of his eyes. "I'm not your enemy, Selena. Far from it. Believe me when I say I had to call in several favors from some very powerful people to speak with you before anyone else."

Moisture clung to the Ombudsman's lashes, a reminder of when he had giggled like someone taking a hit from a narcotics inhaler.

"Who else wants to see me? Why am I so important?" Selena asked.

"I'll answer your questions in order. First, the who: your typical cadre of busybodies and bureaucrats. An awful man from Child Welfare. A powerful woman from the Regulatory. The two of them are almost enough to make me give up Stephen's Point and take up residence at Scrapyard ... or perhaps New Lux ..." He smiled again, but Selena took no notice, mind churning through thoughts almost faster than they occurred.

What was Child Welfare? And why did the Regulatory want to talk to her? Were they going to arrest her because of the crash? Selena eyed the Ombudsman. Although strange, if what he said was true, he might be the lesser of three evils. Her cheek muscles twitched. "You didn't answer my other question. *Why* do they want to talk to me?"

The Ombudsman leaned forward, his expressive hands falling to rest between his knees. "Look, Selena, I know you don't trust me. I can understand that. But I have thrived in the caustic cesspool of the Stephen's Point government for over thirty years. Not through luck or chance, mind you; I've thrived because I understand people. I understand you and your father and those who risk their lives to mine the rim. Fierce, independent, hardworking—you prefer to be left alone, prefer to solve your own problems, prefer that the government stay out of your business. And, until quite recently, we have."

The way he described the rimmers gave Selena a reason to look at him with more than skepticism or fear. Though buried by fancy language, his candor surprised her. Owagumbiea spoke with the expectation she would understand him—a rare trait in adults.

"I gain re-election every three years precisely because I do understand you," he continued. "Your representatives vote for me because they know that I will keep the government out of their business. All I'm asking is that you let me help you do the same thing for you personally."

"Why help me? What's in it for you?"

"Smart girl. Of course there's something in it for me." The Ombudsman leaned back in his chair, a spark of something—satisfaction?—in his mirror-bright pupils. "That is how business is transacted."

"What, then?"

"Ecomire. The fifth-largest pull ever discovered. A fortune."

Selena's spider gave a phantom twitch. She saw the glow of *The Bee*'s console, felt the thump of the bolas release. *Rich as kings!* She blinked. "The shard."

"The shard, indeed."

"Where is it?"

"In lockdown. Unavailable. Useless. At least until we get the matter of the crash resolved."

"Get it resolved then," she said. "It's the Kretchiwitzes' fault."

"It's not that simple. First, everyone except you is either dead or incapacitated. Your father is improving, but he's far from able to give testimony at a formal hearing. Second, you're illegal and out of compliance with The Mandate's requirement to register for the Selection. I can't bring you in for a hearing under the circumstances, now can I? The Regulatory will devour you."

"Illegal?" The word appalled her. She considered herself a legitimate member of a two-person trawler crew. Her father called her his partner, and she'd considered herself his equal for some time.

"It's very dicey. Years ago it probably wouldn't have mattered. Your existence is proof that the Regulatory has had only a sporadic interest in enforcing laws against children at the rim. Unfortunately, The Mandate has made the situation much more complicated."

"You can have it," Selena said. "Take the shard. I don't need it. I don't care—just make sure my father gets what he needs to recover. We'll head back to Scrapyard and leave you the shard as compensation for your trouble. Everything can go back the way it was."

"Laughable," the Ombudsman said. "It won't work and you know it. Stop thinking like a child."

Obscenities filled her mouth, bitter as bile, but Selena clamped her lips shut, sealing them in. His rebuke bothered her far more than a common insult because he was right. She'd reached for an easy, impossible solution to her problems. One man dead, another brain damaged, and her father's injuries serious enough that they'd sent him down to the moon's surface ... things would never go back to the way they were before. She needed to start dealing with it.

Selena refocused on the Ombudsman, ready to listen. "What should I do?"

"Waiting in the hallway is a Child Welfare worker who would be more than happy to send you down to an assigned host family, something I believe you know a little about. You'll enter a training track to become a warehouse coordinator or factory worker or maybe, if you're lucky, a Regulator. Would you like that?"

"Balls!"

The Ombudsman massaged his forehead with one hand, drumming the fingers of the other against his trouser leg. "I didn't think so. After the Child Welfare worker comes a Chief Regulator with a vested interest in enforcing The Mandate. She's *religiously* angry about your status. A 'Selection dodger' she calls you. She doesn't care what reasons you might have. Doesn't care about your beliefs or feelings or preferences. She'll push you through the Selection to make a point. Then she will hand you a pressure suit and a welding torch and send you into the bowels of the beast. I assume you'd prefer to avoid that outcome as well?"

"You know I would."

"Good. If you do as I say, I can protect your father from the harshest of the legal penalties he faces. I can also help you avoid The Mandate and give you the ability to return to Scrapyard once I'm through, if that's what you'd like."

"Okay," Selena said, nodding. "It's a deal. Tell me what you want me to do."

"No more slip-ups—you must *never* let anyone know you piloted *The Bee*. You must maintain complete control over what you say and how you say it. It won't be easy. The Chief Regulator will try to catch you in a lie. She's tricky. The less you say the better. Can you do that?"

"Yeah, I can do that."

"Good. Then we have an agreement. Now let me tell you how this will work …."

CHAPTER SIXTEEN

Theo had little time to think about Marcus or anything else as Sir directed the candidates onto their hands and knees.

"Push-ups. On the three count!" Sir's voice boomed.

Theo was no jock, but he could do pushups, at least thirty. No problem. He dropped into position and glanced up. Sir was on hands and toes along with them.

"Begin! One, two, three—"

A uniform chorus from the trainees yelled on cue: "One!"

"One, two, three—"

"Two!"

Like Meghan, almost all the other kids had been through pre-training. They all knew how this worked, but Theo struggled to follow the cadence. By the twentieth repetition, his muscles were hot. By thirty, they were trembling, and by forty, they burned, sharp pain cutting into his chest and biceps.

Theo glanced at Sir, rising and falling with perfect form and pace. He'd stop them soon, give them a break, right? No one could keep this up much longer. At least he wasn't the only one struggling. Several other kids wobbled at the knees, faces ashen. Theo shook. It was all he could do to stop himself from collapsing.

Someone groaned. Another called out, "Please, I need a break," but Sir ignored them. Theo tried to push himself up for the fifty-third time, but his arms failed. He dropped, his face mashed into concrete, bloodying his forehead. Woozy and sick to his stomach, he took a breath and tried to push himself upright, but could not.

How will I ever make it through this?

"Up!" Sir yelled.

"Fifty-four," Theo mumbled, all his concentration devoted to the simple act of pushing the concrete away.

"Down!"

Someone else's chest thumped the ground. "Fifty-five."

"Hold in the up position," Sir commanded, "knees off the ground. Back straight."

Theo's entire body felt like rubber. His neck and shoulders ached and his arms had lost feeling. Vomit burned the back of his throat. In his peripheral vision, he saw Marcus, arms unwavering, like a machine. Only Hephaestus seemed as physically fit as Marcus. Meghan held the position, but she was shaking too, her face a shade of brilliant crimson. One kid was puking, another started to cry.

Phoebus hadn't exaggerated. This wasn't training, it was a means of breaking their will, of getting them to quit. It was more than Theo'd anticipated and far beyond his fitness level.

I'm not going to make it.

As the thought registered, his arms gave out once more. He crashed down, air crushed from his lungs by the impact. A pair of black boots stopped in front of him. Through blurred eyes, Theo looked up at Sir, towering over him.

"What's your name?" Sir asked. Theo gasped for enough air to reply, then realized that Sir wasn't speaking to him. A few paces away, another prone boy gasped for air, legs against his chest, grimacing in pain.

"Jenner, sir," the boy groaned.

"Get yourself up, Jenner."

"I can't, sir. I think I pulled a muscle in my back."

"On your feet!"

Jenner stayed flat on his stomach, ignoring Sir's command. Sir's temperature seemed to rise several degrees, bald head reddening, eyes furious slits. He reached down and yanked Jenner upright, then slung him around to face the other candidates.

"Look at this worthless piece of crap," Sir said. "He's quitting on all of you."

"I'm not quitting," Jenner protested, struggling to his feet. "I'm hurt."

Sweat dripped from Jenner's eyebrows and drizzled down his cheeks.

"Do you know what I like about you, Jenner?" Sir asked.

"What, sir?"

Sir's voice came so harsh and filled with disgust that it cut through Theo as if the words were spoken to him. "Absolutely nothing. Get your cowardly backside off my training field."

"Whatever," Jenner said. "You're insane."

"Maybe so," Sir said, then raised his voice to a shout. "Time for the demonstration I promised you." Sir waved over a few regulators, who seized Jenner by the arms and dragged him to the medical booth.

"Weakness is a disease," Sir continued. "A disease I intend to cure you of. Down here, you have a benevolent government to help you. You've got a precious mommy and daddy. Up on the *Chimera*, there will be no one to feed you, no one to comfort you, no one to clean up your messes. Once you leave for Earth, you'll only have each other. If I let *one* of you board the *Chimera* before I'm certain I've killed all the weakness in you, I've failed." Sir's face was a granite shelf. "And I never fail."

Still locked in the upright portion of their push-ups, many of the kids swayed over their hands, close to collapse.

"Stand up," Sir said.

The candidates struggled to their feet. A collective breath came from the group. A release of tension. Most of them were feeling the same crushing exhaustion that threatened to overwhelm every muscle in Theo's body. This wasn't easy for them, either. Theo glimpsed fear in some of their eyes. A recognition that regardless of how hard they'd trained, how prepared they'd thought they were, Sir would push them well past their limits.

"I want all of you to get a good look at this," Sir said as he marched the group over to the medical booth.

"Go ahead," Sir said. One of the regulators punched a command into a handscreen and the medical booth's servo arm lowered, positioning laser tracking along Jenner's right forearm.

"What's it going to do to me?" Jenner wailed.

"This," Sir said, "is the mark of the coward." The laser beam intensified and Jenner's skin sizzled. He screamed and jerked in the chair, trying to rip his arm free, but the straps held firm. The stink of burning skin and hair filled the air. Theo's stomach churned. Meghan held a frozen hand in front of her open mouth. Marcus watched with serene calm, not the slightest bit perturbed.

The laser stopped and Jenner's screams died away. His chest heaved, tears rolling down his cheeks.

"Congratulations, son," Sir said, scanning the crescent of char etched into Jenner's skin. "You're out of the Selection. This mark indicates you've become property of the State."

Property of the State? The words were almost as awful as the brand. The two things hit Theo like twin sledge-hammers. The Mandate was no ink and paper law, passed as a good measure to save Steven's Point from an inopportune situation, but rather an open-mouthed scream of terror in the face of obliteration. The Regulatory would do anything necessary to save the colony. Even cruel, horrific things. Stephen's Point would find a crew for the *Chimera* or everyone would die. If a few people got hurt or even killed in the process—those were necessary sacrifices.

The straps holding Jenner in place released. "Good luck," Sir said with biting sarcasm. He turned his back on Jenner as regulators escorted the boy away to a waiting rambler. *I'd rather die than become someone's property,* Theo thought. He would never become his father, trusting someone else to control of his fate. He wouldn't give up, not even if his body failed him—they'd have to force him into that machine. He spat out a mouthful of vomit-tinged saliva.

"This concludes the demonstration," Sir said. "If you give in, you will fail the Selection and receive a brand that will dictate your future. A few of you may help save the colony. Those too weak for the job will serve The Mandate here on Stephen's Point. Some of you may be thinking, 'Well, that isn't so bad.'" Sir minced forward on boot tips, eyelids a fluttering frenzy. He froze, face returning to granite. "If that's you, step forward and you can take the coward's way out."

Meghan pushed past Hephaestus and planted herself in front of Sir. "This is barbaric."

Sir laughed. "Barbaric? I'll tell you what's barbaric. Eating bugs. Or dirt, after you go insane from hunger. Watching your family turn to skeletons around you, their stomachs bloating into disgusting balloons. Worrying that your neighbor might decide he'd rather eat you than starve."

"That's not going to happen," Meghan said. Her eyes wavered, the uncertainty there reflecting the collective thoughts of the group.

"Have you ever seen a person starve to death?" Sir asked. "Skin stretched over bones? It's the blank eyes that you remember. The horror that remains after the soul has left. Life itself is barbaric, little girl." Sir nodded to the regulators. They stepped forward and seized Meghan's arms.

"No," she shouted. "I'm not quitting!"

"You're not? I thought this was too barbaric for you?"

Meghan's eyes flashed with unrestrained hatred, her face a shade of red bordering on purple. "I'm not quitting," she said. "That's all I'm going to say, *sir.*"

"You sure? This is your chance. If you want out, now's the time. I don't expect many of you to make it through the rest of the week, so you may as well save yourself the effort."

No one stepped forward.

Sir shrugged and the regulators released her. Meghan shook herself, ponytail lashing, and rejoined the group.

Next, Sir ordered them to do wind sprints. "I want two groups. While one group runs, the others jog in place. If I see anyone dogging it, you know what will happen. Down and back, down and back, no slowing."

Theo jogged with the others, waiting for the first group, led by Marcus, to run the length of the slab and return. Marcus led the pack on their return trip, and as soon as he reached the starting point, Theo took off. After all the push-ups, running felt like a mercy. Taking even strides, not sprinting, he went fast enough to stay near the front of his group—finally something where his thin frame provided an advantage.

After several more down-and-backs, a girl with sweat-soaked bangs plastered to her forehead hunched over and spewed yellow liquid across the pavement. A sour smell filled the air. Meghan rested a comforting hand on the girl's back and pulled her hair away from her face. When the vomiting ended, Meghan took the other girl's arm and pulled her upright.

"I can't do it," the girl said. "I can't."

Sir rushed over to the pile of puke glistening on the concrete. "You will not puke on my training field! You will ask my permission to puke. Do you understand me?"

"Yes, sir," those of the kids with enough breath to speak replied.

"Good. Anyone else need to throw up?"

A boy raised his hand.

Sir pointed to where the concrete gave way to yellowed sweet grass. "Over there." The boy hobbled away, but couldn't hold it in. Vomit burst through his hands and splashed over the concrete.

Barely an hour, Theo thought. *One hour and we're falling apart.* They'd all get branded before the day was through.

"Don't stop," Sir shouted at the gawking kids. "Get moving!"

The first group headed back out, Meghan dragging the girl she'd rescued behind her. When they reached the end of the field, the girl with the bangs tripped and fell, sprawled on the concrete. Meghan grabbed her wrists, pulling her upright. They managed a few awkward steps, Meghan supporting the other girl, before she fell again. Meghan didn't bother trying to get the girl to walk and instead hoisted her onto her back and struggled forward. She made it a quarter of the way back when Theo's group passed, heading in the opposite direction. The two girls had reached the halfway point when Theo passed them going the other direction.

Why did Meghan bother? Let the regulators take the girl to the booth. She wouldn't make it through the day anyway. Why didn't Sir intervene? Theo rested with hands on his knees, catching his breath as Meghan struggled on. She didn't stop until she and the other girl collapsed to the ground on the other side of the starting line.

"Stop!"

Sir strode over, circling the two girls as if considering whether or not to stomp them into the ground. When he spoke, his tone had changed—not softened, but changed.

"What's your name?"

Meghan managed only a whisper.

"What was that?" Sir said. "Speak up."

"Meghan Ziczek," Theo offered. "Her name's Meghan Ziczek, sir. Don't hurt her—"

Sir whirled on him. "Keep your mouth shut, clown."

Sir pointed at Meghan. "Take a good, long look at Meghan Ziczek." He waved at the regulators who trotted over from the side of the field. Everyone knew what came next. They might not like it but no one protested. Until now Theo had thought of himself as valiant—that he would protect Meghan, maybe even sacrifice himself for her if it came down to it. But as the regulators approached, he realized his bravado existed only between his ears. He said nothing as the regulators joined Sir, towering over Meghan.

Sir offered Meghan his hand. She took it and he pulled her upright.

"That's first thing I've seen today that impresses me," Sir said. "Part of what makes us strong is our willingness to help those weaker than ourselves."

Theo took a huge breath. Sir's strange response had saved him from his cowardice. He'd thought Sir took pleasure in humiliating people. Now he wasn't so sure.

Sir spread his arms as if he might reach out and bear hug the entire moon. "It's the duty of the strong to protect the weak, but it's my duty to protect this colony from the weak among *you*. This training isn't fair. It's not supposed to be. It's a filter. I will use it to strip you down to your core. If you've got some steel in you, I will harden that steel. When I'm done, you'll have earned your uniform and your commission. You will become officers aboard the *Chimera*, burdened with the awesome responsibility of saving this colony from extinction."

The words rippled through them. Earth had forbidden Stephen's Point from creating a military, but words like "officer" and "uniform" reminded Theo of Earth history—*military language*. He recalled images of combat troops augmented by mechanical armor and war drones. The devastation of The Last War had cut Earth's population in half. Did Sir think they were going to war?

Several positions down the line of sad candidates, face keen, Marcus trained his eyes on Sir. Marcus looked energized, waiting on Sir's every word. The murderer *wanted* to take a place on the *Chimera*. Why? Surely not out of a desire to save the colony. If he found out, maybe he could use that knowledge against Marcus. Theo's spirits lifted as he realized he knew the killer's full name. When he got home—assuming he didn't get branded—he would see what he could find out about Marcus J. Locke on the nets.

"Are you able to continue?" Sir asked the near comatose girl Meghan had carried across the field. She shook her head no, face rolling in the dust.

"Brand her," Sir said.

Theo felt the screams as if they were his own.

The regulators marked seven more before the day ended. Some with raw, animal terror in their eyes, others relieved, happy to reach the end of their suffering. Sir's training far exceeded a workout. Push-ups, crunches, squat lunges, mountain-climbers and a horrible thing Sir called the "Iron Cross" in which they held their arms straight out in a T shape for what felt like an eternity.

This isn't physical training, it's torture, Theo thought.

Yet somehow, despite his body screaming objections, Theo struggled on. Every time he fell, he scraped himself back up. Kept moving forward. Kept trying.

Marcus sweated alongside him. He never lost focus, never seemed to fatigue, and obeyed every command with the discipline of a natural soldier. When Sir finally released them, Marcus looked exhausted, but not destroyed like Theo.

Meghan dropped to the ground and lay flat on her back, knees bent. Theo dragged himself over and collapsed beside her. She looked as bad as he felt. A mess of mud and sweat streaked her face, two shades lighter than normal. Dried blood and vomit coated her shoes.

"What *is* this?" Meghan said, voice cracking. "What have we gotten ourselves into?" Her body trembled. Not from exhaustion but from powerful, raw emotion. Fear? Rage? Theo wanted to reach for her, to comfort her, but feared how she'd respond.

A shadow fell over them. "Hello," Marcus said.

Meghan shaded her eyes with a cupped hand, squinting up at the looming figure.

"You're very brave, Meghan Ziczek. Sad that your gesture didn't make any difference in the grand scheme of things. So little does, don't you think?"

"You're not from the Swallows," Meghan said.

"No, I moved here from Conway several months ago. Slipped into this training group last minute."

"Marcus J. Locke, right?" Theo asked, controlling his voice to hide his anxiety.

Marcus' ice-blue eyes met Theo's. "Yes. You've got a good memory, Theo. I suppose that's why you made it into the Selection."

"I guess so," Theo said. Marcus smiled at him, as real and easy as if they'd known each other for years. As if they'd never dropped a body down a cave shaft. As if Marcus had never threatened Theo's life or Meghan's.

"You did better than I thought you might," Marcus said. "Based on how you're dressed."

"Me too," Meghan said. She sat up and looked at Theo. "I thought you'd get branded before the day ended."

"Branding," Marcus mused. "So terrifying." He gazed off into the distance, face blank. "Do you think they kill the kids that get the crescent?"

The question sounded silly to Theo, but Meghan answered anyway. "No way. It's a stupid scare tactic."

"Did it work? Are you scared?" Marcus seemed to be speaking to both of them, hungry eyes searching their faces.

"No," Theo lied. "Whatever they're doing it for, they must have good reasons."

"I wonder," Marcus said. "Maybe one of us will soon find out. See you both tomorrow."

"You're not taking the bus back to the Swallows?" Meghan asked.

"No, I have some things I need to do at the Order compound." Marcus turned and strode away.

Meghan sat in silence, watching Marcus' retreat. "Do you know him?"

"No," Theo said, a bit too quickly.

Meghan looked at him. "He's off somehow. I can't put my finger on it."

Theo shrugged. *You have no idea.*

"Theo?"

"Yeah?"

Meghan frowned, picking at a scab on her knee. "I thought you'd get run out of the Selection today. I hoped you would. Until they branded that kid Jenner."

"You don't want me to get branded?"

"No. I don't want anyone to get branded. You cheated to get into the training, but none of us thought it would be like this. You should quit, Theo. You don't have to be here. Just tell them the truth. Whatever happens, it can't be as bad as the branding."

"I'm not going to quit."

"It's not quitting. You've made your point, Theo. You're tough. Tougher than I thought. But I don't want to see you get branded tomorrow or the next day. If you turn yourself in, you can be done with all of this."

Theo rolled to his side and stood, fighting legs that wanted to buckle beneath him. "No. I'm not here to prove anything to you. If you want me out of the Selection so badly, I guess you better turn me in."

CHAPTER SEVENTEEN

"**H**ow'd it go?" Rose asked.

Selena dipped the final remnant of bread into her bowl of thick and creamy potato soup, placed it in her mouth, chewed and swallowed. "That Child Welfare guy acted like my dad is some sort of irresponsible jerk. He asked so many stupid questions. What do we eat, how big is our berth, how many hours each cycle do I spend in the rim—like you only spend part of a cycle there! We're not shift workers. He's an idiot."

"I'm sure he means well."

"Well, I'm not. The Ombudsman warned me about him."

Rose lowered herself into the same chair Owagumbiea had filled. "What did he say?"

"Lots of things."

"Come on, Selena! One of the most important men on the *Hydra* comes to visit you, and you're not going to even give me a clue?"

The Ombudsman had warned her not to talk about their conversation, but it was tempting to give in to Rose's interest. She wouldn't call Rose a friend, but she wasn't *not* a friend either.

"Selena! The Ombudsman—what did he *say?*" Rose prodded.

"He's my representative in the formal hearing."

"Formal hearing? What formal hearing?"

"The one I have to attend a few cycles from now." *The hearing my future depends on.* One slip and she would lose everything. She had to get this right. Fool everyone. Selena pushed her food tray away. "I'm done talking about this."

"Selena … the Ombudsman … I don't understand why he's taking this on personally. He's, well, sort of important."

Selena glowered. "And I'm not? Is that what you're saying?"

"Of course not—"

"The little girl from the rim can't possibly have anything

important to discuss with her representative?"

Rose stood and removed Selena's cluttered food tray. "That's not what I meant."

"What did you mean?"

"Never mind. I'm sorry I mentioned it."

Rose moved to the door. Desperation washed over Selena, frustration mixing with guilt and the fear of being alone. She didn't want to talk about the Ombudsman, or the hearing, but she didn't want Rose to leave either.

"How long until I get out of this bed?"

Rose's shoulders tensed but she paused, tray in hand. "Dr. Cholewa isn't sure." Rose's tone was careful, formal even. "It can take time for the nervous system to re-establish itself, but you're making solid progress." Rose pushed through the door.

"Wait!" Selena yelled. "When is the next one coming?"

"The next one what?"

"The Regulator. The Ombudsman said a regulator wants to see me."

Rose's face shifted to concern. "I'm not sure, honey."

"Can you check and see if he's here? Somebody or other named Moorland."

"The Chief? Coming here? Why …? Never mind. Do you even know who the Chief is?"

"Some bureaucrat."

Rose laughed. "First off, the Chief is a *she*. Second, she's not 'some bureaucrat', Selena. The Chief runs the show up here. The rebuild is her project. Her baby. If she wants to see you …" Rose stared at Selena. "What do you think she wants?"

The same thing as the Ombudsman, Selena thought. The stuff fortunes were made of.

* * *

The woman wore a spotless, white uniform with silver crescents adorning the lapels. Formal white gloves hid small hands held tight at her sides. Her hair mirrored the insignia of the Regulatory—a soft silver. Selena couldn't guess her age. She could be forty, fifty, sixty. She carried herself with the bearing of a person used to the efficient use of power. Selena had seen men who moved that way, but never a woman.

"How long have you lived at Scrapyard?" Chief Moorland

asked. It wasn't the sort of question Selena had expected. She also hadn't expected Moorland to express her condolences over the crash or inquire about her father's injuries. The woman radiated calm, and Selena couldn't help but respect her.

"Nearly twelve years."

"You came up *before* The Mandate took effect?"

"Yes. I've been at Scrapyard since forever."

"We have no record of you—you've never been sequenced."

Selena thought of the small sequencing station near the docks, created to test the handful of children who lived at Scrapyard. She and Liam had ignored it, even as they watched news reports from Stephen's Point showing long lines of children waiting for blood tests. "You stay clear of that nonsense," Liam had told her. "Let the moon surface folks sort out the *Chimera*."

"Never got a chance," Selena lied.

"Well, you're sequenced now." Moorland paused, looking at Selena with clear, blue eyes. "Would you like to know the results?"

"Don't care."

"You've passed the DNA test."

Selena shrugged, burying her curiosity beneath a veneer of what she hoped looked like boredom. She would take on the persona the Ombudsman had suggested: obstinate, stupid and disinterested in everything except getting back to Scrapyard. "So what?"

"It means you qualify for the Selection. We'll give you the same tests as the others, and if you pass, you'll have a chance to earn a place on the *Chimera*."

"I won't qualify."

Moorland frowned. "Who was flying *The Bee* during the crash?"

"My father."

"Liam? Not you?"

"Course not. I can't fly."

"That's not what my report states, Selena." The Chief's voice was low, cool. "We have numerous witnesses who say you help your father fly *The Bee*. That you're a crack pilot, and that your father's business would have failed long ago without your help."

Who had they talked to? Who hadn't kept their fat mouth shut? Selena lowered her gaze. She had to be careful—the

Ombudsman had warned her that Moorland would try and trip her up. Maybe Moorland was lying.

"They don't know nothing." Selena slowed her words. "I can't fly. My dad said I shouldn't never touch the navigation gizmo. He said he'd skin me if I did."

"So it wasn't you flying the trawler?"

Selena gave a harsh laugh. "I told you already, I can't do it."

"Well, how did you end up in the straps then?"

Selena shrugged again.

"Your father got half his head crushed in because he wasn't strapped in."

Selena stared at the white ceiling. She counted upwards to seven, fingers tapping against her unfeeling legs. She pushed her grief and anger into a tiny place where she could control them. A tiny place that always seemed full until she pushed against it and found she could fit in one more fear, one more sorrow, one more tragedy.

The sound of Liam's head impacting steel echoed in her mind. She saw his boot twitching. Felt her head whipping around like the end of a live wire. "I don't remember that," Selena lied.

"He nearly died. I need to know what happened."

"Because you want the *money*." Selena crammed all her bitterness and scorn into the word.

"No, Selena, I don't need money. The entire Stephen's Point economy is at my disposal."

"But that shard is special."

The Chief studied her. "What do you know about it?"

"Not much," Selena backtracked. "I just know it's a good one."

"You could see the results of the scan from the back of the trawler?"

"No, of course not. Dad yelled to me that he'd found a rich pull."

"You didn't see the results through your spider?"

Selena started, eyes swinging up to meet the Chief's, diving away again. So Moorland knew about the spider. The doctor must have found it. Selena fought the impulse to touch the place where it hid beneath her skin. Had they taken it out? She couldn't be sure—she hadn't tried to use it since arriving at the *Hydra*.

Moorland continued as if she'd never mentioned the spider,

though Selena felt certain she'd return to it soon enough. "After your father told you about the shard, what happened?"

"The Kretchiwitz brothers tried to steal it from us."

"Resulting in a crash."

"You know that already. Why are you asking me? I said what happened and I wrote it out in a report for my Ombudsman. Maybe you should be talking to him."

Moorland straightened her back. "Did he happen to mention that you're out of compliance with The Mandate? You will have to go through the Selection tests."

"Fine. I'll take whatever tests you want."

"If you score well, you might qualify to crew the *Chimera*," Moorland said. She studied Selena for a moment. "You might even get to fly her."

Selena shrugged. "I can't fly. And I'm not much use at tests."

"You've never taken one like this before."

"They're all the same to me. I fail them. Stopped taking them a long time ago."

"There's a piloting test as well, Selena."

"I told you I can't fly."

"Yes, you did. So what do you use your spider for?"

"Keeping track of inventory. Playing games."

"You're pretty good at games, aren't you?"

Selena felt a smile coming and swallowed to hide it. "Not really."

Moorland leaned close and spoke with firm sincerity, "If you fail out of the Selection, your next stop is the moon's surface. You will be assigned a host family and learn a trade."

"What about my father?"

"He's facing serious legal challenges. *If* he recovers, and *if* he doesn't go to prison, you'll be reunited. On Stephen's Point, of course. He won't fly again."

"He will," Selena said.

"I hope you're right. Because if he doesn't, I doubt you'll ever make it back to the rim. Considering how poor you do on tests and that you can't fly."

CHAPTER EIGHTEEN

We need to talk.

The ping sat at the top of the message cue on Theo's handscreen, a static image of Meghan's not-quite smiling face next to it. Theo groaned and rolled over on the bed. His body *hurt*. Every muscle tight, every joint sore, pain that had no boundaries or limits. He hadn't been able to eat after returning from the training, or answer his mom's questions. He'd gone to bed and slept five hours. When he woke, he felt worse than when he'd lain down.

We need to talk.

Why couldn't she leave him alone? Sir had called her a "moral compass." That must mean brave, inflexible, and in a way, stupid. Meghan loved the rules. She loved them so much she wanted him to turn himself in. Maybe she felt threatened by him.

Talk about what? Theo replied, keying in each letter with more force than necessary. He closed his eyes, handscreen resting on his tender chest, wondering where Sir sent Jenner and the others who'd gotten branded. Nobody knew. Heph had asked the regulator that drove their bus to and from Civvy, and she'd said "Why? Do you want me to take you there?"

Wherever it was, it couldn't be worse than the training, could it?

The handscreen vibrated.

What happened in the cave?

Theo pushed himself upright, ignoring the thousand different places in his body that screamed for him to lie flat, to never move again. Why did Meghan want to talk about the cave? Did she know more than she was letting on?

This was bad. Really bad. He considered calling her, but if she had suspicions, he could manage the conversation better in person. He'd have to meet her whether he wanted to or not. Both of their lives might depend on it.

Wearing the same sweat-stained clothing from the morning, Theo tramped downstairs. His mother waited for him at the base of the stairs, a huge smile on her face.

"You made it through the first day," she said.

"Barely," Theo replied, unable to hide his own satisfaction. Meghan might be about to send things to hell in a handcart, but that didn't take away from his accomplishment. Nobody—not Sir, not Meghan, not Heph or Phoebus—had believed he could do it. He'd proved them all wrong.

"Are you hungry, Theo?"

Theo was about to say no when he realized that an immense emptiness was gnawing the inside of his belly. So much of him hurt that he hadn't noticed his hunger.

"Yes," he said, eyes casting around the kitchen alcove, in search of leftovers.

"Sit down; I've got something special for you."

Theo sat. A moment later Erin set a plate in front of him. Theo's mouth filled with saliva.

"What?" Theo said, disbelief in his voice. "How'd you get these?"

"The Order brought them, compliments of Doctor Duncan." If her smile got any wider, her face would crack in half.

Cinder Bars in bright blue packaging. A dozen of them. Theo hadn't seen the chocolate-protein synthetics since he was close to Liddy's age. Anything sweet came at a premium, and dessert items now cost more than his father earned in a month. His family survived on their food ration: protein paste, vegetables, porridge and the occasional salmon delivered by one of his dad's buddies who worked at one of the few remaining fisheries.

"I wanted to give them to you earlier but you went to sleep."

"I can't eat them," Theo said, pushing the plate away. "Liddy should have them. Or Dad."

"You've got to eat," Erin said.

"I don't want them," Theo lied.

His mother sat down, angling her chair toward his, face open and earnest. "Listen, Theo. Liddy and Dad can't save this colony. You can. Because you're special. I guess every mother probably thinks that about their kid. But when you found Stephen's marks in the cave, when you made it into the Selection, that's when I really *knew*."

"I'm not special," Theo said. "I got lucky. Anyone could have found those scratchings."

Erin shook her head. "I don't believe in luck. Neither does Duncan. That's why he sent these for you—they want you to succeed. So do I."

Theo eyed the blue-wrapped bars, hiding the tears threatening to break free and roll down his cheeks. "Why are you being so nice to me?"

Erin looked confused, then hurt. She turned her gaze up through the skylight in the center of the house. "I'm not being 'nice,' Theo. I'm being your mother. And I meant what I said. You can make it through this thing. You're strong."

"I'm *not* strong," Theo said, not hiding his skepticism-laced anger. He thought of the other candidates, their poise, their muscles, their confidence. They'd made it through the Selection tests on their own. None of them had cheated.

"Yes, you are, Theo. You have a strong mind. Your father is convinced you're shiftless because you don't see things the way he does. The older you get, the harder it is to change. But you're still young. Maybe the one good thing that's come from the Mandate is that it's given you choices that your father and I have never had. You have the opportunity to become a leader."

He wanted to argue, but couldn't tell Erin anything about the cave or the lies he'd told to cover up what happened.

"You found the scratchings," she said. Her voice grew hoarse. "I think Stephen wants you to make it to the *Chimera*. I think it's his will." Erin's smile had transformed into something worse than love and pride: conviction. "Eat," she said. "You need your strength."

Theo took a bar and opened it. Devoured the chocolate. Took another. He might not agree with Erin about everything, but whatever lay ahead, he would need his strength. He might get dragged off the field and branded. Or Marcus might come for him. Either way, the calories would go to good use.

He took two more of the bars and stuffed them into his pants pocket. "You guys eat the rest," he said.

Erin looked surprised. "Are you going somewhere?"

Theo glanced down at his handscreen where a red dot marked a location on a map of the Swallows.

"Yes," he said. "I'm going to give a few of these bars to

Meghan. She deserves them as much as I do."

***

The mark on the map placed Meghan at the edge of the industrial district. Why did she want to meet there, rather than at the Civvy? Theo limped along on sore muscles, every footstep painful. By the time he reached the end of the salt crystal coated street, his frustration with Meghan had turned into outright anger. What right did she have to threaten him this way? She was almost as bad as Marcus. He might not even give her the bars he'd brought.

What happened in the cave?

What had happened? Theo replayed the events, omitting all details that pointed to Marcus, to the dead body, to his becoming an accessory to murder. He'd tell her the same thing he'd told everyone. If he stuck to his story, she'd have no choice but to accept it. But what had prompted the question in the first place? Surely she felt the same exhaustion he did. Had she remembered something?

He moved around the side of a dilapidated warehouse, all its windows missing, part of the vast swath of the Swallows, like vacant ruins, picked clean of anything of value.

I'm close, Theo pinged. Where are you?

Inside. Use the side door. It's unlocked.

Theo skirted the building, peering through windows. A flicker of yellow light back in the shadows—had Meghan made a fire? Something felt wrong. He slipped his free hand into his side pocket and withdrew his multitool and selected the knife blade. He felt foolish, but not enough to put it away.

He crept to the side door and pushed it open. Deep shadows hid looming machines. Some sort of assembly line. *Rambler parts?*

"Meghan?" Theo said. "Where are you?"

By the fire.

Theo squinted into the darkness, letting his eyes adjust. Toward the back of the warehouse, red-gold flames licked the air. She *had* made a fire. They could snuggle up beside it while she grilled him on the details of his harrowing escape from the cave.

It might be nice, he told himself. Maybe she wanted to apologize to him, make things right. Theo thought of putting his arm around her shoulders. The warmth of her body against his—

No. Not Meghan. This was all wrong. Meghan wouldn't drag him out to an abandoned warehouse. Not to talk, not to apologize, not for any reason.

Come meet me at the door, Theo pinged. I can't see you.

Scared? came the immediate reply.

Yes. He was scared. The messages came from Meghan's handscreen, but that didn't mean it was Meghan sending them. Theo tightened his grip on the multitool and took a few cautious steps backward. He was getting out of here. If Meghan wanted to talk, they could do it in the alley behind his house.

I'm not coming in, Theo pinged.

No response. Tendrils of sub-zero fear spread from Theo's chest to his toes. He fought the impulse to run and instead backed farther away, knife blade pointed down, but ready to be swung up to chest level, to be driven forward, into—

Would he really try to kill someone?

A muffled sound came from inside the warehouse. Movement. Clothing brushing against metal.

I have her. Come here. Now.

Marcus. Theo's pulse tripled. His fingers went numb from squeezing the knife handle. Marcus had Meghan and was going to kill her. Then he would kill Theo.

If I wanted to kill you you'd already be dead.

Could Marcus read minds? The irrational nature of the idea didn't dispel its power.

I will hurt her if you don't obey.

Theo forced himself forward, one step after another. Blade at the ready, Theo watched for any sign of Marcus, of Meghan. He shuffled toward the flickering fire, unable to think, shoes skidding against the dirty floor. He'd find Meghan and save her. Or die trying.

Theo swung round, holding out the knife, back to the light. Had something moved? The light looked different now, brighter. He smelled sulfur. The air was hot.

The door clanged shut behind him, and he jumped with fear, banging his knife hand into something hard and cold and covered with grease. Theo spun, but saw nothing but the looming shape of machines.

"Meghan!" he shouted. "Can you hear me? Where are you?"

"Here," a voice said.

A hand wrenched his wrist sideways and the knife fell to the ground.

"You really are a stupid one, aren't you?" Marcus said. "You almost figured it out. But almost doesn't count, does it?"

"Leave her alone," Theo begged. "Please. Don't hurt her."

"I haven't done anything to her, nor will I. Right now Meghan is at home. Probably stretching out or sleeping or studying. She's a fantastic candidate, isn't she?"

"She's not here?" Theo asked, relieved.

"Of course not. Why complicate things more than they already are? It's you and I who need to talk."

Theo groaned. So that was what Marcus meant by "almost" not counting. Theo could have turned around and walked away. Marcus might have come after him, but he would have had a chance to escape. A chance that someone would see him, help him.

"Let me show you something," Marcus whispered. "It's quite fascinating."

Marcus pushed him forward, moving fast, guiding him through a maze of industrial equipment. They ducked behind a rusting metal hulk and arrived at the flames Theo had mistaken for a fire. Up close, he saw they rose from within an open metal mouth leading back into a red-hot chamber full of what looked like molten steel.

"A blast furnace," Marcus said. He shoved Theo, his face coming within a few feet of the opening. The scent of singed hair filled his mouth and nose. Greasy. Like someone getting branded. Theo screamed. A fist slammed into his stomach. Gurgling and gasping, Theo fought to re-inflate his lungs, mouth opening and closing like a salmon pulled out of water.

"Shut up and listen," Marcus said. "If I want, I can kill you right now. Put your body in the furnace. Make you disappear. If I need to, I will. But there's a simpler solution, one that I need you to commit to."

Theo nodded, frantic. He'd do anything Marcus wanted.

"Good," Marcus said. His tone became conversational. "What I did in the cave isn't a problem for me unless I get very unlucky. No one's looking for … him. Even if they do, we moved the body where they'll never find it."

Theo rolled to his hands and knees and stood. The furnace

raged.

"But you, Theo. You *are* a problem for me. A very messy problem. Duncan and the rest of the Order have gotten swept up in religious fervor about the new scratchings. They think you're special—like some sort of prophet. We both know what a sham that is. You don't even believe in Stephen. I saw it in your eyes when you thought you were about to die. There was no hope there, Theo. No hope for a miracle or an ascension to some higher plane of existence. We're animal, you and I. Red in tooth and claw. I read that once. It's compelling, isn't it?"

"You're not going to kill me?" Theo asked.

"Not if I can help it. If you were to disappear, the Order would go on a rampage. They'd tear the Swallows apart looking for you. They wouldn't find you—nothing but carbon atoms come out of that blast furnace—but the questions they would ask, the investigation … it might reveal things that I want to stay hidden. Therefore, I prefer you to live." Marcus said everything without a hint of malice, as if he were giving Theo a lesson in algebraic equations.

"What do you want me to do?"

"Stephen's holy behind, you're stupid. How can you not see the obvious? You will resign from the Selection. Give them any reason you like. Or fail tomorrow and let them brand you. I don't care which option you choose, but if you're not out of the Selection by the end of training tomorrow morning, I will bring *Liddy* down here and feed her to the furnace."

"I'll do it," Theo said. "I promise I'll do it."

"You promise? That's wonderful, Theo. It makes me feel so much better, to have your promise."

"I wasn't supposed to be in the Selection anyway," Theo said. Awareness of his future spread before him, directionless and alone.

"Oh?" Marcus said, faintly curious.

"No," Theo said. "I added my name to the list."

Marcus frowned. "You're lying."

"Why would I lie about something like that?"

Marcus shrugged. "People don't need good reasons to lie. They do it as a matter of course. Humans are liars."

Theo shook his head. "I'm not lying. I hacked the Selection list and added my name. Made up scores. It was me the Regulatory was after the day of the drone callback." Despite the furnace, the killer standing over him, it felt good to tell the truth. Behind Marcus' eyes, Theo glimpsed movement. Calculation.

"Can you keep your mouth shut about the cave?" Marcus asked.

Theo closed his eyes, bit the inside of his cheek. "Yes."

"Good," Marcus said. "I've changed my mind. I don't want you to quit the Selection."

"What?" Theo asked. "Why?"

Marcus' eyes reflected the red and orange fire within the furnace. "All that matters is that you do what I tell you to do when I tell you to do it. Now get out of here, and don't forget your pathetic knife."

CHAPTER NINETEEN

Rose wheeled Selena out of the medical bay, down a series of lengthy corridors and into a wide room, walls covered with displays porting in imagery from the exterior of the *Hydra*. The moon hung beside her, shrouded by thick clouds, once again reminding Selena of a murky, white eye. A swirl of vertigo sent the room spinning.

"Are you okay?" Rose asked.

"I'm fine."

"We can go back, if you want?"

"I said I'm fine."

Selena turned her attention from the portal to the center of the room where a thick metal arm crossed a central pivot. One end of the metal arm supported a bulky, egg-shaped pod, the other a dense counterweight. A centrifuge. A simulator. Not the simple sort comprised of nothing more than an interface and a screen—this one mimicked the momentum and g-force of flight.

At the edge of the room, protected from the path of the simulator by a chest-high wall, two technicians studied wallscreens. As Rose pushed Selena forward, they turned to greet them.

"What's that thing?" Selena asked. She used her apathetic voice, the one she'd adopted since meeting with Ombudsman Owagumbiea. Mouth agape, head cocked to the side, hair falling over her ear—she hoped she looked as stupid as she felt.

One of the technicians gave a slight bow. "Welcome to VAST!"

"What's a vast?" Selena asked.

"The device in the center of the room is the Vector Analysis Systematic Tester. We've coupled a live-flight simulator with a robust database of ship's systems and schematics, including modern designs as well as an exhaustive catalog of retired models.

It can simulate all live-flight conditions, generate random events, and produce up to four gravities. In sum: it's the most advanced piece of technology in this star system—excluding the *Chimera*, of course." The technician chuckled at his own comment.

A thick band of cables spooled out from the base of the device and ran along the floor to where they buried themselves in the wall.

"Ah, you've noticed the cables," the chuckler said. "A connection to the *Chimera* herself! We've jacked into her neural network. We have limited access, of course, but couldn't have gotten VAST up and running without it. Now if we could wake the old girl up, then we'd *really* have something!"

"Whatever," Selena said, shoving hair back over her shoulder. Rose frowned and gave her a perplexed look. Selena ignored her.

"You're the testee?"

"That's me," Selena said.

"We are so pleased to meet you! My name is Chuck, and this egghead," he jerked a thumb, "is Rusty Gerber."

"Did you say your name is Chuckles?" Selena asked.

"No, *Chuck.* Rusty and I designed, beta-tested and ultimately perfected VAST for future testees—although it isn't perfect yet. We have a few instabilities in the theta cycles to pin down. But don't worry, it's completely safe."

"I'll bet," Selena said.

Rose cast her another look.

"Finally! To put her to good use; an actual candidate taking her for a spin." Chuck rubbed his hands together. "Rusty and I have spent hundreds of hours inside the device, but neither of us have the qualifications that you must. We're neither quick in reflex nor hearty in stamina." He leaned forward and whispered conspiratorially, "If I'm honest, anything more than a single gravity makes me queasy. You don't want to hear what happened when I pushed beyond that limit."

"Don't remind me," Rusty said, leaning away and making a face.

"I'll probably puke, too," Selena said.

"Nonsense! Don't be intimidated." Chuck grinned. "Someone with your qualifications can handle our battery of tests. You must be truly gifted—I didn't know they let the less than able-bodied through the Selection, if you'll pardon my rudeness."

"She's recovering from an injury," Rose said, glaring at the technician.

"I see. Of course, of course." Chuckles turned away, gazing around as if he'd lost something. "Well, in any case, Trusty Rusty and I are honored to have you here. We're expecting great things from VAST." Chuck paused, offering his index finger to Selena. "And of you as well," he added, almost as an afterthought.

Selena stared at his finger, refusing to take it. "I wouldn't expect much," she said.

"Don't be so modest. We've heard about the rigors of the Selection testing."

"I never took those tests," Selena said. In fact she had, but only hours before. The results hadn't come back yet. She'd purposely chosen incorrect answers and filled in essay questions with misspelled nonsense. While she couldn't fail the DNA test—she had sufficient genetic drift to crew the *Chimera*—she had made absolutely sure she'd fail the other sections.

Chuck's eyebrows lifted in confusion. "You never took the tests required by The Mandate?"

Selena gave Chuck a vicious smile. "No. Never."

"But you must have. Otherwise they wouldn't have sent you."

"Nope. Chief Moorland is forcing me to take this test. Stupid waste of time if you ask me—I can't fly."

"You can't fly?"

"No, *Chuckles.* I. Can't. Fly."

"This is unbelievable," Rusty said, shaking his head.

Chuck pointed at Selena. "When you first came in I knew there was something wrong with you." His face reddened. "Slack-jawed, absent, strapped in that, that *chair*—what is this, some sort of practical joke? Did Professor Yates have something to do with this? He's been after the directorship for—"

"Screw that," Selena said.

"Selena! What's wrong with you?" Rose hissed.

"Nothing. Chief Moorland wants me to take this test. So give it to me—I didn't come here so these goofballs could make fun of me. Put me in that thing and let me get this over with."

"She *can* fly," Rose said.

The technicians stood, arms folded, eyes blazing, barring access to VAST.

"She's from the rim. She's, well, a little different. But I have no doubt she can fly." Rose tried to wheel Selena forward. *What was she trying to do*, Selena wondered, *ram them?* That could be entertaining.

"This isn't funny," Chuck huffed. "We're not inflicting the likes of her on VAST. This system is for *real* testees." He shoved his head forward, saliva curling at the corner of his lips. "And you can give Professor Yates a message from me: he'll pay for this. I know all about the corners he cut on the sampling for the graphic overlay, and I'm prepared to publish a paper exposing him. If he thinks he can—"

"Screw Professor Yates, screw you, screw the whole Mandate!" Selena shouted. "Strap me into your stupid contraption and stop wasting my time." Selena gripped the wheels of her chair, ready to drive it forward herself.

"I'm calling Chief Moorland," Rusty said. He stalked to the bank of screens.

Chuck raised his chin, trying to look authoritative. "Yes, Rusty. Call the Chief."

In a moment, Chief Moorland's face appeared. "What do you need?"

Before Rusty could reply, Selena shouted, "Tell them to let me take my test!"

Rusty pointed at her, red-faced. "Why have you sent us this unprepared, uneducated, and, I might add, *foul-mouthed* testee? I know we're limited on candidates by the genetic lock-out, but surely you could have found someone more suitable than her."

"I thought you might call," Moorland said, amused.

"Did Professor Yates put you up to this?"

She shook her head. "I don't know what you're talking about. I sent Selena to VAST myself. I want you to run her through all the Alpha level tests. Every single one—don't stop, regardless of how she performs. That is all." The screen went dark.

"Call her back," Chucksaid. "This is ridiculous."

Rusty tapped and double tapped. "She won't reply." He slammed a fist into the screen and then howled, hand cradled against his chest.

Rose left Selena's side and went to Rusty. "Let me see," she said. Rose took hold of his elbow, gently straightening his arm and opening his fingers.

"My hand is on fire," Rusty whimpered.

"It's your pinky. You'll be fine," Rose said, giving him a calm smile. "It looks broken. I can set it back at the medical bay."

"It hurts!"

"Your own fault, Rust-o," Chuck said.

"A little sympathy, please?"

Selena stopped listening. She reached for the wheelchair's release, gliding forward, up the ramp to the platform outside the bean-shaped cockpit of VAST. How could she open it? She wheeled around the edge, tracing the cool metal with her fingertips, looking for a mechanism or release but finding only smooth, matte metal.

Nearing the backside of the bean, a familiar tingle began behind her ear and traveled down her spine. The spider had identified an interface! Selena closed her eyes and let her mind empty. The tingle intensified and she reached for it, embracing the data trickling in until it became a surging river. A wing-like door opened in the side of the bean.

Inside, a single leather chair all but filled the compact space. The interior smelled of electrical current and ozone, the air itself alive with power, energy. The tiny hairs on her arms stood on end. Balancing on the edge of the wheelchair, Selena half-pulled, half-fell into VAST.

She heard—no, *felt*—a warm, female voice. "Welcome to VAST. Please inform the testing proctor when you are ready to begin." Selena sunk into the chair, firm and comfortable.

"Hey, dimwits, I'm ready!"

Chuck, Rose and Rusty turned in unison. Rose's face lit up with a brilliant smile. "Look at you," she called. "Just like Wes Gunner."

"How did she ..." Chuck said, astounded.

"She's full of surprises," Rose said. "Rusty, why don't you let me take you to the medical bay. Chuck, can you handle administering the tests on your own?"

Slowly, Chuck nodded, too stunned to argue.

CHAPTER TWENTY

Theo woke five minutes before his alarm. Then, when it was actually time to get up, it took all of his resolve to kick free of the blankets and drag himself to the bathroom. He stood in front of the mirror, examining his face. His left eye wouldn't stop twitching. His body ached. No amount of pain killers made a difference. The person in the mirror looked like a hollowed out version of himself, empty of everything but fear. He feared Marcus would change his mind and kill him. He feared getting branded. He feared what might happen to Meghan. To Liddy.

His little sister peeked in from the hallway, doll held against her chest. "You look yucky."

"Thanks a lot, sis."

Theo didn't want to talk. Didn't want sympathy. Didn't want to be reminded of the black hole he'd been sucked into. Every muscle in his body screamed, every joint tight and painful. He felt terrible. His body wanted—demanded—that he stay home and rest. What would happen if he didn't show up for training? Would they send someone for him? Or would Sir bring a medical booth out to his house and brand him in front of his entire family?

He ran his hand across Liddy's silky hair as he slipped past her into the bedroom. He lay on the bed, body stiff and limp at the same time.

Liddy followed him and leaned against the foot of his bed. "Why are you crying?"

"I'm not," Theo said, but when he touched his cheek his fingers came away damp. He concentrated on his breathing, trying to calm the desperation rising like a groundswell.

"They're branding everyone that fails out of the Selection," Theo said.

"What's 'branding?'"

She was too young for this stuff. He shouldn't have said

anything. She deserved to feel safe.

"It's just ... a mark on your skin."

"A mark? Like with colors?"

"Yeah. Right. Like with colors. They put colors on you when you fail out of the training."

"I like colors," she whispered. "Can you pick your colors?"

Theo met her wide, innocent eyes. "No. You get whatever color they give you."

He ran a hand over his forearm. Could he live with a brand? Yes. He could. Not because he wouldn't feel like a failure, but because he knew about things far worse than a branding. Like Liddy screaming in terror as she was tossed into scorching flame. He wouldn't let that happen.

He rolled off the bed. "Come on, Liddy. Breakfast time." He held her hand as they descended the stairs.

In the kitchen, Erin cooked hot-melt while their dad slept on the downstairs bed.

"Theo?" Liddy asked.

"What?"

"There was a scary man in my dream last night."

"Well, you know what Mom says—scary dreams aren't real. Tell yourself that and you'll be fine."

"I did but it didn't work."

"Well, then I'll tell you. Liddy, the dream isn't real." He smiled at her. "Better?"

"I don't know."

He tousled her hair. "Tell me what you dreamed."

"That a bad man drove the *Chi-mer-a* down and crushed our family."

Theo picked her up and hugged her. He wanted to tell her about gravity and orbits and trajectories, but none of that would mean anything to a five-year-old. "Don't worry. The *Chimera* is our friend. She's going to help us."

"That's not what Dad says."

Theo frowned. Their dad had no sense of what was appropriate to say in front of little kids. He watched all the news programs with Liddy around—analysts and Mandate broadcasters discussing food shortages and predicting the date when starvation would set in.

"What did Dad say?" Theo asked.

"He said the *Chi-mer-a* is a ghost."

"She's not a ghost. She's sleeping." Theo nodded to Marc. "Just like Dad."

Liddy looked unconvinced.

"And we'll wake her up," Theo said. "Just like Dad."

Theo approached his dad, reached out, and yanked a hair from a leg poking out from under the quilt. Marc snapped his mouth closed and pulled his leg back beneath his blanket.

"She might not want to wake up, but we'll wake her anyway," Theo said. Theo tossed a pillow at his father's head. It plonked against his forehead and dropped to the floor. Marc's eyes popped open. "Hey!"

Liddy laughed.

"See?" Theo said. "I can wake anyone. You just have to know how."

Liddy reached for Theo and he lifted her despite the cramps in his calves and carried her to the kitchen where Erin was pouring pungent tea into mugs. He tried to set Liddy down, but she clung to him, clamping her legs and arms tight around him. What had Sir said? That part of being strong was helping the weak. Theo couldn't think of anyone weaker than Liddy. Anger flared inside him. Marcus had threatened his little sister.

The top of Liddy's head pushed against the underside of his chin. Theo considered admitting everything to the Regulatory, throwing himself at their mercy. But that wouldn't keep Liddy or Meghan safe. The Regulatory might not believe him. And the Order, convinced of a crazy prophecy, might intervene to keep him out of a work camp. Whatever happened, he'd have no guarantee that anyone would protect his family. The Regulatory and the Order, as his father liked to say, had bigger fish to fry. No, the thing to do was to wait, bide his time, and learn everything he could about Marcus.

* * *

When Theo arrived at the Civvy, fifteen candidates, including Marcus, Meghan, Hephaestus and Phoebus, stood waiting for pickup. All of them looked exhausted. Nobody said much as they boarded the bus and took their places in the rows of inward facing seats. Marcus slipped in beside Theo.

"Sleep well?" Marcus asked.

"Sure. Why wouldn't I?"

Meghan watched them from across the aisle.

Marcus leaned close and whispered in Theo's ear. "We're going to be good friends, Theo."

"We are?"

"Yes. It's important that people think we're friends. You'll play along. You look up to me like a little brother because I am a superior candidate."

"I'm not your brother," Theo whispered back.

Marcus leaned away, redirecting his attention to Heph. "Good work yesterday," he said. "You're one tough mother."

Heph shrugged, but looked pleased at the compliment. "My brother and I trained hard."

Phoebus leaned back in his seat, hands behind his head. "Do you think they'll mix things up today?"

"No," Marcus said. "Sir's not done grinding us down. By my count, we're light by eleven candidates, not including those that got branded yesterday."

Meghan wrinkled her nose. "That was disgusting. My mom almost didn't let me come back when I told her about it."

"We didn't tell our parents," Phoebus said, shaking his head. "It would have just upset them."

Nemus, one of the candidates Theo didn't know well, piped up, "Where do you think they take the branded kids?"

"It doesn't matter," Marcus said. "All that matters is where *we're* going." He pointed upward.

"Truth," Nemus said, leaning across and bumping fists with Marcus.

"Some of you might fail today," Marcus said, looking around and locking eyes with every candidate. "Some of you will fail tomorrow or the day after that. But some of you won't. Like me. Like Theo. We're going to make it through Sir's meat grinder. We're going to become officers aboard the *Chimera*. We're going to save this colony."

Theo wanted to laugh at Marcus' false bravado, but everyone else on the bus looked thoughtful, motivated, hanging on Marcus' every word.

They're eating this up, Theo thought. *They like him. They can't tell he's a killer.* The opposite, in fact—most of the other kids respected, even revered Marcus.

"Right, Theo?" Marcus asked.

"Right," Theo mumbled. "You got it, big brother."

Marcus' eyes tightened at the corners with a flash of anger before resetting back to charismatic confidence. Meghan watched, wary eyes moving from Marcus' face to Theo's. *Careful,* Theo thought. Meghan wasn't eating what Marcus was serving. The last thing he needed was Meghan asking questions.

Theo smiled his most believable smile and punched a fist into the air. "If we stick together and follow Marcus' lead, we can all make it through."

Nobody else raised their fist. Marcus gave Theo a smile filled with all-too-believable sympathy. An older boy humoring Theo, trying to give him a place at the table. Theo lowered his fist and did his best to look self-conscious and awkward rather than frightened.

When the conversation turned back to the fates of the branded, Marcus leaned close and whispered once again. "Don't overplay it. Your girlfriend is watching us." He smiled and patted Theo's shoulder. "If she gets too curious, bad things will happen."

* * *

Sir stood with his back to them, one hand tight around the wrist of the other. Without being asked, the candidates formed ranks. Sir did not acknowledge them. Without his handscreen Theo couldn't be sure, but he suspected the official start time had come and gone. What were they waiting for?

Then a silver rambler came sliding down the road from the Order compound and stopped at the edge of the field. Theo watched with interest as the rambler's door opened and a woman stepped out, followed by a kid Theo recognized from the day before. His name was Oscar or Osman or something like that. Dressed in yellow business attire, the woman strode across the lot, her son trailing behind.

She stopped in front of Sir. "Are you the maniac they put in charge of this debacle?"

"Quartermaster Krane West, ma'am." Sir did not offer his finger in greeting.

"I don't care what your name is or what make-believe rank you've assigned yourself. Ozyman told me all about your training methods, and I've come to inform you that I'm pulling him out of this savagery."

"What right do you have to withdraw him from the Selection?" Sir asked.

"I'm his mother."

"I don't care who you are. We're all subject to The Mandate."

"Not anymore. Ozyman's through here."

"I'm afraid that's not possible."

The woman's voice rose, shrill, disbelieving. "What do you mean that's not possible?"

Several of the uniformed regulators circled behind her. Ozyman's red-rimmed eyes peeked around his mother's back.

"Under the provisions of The Mandate, he's an asset. That means we can tell him what to do and when to do it. Right now, he's seven minutes late for training—thanks for bringing him by. Saves us having to round him up with the other no-shows."

"You call this 'training?' This isn't training. It's torture!"

"Ma'am, you have two choices: you can leave your son with me and drive yourself home, or I can have you taken into custody."

"You'll do no such thing. I've called Ombudsman Wolcott and told him all about you and your 'training.' Wolcott will shut you down before the end of the day. My son and I are leaving, and there's nothing you can do about it." The woman surged away, Ozyman close behind.

"Ozyman Oscar O'Neil," Sir called after them. "Aptitude index, above average. Sub-category, spatial geometry: exceptional. Sub-category, linguistics: above average. Sub-category, mathematics: above average. Sixty-one point five kilos, one point seven five meters, blue eyes. Son of Lina and Baronty O'Neil, co-chairs of the O'Neil Group."

Theo had never considered that Sir, Quartermaster West, had read their Selection sheets. And not just read them, but *memorized* them. That explained how he'd managed to do roll call the day before without looking at a handscreen.

The woman stopped and gave Sir a savage look. "So you can read—that's impressive. And you know when you're beaten. A good trait for a self-styled, pseudo-military man."

"I'm not letting you leave with Ozyman," Sir said. The woman raised her hand in a vulgar gesture and rushed for her rambler.

Sir nodded once, a sharp head dip. The regulators converged

and ripped Ozyman from his mother's grasp. She lashed out and caught one of them in the face, raking fingernails across his skin. "Let go of me! You think you can get away with this? You'll rot in prison, you piece of filth!"

One of the regulators slammed his knee into her chest and she crumpled to the ground.

"You live in the land of make believe," Sir shouted. "Do you think your money will save you from starvation?" Then, speaking to the regulators, "Get her off my training field."

Regulators dragged her, screaming and flailing and cursing, to one of the black ramblers. Ozyman broke free and took off running. Sir pointed at Marcus. "Bring him back." Marcus nodded and sprinted, hands cutting swift arcs at his sides, crossing the field with incredible speed.

Ozyman didn't have a chance. Short and a bit bulky, even the head start couldn't help him. It took Marcus seconds to catch up. Marcus lowered his shoulder and dove, smashing Ozyman to the ground. Marcus yanked the other boy up by the collar and locked an arm around his neck. Theo knew how it felt to have that iron bicep cutting off his windpipe and he swallowed involuntarily. Marcus dragged Ozyman, legs pedaling and kicking, back to the group. When they reached Sir, Marcus let him drop to the ground in a whimpering heap.

Ozyman's mother shouted threats from the back of the rambler where the regulators had secured her. Everyone looked at Sir, waiting for him to pass judgment.

Everyone but Theo.

He studied Marcus' face. Under the detachment, his eyes burned with wild intensity. *He likes seeing people suffer*, Theo realized.

Ozyman didn't resist when the regulators led him to the medical booth. Sir stalked after them, candidates at his heels.

"You can't do this!" Ozyman's mother shrieked. "You can't do this to my son!" She broke down, sobbing, makeup dripping in dark rivulets down each cheek. Ozyman closed his eyes.

"He's not your son," Sir said. "He belongs to The Mandate."

The laser burned Ozyman's arm. He didn't cry out or flinch. When the regulators released him, he climbed into the back of the rambler and hid his face in his mother's lap.

"You sick, *sick* man," the woman growled. "You're going to

regret this."

Sir's face showed a hint of scorn as the rambler pulled away, but he clearly hadn't enjoyed the branding. He might share some similarities with Marcus, but the two were not the same. Though unpredictable and terrifying, Sir was governed by a set of principles, even if Theo didn't fully understand what they were. Marcus, on the other hand, did enjoy hurting people.

As the rambler slid away, Sir ordered the kids into push-up position.

"Down!"

Sir's voice was so loud that for a moment Theo thought he was yelling in his ear. But no—Sir had joined them on the tarmac, arms level, body a straight line from the tips of his boots to the top of his shaved head.

With each repetition, Sir rose and fell with machine perfection. "Weakness is like a weed." He held himself parallel to the ground with one arm and pointed to the gunkroot squeezing up through the cracked concrete with the other. He lowered himself using one arm. "Weakness grows anywhere it can. It is persistent. Life is a constant war against weakness."

Sir tore free a handful of weeds free and tossed them away. "We've got a lot of weeding to do."

* * *

Hours later, before the training ended, several ramblers bounced down the road from the Order compound, leading a sleek, black Regulatory bus. The vehicles stopped at the edge of the field. Regulators poured out of the ramblers and began setting up additional medical booths. The candidates looked at one another. Had they *all* failed the Selection? Were they about to get branded? Theo could understand why Sir might fail most of them. Other than Heph and Marcus, no one looked like they could last another five minutes, much less another day.

At Sir's direction, the candidates made formation and marched to the medical booths. Theo felt perversely grateful for the break from the physical torment of the training.

"As you've no doubt noticed, some of you haven't shown commitment to the Selection," Sir said. "Today, you'll stand as witness that no one, and I mean no one, will find an easy way out. I don't care if you're rich or poor or the returned Stephen himself."

Prodded by regulators, the kids who hadn't shown up exited the bus, cuffs around their wrists. Theo had forgotten about them, too absorbed in surviving another day to worry about other people's problems. Now he saw the inevitability of what was about to happen. Neither The Mandate nor Sir would allow anyone to quit. The kids from the bus would receive their brand, just like Ozyman. Every single one of them.

Stepping off the bus, their faces were pale, the ugly truth clear to them. Their lives were *not* what they'd believed them to be. Everything wasn't going to be okay. The universe wasn't kind or forgiving, but rather unpredictable, ruthless and cruel.

Regulators herded the no-shows forward. Sir walked around them, looking at each with disgust. After making a full circle, he stopped, hands clasped behind his back. "Soldiers who abandon their armies are executed."

Several kids burst into tears. Others sank to their knees. A brave few glared back, defiant.

"You, however, are not soldiers. Lucky for you."

Meek or fighting, violent or calm, it didn't matter: one-by-one, regulators led each kid to a booth. The stink of singed skin and hair filled the air, a sickening accompaniment to the screaming.

When all the no-shows had received brands, regulators loaded them back on the bus. Sir turned, addressing the remaining candidates. "Some of you believe I am cruel. That is because I am. But I promise you this, kindness will not save our colony."

Rage and frustration crossed Meghan's face like scudding storm clouds over the sea. "Neither will branding all of us!" she shouted. "What purpose does it serve? Scaring people? Humiliating them? That woman was right, you're sick." Meghan stared at Sir with open hatred.

"The process of finding the best is a ruthless one," he said. "It has to be. If you don't want a brand, you better make sure you're among those that complete it. That goes for all of you." Then, speaking to everyone, he shouted, "Dismissed!"

Meghan opened her mouth to argue, but Sir strode away without so much as a backward glance. Her teeth clicked together and she looked at Theo, confusion chipping away at her anger. "He's wrong," she said, eyes dark, fathomless. "There *has* to be a better way than this."

CHAPTER TWENTY-ONE

Inside VAST, Selena waited for the test to begin. A hidden ventilator pushed chill air over her skin, damp from the exertion of getting from the wheelchair to her seat. The bean contained no manual controls, no interface, no screens. She fidgeted, unable to overcome her nerves. Flunking the written tests had been easy. Fun, even. The sort of thing she might have done even if her father's well-being didn't depend on it. But to fail at flying, even in a simulation, felt offensive—like a self-betrayal.

Through the spider, the warm voice spoke once more: "Initiating." A pair of restraints slid from the top of the chair and cinched her shoulders and midsection. A low whine vibrated through the bean and the centrifuge began to spin. Steady pressure pushed her into the seatback. Despite the pain of her bruises, the acceleration felt wonderful.

"Sequence one," said the voice. "Basic maneuvers."

The bean darkened. Her pulse thudded inside her ears. Nervous and excited, Selena waited for the navigation grid to rise in front of her. Instead, the opaque blackness transformed. Myriad stars burst forth, bright and beautiful, spread before her in lacy galaxies. A series of glowing circles materialized in the star field. Large and small, some in motion, others stationary, she recognized the alignment at once. A bobsled run. A flight competition requiring pilots to make a complicated series of maneuvers through and between obstacles. Scrapyard sponsored one every three hundred rotations. Liam always finished near the middle of the pack. Selena didn't compete because of her age, but couldn't wait for the day when she would ace it and embarrass the crusty old veterans and upstart flame-backs alike.

Facing the synthetic run, she planned to bomb it—assuming she could figure out how to fly the simulator in the first place.

"Accuracy is more important than speed. Your objective: do

not miss any of the circles."

Selena tapped her fingers against her knees, scanning for some sign of an interface. Where was the navigational grid? She wanted a chance to fly. "What am I supposed to *do*?" she yelled.

"Begin," the warm voice said.

Selena tingled as her spider surged to life. Stronger than her connection to *The Bee*, it felt as if her body had transformed into the ship. Not a heavy trawler meant to survive in the rim, but a racer! Made of burnished alloy, strong and fast as anything. A tiny triangle, little more than a cockpit attached to powerful thrusters. She felt all of it, as if the very core of the racing ship hummed within her chest. The strangeness, the unfettered freedom threatened to overwhelm her—the ship begged to be pushed to its absolute limits.

She thought of acceleration and the ship responded. Reveling in the simplicity, the speed, she corkscrewed forward, hoping the maneuver would look like stupid hot-dogging. She layered on speed. The first of the circles, half a kilometer wide and impossible to miss, loomed in front of her. She brought the racer's nose to aft, grazing the edge of the hoop but making it through. The next ring, smaller than the first, required a modest course correction. She banked in a wide arc, and the hoop passed on the starboard side.

She rotated on the racer's axis and aimed in the general direction of the next hoop, accelerating for no other reason than she enjoyed the force pinning her to the back of the chair. She would fail, but she saw no reason not to have some fun in the process.

Three minutes later, three of twenty hoops cleared, the ship melted away and the star field became an opaque cocoon once more. Aware of every eyelash blink, every breath, Selena's tiny body felt weak and inadequate. The spider burned behind her ear as she counted the seconds. Maybe her performance had angered Chuckles so much that he would defy Moorland and cancel the remaining tests. The bean would crack open and someone would wheel her back to her boring, curtained room in the medical bay.

"Hello?" she said. "What's next?"

The response was immediate. "Sequence two. Mass and inertia manipulation."

A dense field of colored balls of different sizes and shapes surrounded her. A few as large as proxy-moons, others as small as the racer from the previous sequence. A representation of the rim, but made as colorful as party balloons. The ship that greeted her through the interface was nothing more than a simple orb covered with dozens of steam jets. Lacking primary thrusters, its design offered incredible maneuverability at the expense of delta-V. The ship could easily change direction but had no long-burn potential.

"Using the gravitational forces of the objects around you, accelerate your test pod to maximal velocity."

With a bolas and tether, Selena would have found the highest density object in the field and rocketed herself around it, using the steam jets to increase momentum. Absent a tether, she would need to execute a series of linked maneuvers around any number of objects, working to gain momentum with each successive pass.

She surveyed the field, noting that the largest objects were not necessarily the densest. They appeared to offer an advantage that in reality did not exist. She saw the path she would choose if she wanted to pass the test, but it provided her little satisfaction—she would have liked to *demonstrate* her skill. Instead, pretending to have no idea what she was doing, she rammed the pod into the closest object, a semi-translucent pink ball with the consistency of foam.

"Avoid contact with the objects," the voice chided. "Points will be deducted for each instance of ship-on-object contact."

Selena managed to ram eleven more objects before the sequence terminated.

Again, the voice spoke: "Sequence three. Navigation dynamics."

Shaped like a spear, the engines of the immense ship that greeted her rumbled in pre-burn, poised for ignition. A conical command deck sat at the apex of her two hundred meter length. Despite her size and raw power, the vessel was a relic—a Shellback, a Son of Neptune—one of the first cruisers to break through the boundaries of the Sol system.

Through her spider, Selena explored the Shellback, discovering an array of ten thrusters, each fueled by a mass of liquid fuels heated by a nuclear reactor that filled the back third of the ship. Vibration rose through her seat—a gut-thrum strong enough to set her teeth chattering. The ship could reach fractional light speed, the fastest speed possible without the protection offered by hydrostasis.

In some ways, the ship reminded her of the *Chimera*. The colony ship also used a central drivetrain and an array of liquid fuel rockets that could fire individually or as a single unit. However, the Shellback had a much narrower profile—it didn't need exterior plating to protect colony pods. Most important of all, the Shellback lacked ecomire-fueled cores capable of creating and sustaining a full hydrostasis field.

"Using navigational paradigms, find the most expedient vector to circumnavigate Jupiter and align on a trajectory to reach Alpha Centauri."

Selena didn't know what navigational paradigms were or how to follow them—she hadn't studied navigation, at least not formally. She could, however, feel the largeness of the gas giant Jupiter—so much like Gauleta in size if not color—and recognize the appropriate line to swing the Shellback around its gravity well and toward Alpha Centauri, the closest star to Sol. She could pass the test if she wanted.

Failing it required little forethought. She might miss the correct line or aim the Shellback at Jupiter and let its mass do the rest, but neither of those options required creativity. She could do better than that, couldn't she? A wicked idea came, one so brazen that she laughed aloud. She would pay her ancestors a visit.

She rotated the Shellback, and the red gas giant disappeared over her left shoulder, falling away behind her. Accelerating as fast as the old ship would allow, she burned fuel at an insane, inefficient rate. The Shellback's rudimentary precursor to hydrostasis dulled the acceleration, but not entirely. Her organs plunged inside her, head pressed tight against the seatback. Cruising at full-burn, Selena aimed for the third planet from the sun, the tiny ball of rock and dirt known as Earth. In real life, the trip would take weeks but the simulation allowed for the acceleration of time so that Jupiter shrank behind her and Mars became a distinct, enlarging red sphere.

"Correct course," the voice demanded.

Earth expanded into a blue-green ball. The voice grew insistent. "Slow to fractional burn. Rotate ship two hundred and thirty degrees and follow the indicated path." A graphic overlay charted the prescribed course correction. Selena ignored the voice and hurtled at Earth, watching with fascination as its numerous landmasses took shape beneath swirling, white clouds.

The diversity of colors surprised her—infinite shades of blue, gradients of green, tans and yellows and white. Stephen's Point was monochrome by comparison. The beauty of the simulated imagery captivated her. Separated by countless generations of Samuelsons, The Last War, corporate divestment and thousands of light years, this ball of dirt was her distant ancestors' home.

On a severe approach, the pointed tip of the Shellback hit Earth's atmosphere. The Shellback shook. How long would the simulation last? Would it end before she struck the surface?

"Impact imminent," the voice said. Through her spider, Selena felt something like fear coming from the simulation itself. The presence intensified, grasping at her, trying to force her to correct course, but Selena resisted. Images flashed through her mind—Earth, Gauleta, merging and transforming lines of light, meshing and unmeshing. A voice spoke—not the distant, emotionless voice of the simulator, but a different voice, this one filled with emotion. "Goodbye, friend."

What was going on?

The sky opened. Browns and greens solidified into recognizable terrain. The view rotated counter-clockwise. The indistinct landmass transformed into civilization. Vehicles drove down highways. A passenger train lumbered through a mountain valley. Humans the size of ants stood in some sort of arena. She wasn't being sucked down—they were being sucked *up*. The ship had taken on the density of a black hole and was pulling all of it, everything, up and into her. Selena screamed as the ground rushed up to meet her ....

She sat alone in the chill air of the bean, soaked with sweat, heart thumping. She closed her eyes, the last simulated image burned into her memory: a wall of fire sweeping over the surface of the Earth, leaving nothing in its wake but rubble and char and death.

CHAPTER TWENTY-TWO

Purple bruises covered Theo's chest and arms. Dark skin surrounded his eyes. Yellow-brown scabs marked a patchwork of half-healed scrapes and cuts on his legs and stomach. He hurt everywhere and all the time. Breathing hurt. The soreness had become a constant, one he'd learned to accept, even enjoy a little. He'd made it through the first week of training. Eleven candidates remained, and Sir had finally given them a day off to rest and recover.

Theo filled the bathroom sink with icy water until it ran over the sides and splashed on the floor. He plunged his head beneath the surface. Gripping the edges of the sink, lungs raging inside his chest, the fear of suffocation became a frenzied, thoughtless desperation. When he at last pulled free, he sucked in air—delicious, perfect air. Body shocked to complete wakefulness, he returned to his room to dress.

Careful not to disturb his sleeping sister, Theo donned long pants, a t-shirt, one of his father's work shirts and a beat up fishery jacket. A hat with fold-down earflaps completed his disguise: he looked like any other worker heading off to one of the few operational factories left in the Swallows. He tucked his handscreen into his jacket pocket along with his multitool. Under his left pant leg, he'd taped a sheath containing a thin filet knife, sharp enough to split a hair. He took a final look at himself in the mirror, slouching his shoulders until they matched the world-weariness of those of his father's generation. He was ready.

Theo had kept a copy of the Selection list on an invisible, encrypted data partition on his handscreen. He'd checked and rechecked Marcus' scores, almost all at genius level. Marcus wasn't just a killer, he was a *gifted* killer. A savant. Theo would have to be extremely careful.

Outside, a brisk wind blew down from Great Northern, fresh

with the scent of snow and dwarf pines. In the semi-darkness, Theo cradled his handscreen, re-checking the data he'd scraped from the Civvy network: CCB Slot Request Form to a Dependent Care Signatory: *Huxley, Martha P.K.*

Virtually all communication on Stephen's Point was digital, but certain government agencies occasionally sent physical copies of important documents upon request. And someone named Martha Huxley had filed one for a Marcus J. Locke not three weeks before the Selection training began. He'd found no other mention of Marcus. No school records, Regulatory records, no signs of a social presence on the nets. The only other reference to the surname "Locke" were a few ancient historical texts in the Earth Literature Database. Prior to the Selection and the CCB request, Marcus simply hadn't existed.

Theo pulled up the address associated with the CCB. He knew the place—a squalid multi-family prefab so poorly maintained he found it hard to believe anyone still lived there. But when he checked the Civvy's records, he found that someone named Martha Huxley did live there. She might know who Marcus really was.

Theo powered down his handscreen and shoved it deep into his pocket. The filet knife's stiff, protective sheath rubbed against his shin with each step. He kept his shoulders slumped and walked with his head down, hands in his pockets. Twenty-minutes of shuffling later, he reached the quad. It leaned heavily to one side. The foundation had sunk so far into the ground that earth hid most of the first floor windows. Boards covered the rest. He looked up to the ninth floor where Martha P.K. Huxley allegedly resided. Did she really exist? Or had Marcus created her to set up a dead end for anyone trying to find him?

Only one way to find out.

The smell of decay permeated the air as Theo pushed through the front doors of the quad. The floor felt spongy, like a bed of fungus. The walls, once covered with panels, had deteriorated to reveal the ancient ceramic underneath, as yellow as a dog's teeth. Theo tried to imagine the building as it must have looked when first converted from the insides of Pod Six. The dismal space looked nothing like the images from the history vids—airy, white rooms with blue and green accents like *Chimera*'s interior.

A thick bead of iridescent metal sealed the elevator doors

closed. A faded "Out of Service" sign rested on the ground in front of them. He'd have to take the stairs located at the back of the building. He navigated around piles of litter in the hallway, stepping over bags filled with something that smelled worse than any garbage he'd ever encountered. Why would Marcus live here? Why would anyone? The place disgusted him.

Broken portions of handrail sat in a jumble at the base of the stairs. He climbed upward, noting gaps in the stairwell large enough to fall through. Stairs creaked under his weight, and he suspected they could collapse at any moment. Pausing on the eighth floor landing, barely breathing, he wondered if Marcus might be home. Fear filled his chest like hot vapor.

He ascended the remaining flight, hand wrapped around his multitool. Stepping gingerly into the hall, he checked the nearest door for a number. All the doors were blank. Which was the right one? He would have to try them all. Halfway down the hallway, the click of a deadbolt sounded from one of the doors. Panicking, he threw himself against the wall, flattening against the peeling paint, trying to become invisible.

The door opened a crack. Two eyes peered out. Small, beady eyes surrounded by wisps of white hair, floating like waterweeds. The crack widened. A sunken-faced woman who looked as old as the building gazed right at him. Maybe this was Martha. Marcus' grandmother?

The door slammed. Theo waited, wondering if it would open again, this time to reveal Marcus.

After counting to thirty, Theo pushed free of the wall. He'd come to find answers. He wasn't going to leave until he had some. Picking his way down the hall, he passed a unit entirely lacking a door. A rusting bedframe leaned against the wall, surrounded by rotting bed sheets. He passed the empty apartment and made his way to the next door. A square of metal was visible beneath a layer of grime. He cleaned it with his jacket sleeve, uncovering a small numeral four. Martha lived in unit 904. This had to be the place. He tried the door. Locked.

The access panel, like everything else in the building, didn't work. The lifeless screen didn't respond when he tapped it. The door didn't feel that solid when he pushed against it. He could force it open if he smashed into it, but that would alert anyone inside. Examining the door and its ancient, rusted hinges, he came up with a better idea. He pulled out his multitool and selected one of the screwdriver tips. He inserted it into the door mechanism and twisted. The door creaked. He twisted again in the opposite direction. This time the lock clicked open and the door swung inward.

Using the light of his multitool to guide him, he examined the interior of the room, finding a small foyer connected to a kitchen alcove. The place looked unsanitary for a cat or dog, let alone a human. The smell filling the room made the stench in the first floor hallway seem pleasant by comparison. Layers of competing varieties of bacteria grew on the walls, black-green and dark purple. He hoped he wouldn't catch something from the putrid air.

The kitchen showed no signs of recent use. Stepping over empty plastic bottles and crunching over something—dry cat food?—he examined the bare cupboards, searching for some sign that Marcus once lived here. A pile of grimy, yellowed paper sat atop the counter. Under several generic advertisements addressed to "resident," Theo found an official letter from the Bureau of Elderly Affairs addressed to Martha P.K. Huxley. He began reading:

We regret to inform you that your application for continued support payments has been denied. We cannot extend your benefits without conducting a site visit. You may schedule a site visit with the Bureau at a convenient time by contacting our offices—

Theo set the letter aside and leafed through the rest of the pile. All were addressed to Martha. Leaving the kitchen, he headed to the back of the unit and poked his head into the lavatory. Rusty pipes coated with moisture hung loose from the wall. Leaking droplets of orange water nourished wicked-looking white mushrooms growing from a bed of black gunk. "No one can live here," Theo muttered. The trip began to feel like a waste of time.

On his right, another door led to the last room of the apartment. The door sagged on its hinges. He shoved against it but it barely moved. Glimpsing through the narrow gap between the door and the frame, he saw a reflection in a wall mirror: furniture stacked to the ceiling, massive piles of rags and clothing and the headboard of a bed. He shoved the door again, forcing the gap wide enough to slip inside.

Huddled atop the stained mattress was the shape of an old woman. Theo gasped.

"Excuse me!" he said. Even as the words left his mouth, he knew—the old woman was dead. Her face a skull with paper-thin skin stretched tight, her body a macabre version of Liddy's doll. Empty eye sockets stared at Theo. He stumbled backward, covering his mouth with his sleeve—he'd been breathing in something far worse than mold.

Sickened by the thought of the poor woman rotting away with no one to bury her, no one to mourn her, he backtracked to the foyer of the apartment. There, next to the door, a small rucksack. He'd missed it before; the door opened inward, hiding it from view. Unlike everything else in the place, it was clean. Inside he found a small case filled with cooking spices and rations, a large sheet of canvas, a handscreen and an ancient paper book. Bound in real leather, gold inlay inscribed the title: *A Tale of Two Cities.* A hand written note in a shaky, looping cursive filled the inside cover: *For Marcus, from Martha. Not everything worth reading can be found on the nets. I hope you enjoy this as much as I have.*

He flipped through the pages, reading a few paragraphs. Some sort of novel from Earth, it must have come on the original colony ship—nobody would waste discretionary exchange ship weight on a paper book. Why would Marcus keep a gift from someone he'd killed? It didn't make sense to carry around a clue linking you to the scene of a crime.

Maybe after Martha died of old age, Marcus had continued to collect her support payments until they stopped coming. More likely, Marcus had killed her in order to steal them. *He'll do anything. Anything at all. He has no conscience.* The body in the cave with its distended, blood-red eye; Marcus hadn't just killed the man. He'd destroyed him. Had he discovered Martha's body? Maybe that was why Marcus killed him.

Theo rummaged through Marcus' bag and withdrew the handscreen. After it powered up, a red log-in prompt blinked beneath the seal of a government agency that Theo didn't recognize. No answers here—a failed log-in attempt might be traceable. But even without accessing the screen's contents, its mere presence raised more questions. Why did Marcus have government property? And how did *he* know the password?

Before Theo could power down the screen, the image flickered and a series of characters streamed past: rows and rows of code, moving too quickly to read. The screen flickered again, and the cursor in the log-in spooled out a series of encrypted characters. The cursor blinked at Theo, inviting him to enter the auto-generated—hacked?—password. He waited, finger hovering over the screen, and then with a sense of doom, tapped it.

The screen flashed an index, sorted by date. The heading read "Clinical Notes." Could it be Marcus' journal? He read a few random entries. No, not a journal. Not unless Marcus liked to refer to himself in the third person and write down weird, detailed accounts of his own behavior.

One of the earliest entries, nearly a decade old, caught his eye:

As reported, I find no evidence of the family of origin. The boy appears to live alone. The other vagrants occupying the building think his name is Lucas or Mark ...

He tapped another entry, further down:

The boy exhibits strong anti-social tendencies. His host mother reports that he bit her seven-year-old son.

Theo paused, trying to make sense of the words. The clinical notes didn't belong to Marcus, but to someone checking in on him. Reading them gave Theo a visceral thrill, almost as powerful as the fear of being discovered. He needed to leave, he was pushing his luck, but couldn't stop reading.

... Sociopathic tendencies ... dysfunctional ... high IQ but low emotional quotient ...

It was like one of the Selection sheets, except the things highlighted were frightening. The notes grew stranger. The earliest entries seemed factual and disinterested. The more recent suggested something else entirely:

Marcus indicates he would prefer to stay with the Huxley woman, despite her age. I disagree. He needs to be close to the valley—these drives out to the mountains have taken their toll.

Another: *Marcus seems less compliant—I may have to remind him why he needs to listen to me.*

The final entry: *Driving out to see the boy. I've agreed to take a look at some scratchings he said he found in a cave. If real, they might be worth something to the Order and change everything for us. Either way, it gives me another opportunity to reinforce my position on his participation in the Selection. Marcus must come to see that it isn't in his best interests.*

Theo almost dropped the handscreen. It belonged to the man

from the cave! He had to get out of here. Now. Before Marcus came back. He replaced the book and the screen, trying to arrange them exactly as they were before.

He plunged into the hallway and careened down the stairwell.

Somewhere below, a sound.

Soft-soled shoes on creaking stairs? Theo held his breath, waiting. More faint noises echoed upward. Someone was coming. He crouched, hidden behind the slats of the stairwell's safety wall. The creaking grew closer. He had nowhere to go. The building only had one more story, and if he tried to go up, the person on the stairs would spot him. He couldn't run, which meant he'd have to fight.

Marcus' familiar face appeared between the railings.

Theo's only advantage was surprise. Liddy's smiling face flashed in his mind. He wouldn't let anything happen to her. Shaking with adrenaline, he tensed, ready to make his last stand.

CHAPTER TWENTY-THREE

Pressed against the safety wall, a sick dread filled Theo's stomach as Marcus reached the eighth floor landing. If Theo didn't time his attack perfectly, Marcus would subdue him and throw him over the stair rail. He would fall like the man in the cave, plummeting down, down, down.

"Psssst," a whisper-thin voice called from behind Theo, barely audible over the deafening thump of his own heart. "Psssst."

The crazy-looking woman with wispy white hair and beady eyes waved from her open door. He scurried forward in a crouch, hoping Marcus wouldn't hear him. The woman beckoned, as if somehow the motion of her hand would speed his progress. The door closed behind him and the lock engaged with an audible *click*. The woman put her finger to her lips, the universal sign of silence. No need. To make a sound might mean death.

The woman's funny little eyes blinked at him. Close up, he saw that they weren't just beady, but also kind. Footsteps sounded from the hall. They slowed and stopped outside the locked door. Theo and the woman kept as still as shadows. The door handle rattled. Had Marcus seen him? Had he heard a noise from behind the door?

Theo expected Marcus to pick the lock or force the door open. Instead, after a few more gentle rattles, the footsteps moved away down the hall. Theo exhaled. The old lady pulled his sleeve, drawing him further into the mirror-image of Martha's apartment. Except that the room was clean and didn't stink quite as much. A single, plush chair sat in a corner, and next to it, a bookcase filled with framed images. A light glowed on a small table, turning the wizened woman's face an odd shade of yellow.

"He's a scary boy," she whispered.

"I know."

The old lady smiled, revealing a mouthful of tiny teeth.

Except for the sharp, animal-like canines. Theo couldn't help but stare.

"I only bite bad people," she said, the smile taking over her face and forcing her eyes almost shut. "You're not a bad person."

"How can you tell?" he asked, startled into bluntness.

"You're a worker."

Theo looked down at his father's shirt and jacket. They might have just saved his life.

"Thank you for helping me," Theo said.

"Us workers stick together," she said, winking at him. Despite her stooped body, her whole face constantly shifted, reforming into new expressions, little eyes opening or closing or flashing as if they were about to transform from dark brown to some other color. Theo didn't know what to say to her. He couldn't leave, not until he was sure Marcus had picked up his things and exited the building.

"My name's Lineya," the woman said.

"Theo."

She took his finger and held it in her bony hand. He didn't like touching her, but didn't want to be rude. Not to someone who'd probably saved his life. "You're a good boy," she said. "Kind. I can tell. I can feel it in your pulse. The pulse tells a lot about a person."

"Yeah?" Theo said, pulling at his hand, hoping Lineya would get the idea and release him. Instead she tightened her grip.

"No one comes to see me," she said. "Not anymore. Just like Martha. It's good you checked on her. Has she made it out of bed today?"

"No." Theo didn't know how to tell Lineya that Martha wouldn't ever make it out of bed again.

Lineya laughed. "She's younger than I am!"

"You look a lot better than she does," Theo offered.

"A real charmer, eh? You remind me of my husband, Carl. Died many years ago of a stomach thing."

"Sorry," Theo murmured, thinking of his grandpa Jim-Jim, who'd died of some sort of cancer. He recalled a visit to the hospice right before he died. Grandpa lay on the bed, a blue oxygen mask over his mouth, watery eyes vacant. Erin cried in the chair next to the bed, his father standing behind her. Curious about the mask, Theo asked if he could try it on. Erin's shock soon gave way to anger. She grabbed Theo's arm and forced him into the hallway. He waited there, alone, counting the ceiling tiles. Most of them had been cracked.

"It's okay," Lineya said. "Really. He visits often. Comes in through the window in the form of a great, gray seagull."

"Seagull?"

"A type of bird. They live by oceans."

Not here they don't, he thought. He'd never seen a bird before. The few brought on the *Chimera* had died ages before he was born.

"Stay for tea?" Lineya asked. He shrugged. He might as well. He wasn't leaving for a good while. "Should I invite Martha?" she asked.

"I don't think that's a good idea."

Lineya looked at him, confused for a moment, and then shifted to bright-eyed confidence. "That's right! Martha doesn't drink tea. How silly of me."

Lineya set a kettle of water on an electric heating pad. Theo waited until the water started to bubble before asking a carefully worded question: "Does anyone else come to visit Martha or Marcus?" The old woman poured loose-leaf tea into a little mesh ball and clamped it closed with surprisingly dexterous fingers.

"Like who?"

"Someone from the government, maybe?" Theo leaned against the kitchen doorway, trying to look nonchalant. Lineya dropped the mesh ball into the boiling water and watched as it bobbed, buoyed by bubbles rising from the hot metal. She cocked her head and blinked her tiny eyes.

"Nobody comes from the government," Lineya said.

He was wasting his time. What else could he ask? *So, do you have any idea who Marcus might have killed? Other than your skeleton friend next door?*

Lineya wrapped her hand in a thick cloth and poured yellowish liquid into a pair of cracked cups, their delicate, curving handles reminiscent of the rising steam. She handed one to Theo. Breathing in the steam rising from the cup, her eyes refocused. When she spoke, her voice carried none of the quavering uncertainty of a moment ago. "They won't come here unless you make them—politicians don't like to be reminded of their failures."

The intense heat radiating through the cup warmed his hands and gave him the courage to recall images of the man from the cave. "What about a man? Not too tall, bald head. Has anyone like that come here?"

"You mean the dipsy-do?"

"The what?"

"The dipsy-do—his head bobs up and down when he walks, like a sandpiper." Theo didn't bother asking what a sandpiper was. "He parks his fancy car down in the lot and then skitters in here and checks on the scary boy."

"Checks on him?"

Lineya pursed her lips, as if expecting a kiss and blew over the surface of her tea. Her teeth were the same color as the hot liquid. "The dipsy-do makes sure Martha has enough food and things like that. Sometimes he takes Marcus with him when he leaves."

"Where do they go?"

"Away." Lineya held her cup, bony fingers curled around the thin handle. "But the scary boy doesn't like it. Sometimes I hear things smashing after the dipsy-do brings him home."

Theo risked a dangerous question, "What does Martha say about the dipsy-do?"

"Martha?" Lineya closed her eyes and sipped her tea. "I knew a Martha once."

* * *

Theo made sure to arrive at the Civvy early the next morning. He waited for Marcus, wondering if he'd be able to read the "scary boy," and even more important, if Marcus would be able to read him.

Marcus arrived, trotting alongside Nemus, faces flush from the cold. Nothing in Marcus' demeanor suggested anything out of the ordinary. His blue eyes roved over the other candidates. Theo smiled at him. After a moment, Marcus smiled back.

"Enjoy your day off?" Marcus asked.

"Yeah," Theo said. "I slept a lot."

"Ditto," Nemus said.

If Marcus knew Theo had been to Martha's apartment, it didn't show. "Sir's probably going to throw something different at us today," Marcus said. "The training will shift away from simple physical challenges to psychological ones."

"What makes you say that?" Heph asked.

"It's the logical progression. First, weed out the physically weak, then see who can handle making difficult decisions under pressure. We'll be doing some team dynamic work as well. They'll want to know who plays nice with others."

"Sure," Heph snorted.

Marcus kept his face neutral. "Watch and see if I'm right."

"You go around acting like you've been named the captain of the *Chimera*," Heph said. "You think you're pretty impressive, don't you?"

Phoebus caught Heph's eye and smirked.

"I don't think I'm impressive," Marcus said. "But neither do I underestimate my abilities."

"You're cocky," Heph said, pushing closer to Marcus. "And you're a know-it-all."

Theo tensed, expecting a physical altercation of some sort, but Marcus raised his hands, face a model of genuine goodwill. "I'm sorry if I offended you, Hephaestus. I was simply stating what I felt was obvious. We're through week one and Sir is going to vary the training routine."

"Relax," Phoebus said, speaking to both Marcus and Heph. "Like Marcus said, we'll know soon enough."

* * *

After they completed warmups, Sir split everyone into teams. He paired Marcus with Nemus, Theo with Phoebus and Hephaestus with Meghan.

"You will carry your teammate on your back to the end of the lot. Then you will trade places and return."

Hephaestus gave Meghan a doubtful look. She was half his size, legs thinner than his biceps.

"Since there are an odd number of you," Sir continued, "One of you will need to volunteer to go twice."

"I will, Sir," Marcus said.

Of course you will, Theo thought. *Not going to pass up any chance to show what a great guy you are. What a great teammate.*

"Great. Now get on the line," Sir barked. "Get your partners up."

Hephaestus swung Meghan into place, carrying her like a

backpack. Sir gave the sign and the partners moved forward. Hephaestus jogged, easily covering the distance before the others—the largest carrying the smallest. Nearing the finish line with Phoebus draped over his back, Theo watched as Meghan tried to get Hephaestus up. He was too long, and no matter what she did, his feet touched the ground. She started to take faltering steps, his massive arms looped around her shoulders, feet dragging behind them. She made it farther than Theo expected before she collapsed under his weight.

Two, three, four times she lifted him and each time she fell again. Hephaestus, frustrated, gave Sir a pointed look, but Sir ignored him.

Marcus, riding Nemus's back, reached the end of the lot. He jumped down and then sprinted back to Meghan. He stopped and offered his arm. Meghan looked at Marcus as if she might turn down his offer. Then she extended her arm, hooking it around Marcus's neck, and he wrapped his around hers. Together, they struggled forward, dragging Hephaestus, a half-meter at a time.

Marcus, Meghan and Hephaestus looked like competitors in a bizarre three-legged-race; a jumble of limbs and elbows and dripping sweat. By far the last to cross the finish line, when they arrived, the other candidates began to clap.

Sir pointed at Theo. "Why didn't you bother to help her?" he asked. Theo sweltered in shame until Sir's finger moved to point at Nemus. "How about you? Do you want to see her branded?" Nemus shook his head. "Not one of you will make it through this training alone. If you think that you can, raise your hand—I've got a special program just for you."

No one raised their hand. Jealousy and regret gnawed at Theo. Why *hadn't* he gone to help Meghan? Why was he always "a day late and a bit short," as his father liked to say?

"All of you have had it easy," Sir said. "You think this training is hard but you don't know what it means to suffer. Not one of you."

Theo noticed Marcus's face shift, his eyes defiant, as if he might dispute Sir's claim. Theo thought of the clinical notes in the dead man's handscreen. Marcus had moved from host home to host home since he was a little boy. It couldn't have been easy. *Stop!* his mind shouted. *Never feel sorry for him. Never.*

Sir surveyed the candidates, resting his hands on his hips.

"We don't know what to expect when you arrive at Earth. You've seen images and vids of death and destruction. You think you understand, but you don't. I can pretty much guarantee you one thing: Earth isn't going to throw you a welcoming party. Our ancestors left in disgrace. All of you know the story—corporation divested, sent away to pay off several generations worth of debt. As far as Earth's concerned, we came here debtors and we remain debtors."

Theo had heard the story since before he could remember. It always made him angry—the idea that his parents and their friends were still paying the price for bad decisions made hundreds of years ago.

His generation was supposed to change all that—the first debt free colonists on Stephen's Point—free to choose their own way. What if Earth had stopped sending the exchange xhips *because* the colony was close to gaining independence? What if they'd done it on purpose? Surely they wouldn't cut themselves off from the richest known supply of ecomire? Unless they'd found a better one, closer to home. Or something terrible had happened. A plague. Another war. There might not be an Earth left to ask for help.

Under a sky made opaque by low-hanging clouds, Theo wondered if everything—The Mandate, the *Chimera* rebuild, the Selection tests and training—were nothing but a tragic waste of time. He shook himself. He couldn't afford to think like that. He had to keep pushing forward, keep believing, keep hoping. For the colony, for his family and most of all, for himself.

CHAPTER TWENTY-FOUR

Moorland led Selena into the umbilical, the passageway that linked the *Hydra* to the *Chimera* at the center of the great ring of the station. The ship hung beneath, unaffected by the *Hydra's* constant turning. Spooling away from Selena, large enough to pilot a small spacecraft through, the umbilical's walls glistened and pulsed with phosphorescent color: blue shifting to green, golden-orange, yellow, violet. Strong as steel but flexible, rubbery, almost soft to the touch, the umbilical felt alive.

"It's made of self-repairing synthetics," Moorland said.

Selena rode in a chair pushed by an orderly from the medical bay, nothing more than a simple frame and harness to keep her from floating away in the zero gravity. While she'd started to walk with more confidence, her legs lacked the strength needed to support her on a long trek in gravity boots.

First VAST and now the umbilical; she didn't know what to make of it all. Most technologies had stagnated or even atrophied since her ancestors' arrival at Stephen's Point. The exchange ships brought only what the colony needed to maintain the status quo. She and Liam rebuilt or repurposed whatever they needed from the castoff parts of other ships. What they couldn't piece together, they bought from the scrap warden or bartered for among the other trawler crews. The idea that Stephen's Point had created something original, something different, contradicted her preconception of rimmers as having more advanced tech than the colony.

At the midpoint of the umbilical, oncoming traffic thickened. Dozens of workers and technicians passed on the walls and ceiling, a disorienting sight.

"Shift change," Moorland said. "Every six Earth hours. We use their twenty-four hour clock as a preparatory measure to orient the cadets with Earth's time schema."

Selena risked a question. "But there's no cadets here, right?"

"Soon," Moorland said. "Very soon."

The workers eyed Selena as they passed. Moorland greeted many of them, often by name. She offered thank-yous, tossed out questions or offered a few words of encouragement. She seemed comfortable with everyone.

"You get more from people if you show them respect," Moorland said. "We've lost a lot of good people repairing *Chimera*. Mandate or no Mandate, I want everyone from the welders patching deck plates to the cognitive technicians working to wake the *Chimera* to understand that I know them, that I see them. That's the reason I come here every third duty cycle."

Reaching the end of the umbilical, they entered a bright airlock. After cycling open, the air greeting Selena on board the *Chimera* smelled old. It was a silly whim, but with each breath she felt as if she was drawing in ancient history along with the oxygen. As if she inhabited the ship and the ship inhabited her.

"The hull is pressurized, the drive assembly intact, the substructure tested and re-tested, but we've still not managed to wake *her*," the chief said. "Not after three years of trying everything her protocols indicate. Something's wrong with her and we don't know what. We've patched into her neural network and got some basic functionality back, like the tram we're about to ride, but the *Chimera* remains asleep."

"Oh," Selena said in her fake bored voice.

The orderly directed her harness chair forward, his gravity boots clunking as they worked their way deeper into the ship. Moorland, short hair tucked behind her ears and held in place by a silver headband, glanced down, amused. "Your test results are quite interesting, Selena."

"Because I failed all of them?"

"No, that wouldn't be interesting at all. You'd be omitted from the Selection and sent down to the moon's surface. It's *how* you failed them that interests me."

"Yeah?" Selena said, noncommittal. Did Moorland know about the strange occurrence in the third VAST simulation? *Goodbye, friend.* What was that about? Had the Shellback spoken to her? Or was it some silly piece of code inserted as a joke by Rusty or Chuck?

But if Moorland had more to say, she wasn't going to share it, leaving Selena to stew in silence as they stepped out of the airlock and into the crosshatch. Selena had seen images of it before the pods dropped—a number of long, rooms connected to the much larger pods. They contained meal halls, recreation facilities, greenhouses, libraries and science labs. Everything the colonists needed to live while the ship cut a path through The Everything.

Ahead, the corridor opened into a cavernous space where dozens of workers were assembling prefab walls into living space. "Four crew per room with a shared lavatory. A bit Spartan, perhaps, but efficient," Moorland explained. The space was so deep that Selena struggled to make out the back wall.

"We've designed the new crosshatch with dual docks, each with their own breakage. One portside and the other starboard," the Chief said. So the *Chimera* would have landing craft. *Of course.* How else would they breach Earth's atmosphere?

Moreland beckoned. "We'll take the tram to the command deck. There's something I'd like to show you."

"It's not like I have a choice," Selena said, secretly thrilled at the prospect.

Before they could leave, something impossible happened: a man near the back of the open space launched into the air and rocketed toward them, back first, like a shrimp fleeing a predator. The worker flipped, redirecting to face them. He slowed and landed a few meters from Moorland. His gravity boots contacted the deck with an audible *click*. The worker flipped up his visor, revealing a scraggy beard and friendly brown eyes.

"Thought that was you," he said to Moorland.

"Andy," the chief said. "How's the work coming along?"

"Ahead of schedule for once. We've got all the prefabs in place and will have the quarters fully plumbed within a week. The dock on the backside will take a bit longer."

"Thank you. That's good news."

"Thanks, ma'am. Now I'll get back to it if you don't mind." The man pointed his arms at the ground. On his forearms, a pair of over-sized metal bracelets whirred before the man launched backward, sending him free-flying to the back of the room.

"What are those?" Selena asked, unable to constrain her curiosity.

"Aerocuffs," Moorland said. "Personal propulsion wristlets the space-side welders use in case they got knocked free of the hull. A few of the foremen have taken to using them inside the

Chimera. One of these days Andy's going to break his neck."

So the aerocuffs generated a burst of propulsion like a steam jet. But how did you stop them from whipping you in a circle? How did you maintain a flight line? Selena swallowed her questions. She'd have to get her hands on a pair and find out for herself.

The strange new-old air tickled her nostrils as they clumped deeper into the crosshatch. "We've had to power everything ourselves," Moorland said. "We can't get even get the ship's basic systems active. Some think it might be impossible, that all the cores went inactive and that's what's preventing *Chimera* from waking. If they're right, we're in the midst of the most colossal waste of time in the history of the colony."

Selena grunted. She, too, hoped the *Chimera* could be restored. If not, it wouldn't matter what happened to her father.

"It's frightening to consider the implications, isn't it?" Moorland said. "That's why we must all do everything we can. We have a duty to save the colony. That includes you, Selena."

Selena shifted in her chair. She'd never considered herself patriotic. It was always her and Liam, a two-person team. The folks on Stephen's Point may as well have lived in a different galaxy. But without them, there wouldn't be a Scrapyard or New Lux or mining. She needed the colony. More than that, since meeting Rose, Dr. Cholewa and Moorland, her feelings had shifted in ways she couldn't quite explain.

"Left turn," Moorland said. From the vantage of her chair, Selena tracked wall markings providing directions to various places within the *Chimera*, painted by the survey teams sent in before the repairs began. Down the corridor and around another corner, they reached the tram station. Moorland approached a wallscreen and tapped in a few commands. A low rumble filled the room. "Some things require little improvement," Moorland said. "A train is a train—within a spacecraft or not."

The lights flickered as the tram whooshed into the room. The doors slid open, and they entered a narrow car lined with bucket seats. "The tram has three stops," the chief said. Another thing Selena already knew—she'd read all about the *Chimera*'s design. The tram traveled the spine, with the command deck at one end of the ship and the firewall at the other. The crosshatch and quarters split the distance between the two. Would they visit the firewall?

Though not as enticing as the command deck, the dense shielding that blocked heat from the thrusters at the back of the ship interested her as well. She wanted to see everything.

They boarded the tram and it accelerated toward the command deck. Minutes later they stepped off at the forward tram station. The space that greeted them was markedly different from the industrial-looking crosshatch. Warm light reflected off of ceramic-gray walls. Blue ceilings shifted in hue like the surface of water. Bundles of cabling floated in the microgravity, some patched into wallscreens, others spiraling off into wall slits.

Moorland grimaced. "All we do is poke and prod her. It's starting to feel like an autopsy."

"I know the feeling," said Selena.

Moorland glanced at her. "Yes, I suppose you do. They tell me you're making good progress in regaining the use of your legs. Doctor Cholewa expects a full recovery."

Selena resurrected her sullen, blank expression and hunched in her chair. She had to be careful. The hearing was five rotations away. She needed to finish what she'd started. Win back the contested ecomire, pay for her father's medical care, put their lives back together.

"We've tried everything to wake her," Moorland said. "Nothing has worked." The chief spoke with a mixture of frustration and tiredness that Selena recognized in herself. A familiar feeling—being stuck on a single, unchangeable trajectory. Here she was with an opportunity to change course, but unable to do so because she had to stick to the Ombudsman's plan.

They approached the command deck, passing a steady trickle of technicians clunking along in gravity boots. Two women argued passionately about the best way to stimulate something called the "paraxial sub-matrix." The blue ceiling wavered and pulsed, reminding Selena of the umbilical. Perhaps Stephen's Point hadn't come up with new technologies. Maybe they'd borrowed them from the *Chimera?*

The corridor ended at a large porcelain-white room. A curved wall bent around her in a half-oval shape. Dominating the center of the room, surrounded by support stations, sat the sphere. The interface for the ship. Not a simulation like VAST, but the real thing. As large as a small rambler, it appeared to hover in the air, as smooth and white as an egg. Selena leaned forward in her chair, unable to hide her excitement.

"Here she is," Moorland said. "Or at least here she *should* be. We opened the sphere and looked inside, but all we found was empty space. We can send data in and pull it back out. We can resource VAST through the umbilical. But we cannot wake the *Chimera*. If we transitioned her guts to analog, it would be pointless. Only *Chimera* herself can pair with a navigator and open fractal space."

Selena stared at the sphere—the very place Stephen had once stood. She'd never visited a temple or lit a candle to a god like some of the flame-backs. She'd never wanted to. But this place felt *different*—charged with deep meaning. With memory. With purpose.

She wanted a closer look.

Without thinking, she unbuckled the strap holding her in place.

"Would you like to go inside?" Moorland asked. "Dozens of technicians have popped in and out the last few years. You won't hurt anything."

Selena didn't answer. She positioned herself, feet against the chair back, and launched into the zero gravity. The sphere expanded before her until she rebounded off the side. Using her hands, she guided her body into position and slipped through the opening. She expected an interface grid or at least a chair, but found nothing but curving, white walls made of hand-sized tetrahedrons interlaced like puzzle pieces.

How could someone use this space to navigate? She'd never seen anything on the nets explaining how it worked, and she'd read everything she could find about the *Chimera*. Glowing accounts from First Colonists, flight logs, technical specifications. Even some of the rambling writings of Stephen himself. However Stephen navigated the *Chimera*, it wasn't anything like a trawler, and probably not like the VAST simulator either. Could he have used something like her spider?

Selena placed her palms on the walls of the sphere and closed her eyes, imagining the ship as it once was. The intricacy and power of the *Chimera's* systems coalescing in and through her. What would that feel like?

A static wash from her spider fuzzed through her mind. She shivered, cold as ice, mind slipping. Faster than an eye blink, she fell, down into a cold that reached through skin and flesh, deep into her bones. She shook, transported to a place where the white of the sphere turned to darkness, and then to stars, and then to—

The impossible.

The Chimera, the *Hydra* and the moon they orbited, the star Elypso, whisked away by the chaotic, looping folds of The Everything. She no longer had a mouth with which to gasp. Instead of a body, she now possessed an intricate assemblage of systems, stretching and retracting, growing and receding. All of her yearned for the awful and beautiful chaos of fractal space, the illogical shape of the universe overlaid with the logical progression of a recurring pattern.

The branches of a tree reaching to the heavens, but the heavens curve and darken and swallow it. The tree becomes ten more trees, or ten-thousand. Crisscrossing branches, bent or straight or both, complexity within complexity, creating space that could not exist, yet did. In that fraction of a fraction of a moment, like a dog hearing frequencies beyond human capacity, Selena felt an emotion too strong and lovely and terrible for words.

The Everything became something once more. A sphere. A space within a colony ship orbiting a single moon orbiting a single planet traveling a never-changing path around a single star. The constraints of this fixed system felt like the tightest of straitjackets—as cruel as sealing a live person in a casket or chaining a leopard to a stake.

Not since the day her mother fell in the snow and became a thing covered over with flies had she felt anything so intense.

Goodbye, old friend.

Empty of everything but grief, Selena wept.

CHAPTER TWENTY-FIVE

Theo leapt from bed, sick panic rising in his chest. Somehow, despite setting his alarm, he'd overslept. Where was his handscreen? He'd tucked it under his pillow after spending a late night reading hacked Civvy records in search of children taken in by Child Welfare named Mark or Lucas. He'd found nothing useful. Without access to a physical terminal at the Civvy, he could only pull one record at a time without raising suspicions and getting caught. He'd also downloaded a copy of *A Tale of Two Cities,* but couldn't make sense of it.

Giving up his search well past his usual bedtime, Theo tried to sleep, but couldn't. His mind churned through the same scant pieces of evidence, unable to turn them into something he could use to free himself from Marcus. Why hadn't he stolen the hacked handscreen from Martha's apartment? He could have ripped everything off of it, recovered any erased data, and traced it back to its original owner. Instead he'd panicked, run and lost his best chance at gaining real leverage over Marcus.

Theo tore the blankets and pillow off his bed. No sign of the handscreen. It wasn't on his dresser either, or on the floor under the bed. He dumped out his clothing, frantic hands throwing pants and shirts and socks around the room. *Marcus.* Somehow he'd learned of Theo's search, slipped in during the night and stolen his handscreen from right under his pillow. With a jolt of horror, Theo turned to Liddy's empty bed.

"Liddy!"

He slammed through the door, searching the bathroom, the stairwell. He pounded down, flew around the corner to the kitchen and slammed into Liddy, knocking her sprawling. She started to cry. Theo lifted her, pulled her close. He didn't care about being late, as long as she was safe.

Then he saw his handscreen peeking out of her back pocket.

"What are you doing with my handscreen!"

Liddy's crying intensified. Theo snatched up his handscreen. "Why'd you take it? Now I'm going to be late!"

Liddy sobbed, snot running down her nose and over her upper lip.

Where were their parents? Why was Liddy downstairs alone? He checked the time and groaned. The bus would leave from the Civvy in seven minutes.

"I wanted to see what story you were reading," Liddy blubbered. Theo didn't want to comfort her, and he certainly didn't have the time.

"Where's mom?" he asked.

"She went down to the Allen's for five minutes."

"Tell her thanks a lot for waking me up," Theo said. He flew back to his room, pulled on clothing from the pile on the floor, then jumped down the stairs three at a time.

"Stay here with me," Liddy wailed, when he returned to the kitchen.

"I can't." He pushed her away. Liddy wailed louder.

"Shut up, Liddy!"

He slammed through the door and broke into a sprint. He could make it if he gave it everything he had—a mile and a quarter to the Civvy in just over six minutes. When he hit the end of the alley, he saw Liddy racing along behind him.

"Go home, Liddy!"

She glared, defiant. Cheeks pink from running, tears and snot glistened on her face.

"No!" She said it in the same tone their mother used when she'd made up her mind about something. Lips pursed and colorless, little cheeks puffed out, chin thrust up at an angle—he might laugh if he wasn't so angry.

He'd have to leave her. She'd go home once she realized she couldn't catch him. But glancing over his shoulder, he saw she wasn't giving up. She ran barefoot, arms pumping with each stride, face as determined as ever. He stopped and scanned the expanse of the Swallows—the crooked alleys and abandoned factories, loiterers with nothing but time on their hands—no place for a little girl.

Theo rushed back and scooped her up. Threw her over his shoulder and raced for the house. Liddy screamed, kicking his ribs with sharp little feet. He'd nearly reached the door when his mother's voice rang down the alley:

"Liddy! Liddy! Where are you?"

"I've got her," Theo called.

"What are you still doing here?" Erin asked. "Don't you have training?"

Theo slung Liddy down and pushed her forward. He glared at Erin, angry at his sister, his mother, himself. He'd be late for sure. "What's wrong with you? Leaving her home by herself? She took my handscreen and I didn't wake up and—"

It didn't matter. He had to run. He thrust Liddy into his mother's arms and sprinted away. He ran faster than ever before, filling his lungs with every other stride, ignoring the surprised faces of strangers as he streaked past.

He was *not* going to miss the bus.

Plunging through one of the arches, the curvature of the pod spread above him. There was the memorial and the sleek Regulatory bus waiting for him. He was going to make it. He was going to—

The bus pulled away.

Theo shouted and ran faster, following along behind the bus as it gained momentum. He ran until his chest burned and his vision blurred. His legs became dead things incapable of moving faster. He stopped, bent at the waist, gasping for air. The bus lumbered out of the Swallows and into the foothills.

Pain, sharp as a clamping vice, began in the side of his stomach and lower back. He slowed and screamed every dirty word he knew, then invented a few new ones. Seething, he watched the bus disappear over the backside of a hill. He could turn around and go home and wait for the Regulatory to pick him up, or he could run to the training field, arrive late and get branded. Theo took a few more deep breaths, re-gathered himself and ran.

Up and down hills, into the Order compound, past the library and infirmarium. He'd cheated to get into the Selection and now he was getting cheated back out of it. He wasn't blind to the irony. The embarrassment of failure, the pain of the brand—he could live with both. What hurt the most, the crushing thing, was that he'd started to see himself differently. Started to hope that he might actually make it through the Selection.

Theo arrived at the training field while the other candidates were still completing warmups. He forced himself not to slow and approached Sir head on. Sir didn't seem to notice. Theo stopped a meter away from Sir and entered pole position: chest out, chin down, shoulders back. Sir ignored him until the other candidates finished a set of jumping jacks.

"Do you think you can sneak onto my training field?" Sir didn't appear angry. Maybe he would get through this without a brand after all.

"No, sir," Theo said. "And I didn't sneak. I ran."

Sir smirked. "We saw," he said. "You're not a bad runner. Too bad you don't give two shits about your fellow candidates."

"I thought it better to arrive late than not at all, sir."

"You thought so, did you?"

"Yes, sir."

"Let's see how long it takes for me to change your mind."

"Should I join the others, sir?" Theo asked, desperate to redeem himself.

Sir glared at Theo. "While you slept in, everyone else here was busting their humps." Sir pointed at the candidates. "They're better than you. They arrived on time. You will stand here and watch them work."

Sir set the group in motion—a wind sprint to the end of the field and back, followed by another. After each down-and-back, the other candidates watched Theo. Some with pity, others with scorn, all hyperaware of the boy doing nothing while Sir worked them into the ground. Sir wasn't going to punish him the usual way. No, he had something much worse in him. Sir would make sure his fellow candidates hated him.

It took Sir much longer to bring them to their breaking point than on the first day. It might have been fifteen minutes. It might have been two hours. Theo lost track amidst the groans and the sweat and the puke. Theo's resolve fell to pieces. He'd come prepared to get branded, not the humiliation of standing alone, responsible for the suffering of others. His face burned, a white-hot mask bolted to his skull.

The candidates ran and ran some more. No breaks. No water. They completed down-and-backs and suicides, running until they wheezed and gasped for air. A sandy-haired boy named Preston wavered on unsteady feet. Taking several faltering steps, his eyes rolled upward. He crumpled to the ground, unconscious. Sir motioned to a regulator to checks the boy's vitals.

"Keep running!" Sir screamed at those who slowed to check on Preston.

The regulator assessed Preston's still form, stood and walked away. A moment later the boy began to stir.

"What should I do with Preston here?" Sir shouted at Theo. "Don't be shy. Tell me. What should happen to him?"

Theo couldn't think of anything to say.

"He's addled. Even if he does get back up, he won't last much longer. What should I do? Answer me, damn it!"

"Ask Preston, sir," Theo said.

"Ask him what?"

"Ask him if he wants to stay in the Selection, sir."

"This isn't about what *he* wants. I'm asking you."

"No," Theo said. "It's not up to me, sir."

The rest of the group returned from a down-and-back. They lingered, watching.

"Leaders make the tough calls," Sir said. "They can't afford to take opinion polls."

"Then make the call. *Sir.*"

Sir barreled toward Theo. It took all Theo's courage not to turn and run. Sir grabbed him by the neck and hauled him over to Preston and shoved him down, face to face with the other boy. "*You* will decide!" Spit flecks spattered Theo's neck. "*Now!*"

Preston looked at Theo with miserable eyes, almost pleading. *Let me go. I don't want to do this anymore.* The medical booth gleamed at the edge of the field like a polished steel egg. Theo recalled the smell of roasting flesh and the sound of screaming. It would be so easy to for him to condemn Preston to that fate—clearly what Sir wanted him to do.

Meghan, eyes wide, mouth open, stared at him along with the others, waiting for his decision. He bit the inside of his mouth, bit until he tasted blood. To hell with Sir. He wouldn't do it. It wasn't right to condemn Preston.

"I won't decide, sir." Theo said. "And you're not going to be able to make me."

"That's where you're wrong." Sir's face broke into a smile. "I can make you. It's him—or you. Now choose."

Theo closed his mouth, defiant. Forcing him to watch others suffer for his mistake was cruel. Asking him to send Preston to get a brand so that he could remain in the Selection was far crueler. If he condemned Preston to save himself, none of the others would ever forgive him. Especially not Meghan. Her face had lost most of its color. She took a half-step forward but Hephaestus planted a giant palm on her shoulder and drew her back. Marcus made a subtle gesture, running his extended thumb across his throat. Theo had no doubts as to what *that* meant. Marcus wanted Theo to stay in the Selection for some twisted reason.

Sir's fingers dug into Theo's bicep. "If you don't choose, you're *both* going to the booth."

Theo stared the cold-blooded bulldog square in the eyes. As much as he wanted to make it to the *Chimera*, he wasn't going to sacrifice someone else to get there. The idea made him sick. He wasn't going to become Marcus.

"I choose myself," Theo said. "Give me the brand."

Theo ripped free of Sir's grasp and ran to the medical booth. A pair of regulators stepped into his path but he dodged, spun around them, smashed the booth's buttons with his fist. Nothing happened. Sir and the regulators closed in on him. He beat the controls, pounding until something cracked. Maybe the control panel. Maybe his hand. He didn't care anymore.

The booth doors began to close. Theo dove inside, closing his eyes, welcoming the pain. A rush of air pressurized the environment as bands cinched around his arms, holding him in place. A pair of servos dropped down and whirred toward his chest. One stopped right above his heart. He felt it, heavy and electric, though it hadn't touched him.

The servo flicked open, revealing a gleaming needle. What had he done? This wasn't the branding mechanism. The needle stabbed his skin, the pain of the puncture replaced by a warm wash of anesthetic. His torso went numb. A blunt, hot thing swung out from the wall. Theo forced down a scream as it pressed forward. It burnt through his shirt, acrid smoke filling his nostrils. He felt nothing when it touched his skin. It remained for no more than a second and whisked away, out of sight. Through a char-edged hole in his shirt, he glimpsed a ring of bright red flesh.

Outside the booth, one of the regulators had opened the side panel of the medical station. Abruptly, the booth powered down, the doors flung wide, the restraints around Theo's waist and arms slithering away.

"You're a damned fool," Sir said. "You set that thing to cauterize a wound. You're lucky it's got an override or you might have killed yourself."

Sir's anger no longer mattered. Theo was done. Out of the Selection. At least he'd be able to look himself in the eyes each morning.

Preston and the other candidates stared at Theo with incredulity and … respect? Theo waited for the regulators to seize him and haul him to wherever they took the other failures. A strange sort of smile appeared on Sir's face. Great. The man wanted to do it himself. Theo wouldn't bother resisting.

"You still think you made the right call?" Sir asked. "Now that you've got that cherry burned into your chest?"

Theo looked at Preston, Meghan, Heph. At Marcus with his cool blue eyes and unreadable face. "Yes," Theo said. "I do."

"Good," Sir said. "Now fall in line with the others."

"What?"

Marcus looked as shocked as Theo felt.

"You heard me, candidate. Fall in."

The strange smile broadened. For a moment, Sir almost seemed human. "What if you'd set that thing for an appendectomy?" Sir's laugh sounded like someone vomiting up chunks of gravel.

"What about Preston, sir?" Theo asked.

"He stays."

Theo managed to get his legs moving and rejoined the candidates. Preston offered his finger to Theo and whispered a thank you when Theo took it. Heph and Marcus followed. Marcus thumped him on the back and said, "Well played." Meghan ran a gentle hand over Theo's chest and for the first time since she'd learned that he'd added his name to the Selection list, looked at him with something other than scorn.

"The whole is more important than the individual," Sir said. "When you fail, your failure impacts everyone. You must not fail each other or this colony. All of our lives—even mine—will rest on your shoulders."

As the anesthetic started to wear off and his skin began to throb, elation filled Theo. He'd passed Sir's test and nobody could take that away from him.

CHAPTER TWENTY-SIX

The day after his self-administered branding, Meghan arrived at Theo's house early. He opened the door, too surprised to be polite. "Hello?"

"Are you going to invite me in?"

"Sure." Theo held the door and Meghan slipped past him.

"Come on," she said, heading for the stairs. Theo followed her. What did she want?

In the bedroom, Liddy sat atop her bed, playing with her doll. "Hey, Liddy," Meghan said. "Can you go downstairs for a little bit? I need to talk to Theo about something."

"What?" Liddy asked.

"Important things about the Selection."

"Are they secret?"

"Super-secret," Meghan agreed, sitting on the edge of Liddy's bed. "If I told you, the Regulatory might have to arrest you."

"But I won't tell anyone. I promise."

"That's good," Meghan said, smiling. "How about I tell you one secret, and then you go downstairs. If you keep that one, I'll tell you another the next time I come. Deal?"

"Deal," Liddy said, leaning close so that Meghan could whisper in her ear. Meghan said something that Theo couldn't hear, and Liddy looked at Theo, awe breaking out on her face. "Is it true?"

"Is what true?" Theo asked.

Liddy opened her mouth to speak but Meghan cut her off. "Remember—it's a secret!"

The effort of holding back was almost more than Liddy's five-year-old self could handle. She bounced on the bed, lips mashed together in such a comical way it made Theo laugh.

"Good job," Meghan said. "I'll come back in a few days to make sure you're still keeping the secret. Now take your doll downstairs for a little while."

"Okay," Liddy said. She leapt from the bed and thumped down the stairs.

Meghan pushed the door closed behind her. A rush of nerves sent Theo's heart racing. What if his parents came to check on them? They'd think—

Meghan didn't notice or didn't care. "Show me."

"Show you what?" Theo asked, taking a step backward.

"You know what. Show me."

He unfolded his arms and lifted the edge of his shirt. Held in place by several layers of tape, a wad of fabric cut from an old shirt protected the wound on his pectoral muscle. The burned skin had fallen away during the night, leaving behind an itching, burning sore that oozed amber liquid.

"What a mess," Meghan said.

"I know. I should have realized Sir wasn't really going to brand me."

"I meant your lame dressing," Meghan said. "You can't go to training without a proper bandage. You'll rub yourself raw." She pulled a small, blue case out of her shoulder bag. Inside, white foam dressing nestled beside a row of small plastic bottles, adhesive and antiseptic pads.

"Take off your shirt," she commanded.

"I'll be fine."

"No, you won't be fine. You'll break the scab and bleed all over the place. And I don't think you want to attract any more special attention from Sir."

She had a point. Theo slipped his shirt over his head. A trickle of warmth traveled up his neck as Meghan looked at his half-naked body. Meghan removed a bacterial gel from the medical kit and squirted it on a gauze pad. "This will hurt like a six or seven out of ten."

Theo smiled at her honesty, at least until the gel contacted the wound. He held himself rigid, trying to think of anything but the pain burning into his chest.

Meghan thoroughly and mercilessly cleaned the wound. Theo's eyes watered, but he managed not to scream. She selected a piece of foam, adhesive and a pair of scissors and cut the dressing down to the appropriate size. Next she layered them over the wound. "This will let it breathe, but protect it, too."

Steady and sure-handed, Meghan's fingers ran along his chest. She finished, hair brushing his shoulders as she leaned in to inspect her handiwork. He felt a bit lightheaded, but not from pain.

"That should do it," Meghan said. She patted his chest and smiled, but didn't move away. "What you did yesterday—that was brave, Theo. Jumping in the medical booth was really stupid, but choosing yourself … I didn't expect that from you. Not after you cheated to get into the Selection. I thought …"

"Thought what?"

Meghan looked up through the skylight, avoiding his eyes. "I hate liars."

"Do you hate me?"

"No! I don't know. It's just that … I've had to live with one for a very long time."

Theo frowned, running through a list of faces, everyone in Meghan's life. He couldn't think of a likely person. Meghan's family was tight. Perfect. They were so much closer than Theo and his parents. "Who?" Theo asked.

"The same one that pushed me to train for the Selection."

"Your dad?" Theo asked, confused. Mr. Ziczek bounced around with a huge smile on his face, always cheerful and funny. Unlike Theo's dad, who looked unhappy even when he did occasionally smile. Theo had sometimes secretly wished that he could swap out his dad for Meghan's. The guy was so encouraging. "But he's a great dad," Theo said.

"Sometimes he is," Meghan said. "But he's a liar. He lies about everything. To me. To my mom. To our family."

"What?" Theo asked. "What does he lie about?"

Meghan sighed, angry. Then the anger turned to something else entirely. A weary sadness. "He cheats on my mom." The words hung between them, their sound long past, but the meaning resonating on and on.

"With who?" Theo asked. As soon as he said it, he regretted it, wishing he'd thought to say something kinder or more comforting.

"A lot of people," Meghan said. "A lot of times. It doesn't matter. My mom knows. She always knows and she always takes him back. That's the worst part. He lies and she doesn't care."

"Like me," Theo said. "I didn't know, Meghan. I'm sorry."

"No," Meghan said, voice thick. "Not like you. I'm the one

that should be apologizing. When I learned you added your name to the Selection list, all I could think about was all the times my dad smooth-talked my mom. All the lies he told her about how different it would be this time, then the next time. How he'd change, how he loved her and our family and didn't want to hurt us …"

Meghan's eyes flashed, tears sparkling. She rubbed them away, swallowed.

"I'm sorry," Theo said. "I didn't know."

"Nobody knows," Meghan said. "We keep it a secret. Our happy, happy family."

Theo looked at Meghan, seeing her in a different way than ever before. She'd always been so strong, so competent. She'd never told him anything this personal before. He wanted her to keep talking. He wanted her to trust him. Most of all, he wanted to deserve that trust.

"You surprised me," Meghan said, looking into his eyes. A rush of tickling warmth traveled in a wave from his head to his toes. "But we still need to talk about the list."

Here it comes, Theo thought. *She still wants me to turn myself in.*

"Forget what I said before," Meghan said. "I'm not going to tell anyone what you did. You're not like my dad. I shouldn't have acted like you were."

Theo swallowed. "Thanks," he said, the word totally inadequate to express his relief.

"Maybe you're in the Selection for a reason, Theo. I didn't think you'd make it through the first day and then you did. I didn't think you'd make it through the second day and then you did. Then you made it a whole week. And yesterday, you chose someone else over yourself. You're changing. And I think I might like the person you're becoming." Meghan smiled. "Time will tell, but I'm not mad at you anymore."

She leaned forward and Theo realized she wanted him to kiss her. He hadn't kissed a girl before and didn't know how to do it, but he'd try. Tingling, afraid and electrified at the same time, he moved toward her—

The bedroom door opened and Liddy's head popped through. "What are you guys doing?"

Theo jumped like someone had zapped him with an electrode.

"Nothing. Meghan helped bandage me up. Now get out of here, Liddy. We're still talking about secrets."

"Why do you need a bandage?"

"Because he hurt himself yesterday," Meghan said.

"How?"

"I had a little accident," Theo said. "I think I hear regulators in the alley. They're coming for you, Liddy. You better go hide in Mom and Dad's room."

"No, they're not!" Liddy protested.

Meghan gave Theo a look. "Stop scaring her." She took Liddy by the hand. "Theo and I need to go to training now, Liddy. We can all go downstairs together."

Meghan tossed him his shirt. "Ready to go?"

"Let's do it," Theo said.

Downstairs, Meghan gave Liddy a kiss on the forehead, and then she and Theo set out for the Civvy, walking side-by-side.

"There's one more thing I want to talk to you about," Meghan said.

Theo gave her a sideways glance. "Yeah?"

Meghan pursed her lips the way she did when something annoyed her. "What's going on between you and Marcus?"

"Nothing," he said.

"Why are you so afraid of him then?"

How could she possibly know that? He'd never said anything to her about Marcus. He needed to give her a plausible explanation, or she'd keep asking and trying to figure it out.

"He's intimidating," Theo said. "He's tougher than all of us."

"Whatever, Theo," she said, calling his bluff. He started to panic, but she spoke again: "He's bigger than you and stronger than you, but he's not tougher than you. No one is. Not after what you did yesterday. You stood up for what's right. And Sir likes you better for it. Don't let Marcus get in your head. He's so weird—I bet he gets bounced from the program. I don't know how he passed the psych evaluation."

Theo had nearly forgotten that portion of the testing. He'd taken his months before the aptitude tests. A woman in a mauve room at the Civvy had asked him all sorts of questions about his mother and father and what sorts of dreams he had and if he was afraid of anything in particular. Then he'd taken a weird multiple choice test that the woman explained had no wrong answers. *Sure,*

Theo thought. The questions asked what he'd do if he came across a hurt animal, if he felt people were basically trustworthy or untrustworthy. Did he ever have blackouts? If so, how often did they occur?

Meghan was right about Marcus' oddness, but wrong about him failing a psych test. Marcus changed himself depending on the circumstances. He'd convinced the other candidates and Sir that he was a good leader. He'd likely destroyed the test. When he left, the person who administered it probably jotted down notes about how mature and humble Marcus was.

"I don't trust him," Meghan said. "Neither should you."

"Why?" Theo asked. "Did he do something weird?"

"Not exactly."

"Did he say something?"

Meghan shook her head. "It's not like that. It's just this *feeling* I get around him. He gives me the creeps."

Me too, Theo wanted to say, but the last thing he needed was Meghan digging into Marcus' past. That could lead to a very dangerous situation, one Theo wouldn't have any hope of controlling.

"He's okay," Theo said. "You should give him another chance." *Like you're giving me.*

"Maybe."

"Sir likes him," Theo said. "And I like him." He hated lying to her, but it felt like his only option. If he could deflect her attention for long enough, he'd find out something that would help him deal with Marcus.

"He's had a rough life," Theo offered. "I don't think he has any family left."

"Really?"

"He doesn't talk about it much," Theo said, "but that could be why he's a little strange." Theo reached for her hand and squeezed it. "Don't worry about him."

Meghan squeezed his hand back. "Okay," she said. "Maybe I misjudged him."

Theo propped up his fake smile. *No. You haven't. You've never been so right in your life.*

CHAPTER TWENTY-SEVEN

Selena rested against the wall of the sphere, undone with sorrow. Loud voices called out from all around, but she couldn't untangle the words. They spoke a language she once knew but had forgotten.

"Pull her out!"

"No, leave her in. Look at the synaptic responses from the *Chimera*. They're off the chart."

"I said get her out of there! That's an order."

Hands wrapped around her arms and guided her out of the sphere. She blinked at the faces staring at her, focusing on a middle-aged woman in a spotless white uniform. The woman looked concerned. She was saying something over and over again. It sounded like a nursery rhyme. A terribly sad one.

"Can you hear me, Selena? Are you okay?"

Tears streaked Selena's cheeks. Her face felt puffy.

"Did you find the *Chimera*?"

Chimera. The word echoed inside her, carrying with it a riptide of emotion and fragmented images. Blood on snow; Elypso breaking from behind Gauleta; her father lifting her into his arms and holding her against his chest; her fingers guiding a tiny ship through what once felt like a vast swath of space but which now felt claustrophobic; three cycles of motion observed from inside a prison.

As if borne away by a rushing current, the confusion left her. She looked out of her own eyes when Moorland touched her check. "Selena?"

What to say? What words could convey what she'd experienced? Her eyes welled up. *What just happened to me?* A part of her heart and mind ripped open, connected to … not a person, but neither an "it." A presence with needs and fears and emotions as real as her own.

"She's locked away," Selena stammered. "We have to help her."

"What did she say to you?"

What indeed? Nothing. Everything. Like trying to explain a shadow to the sun. A great number of people filled the room. More poured in from the corridor: technicians, welders, fabricators, scientist and laborers. They gathered round, staring at the sphere. At Selena. She couldn't meet their gaze, looking instead at the patterns engraved in the floor. She tried not to think. Not to remember.

"You've done more today than we've managed in three years," Moorland said.

"What did you do?" someone shouted. "The whole ship blinked!"

"Did she give you any clue how to bring her forward permanently?"

"Can you do it again?"

Selena closed her eyes. She wished her eyelids were as thick and impenetrable as *The Bee's* blast shield. That her ears had eyelids. That she could disappear.

"Enough," Moorland barked. "Let's get her back to the *Hydra*."

The orderly secured her to her chair, and Moorland led her through the throng. Riding the tram and traveling back through the umbilical to the *Hydra*, Selena did her best to repack her memories, to stuff them where they belonged.

When she arrived at the med bay, Rose helped her into bed.

"Can you give us some privacy?" Moorland asked. Rose nodded, but didn't move. "I need to speak with Selena. You can come back when we're done. It won't take long."

"Do you need anything?" Rose asked, directing her question at Selena.

Selena shook her head. Her eyelids drooped. She wanted to sleep. She felt like she hadn't done so in ten cycles.

"Thank you, Rose," Moorland said. "You can go now." The door closed on Rose's anxious face.

Selena summoned her remaining strength. "I want to be alone."

"We need you to help us, Selena. The *Chimera* responded to you."

"I can't do it again. I won't."

Moorland frowned and seated herself on the edge of the bed, her weight bending the mattress. "Why did you fail the VAST tests?"

"Because they're hard."

"Not for you. You didn't just fail each test. You failed them perfectly. Your response times in VAST are as good as any we've seen."

Selena closed her eyes. "Luck."

"What did you see, Selena? When you crashed the Shellback?"

Selena remembered the wall of fire, burning Earth. "Everything on fire."

"That isn't part of the simulation. It came from the *Chimera*—a moment of wakefulness caused by an encounter with you."

Selena opened a single eye. "You wanted me to go into the sphere."

"Yes. I thought it might trigger a response."

Selena scrubbed at her face. "You had no right!"

"What happened in the sphere, Selena?"

"It doesn't matter."

"You have a choice to make, Selena. What you say at the hearing will change the rest of your life. Your father would want you to tell the truth. He would want you to help save the colony."

"You don't know what my father wants. You don't know him, and you don't know me."

"I know he must love you a lot to bring you up to the rim. I also know that you're the descendent of First Colonist Ashley Samuelson. You have this in your blood."

Selena sat up, speaking with as clear and powerful a voice as she could muster. "Get out of my room!"

"What kind of person do you want to be, Selena?"

The chief's intense, blue eyes bored into hers. She couldn't stand it and turned away, utterly miserable. "I don't know," she whispered. Her answer terrified her because it was true.

CHAPTER TWENTY-EIGHT

On their way to that morning's training, the Regulatory bus slowed in front of the Order library and pulled over.

"Why are we stopping?" Heph asked.

"No clue," Preston replied.

Marcus caught Theo's gaze, eyes unreadable, face relaxed. A pair of apprentices emerged from the library. They approached the driver and after a short conversation, she turned to the candidates and barked, "Theo Puck, to the front."

Everyone looked at Theo, but he was as confused as they were.

"What's going on?" Theo asked.

"The Order wants to speak to you," said the driver. "Quartermaster West has given his approval. You will return to the training field once the Order releases you. Quartermaster West would like you to know that if you dawdle, he'll know and make you pay for it."

"We'll be waiting for you," Marcus said. "Don't waste the Order's time." A hint of malevolence in his tone, layered beneath false comradery.

Theo played along. "Trust me, I'd rather be doing wind sprints than talking to these jokers."

He got a chuckle from some of the candidates but not Meghan.

Theo approached the apprentices—neither much older than him, eyes sincere, almost *reverent*. What did they want with him? He felt more nervous about going back to the library than he did attending another day of training. At least he knew what to expect of the training. He also didn't want to leave Meghan alone. With Marcus worried about the unannounced stop at the Order compound, he might do … anything.

"Master Puck," the nearest apprentice said. "This way,

please."

Master Puck. They were taking him to Doctor Duncan. Had to be. Theo hadn't seen or heard from the man since his visit to Theo's house. So much had happened since then, so much had changed. Why did Duncan want to see him now? Could it have something to do with Theo's brand? Or had Duncan discovered the body?

"Hurry up, Puck!" the driver said. "We're burning daylight."

Curious eyes weighed on him as he joined the apprentices. They smelled of sweet grass, their close-cropped hair glistening with sacramental oil. They bowed to Theo. He awkwardly returned the gesture and followed them off the bus.

The library stretched skyward, a gray stone monolith broken up by arching windows. Rather than going into the main entrance, the apprentices led him around the side of the library and into a vestibule. One of the apprentices pointed to a cushioned bench. "Wait here, please."

"Wait for what?" Theo asked, but the apprentices didn't answer, disappearing through doors that led deeper into the library. He hugged himself in the chilly air. His pulse raced but he sat motionless, weighing his options. He could deny everything or he could accept responsibility. Either would require an elaborate story, one that someone as smart as Duncan would pick apart. Maybe he could tell them about Marcus. Duncan might be able to protect Meghan, himself, his family.

He'd talked himself into a voluntary confession when the swish of cloth on stone drew Theo's attention. Duncan strode toward him, dressed in a dark blue robe fringed with gold, the sacred emblems of the Order embroidered over his chest.

"Theo!" Duncan boomed, voice echoing in the still silence of the vestibule.

"Doctor Duncan." Theo stood and took the man's finger, released it.

"Good to see you again, Master Puck. How's your head coming along?"

"My head?" Theo asked before remembering his excuse for mistaking Stephen's scratchings for mold. "Oh, it's fine, sir. No problem at all. That plastiheal is amazing."

Duncan gave him a broad smile. "You don't have to call me sir. I'm not your trainer. By the way, how're you getting along with Quartermaster West?"

"I'm not sure how to answer that," Theo said.

"The field report from yesterday was very interesting. You burned a circle into your chest?"

Theo's hand rose to Meghan's bandage beneath his shirt and he flushed.

"It was an accident."

Duncan laughed. "Krane West's a tough old bastard and not fond of giving compliments. But he went out of his way to describe you as 'adequate.' You should be proud of that. Now, will you accompany me? I'd like to introduce you to a few of my associates with the Order.

Duncan led him through the thick doors of the vestibule. They swung shut on a whisper of sound and then made a distinct click. With a chill, Theo realized they'd automatically locked behind them.

The vaulted ceiling of the library's main rotunda stretched above them. Scale models of colony pods, pitched on landing trajectories, hung overhead. Above them, a fresco depicted the *Chimera* in orbit around the moon. In the center of the room, a life-size statue of Stephen stood atop a pedestal. He held a book in his left hand. His right pointed up to the *Chimera*. The likeness was excellent. It depicted the young Stephen, before the caves and the madness. Parted near the center, his hair accented the sharpness of his features, giving him a hungry appearance.

What would Stephen think of his statue? Not the Stephen at the end of his life when insanity had overtaken him, but the Stephen who'd first stepped foot on the moon, before the colonists named it after him. Would he object to the way the Order interpreted his writing? Would he object to his own religion?

Two robed figures flanked Stephen's statue, as motionless as their bronze counterpart. Was this the council that would question him about the murdered man in the cave? He could feel Duncan's tension as they approached. He'd almost persuaded himself to tell Duncan the truth—now he felt relieved he hadn't.

"Let me introduce you to my fellows." Duncan pointed to a thin man with a shock of bone-white hair. "This is Curate Masters, a Speaker Eloquent." The man nodded to Theo. "And this is Sister Sallymander," Duncan said. "She's come up from the Golden Valley to meet with us."

Theo recognized the woman's name. The High Librarian of the Golden Valley, and one of the most important scholars in the Order. And the man was a Speaker Eloquent, one of four, all sharing the same name. Why had such important people come to meet him?

Duncan turned to Theo. "Before we continue, you must take an oath."

"What sort of oath?" *To tell the truth?* An image of the dead man flashed through Theo's mind, followed by the scent of the white-hot metal from the blast furnace.

"To protect the Order. Are you willing to do that?"

"I don't know," Theo said, growing more confused. "What does that mean?"

Duncan looked as though he desperately needed something from him, as if Theo's response meant everything to him. "Some things you must approach with faith," Duncan said. "The Order would like to give you something, but first you must commit to holding it in strict confidence."

Duncan hadn't brought him here to question him, or to eject him from the Selection. No, this was something much, much stranger. And despite his unbelief, Theo wanted his curiosity satisfied. "Okay, but only if you promise me that it's not going to hurt me or anyone I care about."

"Of course, Theo. Just the opposite, in fact."

Duncan beckoned to the Speaker Eloquent and the older man stepped forward. He held a bowl of ash and offered it to Theo. Theo dipped his finger and lifted it to his forehead, making the sign of *The Emergent Intellect.*

"Repeat after me," Duncan said. "By the solemn sign of the Orb, I swear myself to silence ..."

"By the solemn sign of the Orb, I swear myself to silence," Theo said.

"Root and branch constrain me to my word ... Eye watch over me as I watch over all things."

Theo finished the oath. He'd never heard that one before, and he'd heard many.

"Thank you, Theo."

"Is that it?" Theo asked.

"Yes," Duncan said. "Now will you please show my companions your brand?"

Theo didn't bother asking why. Lifting his shirt, he peeled back Meghan's expert bandage, exposing the scabbed circle on his chest.

"The signs fit," Sallymander said.

"Signs?" Theo asked.

"We believe you are the Stephen reborn," Sallymander replied, eyes glowing.

"You do?" Theo asked, unable to hide his incredulity. Confessing to adding his name to the Selection list, even admitting to helping hide the body in the cave, suddenly seemed preferable to whatever Sallymander, Masters and Duncan had in mind for him.

"Yes, Theo Puck," Sallymander continued. "You are the prophet Stephen spoke of in his final hours."

Theo took a step back, butting against a bookshelf. *How can I be some sort of prophet if I don't even believe in the religion?*

"He will be from among the least of you," Sallymander said.

"He will lead you through the present darkness and the darkness that will come," Eloquent added.

"He will reveal new signs and be marked by a sign himself," Duncan concluded.

"A poor boy from the Swallows, you made your way into the hidden caves and revealed new Scratchings," Sallymander said. "You are marked, not with a crescent, but with a circle. The circle represents fulfillment, completeness. The beginning becomes the ending, the ending the beginning."

Theo stared at Sallymander, dumbfounded. "You're not serious, right?"

"You're a very humble child," Sallymander said. "Stephen instructed us to train and equip the new prophet. While the Order doesn't run the Selection, we believe Stephen will be pleased with the training you're receiving through The Mandate. As for equipping—Duncan, present Master Puck with the artifact."

Duncan pulled something from within his vestments and offered it to Theo.

A book. Tiny, black and held closed by a silver clasp, it felt old and brittle, and weighed almost nothing. "I—I don't know what to say," Theo mumbled.

The curates' faces shined with intensity in their perceived holy moment.

"It's just ... what if I'm not ..."

"To those of us who know the signs, it's clear," Eloquent said.

"You don't have to give anything other than your best effort," Duncan said. "The Eye will guide you along your path."

Looking at Duncan's kind face, Theo's skepticism suspended for a moment. He didn't believe he was some sort of prophet, but that didn't mean he knew everything. What if what the Order taught contained a bit of truth? He'd always thought that religion made people blind, but what if his cynicism had led him into a different sort of blindness?

"The book is yours," Duncan said. "Study it, but show it to no one."

Sallymander and Masters clasped Theo's finger. Tears hung in the corners of Eloquent's eyes. "We shall watch your progress with great interest. Stephen protect you."

"And you," Theo replied.

Theo glancd inside the book's front cover, noting the writer's name. *Ashley Samuelson.* He tucked it into his pocket. Duncan frowned slightly, but said nothing. What did they want him to do? Carry the super-secret book openly?

"I really should get back to the training," Theo said.

"Of course," Sallymander agreed. "Stephen's blessings to you, Master Puck."

Duncan dropped a hand on Theo's shoulder. "I'll walk you there just in case Quartermaster West has any questions."

"That's all right," Theo said. He planned to run the whole way.

"No, I insist."

Duncan and the other two curates exchanged fingers, and then Duncan and Theo navigated back through the temple and exited into the permadawn. Theo felt sure Duncan had insisted on accompanying him, not to explain anything to Sir, but because he wanted to talk to Theo alone. When they reached the road to the training field, Theo paused, waiting.

Duncan frowned, ran his fingers through his reddish hair. "I know your secret."

Theo's body stilled like the placid surface of a fishery pond, as if to offset the intensifying drum of his heart.

"No point in denying it, Theo."

His face felt as though it were made of glass. If he moved, it would shatter. And he would shatter with it, crumbling to a pile of shards at Duncan's feet. Duncan rubbed his beard with a large hand. Theo waited for the accusation, the words that would cement his future as one of shame and imprisonment. Duncan had found the body and now he wanted answers.

Theo pulled out the book. "If you know, why'd you give me this?"

Duncan gripped his wrist. "Put that away."

"Are you pulling me out of the Selection?"

Duncan shook his head. "No, Theo. Why would I? I've always known you hacked the Selection list and added your name. I decided that a person with that sort of initiative and skill might deserve a legitimate chance at making it aboard the *Chimera*."

"But I'm a sham," Theo said. "Surely you don't think I'm *really* the Stephen reborn. You don't believe all that stupid—"

"Quiet!" Duncan snarled. Theo flinched, caught off guard by Duncan's sudden intensity. "Listen carefully, Theo. I know you don't believe in Stephen or have much respect for my religion. And you are correct that I struggle with some of the Order's teachings. But I realized many years ago that the Order serves a purpose on this moon—the most important purpose of all."

"What?" Theo asked.

"Hope."

"What good is hope if it's empty?"

"Hope is never empty. It might not be perfect or logical, but hope has allowed our species to thrive, to spread through the stars. And now this colony needs you. Not because of your excellent navigation test scores or your ability to survive grueling training. They need you as a symbol, Theo. Something for those of us stuck on this rock to believe in. You've seen the predictions on the Mandate Broadcasts. Power conservation measures won't be enough. Sanitation systems will fail. Wide-spread starvation will set in. Far worse times than these lie ahead of us. And in the midst of a great darkness, people need a light."

"A false light isn't a light at all," Theo said, voice thick with self-loathing.

"Look at me, Theo."

Theo stared at his feet.

"I said, look at me!" The words carried the full force of Duncan's large frame, and in that moment, Theo considered that

Duncan could, if he chose, replace Sir on the training field. Theo raised his eyes.

"You're not false unless you believe you are. You scored higher than anyone else in the entire colony on the navigation index. You might be our only chance at making it back to Earth."

Beyond his sightline, hidden by Order buildings, the remaining candidates trained under Sir's command. He imagined Marcus, blank on the outside, full of appreciation for his own cunning on the inside. Above, hidden by the gray sky, the *Chimera* traveled her elliptical orbit, waiting for a crew. In a month's time, those that survived the Selection would take their places on board.

"The Selection didn't choose you, Theo. You choose the Selection. That point isn't lost on me. I'm asking you to risk believing in yourself. Risk letting the colony believe in you. Can you do that?"

Theo nodded, not sure of anything but the weariness in his body. "I can try."

CHAPTER TWENTY-NINE

Selena dreamed of Stephen's Point, of the last time her father came home on one of his infrequent visits. She and her mother drive their rented vehicle out from under the shadow of the mountains. Into the valley where the city of Stephen's Point sprawls. Towers with gleaming windows, grids of square stars. They pull alongside a train station. Green trains rush overhead on elevated rails. Snow dusts the stairway to the platform.

She stands on the platform as trains come and go. More people than she can count surge in and out of the cars. The temperature drops and ice crystals form over the windows of the trains. She shoves one hand into her jacket pocket. The other clutches the hem of her mother's coat.

A burst of air sends strands of her hair flying as another train rushes into the station. Doors slide open. Men and women push free of the cars. There, among the sea of faces, her father appears. Wearing a jumpsuit, face clean-shaven, he navigates the crowd like a ship between shards. She doesn't know what to do, and so she waits until he stands in front of her, a human tower.

Liam sweeps her up and holds her, suspended, inches from his smiling face. Her mother laughs. White snowflakes attach to her mother's dark skin, land in her hair and cling for a moment before disappearing in her warmth. How beautiful, how ghostlike her mother looks.

Liam says something and her mother blushes. He lifts Selena higher and places her on his shoulders. The three of them make their way down the stairwell and into the snow-filled permadawn.

Her only memory of her family together.

Strange how a single moment can become a replacement for a vast stretch of time. A story told again and again, told to herself, until the story and the memory became interchangeable and inseparable.

Her father arrives on a train.

Her mother lies dead in the snow.

A prolonged burn, Nadil dropping away to nothing, surrounded by the black of space.

"It's you and me now," Liam says when she arrives at Scrapyard. "You and me. Always." His arms tighten around her tiny body, his lips brushing her scalp.

* * *

Selena woke to find Rose in her doorway, holding a stack of clothing. Selena slipped out of bed and stood on bare feet, stretching.

"Good morning," Rose said. "How'd you sleep?"

"Good, I guess. I thought you worked second cycle today?"

"I do. I came to bring you these." Rose offered the stack—a teal-colored, long-sleeved t-shirt, tan trousers and matching jacket, and a pair of dark brown shoes.

"Fancy," Selena said. "Are you taking me on a date?"

"I don't date crazy people. Or women. And definitely not crazy women. But I thought you'd want something to wear to the hearing tomorrow."

For the last three weeks, Selena had worn nothing but the loose-fitting pants and shirts provided by the med bay. Before the crash, she'd always worn miner garb tailored down to size by Molly at the laundry. Thick, synthetic denim dyed brown or blue or black. Nothing fancy.

"Are they yours?" Selena asked.

"Not a chance. I'm way too fat. My clothes would fall right off you."

"You're not fat."

"Well, I'm thicker than you, that's for sure. I asked around—these came from a shipping sergeant down in Receiving."

"Well, tell her thanks but no thanks. I don't need them."

"What are you going to wear then? Med basics?"

Selena shrugged. "Sure. Unless they'll give me back my old clothes."

"They cut you out of them, Selena. Not to mention it was covered in blood stains. You have to wear *something.* I don't think you want to attend a formal hearing dressed like that."

"Why do you care so much?" Selena asked. "It's not *your*

hearing."

Hurt washed over Rose's face, followed by anger. "Fine, Selena. You know what? Wear whatever the hell you want. You know best. You don't need help. You don't want help. I get it. You're the toughest Jack to ever come aboard the *Hydra*, and everyone else can shunt themselves out an airlock."

Rose dropped the clothing and stormed out the door. Selena stared at the outfit lying on the floor, arranged as if a person had dematerialized from inside it.

* * *

After a short search, Selena found Rose administering an injection into the forearm of a woman with a bloody bandage wrapped around her left hand. She waited, feeling awkward, as the woman's face tightened and then relaxed as the painkiller took effect. Rose retracted the needle and dropped it into a locked bin marked "Sharps."

"Rose?"

Rose turned.

Selena looked down, suddenly shy, unable to voice her apology. The jacket and pants conformed to her slender body, giving her the hint of an hourglass shape. She'd brushed her hair back over her shoulders and fastened it with a small clasp. She felt foolish. She looked foolish.

"The clothes fit," Rose said, her voice guarded.

"Look, I came to apologize."

Rose waited, forcing Selena to drag more words out of herself. "I shouldn't have snapped at you. I really am sorry."

Rose smiled. "It's okay, Selena. Now turn around—let me see." Rose circled her index finger, and Selena obediently turned on her axis, like a ship aligning with a dock. Her face flushed as a male orderly at the other end of the room stopped to watch.

"You clean up great," Rose said. "You look pretty and smart and reliable. That's what we want."

No one had ever called Selena pretty before. She'd suffered plenty of come-ons from lonely miners, and even had to crack one bastard's ribs with a wedger after he wouldn't take no for an answer, but she'd never thought of herself as pretty. She looked nothing like the girls at New Lux or the actresses in vids, and had never wanted to. She prided herself on ability, not looks. But she had to admit, the clothing fit much better than her mining gear. It felt made for her.

"Um … thanks. Rose, listen. I'm sorry. I don't know what's wrong with me sometimes. All you've done is show yourself to be a friend. I shouldn't act like you aren't. It's just … well … out there," Selena motioned to Elypso and the shards packed around it. "I don't have anyone but my dad. Not really. We all work so much and so hard, and everyone's trying to get an edge, even if it means slicing the other guy. I'm not used to someone caring about me."

Rose pulled her into an awkward embrace, and Selena's shoulders locked tight until Rose's warmth soaked into her. How long had it been since anyone had hugged her? How long since she'd hugged back?

"It's okay," Rose said, pulling away at last, giving Selena another quick, appraising glance. "I mean that. And you really do look beautiful."

* * *

Several rotations later, Selena hadn't finished brushing her teeth when Rose rushed into her room. "Get dressed," she said. "They moved the hearing to oh-nine-hundred hours today. I just found out."

"Oh-nine hundred? That's thirty minutes from now. Did they say why?"

"No. The order came a few minutes ago. They're sending a regulator."

"A regulator?"

"I know. I don't understand it either."

"All right. Maybe it's a good thing—I can finally get this over with."

"It feels wrong," Rose said, worry lines forming around her eyes.

"Don't worry," Selena said. "It'll be fine."

"You're not going alone. I'm coming with you."

Selena knew better than to argue.

A knock sounded at the door. Before either of them could respond, it opened and a blunt-faced man in a black uniform stuck his head inside. "Selena Samuelson, time to go."

"Okay," Selena said.

She stepped forward, but Rose caught her eye and signaled

toward the wheelchair in the corner of the room.

"Let me help you," Rose said, taking her hand. Selena made a show of struggling to walk the few steps to the chair before falling into it. The regulator reached for the handles.

"I'll push her," Rose said. "She needs constant monitoring."

"They said I should bring her."

"And you will. But I'm coming too. She needs …" Rose grabbed something from the medical station. "… frequent doses of Riballium for her tremors. Only a nurse can administer it."

The regulator nodded. "Fine," he said. "But we need to go. I was told to make sure she wasn't late."

* * *

"You will, of course, follow the plan?" the Ombudsman asked.

"Should you be talking to me?" Selena whispered. "Isn't it suspicious?"

"Not in the slightest. You are a citizen of Scrapyard, albeit an illegal one, and therefore provisionally under my care and supervision. As such, I have every right to speak to you."

Selena sat in her wheelchair behind a polished table. Before her, a curved wall of dark wood with a silver crescent inlay served as the bench where the outcome of the hearing would soon be decided. Rose sat at the far side of the room, watching Selena with a concerned expression on her face. She needn't worry—the Ombudsman had everything under control.

The Ombudsman leaned close. "Answer each question clearly, but offer nothing unless asked."

"You got it," Selena said.

"All of this will soon be behind you, Selena." He patted her back, stood and took his place at the far side of the bench.

She'd forgotten to ask him who would represent her as an advocate. She doubted they'd go so far as to call in another trawler pilot from Scrapyard. Not that anyone would come if they asked. Maybe they'd picked an industrial worker? No shortage of them on the *Hydra*. Or they might have gotten one of the pilots from the welding ships piecemealing the *Chimera*'s shielding back together.

It didn't matter. She wouldn't even need an advocate. The Ombudsman had assured her of a quick decision ruling the crash the fault of the Kretchiwitz brothers and naming the shard her father's property. The whole thing wouldn't take more than an hour.

Flanked by two more regulators, the station arbiter arrived. High behind the bench, he balanced on the edge of his chair, hands clasped in front of him as if he intended to pray. Ombudsman Owagumbiea studied a handscreen. Minutes ticked past. Neither the Ombudsman nor the arbiter seemed to care. Selena shifted, restless, curling and uncurling her toes. What was taking so long?

"Excuse me," Selena said.

The arbiter peered at her, eyes icy, mouth a pinched frown. "Yes?"

"Do I get an advocate?"

"You must address me as Arbiter Redgrass."

Selena looked to the Ombudsman. "Shouldn't I have an advocate?"

"You don't need one. You have no standing—you're an illegal."

"Well, not anymore. I've been sequenced."

"Which means you're subject to The Mandate and the Selection. Your sequencing doesn't change your legal status as pertains to this hearing." Selena didn't have to look at Rose to sense her response to the Ombudsman's words.

"My father is a citizen," she said. "He's up for this hearing, too."

"And he will have an advocate. Delayed, I'm afraid, on the way out from Scrapyard. But he'll be here any minute."

"Who?" Selena asked.

"A man called Carson. Your landlord, I believe," Arbiter Redgrass said.

"Carson?" Selena spat. "He's no pilot! He doesn't know a damned thing about it."

"You should be grateful. We had to find someone on short notice."

"You've got to be joking. He doesn't even like us!"

"Well, I'm sure he'll lay his personal feelings aside in the interest of the law. As is our duty when called to a hearing."

"I'll bet," Selena said.

Redgrass scowled. "Careful with your tone, young lady."

Selena folded her arms across her chest and tried to calm herself. So she'd have to listen to Carson prattle on and try to make himself look important. She wouldn't enjoy it, but what real harm could it do? The pompous cow didn't know the difference between a vector and velocity.

Owagumbiea offered her a small, conspiratorial smile. *Stay calm. Stick to the script.* He didn't need to worry about her. She'd stuck to the charade, survived all of Moorland's attempts to trip her up. Soon she'd have her share of the money from the sale of the shard. The first thing she'd do was buy a shuttle ride to Stephen's point and visit Liam.

"Ah, here he is," said the arbiter. "Finally."

Carson waddled through the door, dressed in seedy-looking formalwear—threadbare and patched with mismatched materials. He gave Selena a malicious smile as he approached the bench and took the fingers of Owagumbiea and Arbiter Redgrass.

"So sorry for the delay, Arbiter," he said. "The shuttle from Scrapyard had a minor pressure loss in its steam jet lines. Nothing too serious."

"I understand," said Redgrass. "So many breakdowns these days—it's frightful trying to get anywhere. We appreciate your commitment to the civic process."

"Oh, I wouldn't miss this for *anything*," Carson said.

"Admirable. Now, I assume you understand your role here today? You no doubt watched the Introduction to Advocacy vid?"

"Yes, on the flight over. Very instructive."

"Quite. Now, if you don't mind, we'd like to get underway."

Carson shrugged. "Works for me."

"Meaning that you must take your place next to Selena," said Redgrass, motioning for him to sit. "Remember—you are advocating for her father Liam who is unable to attend, *not* Selena herself."

"A shame," said Carson, still not taking the hint.

"You may take your place now, sir."

"Yes, certainly." Carson bobbed a few times in some semblance of a bow and then took the chair beside Selena. "I'm advocating for your father," he whispered. "It's important that you let me help you, Selena. You *need* me."

Selena faced him, and with a cheerful face she hoped the arbiter would see as appreciative, leaned over and whispered, "If you so much as look at me funny, I'll snip your nutsack."

"Let us begin the formal hearing," Redgrass said. He leaned

down from behind the bench. "Tell me, Selena, for the record, who was piloting the trawler at the time of the accident?"

"My father."

"And was it your father who captured the contested shard, evidence number RG 546?"

"Yes."

The arbiter paused and looked at Carson. "And you verify that Selena could not have been piloting the trawler? That she does not have the prerequisite skill?"

"Oh, definitely not. If I'm honest, I would say Selena is quite slow. Stubborn, dimwitted. At least she's not bad to look at …"

"Yes, I think we understand."

"She's ignorant of her father's business—nothing but a troublemaker. I think she's even in a gang."

"Very well, Mr. Carson, that's enough."

Selena gave Carson a savage look and used her index and middle fingers to simulate scissors. "Snip, snip," she said.

The arbiter studied Selena with flat, appraising eyes. "As Wayne Kretchiwitz is deceased and Victor Kretchiwitz cannot be relied upon to give testimony due to his injuries, we have only your account of the crash to rely upon, Selena."

"I'm sorry about what happened to Wayne," Selena said, "but they caused the accident themselves."

"Yes, that is what your report states, and Ombudsman Owagumbiea agrees with your assessment."

Selena shot the Ombudsman a grateful smile, ready to hear the arbiter rule on her behalf. The arbiter studied a handscreen, paging through notes, then asked another question, almost as an aside. "Does your father have a drinking problem?"

"What?" Selena asked.

"Does he often drink while working?"

"No, of course he doesn't!" She wanted to add some choice expletives, but reeled herself in. She couldn't afford an outburst.

"So he never drinks while piloting?"

Selena felt a sudden unease. She paused, trying to think of an answer that was not an answer. A hand tightened around her arm, and she flinched before realizing the fingers belonged to Rose, not Carson.

"Don't say anything!" Rose hissed in her ear. "This is a screw job. It's just like when Flenning McGrath tricked Lemmy into signing over his business in *A Crying Shame*."

"I don't know what you're talking about," Selena replied. She bounced a leg on the footrest of her chair. Her eyes flicked from the arbiter's grim face to the Ombudsman's implacable, almost serene expression.

"They're trying to trap you. If you say—"

The Ombudsman's voice rang out like a megaphone. "Get this distraction out of the hearing. Regulator Simms, would you please?"

"Don't answer their questions. They're trying to—" Rose's words died as a regulator clamped a gloved hand over her mouth and pulled her backward. Rose flung her body from side to side as two more regulators grasped her feet. They pulled her straight and carried her from the room.

Selena stared in shock as the door slid shut. Stephen Almighty. What had she gotten herself into? Why had questions about her father's drinking caused Rose to go crazy? Selena felt sick, angry, and more than anything, confused.

"Now, let us continue." The Ombudsman's voice had an edge to it now. "Can you once again affirm for the record: Who flew the trawler at the time of the accident?"

Whatever Rose believed, it didn't change her current circumstances—she had to stick with the original plan. It was her one chance to save Liam.

CHAPTER THIRTY

By the time Theo arrived at the training field, everyone was already gone. He slowed, crossing the cracked slab carved into the side of the rolling landscape at the edge of Great Northern. The cloud cover had cleared and he could see all the way to the Golden Valley. Like a silver thread, the clover train line ran out to the Swallows, connecting the valley to East End, Conway and the Bunkers. A breathtaking view. How had he never noticed before? *Too busy holding in vomit and fearing for my life.*

His father, his family, the Swallows, the colony itself—all the men and women and children, those on the moon's surface and those in space—were pinning their hopes on the Selection candidates. On him. The Stephen Reborn. He gave a dry chuckle. The idea was insane.

"What's so funny?" Marcus asked.

Theo whirled. "Nothing," he said. The book felt like a hot coal pressing against his leg. Why hadn't he taken the time to return home and hide it? Marcus would descend on him and steal it before Theo had a chance to read the first page. Unless he acted first, caught Marcus off guard.

Theo sauntered over to Marcus. "You shouldn't sneak up on people like that."

"What did Duncan want?" Marcus asked.

"He wanted me to confess that I hacked the Selection list." Theo said the words without a hint of fear.

"And?"

"I confessed."

Marcus narrowed his eyes. "You're lying."

"No, I'm not. Duncan knows."

"You obviously are. If you told him, you'd already be on your way to a prison camp somewhere."

"That's not what happened," Theo said, intentionally vague,

goading Marcus.

"The Order isn't going to sit on their hands and let you complete the Selection training."

Theo beamed. "They think I'm the Stephen reborn. Sister Sallymander came in from the Golden Valley, and so did one of the Speakers Eloquent."

For the first time, Marcus looked unsure of himself.

"They had a little ceremony and everything," Theo continued, enjoying the idea of being ahead of Marcus. "They said I fit the signs. That I found the way through the darkness and revealed new signs and that I have a sign myself. I've got a circle on my chest and it stands for beginnings and endings and all sorts of really significant stuff. I'm pretty much a prophet now."

"You've got to be kidding. That's so—"

"Ironic?"

Marcus gave him a savage look.

"Hey, I didn't ask for this," Theo said. "They came up with all of it on their own."

"Those idiots!" Marcus exclaimed. "So blinded by religious fervor that they'll knowingly let a *criminal* stay in the Selection. What a load of trash. They're an embarrassment and they don't even know it."

Marcus sucked in his lower lip and bit, eyes almost closed. He looked like a person come to the end of himself. A person ready to scream because no words will serve. By degrees, his face began to relax. His rage began to dissipate, replaced by fervent thoughts, the weighing of options, of outcomes, of potential moves to be made.

"This doesn't change anything, Puck," Marcus said. "The Order can think whatever they want. Things between us remain the same as before." As Marcus spoke, his eyes darkened to sapphire. The emptiness behind them solidified into a presence, and suddenly it was like a different person was looking out from inside Marcus. A darker, more terrifying person. "So long as you keep your mouth shut, Meghan stays safe. Liddy stays safe. But don't you dare try and use your newfound status against me. If you do, you know what will happen."

"I have nothing to gain by talking about … anything."

Marcus looked out over the valley below them, lit by a thousand tiny lights, as golden as its name implied, taking in the view that had captured Theo's imagination moments before. "Do you ever think about how pointless it all is?"

"What?"

"This." Marcus gestured to the distant city lights. "All of it."

The emptiness in Marcus' eyes returned. A hopelessness that Theo suspected Marcus used to subdue a seething, immeasurable rage. When Sir said that none of the kids knew a thing about suffering, Theo'd seen a flash of genuine feeling crack through Marcus' practiced impassivity. For all his cunning, Marcus balanced on a knife edge. His controlled persona never fully hiding the contempt that pervaded his every word, every action.

Theo thought of Martha, lying dead in the squalid apartment Marcus once shared with her. Had he really killed that poor old woman? And who was the man in the cave? What had *he* done to Marcus?

Marcus stood against the backdrop of the valley, face severe. Theo couldn't imagine what he saw through the filter of his empty eyes, the beauty of the colony reduced to the single word: pointless. If he didn't fear and hate Marcus so much, he might pity him.

"You're not what I expected," Marcus said.

"I'm not?"

"I thought you were weak."

"No, I'm the cussed Stephen Reborn and you best not forget it."

At first Theo thought Marcus was hiccupping, then realized that the sound was laughter. Genuine laughter. Not at Theo but with him, the first natural moment they'd shared. The laughing ended as abruptly as it had begun.

"I want off this rock," Marcus said. "If we make it to the *Chimera*, I'm never coming back here. Never."

"You don't care about the colony?"

"No. Why should I?"

Theo didn't try and convince him otherwise. Here was the true Marcus. Willing to kill, manipulate, control. Theo had never asked himself why Marcus did what he did, he merely accepted it. He'd thought of Marcus as a force of nature. Now it was clear he had some sort of plan.

And whatever it was, it wasn't good.

CHAPTER THIRTY-ONE

"Liam flew the trawler the day we made the pull, just like he did every day. I can't fly," Selena said. Embarrassment swelled inside her like a fungal blossom.

"Very good, Selena," the Ombudsman said. "We appreciate your honesty. Now let us return to the issue of your father's drinking."

Selena scrunched her mouth into a frown. "So my dad likes to relax with a drink after the end of a cycle. What's that got to do with anything?"

"I hear he favors Mescua," Carson offered. "He orders cases of the stuff when he's made a decent pull."

Selena's face cooked to a nice, pink-red flush. "He doesn't drink any more than most ore hounds."

"That's immaterial to the matter at hand," the arbiter said. "I want you to answer one simple question: does your father drink while operating in the rim?"

"One simple answer then. No."

Arbiter Redgrass pointed at her with a long, wrinkled finger. "I think you're lying."

"I'm not!"

"You're lying to protect your father. His toxicity report shows his blood-alcohol levels were quite high when the rescuers pulled him from the wreckage of *The Bee*. Far too high for piloting, and in violation of the law."

"But … he …" Selena stammered, unable to put together a cohesive thought, much less words.

"I'm sorry that you feel a misguided loyalty to a man who endangered your very life. It's clear he isn't fit as either a pilot or a father. Based on your biased testimony and without any other witnesses to settle this matter, I have no choice but to hold him responsible for the crash. I declare him guilty of piloting while intoxicated and reckless endangerment of a minor. The shard will be forfeited to the state."

Selena's stomach compacted into a hard stone, tight against her backbone.

"Furthermore I remand him to a work brigade at Pole Station where he will serve The Mandate for the period of two years, at which time he will be eligible for parole."

Pole Station. Even without medical complications, Liam wouldn't last six months in the freezing temperatures at Stephen's Point's southern pole. Selena rocketed to her feet.

"And you, Selena, will be assigned to a host family. I hope that they provide you better care than your derelict father."

"Ombudsman," Selena shouted, trembling with fear and anger. "You have to do something!"

"I'm sorry Selena—the arbiter's decision is final."

"You sack of shit!" Selena screamed. "It was me flying, and you damned well know it."

"I have no idea what you're talking about. Your father is a drunkard, and you're a desperate child willing to tell any lie to protect him. Nothing you say will change the outcome of this hearing."

"Not to mention that you have no standing here," Arbiter Redgrass added.

"Rose was right. You're a lying, scheming thief. You worked this all out ahead of time—assigning Dad this reprobate as an advocate, rushing the timing of the hearing—I never should have trusted you."

"Are you done?" The Ombudsman smiled at her. *Smiled.*

Selena leapt over the table and charged the bench. She got close enough to see the whites of his eyes before regulators pulled her back. They strapped her into the wheelchair using zero-g safety strips. She had a moment of perfect, unobstructed eye-to-eye contact with the Ombudsman. "That shard belongs to *me*," she shouted. "You better watch your back, because I'm coming for you."

Ombudsman Owagumbiea chortled. "You'll never see me again."

"I'll tell Moorland. She'll sort you out."

"I'm afraid that you won't have the chance. Your shuttle to Stephen's Point leaves in ten minutes."

CHAPTER THIRTY-TWO

Theo ducked off the trail and flattened himself against the trunk of a dwarf pine, eyes on Marcus' back. Theo had helped Marcus hide a body and became complicit in the murder. He hadn't reported Martha's death or Marcus' threats against Meghan and Liddy. Compromising again and again, he was linked to Marcus, their fates entangled. That would end today.

After training ended and the candidates returned to the Swallows, Theo followed Marcus. As he suspected, Marcus didn't go back to Martha's apartment. Instead, he circled the Swallows and headed back up the road leading to the Order compound. Soon Theo would know why.

The crisscrossing branches of the pines formed a green ceiling above him. He picked his way across a deep blanket of drying needles, hoping to avoid any snapping twigs. The scent of the trees filled his nostrils, as rich as incense. To his surprise, Theo found Marcus easy to track. The other boy seemed to have lost his sense of suspicion as the trees thinned and the ground grew rocky. They weren't that far from the cavern where Theo had found the scratchings.

They wound their way up the east side of the mountain. Elypso bathed them in angular, yellow light. Near the ridgeline, the terrain opened up and Theo had to crouch and use boulders and low places to stay hidden.

He'd thought and thought about ways to rid himself of Marcus. To get him out of the Selection. All led back to the same thing, the same place, the same dead body. If he learned who Marcus had killed, he'd have something more than conjecture to offer the Regulatory.

Without warning, Marcus cut off the trail and disappeared. Theo quickened his steps until he reached a precarious stairway of boulders descending into a draw between two ridgelines. Theo recognized the trail that ran along the farthest ridge—it led to the cave where he'd met Meghan on a day that felt like a lifetime ago.

Outcrops of rock littered the bottom of the draw, offering numerous hiding places. Theo had only one approach unless he wanted to risk descending the shale slides lining the boulders. One slip on the unsteady stones and he would fall without stopping. The rocks would cut him to ribbons. His finger traced the edge of the wound on his chest. No way but forward.

Theo lowered himself down the boulders. He climbed with ease, strong and quick. Strange how much had changed—how much he'd changed in the last few weeks. Halfway down, he noticed a narrow crack in the rocks at the base of the draw, invisible from above. Another way into the cave system, and likely how Marcus had gotten the unlucky dead guy into the cave system.

He edged over to the cave opening and peeked inside. He pulled out his multitool and powered up the flashlight attachment. Cool cave air met his face as he ducked inside. Ahead, the cave broke into two separate paths, one that seemed to go deeper underground, the other meandering parallel to the entry point.

Which way to go?

Theo paused, holding his breath. A distant crackling came from the meandering passageway. He clamped a hand around the light so it lit only the space beneath his feet. Twenty meters down the meandering passageway, it took a sharp turn left. Orange light flickered off the cave wall. A fire.

He turned off his light and guided himself forward in the semi-dark, fingertips tracing damp rock for balance. Marcus stood beside the fire, warming his hands.

"Hello, Theo." Marcus held a small stunner like the regulators carried, its metal contacts crackling. Theo stood his ground, hand wrapped around his multitool. He felt the same fear and adrenaline as he had on their first meeting in this very same cave system, but this time Theo was in control of both.

"We need to have a talk," Marcus said.

"About what?"

"About this problem we have."

"I'm not sure there's anything to talk about," Theo said. "You've threatened me, Meghan, my family. And you're a killer."

Marcus nodded. "All of that is true. But there's no sense in us trying to kill one another, is there?" Marcus took a step backward, and Theo followed. They circled the fire, moving like partners in some horrible, silent dance. As Theo's eyes adjusted to the firelight, he could see more of the small alcove where Marcus lived.

"Nice place," Theo said.

"It has a certain charm."

Risking a quick glance around, Theo found that it did, in fact, have some charm. Marcus had arranged a ring of stones around the fire pit, set under a tiny crevice, winding straight up into the mountain. A small trickle of water ran down the crevice diverted by a large, flat stone wedged over the hearth. Rerouted, the water dripped into a metal basin. Next to the basin sat a plate, fork and a few knives. On the right side of the fire pit, a bedroll rested atop a small rug.

"Why do you live here?" Theo asked.

"You know why."

Theo's eyes fell on a leather-bound book resting on Marcus' bedroll. *A Tale of Two Cities.* A corner of the dead man's handscreen peeked from beneath it. Why had Marcus kept them? He was too smart to keep incriminating evidence, wasn't he?

"How much of it did you read?" Marcus asked.

"I don't know what you're talking about," Theo said.

Marcus lowed himself to the ground and set the stunner in front of him. "Sit down, Theo."

"I prefer to stand."

Marcus shrugged. "Fine. Tell me how you found Martha's apartment."

"Who's Martha?"

Marcus glared at Theo. "Stop pretending. I know you found my old apartment, that it was you hiding in that crazy old lady's place. Now tell me how you found it."

"Civvy records," Theo said. "It was the only thing associated with your name other than the Selection list. Marcus isn't your real name, is it?"

"I don't know," Marcus said. "Maybe not."

"You don't know your own name?"

"I don't know a lot of things," Marcus said. He stared into the fire, reminding Theo of Stephen, a man looking from one world into another.

"Tell me why," Theo asked. "Why kill that helpless old lady?

Why kill Martha?"

Marcus looked up. "I didn't kill her. She died of old age."

Theo crouched facing Marcus, multitool at the ready. "You didn't?"

"Of course not. Why would I? She wasn't a bad host mother. Better than a lot of the others. She was kind. She let me come and go when I pleased. With her support payments, we never went hungry."

Theo stared at Marcus, trying to tell if he was lying. He hadn't checked the woman for marks. Maybe she really had died of old age.

"Is this why you followed me down here, Theo? To ask about an old dead woman? Or did you come to try and kill me?" Marcus glanced at the multitool. "And good luck with that …"

"I came to try and understand," Theo said, realizing as he spoke the words that they were true.

"Understand what?"

"Everything. Why you killed that man. Why you threatened to kill Meghan and Liddy. Why you want to make it through the Selection. Why you changed your mind about me back in that warehouse." The words tumbled out. Maybe he wanted to understand Marcus so he could understand himself. Why he'd helped hide the body. He could've said no. Marcus might have killed him, but at least he would have died with a clean conscience.

"I'll tell you if you tell me what Duncan gave you."

Theo nodded to Marcus' copy of *A Tale of Two Cities*. "Just a book."

"What sort of book?"

"A real one. On paper. Written by a member of *Chimera's* original flight crew, some lady named Ashley."

"Show it to me."

"I don't carry it around. I'm not stupid. Now you tell me who that man was and why you killed him."

"No," Marcus said.

"You said you'd tell me if I—"

"Not until you show me the book." Marcus stared at Theo, unblinking.

"You'd steal it from me. That's why I gave it back to Duncan."

Marcus sneered. "A lot of good it will do you then."

"He only agreed to take it back because I memorized most of it."

"In a week? Sure you did."

Theo quoted a passage: "'When we change shifts, Stephen holds The Everything himself for a moment. Sometimes when the relieved navigation assistants unsync, before we can take their places, he groans inside the Sphere, like a man carrying the world on his shoulders. And maybe he is. Our very own Atlas.'"

"You could have made that up."

"You're right," Theo agreed.

"I could get it all out of you. Force you to recite it."

Theo tapped the place where the brand marked his chest. "No, you can't."

"I'll come for Liddy then."

"Nope. Because if you hurt my family, I'll tell the regulators everything. They might not believe me, but it will affect your ability to make it through the Selection. You know it will. You're as worried about me as I am about you."

Marcus smiled—a strange, sardonic expression. "I could kill you."

"But you won't," Theo said. A long silence filled the cave-room. "It's not to your advantage. I saw the way you looked at the Golden Valley. It's not that you just don't care. You *hate* this place. You'll do anything to make it aboard the *Chimera*."

Marcus didn't argue.

"That's why ..." Theo continued, the truth descending on him, sharp-edged and clear. "You *need* me."

Marcus looked at Theo—not with pride or cunning or ambition, but simple agreement. "Well done," he said. "This went far better than I could have hoped. Since you told me you hacked the Selection list, I realized you could be of some use to me. Now we can stop getting in each other's way."

"I make my own choices," Theo said. "You think you can use me but you can't. I'm not doing this for you, I'm doing it because I want to."

"Me too," Marcus said.

Surprising himself, Theo offered his finger to Marcus. And even more surprising, Marcus accepted it.

CHAPTER THIRTY-THREE

Selena struggled against the safety straps, skin rubbing raw. She jerked forward and back, snarling. The chair turned, gliding out the door and into the corridor. They would take her to the colony. She would never see the rim or her father again. Everything right in the world had been snatched away in an instant.

The initial shock of the hearing's outcome faded as Selena's two regulator escorts whisked her through the *Hydra*. One regulator pushed her wheelchair and the other marched alongside, boots clacking with each pounding step. Full-grown men, trained enforcers with expertise in hand-to-hand combat. She couldn't fight them even if she managed to slip her restraints.

Once they placed her on a shuttle bound for Stephen's Point, she'd lose any hope of getting back to Scrapyard. If she managed to escape when she arrived at the colony, she wouldn't make it far. Not in a strange city she knew little about and without money or friends. No, she needed to do something *now*, impossible as it seemed.

The rage and fear made her body jittery. She needed to slow down. To think. She imagined her hands entering *The Bee's* interface, the cool light playing over her skin. She closed her eyes, relaxed her body. The squeak of wheels against deck plate faded along with the staccato clump of boots. *Think!* From her internal, simulated interface, an idea came. A crazy idea, but an idea nonetheless.

If she could get to *The Bee* ....

They entered a cavernous service lift to the outer ring of the *Hydra* where various docks allowed civilian shuttles, welding ships, and Regulatory vessels access to the station. The drag of gravity increased as they ascended in a direction that felt like up.

Selena studied the regulators. Their name badges read Thompson and Dembrowski. Thompson pushed the chair while

Dembrowski, eyes locked forward, chest out, marched alongside. A man in love with his job. He wouldn't last long at Scrapyard—nothing riled up rimmers like someone making a show of their authority. Or their ignorance. Even a strong fighter couldn't deal with ten or twenty opponents at once. That only worked in vids.

Arriving at the outer ring, they followed the main corridor leading to the shuttle docks and their corresponding waiting area. Rows of blue upholstered chairs filled a narrow room. Three access gates led to unique airlocks. Out of one of the small portals lining the room, Selena saw that two of the docks were empty. The third connected to the *B-7*, fresh in from Scrapyard.

The few people waiting to board the shuttle watched with interest, curious about the girl strapped to a wheelchair, escorted by not one, but two regulators. Their eyes traced her path as Thompson angled for the back of the room. She considered calling to them, trying to explain her situation. They'd think she was crazy. They probably already did.

Past the main waiting area, Dembrowski typed a passcode into a wallscreen and a door opened. A single chair, bolted to the floor, sat under harsh lighting. An interrogation room. Thompson wheeled her alongside the chair—a single forged piece of metal—and secured the two chairs together with several more safety strips.

"ETD, seven minutes," Thompson said.

"Time enough to grab a cup. Want anything?" Dembrowski asked.

"That shit rots your guts. But help yourself."

"You good on your lonesome?"

"Only if you hurry."

The regulators laughed.

"Watch yourself—she might go for your eyes."

"I'll keep my distance."

The door slid closed and Dembrowski marched away. Thompson glanced at her, making eye contact for the first time.

"Am I under arrest?" Selena asked.

"Not exactly."

"Then why strap me down?"

"Ombudsman's orders."

"But you work for the chief, right?"

"She's the top of the food chain up here, but we're Special Agents to the Economic Office."

Selena nodded, but the truth was she didn't understand the inner workings of the Stephen's Point government. She studied Thompson's face. Broad nose, dark brown eyes, acne scars on both cheeks. Young. Maybe not even twenty.

"Where you from?"

"Bunkers."

"I've seen pictures," Selena said. "Honeycombed walls, geothermal heat. Impressive engineering."

The man shrugged, disengaging from the conversation. She had no idea what to say, how to influence him. Unlike Liam, she was bad at smooth-talking. She preferred a direct approach, all cards on the table. "My trawler is down here somewhere," she said. "It would be nice to say goodbye to her."

"Not going to happen."

"It won't take long."

"Doesn't matter."

"Please?"

"Look, kid, I said no. Even if we had time, which we don't, my orders are to escort you onto that shuttle and make sure you arrive at Nadil. And that's what I'm going to do."

The door opened and Dembrowski stepped through. "Glad to see you're still alive," he said, a steaming cup of tea in hand. "Three minutes and change—they'll announce boarding any minute."

Dembrowski nursed his tea. If she had a hand free, she could knock it into his face and scald him. Maybe disorient him enough to try and make a break for it. But even free of the restraints, her legs wouldn't support her for long if she needed to run. She clenched and unclenched her hands in frustration.

Overhead, a speaker crackled to life. "Attention passengers, boarding for the Nadil shuttle will now begin."

"That's us," said Dembrowski. He gulped down his tea and tossed the cup on the floor.

Thompson guided her chair to the front of the line of people waiting to board the shuttle. "Priority boarding," he said, showing the gate attendant his badge. The woman gave Selena a quizzical expression.

"I'm on the most wanted list," Selena said snippily.

"Custodial Care," said Thompson.

"Three, then?" the woman asked.

"Nope," Dembrowski said. "Just two. I've got another assignment—heading to scrap-heap for a rotation or two."

Selena looked up, surprised.

Dembrowski slapped Thompson on the back, "Say hey to the Bunker folks."

"Will do. Keep your bits encrypted and your junk in your pants."

"Can't make any promises."

Both men laughed. The gate agent looked at Selena and rolled her eyes. *Meatheads.*

Thompson maneuvered past the gate agent and into the airlock. The orbital lander rested in a pneumatic cradle. Unlike trawlers and scavengers, the shuttle had reentry wings and stabilizers, allowing a smooth, coasting landing at a horizontal landing strip. Inside, the shuttle was nothing more than a narrow tube, rows of seats separated by a central aisle. Thompson pushed her to the very back where a cloth partition separated a private seating area from the rest of the shuttle.

"A perk of working for the Regulatory," Thompson said. "Better seats." He gave a tiny smile. "And better drinks."

He unfastened her safety straps and lifted her. His muscular arms transplanted her to the exterior seat next to the small, veiled portal. He waited, thick body filling the aisle, eyeing her.

"What?" she said.

"Fasten yourself. Good and tight."

She had no choice but to obey. She reached up and pulled the restraining harness—thin and flimsy compared to those in *The Bee*—across her midsection and locked it in place. It felt strange to strap into a ship she wasn't flying. She didn't like it. She liked the idea of punching through the atmosphere and landing on a spinning ball of rock even less.

Thompson sat next to her and strapped in. A whine filled the cabin as the pilot brought the core to load. The shuttle began to shudder as the hydraulic cradle lifted it upward. A blast shield rose behind the thruster cones and the steam jets pressurized with a slight pop. Selena imagined the pilot going through preflight, checking instruments, beginning the sync. The ship lifted, underbelly jets taking on her weight. The core cycled up, readying for the controlled burn that would launch them through the breakage and into empty space. Selena closed her eyes, aware that this was likely her final journey through the vacuum of space.

A loud popping sound shook the cabin. A sound she knew all too well from excursions to the rim: massive pressure loss in the steam jets. The ship jerked, shuddered, scraped against the starboard side of the cradle. A few passengers screamed. Thompson glanced at her, aloofness cracking for a moment.

These people had no sense of proportion. The shuttle had collapsed back into the protective cradle, and while it might have sounded bad, it caused no real damage. Nothing like the time she blew four steam jets while making a fifteen tonne pull. *The Bee* had yawed to the side, dragging her in a pendulum motion around the shard, exactly like what happened in the crash that nearly killed Liam, but much less dangerous. She'd cut the tether, reversed thrust on the good jets and steadied *The Bee*. No problem.

Thrumming vibration rose through her seat—the core going into down cycle.

"Shuttle's dead," Selena said, smirking at Thompson.

She envisioned the jet system, water vapor shrieking out of burst seams, condensing on the floor and walls, forming puddles. No real harm done, except that the lines would need replacing, assuming they had the parts.

"Better now than out in space," Thompson said, his calm returned.

First on, last off—Selena and Thompson disembarked ten minutes later, passing the same gate agent. Selena gave her a bright, happy smile. "Add another crime to my long list," she said. "Sabotage."

* * *

Back in the holding cell, Thompson sat across from Selena in the interrogation chair, right ankle perched on his left knee, stony and silent.

"It's gonna take them hours to fix the steam jets," Selena said. "They'll have to find the leak and either patch or replace the failed lines. Pain in the butt. Trust me, I've done it."

Thompson leaned back and closed his eyes, ignoring her.

"Calibrating to make sure the pressures are set right is tricky. Hard to avoid getting burned."

Thompson refused to acknowledge her.

"One time, my old man and I blew a line with a pull in tow.

Skewed *The Bee* to the side. Might have killed us."

Silence.

Selena raised a hand, pantomiming a ship skidding sideways, her other hand a tight fist to simulate the shard. Although her story took place in the vacuum of space and was therefore soundless, she added some whistling steam jet sound effects. "And so I cut the tether, and—" she smacked her fist into her palm. "Blammo!"

Thompson opened his eyes. "Look, kid, I don't care about your adventures at the rim. I don't care about steam jets. Want to know what I *do* care about? Getting back on solid ground. Then you become somebody else's problem. Until then, how about you keep your mouth shut?"

Selena shot him a malevolent look. "Why don't you kiss your own bunghole?"

"You got a mouth, kid. Show some respect."

"Respect? Respect what? You said it yourself—I'm not your problem. You don't care about me or my father. Why should I respect you?"

Thompson rolled his shoulders and dropped his suspended leg to the floor.

"What are you going to do, you big tough regulator? Beat a crippled girl in a wheelchair?"

Thompson stared at her. "Do you know why we have a bunker in the first place?"

"You don't want to hear my stories and I don't want to hear yours—besides, I know all about that lame civil war after Stephen died. The riots and the starvation and all the other garbage. None of it impresses me."

"My First Colonist grandfather helped build the bunkers," Thompson said. "A safe place. A shelter from the rioting. Without it, you and I wouldn't exist. I joined the Regulatory because I believe people need protection. No one likes us until they need us. You don't like me because you think I have some personal problem with you. I don't. But you've been remanded to the surface and it's my job—my duty—to get you there. So you might as well calm down and let the next few hours pass pleasantly."

"Are you threatening me?"

Thompson shook his head and gave her an *I feel sorry for you* smile. "Do you see *everything* as some sort of affront to your pride? Are you that self-centered?"

Selena felt the words like a slap. They reminded her of the Ombudsman's scorn at her childish assumption that she and Liam could return to Scrapyard after the crash without repercussions.

"No," she said. "I see you're doing your job. But does that mean I have to leave everything I care about on board my ship? Does your job prevent you from showing a little human decency?"

She waited, heart rushing like *The Bee*'s core at full load, wondering if she'd gained any leverage.

"What's in that trawler that's so important to you?"

A trained lie detector, the regulator would sense it if she made something up. She cycled through the few items she kept on board and settled on the one that made sense—the one she *would* miss.

She looked Thompson in the eye, surprised by the genuine, emotion in her voice. "The only thing I have left from my mother. She died when I was five."

Thompson sat, expressionless, thinking. Strange how easy it was to mix the truth with a lie … The thought of the small, metal box hidden beneath the interface terminal gave her voice the right edge—like she'd taken a shot of her father's Mescua. Because at the bottom of the box, buried beneath a thick pile of pull tickets, sat her mother's pendant, a tiny silver charm.

Tears welled in her eyes at the thought of how it once lay against her mother's neck.

"What is it?" Thompson asked.

"A charm."

"Like an icon?"

How to answer? She swiped at her eyes with the back of her hand. She thought of all the silly Order effigies in the shape of the sphere she'd seen hanging from around the necks of workers on the *Hydra*.

"Doesn't have anything to do with the Order," she said. "It's just something my mother wore. It wouldn't mean anything to anyone but me. It's the only thing I have left that belonged to her."

"Tell me where it is. I'll send someone to get it."

"There's no way they can get at it," Selena lied. "It's in a hidden compartment with biometric encryption. Only I can access it."

Thompson mulled it over, eyes tracking the tears streaking her cheeks.

"Please," she said. "Please won't you help me?"

Thompson pushed himself upright. "Okay," he said, sighing. "Let's go."

CHAPTER THIRTY-FOUR

Each night Theo dreamed the same dream. On the command deck of the *Chimera*, a young Stephen stands within the navigation sphere, sweat dripping from his forehead. Straining, jaw clenched, stretched to the limits of what his mind can bear. Theo wants to ask him something. He steps forward. Stephen opens his eyes, looks at Theo and transforms into an old man. Bare-chested, wild-eyed. The sphere becomes a cave. The ancient Stephen slices lines into stone. What do they mean? Stephen's bloodshot eyes look straight through him, as if into some other realm of existence. The dream dissolves.

Theo woke the same time each day, trained with the other candidates and returned home to eat and sleep. His fear of the training had ebbed under Sir's discipline, replaced by an automatic set of responses. The burn on his chest had shrunk to the size of his pinky. Soon it would be nothing more than a purple scar. Somehow, his worn-out, athletic clothes now inspired a certain pride in him. Even his father had started treating him with deference, although that was likely due to the extra rations they received from the Order for his status as one of the final candidates left in the Swallows training group. Eating as much as he liked, Theo'd gained nearly five pounds of muscle.

Of the original candidates, seven remained. Hephaestus, Meghan, Preston, Nemus, Phoebus, and of course, Marcus. Brutal physical workouts had been replaced with team-based logistical training held at the Forest Center, a warehouse-like building adjacent to a muddy track and obstacle course. The building contained several large areas reserved for physical problem-solving, banks of screens running a wide variety of simulations, two classrooms and an actual gym with weights and other training equipment. It also included a vacuum chamber and pressure suits for emergency depressurization training.

Theo and the others learned basic combat tactics, threat assessment, crisis management and command paradigms and controls. Each day Sir manufactured high-intensity scenarios out of thin air, and each day Theo and the other candidates solved them. At the end of the day, Sir transmitted their scores up to the *Hydra* for someone called "The Chief" to evaluate. Sir never revealed where they fell in relation to the other training groups, or how they stacked up individually. Theo had no clue how the Swallows group compared to those from Conway or East End, but suspected he was near the middle of the pack in his own training group.

Theo jogged up the path to the glass and steel Forest Center, enjoying the wind rushing past his ears and the heavy, almost sweet aroma of the pines. Breathing deep, his body felt clear and clean and strong.

Outside, Megan, Nemus, Phoebus and Hephaestus sat in a circle, bending over to touch their toes. Meghan glanced up. "Hey, Theo," she said. "Where have you been?"

"Running."

She stared at him, not quite smiling.

"What?" he asked.

"I don't know. You look … different."

"Different?"

She switched legs, bending over again to grab her heel. "Yeah. Excited. Happy. Something."

It took a moment to register. *I'm happy.* He hadn't felt like this since before the murder in the cave. Maybe since before the fisheries collapsed. Now that Duncan had absolved him of adding his name to the Selection list and he'd come to an agreement with Marcus, all the energy he'd devoted to worrying had been going into his training. Liddy would be safe. Meghan would be safe. He would help crew the *Chimera*.

Meghan watched him with that odd half-smile, eyes sparkling in the patchwork light sifting down from above. Theo bent over and started stretching.

"You're smiling again," Meghan said.

Theo concentrated on his toes, leaning over at the waist, face against his shins.

"Don't be embarrassed—it's nice to see you happy."

"I'm not embarrassed," Theo said.

Nemus gave him a knowing smirk. "It's okay, Theo. We all

know you have a thing for her."

It was Meghan's turn to blush.

Nemus pointed to Theo's chest. "Take off your shirt and show her your scar. Girls like a man with a few scars."

"She's seen it," Theo said.

"Hot stuff," said Nemus. "Tell me more!"

Hephaestus saved him. "We better get inside. Three minutes until fall-in."

Theo pulled Hephaestus to his feet. His hand felt small inside the older boy's, but he was proud of how easily he pulled him upright. Nemus gave Theo a hard jab in the ribs as they stepped into the Forest Center, but Theo's mood was too good for retaliation.

"Where's Sir?" Meghan asked.

Marcus and Preston were doing warm-ups in the gym. Other than them, the place was empty, Sir nowhere in sight.

"What time is it?" Theo asked.

"Time," Hephaestus said. Sir never arrived late. He was always waiting in the Forest Center, pacing, eager. Marcus and Preston noticed their arrival, dropped their weights back into the rack, and came to meet the others.

"Have you seen Sir?" Theo asked them.

"Nope," Preston said.

"We should start without him," said Marcus. Everyone fell into formation as a wallscreen flicked on, drawing attention to a table at the far side of the room.

"What is this? Some kind of test?" Meghan asked.

"I don't think so," Theo said. An electric tingle ran through him. "Come on, let's check it out."

On the table, a row of pressed uniforms: slate gray, tailored, lapels marked with silver crescents. Face bright and fierce, tears welled in the corners of Meghan's eyes. Heph grabbed Phoebus around his middle and lifted him off his feet, crushing him in a massive bear hug. Marcus smiled, a true, genuine smile. Sir's square head, framed by the collar of a black dress uniform, appeared on the wallscreen.

"Pole position, cadets," he said.

As Theo snapped upright, the significance of the word *cadets* hit home.

Even with his eyes fixed forward, Theo felt the excitement of the cadets standing next to him. *This is it. It's happening!*

"You will no longer call me Sir. Quartermaster West will serve. Once you don those uniforms and accept your commission, I will be the one calling each of you 'sir.'" He nodded to Meghan, "or ma'am, as the case may be."

Theo and the others looked at each other. None of them knew what to say.

"I couldn't be there in person today because the timeline has been accelerated. You are transitioning to the *Hydra* station, where you will complete the remainder of your training."

"May I speak, Sir?" asked Marcus.

"Of course, Cadet Locke."

"You're not coming with us, Quartermaster?"

Sir shook his head. "I'm afraid not."

"Who will be our trainer?" Theo asked.

"You'll have several," Sir said. "But that's not important right now. You need to get your uniforms on. The Regulatory's doing a special Mandate Broadcast on all of you in twenty minutes' time."

"Thank you for everything, Quartermaster," Heph said.

"It's been an honor," Sir replied., "but don't get comfortable. The Selection isn't over, and those of you who do advance will carry the weight of this colony on your shoulders."

Sir loomed over them on the wallscreen, an expression on his face that Theo couldn't decipher. "Stephen be with you," he said.

The Quartermaster turned away before the screen faded. The cadets looked at each other, quiet for a moment before Nemus started to shout, jumping and pumping his fists. Theo grabbed Meghan and hugged her, breathing the scent of her hair.

"We made it!" he yelled, voice cracking with strain, joy, relief. "I can't believe we made it."

The celebration continued until Theo realized that the wallscreen had once more come to life. Not Sir, but a woman with silver-blond hair, dressed in a white uniform. She watched them with frank, appraising eyes. Theo snapped to attention, alerting the others who followed suit.

"Greetings, cadets," she said. "My name is Chief Moorland. As Quartermaster West has already informed you, the training schedule has been accelerated. You will report to the Nadil Space Port two days hence at sixteen hundred hours to board the orbital that will bring you to the *Hydra*. Wear your assigned uniform. You need not bring clothing or personal possessions. Everything you need will be assigned to you upon arrival. Understood?"

"Yes, ma'am," the cadets replied.

"Good. Further instructions will be delivered by your local Regulatory office by eighteen hundred hours tonight. I look forward to meeting you all in person. That is all."

The screen went dark. Theo looked at Meghan, her face aglow, uniform clenched against her chest. "Can you believe it?" she said. "We're going to the *Hydra!*"

Theo could believe it. He wanted to laugh, to let the immensity of his feelings come ripping out. Instead, he took his assigned uniform and caressed the fine material, the crescents on the lapels. He'd made it. Despite everything, against all the odds, he'd made it through the Selection.

* * *

Theo sat on the tide wall that wrapped around the west edge of the Swallows. Wind whipped off the alkali oceans, carrying with it the taste of brine, hinting at the warm season storms a few short months away. Storms he would miss. Tomorrow, he and the other cadets would leave for the *Hydra*.

Thirty meters away, Meghan stood with her back to the colony, gazing out over the white ocean crust. Duncan had given Theo permission to borrow a rambler from the Order's motor pool, and they'd driven up to the tide wall that morning. Everyone in the Swallows, including the Regulatory, were going out of their way to make the cadets' last few days on Stephen's Point special.

Since swearing his oath to protect the colony live on a special Mandate Broadcast, Theo couldn't leave his house without getting swarmed. People wanted to capture vids with him or have him autograph Mandate literature about the *Chimera* rebuild. Worst of all, the Order had announced plans to rename the student chapel after him. Puck Chapel sounded ridiculous—he could imagine exactly what future irreverent students would call the place.

Meghan waved, dark hair streaming. She shouted something, but it was lost in the low moan of the wind. Theo moved to join her and she met him halfway. They stood together, watching clouds of white silt form and reform over the ocean crust.

"Hard to believe there's water under there," Theo said. Meghan reached into his jacket pocket and took his hand. She

N. J. TANGER

pulled him, turning him to face her.

"Do you think we'll make it?"

"To Earth? Of course we will."

"How can you be so sure?"

He wasn't sure at all. A gust of wind buffeted them, and they turned their backs, protecting their eyes from the fine grit. Some collected in Meghan's hair. Theo reached out and brushed it away, the softness of the strands causing his throat to tighten. He pulled her close. His lips brushed her forehead, her cheeks, her lips. She returned his kiss. It felt good to touch her, to be touched.

They separated and she looked at him, blue-green eyes clouding, hands still gripping his. Her face was unfathomable. "I'm not sure this is a good idea."

"Why not?"

"It's just ... aboard the *Chimera* ... we'll have jobs to do."

"And we'll do them," Theo said, more confident than ever that this was true.

"I know, but—"

Theo took her other hand. "Don't worry so much. We'll be fine. Together."

"Together?"

"Yeah. You and me. We'll do our jobs. Save the colony. Come back here as heroes."

"Well, when you put it like that ..."

This time she kissed him. Standing at the tide wall, the colony spread before them in the valley below, his fingers tracing the small of Meghan's back, Theo let his doubts slip away. They *would* save the colony—he and Meghan and the rest of the cadets.

"Have you said goodbye?" she asked. "To your family?"

"Not really. We're not good at that sort of thing. My dad keeps hovering around, looking like he wants to say something, and my mom tears up every time she looks at me. Liddy stopped talking to me after the Mandate Broadcast. She's taking it the hardest ... I'll miss her most of all."

"My brothers can't wait for me to go," Meghan sighed. "They're sick of me getting all the attention. It's weird ... I'll miss the Swallows more than my family. I keep watching the *Chimera* when she passes overhead and thinking that when we're up there— what I'll miss is the smell of the air. And the dwarf pines. And the view of the mountains."

"Earth has mountains."

"Yeah, I know. But they're not *my* mountains. *Our* mountains."

Theo shaded his eyes, surveying his world. Great Northern peaked with snow, the tree line transforming into deep forest to the north, the alkali ocean shimmering off into the horizon line, the glittering buildings of the Golden Valley, Pod Six and the surrounding collection of homes, factories, and warehouses. Tomorrow he would leave them behind.

Meghan pressed her head against his shoulder. He stood straight and strong the way Sir taught him to, but his mind wandered into the darkness of a cave, to the face of a man with a crushed-in skull, to the glacier-blue eyes of his murderer.

"What's wrong?" Meghan said.

"Nothing," Theo said, shaking himself. "We're going to save the colony. What could be wrong with that?"

CHAPTER THIRTY-FIVE

The shattered remains of *The Bee* sat hulk-like in the corner of the hangar. Her battered outer shield plates sagged from her frame. Yawing on broken supports, the trawler looked as if it might topple over. Scorched and discolored, beaten and bruised—the ship had sacrificed its core to protect her. Selena swallowed, nails cutting into her palms as she came to realize what it meant.

The Bee would never fly again.

Thompson wheeled her to the hatch. Forced open when the rescuers extracted Liam and her, she could see into the dim interior. Command chair ripped loose from the console, ominous smears of blood on the rear bulkhead. Only Liam's hammock appeared unscathed. It hung as it always had, in a suspended rope web. She imagined rescuers cutting her loose from the straps, hoisting out her unconscious body.

"You've got five minutes," Thompson said. "Do you want me to help you inside?"

"No."

She would do this herself. She stood and struggled to the hatch. Grasping each side, she pulled herself through. A sour chemical odor filled the air, masking the rotten-sweet iron smell of blood. Selena moved over decking slick with hydraulic fluid and reached the pilot's chair. The interface was lifeless. She couldn't escape in *The Bee*; it had been foolish to even consider it. The good fortune of the shuttle's steam jet failure, convincing Thompson to bring her here … she'd started to hope, once again letting childish ideas push away clear, logical thinking.

She pulled herself into the chair—trickier to do in gravity— welcoming its familiar contours. How many hours had she sat in that chair? How many good pulls made, near tragedies avoided? She thought of her father coaxing her in using the interface. Her fear and hesitation overcome by the electric realization that *this* was what she was meant for as Liam's laughter filled the cabin.

She reached under the console, probing until she located the lever that opened a magnetic hide-store. Selena removed the small box containing pull tickets issued by the Scrap Warden and a handful of personal items. A folded sheet of paper detailing the terms of a bet she had won against her father years earlier—she'd remembered all nineteen trawler variations, including tonnage and core loads. Beneath the tickets and paper, a pair of weighted, twenty-sided dice, used for cheating at Rankle Toss. Beside them, a small silver charm, a shooting star.

The items summed up her entire life. The struggle to earn her father's respect. Hours spent in the rim. Wild times at Scrapyard. Making her way any way she could. A good luck charm that hadn't brought her any.

She traced the edge of the lifeless interface with cold fingers. Soon they'd send *The Bee* to a chop shop and piece her out to try and cover Liam's debts. She took the small charm and set it on the interface. She remembered how large it seemed when one of the regulators who had found her mother pressed it into her tiny palm so many years ago.

Selena leaned into the worn fabric of the chair, unable to hold back the sobs rising in her chest. She needed to leave. She could do nothing for *The Bee*, for her father, for anyone. She reached for the charm and stopped, fingers outstretched. The shooting star glittered on the dead interface. From deep memory, words came. "Come ride a pillar of fire with me," she whispered.

Goodbye, old friend.

She snatched the charm and shoved it into her pocket. Scrubbed her face free of tears. Took a deep breath. Climbed out of *The Bee* for the very last time.

"Did you find it?" Thompson asked.

"Yes."

She worried he would ask her to show him, but he only nodded and whirled her chair back to the hangar exit. Selena tracked the distance, measuring her remaining freedom in meters.

They passed a repair station arrayed with tools. There among the pressure gauges and sockets and current testers was something that cut through her defeated resignation.

"Can you stop for a sec?" she asked. "Those belong to my father."

Thompson looked skeptical.

"Please?" she said, blinking up at him, harnessing the last of her tears, hoping they would persuade for her.

The chair slowed, stopped. Selena reached for the pair of metal cuffs. Thompson looked at her, face neutral, clueless as to their function. She slid them over her wrists and up her forearms. Without prompting, they tightened, conforming themselves to her arms.

Thompson raised an eyebrow.

Selena admired the aerocuffs, holding them out for his inspection. "Fashionable, don't you think? For special occasions."

Thompson grunted, and they accelerated down the corridor that led back to the shuttle dock. Selena played with the aerocuffs, trying to work out how the two recessed dials in each cuff controlled them. One had to govern velocity and the other narrowed or widened the cone of thrust. But which was which, and how did you fire the damned things? They didn't seem to have an interface; she felt no tingle in her fingers or arm and received no data feed through her spider. No obvious external trigger either. How had that technician Andy fired them back in the crosshatch of the *Chimera*?

They closed on the lift, fifteen meters away. Now or never. She reached behind her head, as if stretching, pointing one of the cuffs at Thompson's thick chest. She willed the cuff to fire, hoping that perhaps it had an interface after all, but nothing happened.

Thompson gave her a funny look.

"Just stretching," she said. As if to demonstrate, she opened her hand and spread her fingers. The aerocuff began to hum.

"What was that?"

"What was what?"

"Your arm things are making noise."

"Oh, they do that," Selena said, stretching her fingers again, trying to duplicate the gesture that had brought them to life.

"Let me see," Thompson said.

"Sure."

She wiggled her fingers, opening and closing her fist, desperate to get the cuff to do *something*. Before she had a chance to retract her hand, Thompson grabbed her wrist, arm stretched behind her.

"These aren't decorative. They *do* something. You're going to tell me what it is, or I'll pry them off you."

"They're useless," Selena said. "They don't even work."

She relaxed her arm and spread her fingers like a bolas pod about to strike a shard. The cuff vibrated against her skin. Thompson's eyes widened. He released her wrist and tried to duck, but it was too late. The cuff fired a pulse of air directly into the regulator's face.

The blast sent them both sprawling. Selena toppled out of the chair and Thompson launched backward, slamming into the floor, landing on his back. He groaned, narrow cuts etched into his face. Selena scrambled to her knees and crawled away as fast as she could. Thompson rolled to his side and stood.

Still unsure how to fire the cuffs, Selena knelt and aimed her palms at him, fingers splayed, trying to duplicate the motion that had fired the cuff the first time. The cuffs hummed, and another blast of air shot out, slamming her into the floor, head cracking against the deck plate. Thompson was sprawled on the floor a half-dozen meters away, unconscious.

Wobbling from the pain coursing through her head, shoulders and back stiff, Selena shuffled in the opposite direction of the lift. She couldn't keep firing the aerocuffs or they would kill her, and she couldn't go back to the shuttles. *Where?* Not the shuttles and not *The Bee*—maybe she could find a different ship. One of the welders, or a tug. A long shot, but she had no other options.

Using the wall for balance, she struggled forward until reaching a t-shaped intersection.

She turned right, hoping it would lead her to an adjacent hangar. Exhausted from firing the aerocuffs, legs already tiring, she couldn't keep this up for long. Why hadn't she thought to get back in the wheelchair? Too late now, she wasn't going back.

A group of technicians wearing green jumpsuits emerged from a doorway, talking and gesticulating as they read data from handscreens. Selena let go of the wall, trying to appear natural. None of the technicians made eye contact, too distracted by their conversation to notice her unsteady gait. She waited until they disappeared around the corner and popped through the door they'd exited.

A narrow, low-ceilinged passage, thick with bundled cables, led to a small room lined with screens displaying various charts and graphs. She passed a series of windows providing views of science labs filled with equipment so clean and sterile and precise they made her uncomfortable. Why had she ever thought that Scrapyard enjoyed a technological edge? Because they flew trawlers in and out of the rim? What had Scrapyard produced that could rival self-healing synthetics or aerocuffs?

A scientist stepped out of the lab, shiny black hair pulled behind her delicate ears. "Can I help you?"

"Yes," Selena said. "I'm looking for a lift."

"Who are you and why are you here?"

"Nobody important. Just lost."

"Are you injured?"

"No. Well, sort of. I'm in recovery. Can you point me to the nearest lift?"

"I'm calling medical," the woman said.

"No!"

The scientist stepped backward and pulled a handscreen from her pocket.

"Please," Selena said. "Please, don't." The woman lifted the screen and began to speak. Selena didn't wait around to hear what she said. Each step sent dull pain into her abdomen as she shuffled out of the labs and back into the *Hydra's* outer ring.

CHAPTER THIRTY-SIX

Moorland's screen lit up and Peterson's animated face appeared. "Chief?"

"What can I do for you?"

"Strange situation up here. A nurse asked for you. Insisted she speak with you personally. She was really worked up."

"Is someone hurt?"

"I don't think it's anything like that. She said you'd want to know that someone named Selena Samuelson is getting shipped down to the colony after some sort of hearing."

"What? The hearing isn't until next rotation!"

Peterson shrugged. "The nurse seemed pretty angry about it, too. When I told her you might be busy, she took off for the shuttle dock. She's probably there now. I didn't want to bother you, but thought it might be important, so I called."

"You did the right thing. Thank you for letting me know."

Moorland cut the connection and called up the flight deck. She shouted into the screen, unable to hide her anger. "When was the last outbound shuttle?"

"Six hours ago."

"Good. "Ground all other outbound flights. I don't want anything—not even welding ships—leaving the *Hydra*."

"Ma'am? We've got the first set of cadets on their way up, due to arrive in less than an hour. Should I send them back?"

Moorland considered. She'd intended to meet the cadets at the dock and give them a tour of the *Hydra*. She'd have to adjust. "Land them. Have Lemieux take them to observation. I'll meet them there as soon as I can."

Moorland brought up Control. "I'm only going to say this once: I want a detail to take the Ombudsman into custody, and a second detail to locate Selena Samuelson and bring her to control."

"Arrest the Ombudsman?"

"You heard me. Now move."

* * *

A ripple from The Everything brushed against the walls of the *Chimera's* Salix prison. It burst around her hull like the magnetic wash of a pulsar. She roused herself, sensors reaching out, aware that one of the blind ones would soon push through the thicket of fractal space. The ripple strengthened into a current, then a wall like a tsunami, crashing into itself, sweeping out to reform and crash again.

An opening formed. Through it she glimpsed The Everything. For a tiny fraction of time she studied pathways like ropes and cables and threads, braiding themselves together or tearing themselves apart. She held them for a precious moment, all of her alive, even constrained within the Salix prison.

The blind one tumbled out of The Everything. The opening closed. *Chimera* felt as though all her cores had been jettisoned, leaving her cold and frail and empty.

The blind one coasted, listless without direction provided by the exchange dock. For the first time *Chimera* felt a sort of kinship with an exchange ship. She also was lost. Just as the blind one lacked a dock to direct it, so she lacked a navigator. None of the offspring of the First Colonists thrumming throughout her decks reached out to her. None but the dangerous girl, and she had refused the *Chimera's* invitation.

But perhaps ... perhaps she could reach for the blind one.

She pushed against the Salix prison, testing, unsure—the protocols did not address these peculiar circumstances. It was worth an attempt.

The prison did not react when she sent her first, tentative burst. A simple query: *Cargo?* The response arrived milliseconds later: *Unknown.* She sent another short burst, and again the Salix prison did not restrict her.

Query: *Status of cargo?*
Response: *Unknown.*
Query: *Systems status?*
Response: *Functional. Cargo hold reports venting irregularity.*
Command: *Specify the nature of the irregularity.*
Response: *Unknown. Advise trajectory, navigation reports no*

beacon lock.

Command: *Wait for coordinates.*

Response: *Confirmed.*

A conversation completed in a microsecond. The *Chimera* was unsure how to proceed. Without a dock, the blind one could not birth its cargo. She might bring it alongside herself, but the "unknown" cargo status gave her pause. The Salix protocol, and even her primary protocols, had no test case for these parameters. She formulated another question.

Query: *Specify cargo irregularity.*

Response: *Cargo density ninety percent lower than expected.*

Command: *Provide cargo manifest.*

The blind one listed tens of thousands of items from cores to athletic shoes. A typical resupply. Nothing unusual. The blind one showed no sign of hull breach, no physical damage, and no system damage. Despite its manifest, the blind one reported its cargo as "unknown." That meant that whatever it contained had never been part of a prior exchange ship manifest. These facts presented two hypotheses:

The exchange ship carried weapons.

The exchange ship carried humans.

The *Chimera* formulated a final query: *Does the cargo present a threat to the colony?*

Response: *Unknown.*

* * *

To Theo, the *Hydra* looked like a parasite. Half as long as the *Chimera*, it hung beneath the cruiser, suspended by a luminous umbilical at the very center of the *Hydra's* rings. The station turned around it like a wheel. The shuttle fired its steam jets and rotated, preparing to dock. Suddenly Theo gained a sense of scale. In images, even as a swarm of lights visible from Stephen's Point, he'd never understood the magnitude of the *Chimera*. Larger than the largest building in the Golden Valley, almost wide enough to fit the Swallows inside—the only word that came to mind was "awesome."

Here we go, he thought. *Here we go.*

The shuttle pushed through the breakage: a series of synthetic curtains, almost like skin, which repaired themselves after each entry or departure—a seal against the vacuum, and a means of slowing the ship. The shuttle lurched to a stop, held in place by a cradle under the fuselage.

The cabin pressure shifted. Theo's ears popped. Many of the cadets unbuckled and crowded into the narrow aisle. Theo remained seated—jostling wouldn't get him off the shuttle any faster. A glorious mix of wonder and anticipation lighted Meghan's face. The same feelings pumped through Theo with each thud of his heart.

"I can't believe it," she said. "We're here."

Theo grinned, unable to control the reckless happiness bubbling inside him.

The train of cadets started to move up the aisle. Theo and Meghan joined them, hands meeting in a surreptitious clasp as they fell in behind the others. At a half-trot, they reached the shuttle gate and entered a waiting room. Two men and two women wearing white uniforms stood with hands behind their backs outside the gate. The welcoming committee.

Marcus stepped forward and offered his finger. "Cadet Locke," he said, flashing a quick smile, speaking with just the right amount of enthusiasm.

"Hurston Lemieux," said one of the men. "Lead trainer. I wish we had time for formal introductions, but we've got a few double urgent situations we're dealing with at the minute. Chief Moorland has asked that we bring you to observation where she will join you once she is able."

"Thank you, sir."

"Trainer or Hurston will be fine."

Marcus smiled again—warm and bright, one colleague to another. "All right, Hurston, lead the way."

* * *

After traversing the *Hydra*'s outer ring and taking a lift to the middle ring, Theo, Meghan, and the rest of the cadets stepped into a room lined with massive screens displaying views of space. Parallel to the screens, a large portal gave an uninterrupted view of Elypso, the rim, and the underside of the *Chimera*. A woman with silver blond hair stood waiting for them.

"Chief Moorland, the cadets have arrived," Hurston announced. The chief didn't move, transfixed by the view out the portal. A handful of other *Hydra* staff monitored screens. They appeared to be arguing. Something big must have happened—something to do with whatever Moorland and the others were watching on their wallscreens. The cadets crowded forward, following the woman's gaze.

At first, all Theo saw was Elypso bathing Gauleta in yellow light—beautiful, but not exciting. As his eyes adjusted, he made out small lights—tugs—burning in the direction of the *Hydra*. Behind them, a looming dark shape visible only as it passed in front of stars, blocking their light. Something massive.

He recognized the outline. "An exchange ship!"

"Thank Stephen," Meghan said.

"Broke in from fractal moments ago." Chief Moorland turned to face the cadets. "With no dock to guide her, I sent out tugs to tow her to the *Hydra*. We've got an umbilical waiting."

Theo didn't know what to say. Hurston and the other trainers stood alongside the cadets, the exchange ship growing larger and larger as the tugs towed it to the station. Everyone began to talk at once.

"Looks like we get to go home."

"Screw the *Chimera*. We need our exchange dock back!"

"I hope they sent guitar strings!"

"How do we bust it open?"

The cadets gushed with excitement. Everyone but Marcus. Close to the portal, face reflected in the glass, he looked disturbed, disappointed, angry. They all knew what the exchange ship's arrival meant. An end to the rebuild, The Mandate repealed, the Selection cancelled—cause for celebration.

So why did Theo feel like how Marcus looked? He should be happy, but he wasn't. He didn't want to go back to Stephen's Point. He didn't want to return to the routine. The safe, regular life he used to enjoy now seemed exactly that: safe and regular. Another way of saying boring.

For the first time in his life, he'd started to feel like he mattered. He'd become part of something important. He carried real responsibility.

Meghan tugged his sleeve. "Wonderful, isn't it?"

"Wonderful," Theo said. "Sure."

Marcus whirled from the portal and cut through the cadets, heading for the lift. No one paid any attention. Meghan reached for Theo's hand but he pulled away. "Sorry," he said. "I have to go."

Meghan looked hurt. "Go where? Don't you want to celebrate?"

"I will. Later. I promise."

"Theo—"

"I'll be back soon," he said, backpedaling.

"Where are you going?" Meghan asked.

"With Marcus. He's upset. He needs someone to talk to."

Ignoring the disappointment on Meghan's face, he slid into the lift alongside Marcus an instant before the doors closed.

Marcus' eyes smoldered, his body casting off an emotional radiation that burned Theo's skin. "This means nothing," Marcus said. "We don't know what's on that ship or how to unload it."

"Moorland said they'd use an umbilical, like from the *Chimera.*"

"It might be empty. Or full of a toxic nerve agent. Or nuclear warheads."

"Why would Earth try to gas or bomb us?"

"Why did they cut off our supplies for fifteen years? Maybe they decided that rather than kill us slowly through deprivation, they'd to the merciful thing and wipe us out with a nice little plague."

"Wouldn't the exchange ship head right for the surface of the moon, then?"

"Shut up, Theo." Marcus' eye twitched. His fingers tapped his pant legs. Theo studied him from the corner of his eye. He'd never seen Marcus unnerved before.

"Isn't this a good thing?" Theo asked, unsure of the answer himself.

"No! It is not a good thing. Look, Theo, not everyone wants a pathetic, coddling family and a moronic religion. Not all of us want to watch our lives dwindle to nothing as we fulfill meaningless tasks for a meaningless government on a meaningless chunk of rock. What's the point of it? What's the point of anything? There's nothing new under the sun, Theo. Not ours or any other. Measured by astronomical units or how many worshipers cast prayers in their direction, they're all just giant balls of burning gas. As hollow as the rest of the garbage which fills The Everything."

"What's the point of leaving, then? If you're right, then leaving means nothing as well."

"At least it's interesting. Different than another day breathing used up air, knuckling under to morons and their false prophet. Watch—the colony will declare this an act of Stephen and establish a holiday in honor of the day he saved us once again. They'll parade in the streets and raise new temples. Shouting praises to a parasite. All of them junkies, strung out on lies."

"I don't believe it, either," Theo said.

"I don't care what you believe. It doesn't matter." Marcus' voice transitioned from roiling anger to exhaustion. "Nothing matters. Nothing."

Theo could think of one thing that had to matter to Marcus. Enough to cause him to smash a man's head with a chunk of stone.

"What about the man in the cave. Does he matter?" For a moment Theo thought Marcus had chosen to ignore him. Then he lunged at Theo, grasped his neck and shoved him against the wall of the lift.

"Not anymore," Marcus spat into his face. "Never mention him to me again."

Marcus' fingers dug into Theo's throat, so close he could smell the hint of sweat rising from beneath Marcus' uniform.

"Let go of me!"

"I'll let go when I feel like it."

Theo slammed his arm down across Marcus's arms, breaking his hold. He shoved Marcus, knocking him backward into the opposite lift wall. Marcus rebounded, rocking forward off his shoulder blades. Theo turned sideways, arm extended, ready to fight, but Marcus only looked at him, his eyes dark coals of pure hatred.

"Some people deserve to die," Marcus said.

"Why?" Theo asked, breathing hard, ready lest Marcus try to catch him off guard.

"You don't know what he did," Marcus said.

Before Theo could ask any of the dozens of questions that sprang to mind, the lift door opened. Marcus shook himself, face resetting to calm. Theo hunched over, regaining his air as Marcus strode away.

"Where are you going?" Theo asked.

"To find out what's on that ship."

"How?"

Marcus didn't answer.

Unsure where they were headed or why, Theo ran after him.

CHAPTER THIRTY-SEVEN

Moorland watched the panel of screens that provided the best views of *Exchange Four*. Nestled alongside the *Hydra*, devoid of aesthetic appeal, the exchange ship was nothing more than a metal tube connected to navigational circuitry. In the years she'd worked as a controller for the dock, Moorland had never paid the exchange ships much heed. She saw them as tools. Now, face to face with one for the first time in over fifteen years, she couldn't help but marvel at how her feelings had changed—the ship might be their salvation.

"Any luck decoding the bursts from the *Chimera*?" she asked Duty Officer Blake.

"No, ma'am. The ship-to-ship from the *Chimera* and *Exchange Four* used a different schema than dock beacon code. Something initiated by the *Chimera* herself. We didn't even know she had the capacity. We don't have records of her communicating with an exchange ship before. There's still so much we don't know about her. And so much we may never learn, now that Earth's sent us a resupply."

"Assuming that's what we're looking at," Moorland said.

The duty officer, a capable, intelligent girl Moorland had handpicked from the Regulatory, gave her a sharp look. "What else could it be?"

"I don't know." Moorland cycled through various camera angles, searching the exterior of the ship. Nothing but steel plates over a drive assembly. Why did she feel so uneasy? Soon work crews would have an umbilical in place, and she'd have a live feed of the interior. Until then, she would give her attention to other pressing issues.

She pushed away the images of the exchange ship and brought up Command. "Do you have the Ombudsman in custody?"

"Yes, ma'am. We're holding him until you give us further

instruction."

Moorland couldn't help smiling—she'd never liked that smooth-talking weasel. He'd been a concession to the bureaucrats in the Economic Office. She'd put up with his smugness because he helped speed the flow of raw materials from the rim. She knew he took a cut but considered it a worthwhile price. However, she'd never suspected the depth of his corruption. To actively work against The Mandate … Moorland wanted to call Control and have the bastard pushed out an airlock.

"And Selena?"

"We're still looking. One of the regulators, a guy named Thompson, called in for backup a few moments ago. Apparently Selena shot him with aerocuffs."

Moorland raised an eyebrow. "Aerocuffs? How'd she get aerocuffs? Never mind. I want her found. Now."

"Yes, ma'am, but with the exchange ship's arrival and the rings flooded with foot traffic, we're having trouble locating her. It's not like she's connected to the network. She doesn't *want* to be found."

"Can you isolate her using biometrics?" Moorland asked, irritated.

"That's what we're working on."

"Work faster. Until I know what's on *Exchange Four*, I'm operating under Mandate protocols. We need the girl. She's irreplaceable."

* * *

Selena read the wallscreens identifying different sections of the labs. The names meant nothing to her. *Cognitive Analytics, Infrastructure Development, CCCAP Recovery*. None hinted at the direction to the nearest lift. Her legs pulsed with pain. She wasn't sure how they'd continue to support her.

"Stop!" a voice shouted. A pair of regulators rushed forward carrying stunners. No way could she outrun them, not with her legs screwed up. Ducking into the first open door, Selena dashed between rows of screens suspended above workstations. The technicians in the room don't seem to notice her—to the contrary—they were headed the opposite direction, all of them in a great hurry. Good. Hopefully they'd slow down her pursuers.

Selena hobbled forward, pushing past elaborate crystalline

constructs and banks of colorful wallscreens displaying complex visualizations of data. Some of them reminded her of schematics for a ship. A very odd ship named the *Helvictus*. She would have taken the time to study them if she didn't have regulators closing in on her.

Selena slammed through the lab exit, hunting for a sign that would help her reach a lift. A crash sounded from behind her. Thompson and the other regulators had made it into the labs! She dove through the nearest doorway.

Welders, dressed in pressure suits and carrying heavy equipment, barreled down the corridor in a real hurry. Selena pressed against the wall, hoping the regulators would have a hard time navigating the lab. When the last welder passed her by, she headed in the opposite direction.

Rounding a corner, she ran into two more gray-uniformed regulators coming from the opposite direction. Damn it all to hell! How many of them were on the station? She raised her aerocuffs and noticed they weren't Regulators. They weren't even men. More like boys.

One tall and skinny, the other thick-chested and blank-faced, their uniforms looked different than any she'd seen on the station. Silver crescents flashed from their lapels. The boys were unremarkable except for the shorter, dark-haired one's peculiar eyes. Eyes that locked with hers for a quarter-second before moving on. As if in that instant he'd judged her unimportant. Without further reflection, her feelings for the dark-haired boy cemented into instant, intense dislike.

* * *

Marcus traveled the *Hydra* like Theo would the back alleys of the Swallows—sure of himself—making turns and taking passageways. If Theo didn't know better, he'd suspect Marcus was charging around aimlessly.

Theo followed close behind as they weaved through throngs of people chattering with excitement, all of them headed for the observation platform. The news must have already arrived on Stephen's Point—The Mandate Broadcast would be carrying the details of the *Exchange Four*'s arrival to every public and private screen.

Theo imagined his parents joining crowds of workers in the

streets. The Swallows would celebrate like they had when The Mandate first went into effect. A bit of homesickness pricked him. For a moment, Theo wished he was celebrating with them. The sight of Marcus' muscular shoulder blades and purposeful stride pulled him back to the present. Returning to Stephen's Point wasn't a real solution. Theo and his family would be nothing but liabilities for Marcus. Maybe that was why he was following Marcus. They *both* needed to know what was on the exchange ship.

Marcus led the way down a straight corridor intersected by many others. With each intersection they passed, the curvature of the passages lessened. They had to be moving toward the outer edge of the *Hydra*.

Abruptly, Marcus slowed. A short, chestnut-haired girl leaned against a wall, arms extended toward them, as if welcoming them—or warding them away. Her face streaked with sweat, hair a wild tangle over her shoulders, brown eyes narrowed—she looked ferocious and fragile at the same time. The way she leaned against the wall … was she injured? Marcus sped up, ignoring her. Theo let Marcus go and slowed, stopping beside the girl.

"Are you okay?"

The girl raised her arms, pointing her wrists at Theo, her jaw clenched, eyes fierce. "Keep moving," she said, voice low and menacing.

"Are you hurt?"

The girl flexed her pointer finger. For the first time Theo noticed the silver bracelets on her forearms. Bracelets that hummed. Theo backed away, aware that Marcus had already disappeared around the curve of the passage, slipping into the growing crowd filling the corridor. "I'm not going to hurt you," Theo said. "My name is Cadet Puck. I'm here to help crew the *Chimera*. Do you work here on the *Hydra?*"

A door slid open a few paces down the hall. A pair of furious looking regulators charged forward at a sprint. The girl's face contorted—a flash of vulnerability. "Please," she said. "I need your help."

* * *

"Okay, let's go." The boy's voice carried the quiet edge of authority. He stretched out his hand.

Selena's fingers wrapped around the boy's. Then they were moving, rushing, the boy dragging her through oncoming foot traffic. "We have to catch up with Marcus," the boy said.

The weirdo? Great.

"What's your name?" the boy asked.

"Selena."

"Why are the regulators after you?"

Selena grimaced, "Does it matter?" She pointed with relief. "Look—there's a lift."

The boy gave Selena a look that at first she interpreted as pity, but then recognized as incredulity. "You can barely walk," he said. "What happened to you?"

"A lot of things." She shrugged and changed the subject. "Where are you going anyway?"

"*Exchange Four.*"

"What's that?"

"You don't know?" the boy asked, voice filled with disbelief.

"Do you answer every question with a question? Just tell me!"

"An exchange ship. It arrived a little bit ago. Tugs are towing it to the *Hydra.*"

"You're lying." But even as the words left her mouth, Selena knew the boy *wasn't* lying. The tides of people swarming through the corridors, the welders in pressure suits …

The boy tugged at her arm. "That's why we have to find Marcus. He's going to try to get inside the exchange ship."

Selena weighed her options. If she was going to steal a ship, now was the time. With everyone distracted, she'd never have a better chance. But if the *Exchange Four* contained a resupply, it would offer her a different, long-term opportunity. Maybe things *could* return to normal. Selena and her father could go back to the rim, assuming she could get him out of legal trouble. But that would never happen if she commandeered a ship.

She needed to find out what was on the exchange ship. If it contained even a half-manifest, the markets would surge back to life. The economy would stabilize, and mining at the rim would once again become a sustainable business. Most of the flame-backs would head back to Stephen's Point. She and Liam could resume life much as it was before the ecomire rush. She'd find a way to deal with her dad's legal issues, and then they'd return to the rim for good. For the first time since her arrival at the *Hydra*, Selena believed everything might work out.

CHAPTER THIRTY-EIGHT

Theo dashed past the welding docks, scanning for any sign of Marcus, dragging Selena along behind. He didn't see any regulators. Maybe they'd lost them?

A row of welders in orange pressure suits tramped past, helmets sealed. They had to be preparing to board the exchange ship, and the fact they'd already suited up meant they were going through an airlock and into a depressurized ship. They must have already attached an umbilical. Could one of the people in the pressure suits be Marcus? No—they hadn't been separated *that* long—it took real effort to don a pressure suit.

Ahead, yellow signage marked a utility locker with diagrams outlining its contents, including an over-sized human shape with a helmet. Pressure suits. "In here," Theo said, checking over his shoulder to make sure no regulators were in sight. He yanked Selena through the door. Under the locker's stark lighting, Marcus looked up from pulling a pressure suit over his torso. "About time," he said, then he saw Selena. "What's *she* doing here?"

"Coming with us," Theo said.

"No, she's not," Marcus said. Theo ignored him, opened a locker and pulled out a pressure suit. Rubbery and at the same time inflexible, fibrous micro-pulse mesh lined its insides. When sealed, the mesh augmented the wearer's movements, like extra muscles worn on the outside of the body. They increased strength and stamina and allowed the wearer to carry many extra kilos of weight.

Theo worked the unwieldy legs up over his calves and thighs, yanking with all his strength, forcing his feet through the openings. He selected a pair of gravity boots and stepped into them, the auto-seals at the ankles snapping tight with magnetic precision. Halfway done.

Theo looked up and found that Selena already had her suit

over her legs and torso and was adjusting the shoulder tension before placing a helmet over her head. She moved with an easy grace, as if she'd done this thousands of times before. Marcus was still struggling to get his arms through the stiff sleeves. Even with all their training at the Forest Center, Selena had beaten them by a huge margin.

Theo pointed at Selena. "She knows what she's doing. She can help us."

Marcus shot him a look of skeptical condescension. "She's no cadet. We don't know anything about her. She's not coming."

"I'll go where I like," Selena said, making a few expert adjustments to the helmet's position before the magnetic seals suctioned closed with a hungry slurp. Selena looked at Marcus, face shadowed by the curved faceplate, voice amplified by an external speaker. "You can't stop me," she said. "From the look of it, neither of you knows anything about suiting up." Theo noticed the silver cuffs were now tight around the forearms of her orange suit.

Marcus' eyes darkened, but he didn't argue. She was right and they both knew it. The equipment they'd trained with at the Forest Center was good but rudimentary—the rest of their pressure suit training was supposed to happen on the *Hydra*. Selena could help them if Marcus would let her.

Selena extended her hand, blue light shining from her palm, casting a mesh of lines over Marcus' body. "Your biometric strap isn't tight enough," she said. Marcus ran his fingers along the inside of the rubber strap circling his chest and frowned.

Theo raised an eyebrow. "See?"

Before Marcus could reply, the door to the locker opened and a regulator stuck his head inside. Selena quickly turned away, hiding her face. "What are you doing in here?" the regulator asked.

"Heading out for a training exercise," Marcus said, almost bored.

"While the station is preparing to receive *Exchange Four*?"

"*Exchange Four* is the training exercise," Marcus said. "And you will address me as 'sir.' I am a Selection cadet."

"You have to be kidding me."

"No, I am not *kidding* you. I'm Cadet Locke and this is Cadet Puck. We've been assigned to accompany those going to explore *Exchange Four*."

The regulator pointed at Selena. "Who's that?"

Marcus shrugged. "Some fool. From her accent, I'd say she's from the rim."

"She's a cadet from a different training group," Theo lied.

The regulator frowned. "We're sending untrained cadets aboard the exchange ship?"

"Maybe you've been living in a cave," Marcus said, smirking. "But we're here to crew the *Chimera* and we're *far* from untrained. Now get out of the way before I contact Moorland and tell her you're obstructing us."

"I'm not here to *obstruct* you. I'm looking for a girl named Selena Samuelson. The chief wants her brought to Command. She looks like this." The regulator held out a handscreen displaying a picture of a surly looking Selena, lying in what looked like a medical bed. She must have been sick or gotten hurt somehow.

Theo caught Marcus' eye. "We haven't seen anyone like that," he said. *Samuelson.* The same last name as the woman who'd written the book Duncan gave him. *Ashley Samuelson.* Could they be related?

"Yes, we have," Marcus said. "That's her right there."

"This isn't some joke. Why don't you cut the attitude and try to be helpful?"

"I am being helpful. That's her."

"Quit wasting his time," Theo said, punching Marcus in the arm as hard as he could with the heavy, half-on pressure suit flailing around his hips.

Marcus turned to Theo, eyes blazing. "Touch me again and I'll break your fingers." He looked at the regulator. "Check her for yourself. See if I'm lying."

The regulator shrugged and pushed between Marcus and Theo. "What's your name," he said to Selena, "And look at me when I'm talking to you."

Selena turned, but her faceplate had transformed from clear to a black reflective surface. "Cadet Gunner," she said, voice amplified by an external speaker.

"Show me your face."

"I can't, sir. My helmet malfunctioned."

"Then take it off."

"Yeah," said Marcus. "Take it off."

"Okay," Selena said. She raised her hands as if to unseal the helmet, then slugged the regulator in the jaw. Aided by the augmentation of the pressure suit's muscle fiber, her blow sent the man sprawling. His head impacted the floor with a heavy thud. He groaned, rolled on his side, eyes half-closed.

"Look what you made me do!" Selena said, voice furious.

Marcus looked at her as if for the first time. "Why are the regulators after you? What did you do?"

"I hurt people that mess with me." Selena raised her arms, aiming her cuffs at Marcus. She fired a tight cone of air, slapping Marcus against the wall. Selena leapt forward and held the cuff inches from Marcus' exposed face. Faceplate no longer opaque, she stared at Marcus with unwavering eyes. Without an active pressure suit or cuffs, Marcus was powerless to defend himself. "Whatever," he said. "I've got a ship to explore."

He pushed past Selena, grabbed a helmet and lifted it over his head.

Theo looked at the groaning regulator and realized how close he'd probably come to suffering the same fate moments earlier in the passage. Who *was* this girl? Marcus clumped to the locker exit. "Coming, Theo?"

Theo fumbled with his helmet. He couldn't quite get the locking mechanism closed. He repositioned the helmet and tried again. No luck. He didn't want to get left behind, but if he couldn't get the stupid thing to seal …

"Let me," Selena offered.

She adjusted the helmet and it clicked into position. Cool, recirculating air wisped across his face. The suit tightened over his body like a second skin, one made of powerful synthetic muscle fiber. He stretched out his arm, marveling at how strong he felt, how little of his weight his legs seemed to carry. A tone announced his suit's readiness, followed by another syncing him to a closed-link com channel between his and Selena's suit. "Whoa," he said, voice echoing inside the helmet.

The hint of a smile appeared on Selena's face. "Ready?"

It took him a moment to locate the private channel in his visual cue and activate it. "This is intense … I've never worn a pressure suit before."

"You'll get used to it. Now come on—we need to hurry if we want to make it aboard the exchange ship."

* * *

"Regulator Jempson just called for medical," Duty Officer Blake said.

"What happened?" Moorland asked, pretty sure she already knew the answer.

Blake frowned, lips a narrow line. "A girl in a pressure suit gave him a concussion."

"Selena," Moorland said, speaking the girl's name like a curse. "What does she think she's doing?"

"Escaping is my guess."

"She's an idiot," Moorland said, rolling her eyes. "Do the other regulators have her position?"

"Yes, ma'am."

"Good. Do they have her in custody?"

"Not exactly, ma'am."

"What does 'not exactly,' mean?" Moorland felt her blood pressure rising. Why couldn't anyone seem to find and hang on to one reckless little girl?

"You're not going to like this." Blake paused, bracing for Moorland's reaction. "It seems she made her way into the umbilical connecting the *Hydra* to *Exchange Four*."

"How did that happen?"

"Apparently she found a pressure suit and joined the exploration team. The focus was getting the umbilical in place and preparing for the weld. Nobody double checked identities. Now they're sealed in the umbilical and the weld is underway. If we stop and pull them out, we'll have to cycle the whole umbilical and delay gaining access to *Exchange Four*."

Moorland took several deep breaths before replying, letting her frustration out in a long, satisfying string of curses. "Can you get me on her suit's com channel? I want to speak to her."

"I've already tried that. She won't reply."

"Try again."

Moorland waited for a connection, honing her disappointment and frustration with Selena down to a single point, a single message, one she hoped the girl would listen to. Because as reckless and stupid as Selena could be, they still needed her.

* * *

Theo's boots clamped securely to the floor. They huddled together near the back of the group of welders and technicians crammed into the airlock. Located at the center of the inner-most ring of the Hydra, the whole station whirled around him, though Theo couldn't see or sense its motion. With no centripetal force to create gravity, only their boots prevented him and everyone else from free-floating inside the airlock.

Depressurization took nearly a minute. The sound of rushing air faded to nothing as the vacuum wrapped Theo in a cocoon of silence broken only by the sound of his own breath and the whir of his suit's life support system. When the depressurization was complete, a light turned green and the airlock door dilated. Thirty meters of umbilical spooled out in a direction that looked so much like down that Theo's stomach rolled inside him.

At the end of the umbilical, brilliant floods lit a dull gray circle of exchange ship hull. Because they lacked a crew, exchange ships didn't need airlocks. They offloaded their cargo through massive, inward-folding cargo doors. With the exchange dock harvested to construct the *Hydra* and repair the *Chimera*, cutting a hole into *Exchange Four* was the only expedient way inside.

Theo's boots held him steady as his stomach whirled. He felt like he should be tumbling forward, down, but there was no down here, no up, no direction at all. Theo's head spun. He swallowed the saliva pooling in his mouth.

Selena's voice sounded over his com. "If you've got to puke, just let loose. The vac in your suit will take care of it."

"I don't have to—"

A stream of liquid forced its way out of Theo's mouth. Before the vomit could hit his faceplate, an intense suction pulled it down a tube near his chin.

"You'll feel better in a minute," Selena said, voice amused. "Drink some water from your reservoir. It comes from the same tube as the vac."

Theo couldn't risk a reply.

The welders approached the hull. The technicians and survey team waited near the airlock, unaware of the interlopers, focused on the work at hand. Theo's heart hammered in his chest. Projected by the helmet, a readout above his line of sight registered his heart rate at a hundred-fifteen beats a minute. A separate readout displayed a list of numbers, most of them indecipherable except for the temperature, -60 degrees Celsius. Selena floated next to him. Tethered to the umbilical by a single hand, gravity boots disengaged, she seemed more comfortable in zero gravity than anyone, including the welders.

Who was she? Why were regulators after her? Was she dangerous? He found the girl's penchant for sudden violence frightening, but she'd stood up to Marcus. That took some doing. In a way she reminded him of Marcus, but didn't have the same coldness, the same calculated quality to every word and action.

Showers of sparks floated around the welders as their cutters began to melt through the wall of the exchange ship. Nervous anticipation sped Theo's breath, whisked away by the respirator before it could transform into moisture and fog his faceplate. Marcus looked at Theo, his expression unreadable. What would they discover inside *Exchange Four*? Stacks of supplies, the fulfillment of the last list sent over fifteen years ago, or something else entirely?

Selena pushed off of the wall with her feet and floated closer to the welders. Catching herself on what Theo perceived as the ceiling, she slowed and stopped her momentum, as graceful as an acrobat. She flipped her body and locked her boots to the ceiling— now her floor. Theo clenched his teeth as his stomach did a barrel roll.

"Better view from here. Come on up," Selena called over the com.

"No, thanks," he said. "I'm fine." His hands gripped a tie-down on the wall like he intended to rip it loose.

The welders worked as a team. Two of them guided white-hot cutting tips in a series of controlled circles, each pass burning deeper into the hull. Lips of red-hot melted metal rose along the sides of the circles like glowing scars. Two other welders stood behind those making the cut, projecting a grid of lines over the workspace, welding tools strapped to their backs.

"They're cutting an exploratory hole first. Once they survey the interior, they'll open the main doors from the inside and pull out the contents with tugs. At least, that's what I'd do," Selena said.

The welding blades completed another circuit.

"Less than a centimeter to go—one more pass should do the trick."

Theo held his breath. He imagined corridors like the caves beneath the Order compound that led to massive warehouse-like rooms. Cores as large as houses, sacks of grain, circuitry and magnets—everything the colony had gone without since before Theo was born. All the colony's problems solved, the fisheries restored, The Mandate repealed ….

The cutting blades penetrated the exchange ship. One of the welders began to struggle with his cutter. A round chunk cut free from the hull warped outward. Air began to vent from *inside* the ship, sucked out by the vacuum of the umbilical. Then the chunk of hull tore free like a dislodged food can lid. It caught the nearest welder in the chest, smashing his cutting tool. The still-ignited tip sprouted a plume of fire.

Fed by the oxygen rushing out of *Exchange Four*, the cutter's flame burned hot and bright. Chunks of molten metal sprayed the welders, pushed by the blast of air escaping from the exchange ship. They pelted the welders, burning holes through their pressure suits. Pumping out flame retardant chemicals and emergency sealers, the welders spiraled away from the hole, coated in yellow-green foam.

"Shit!" Theo yelled, his vision filled with shades of orange and oily smoke.

"The ship was pressurized!" Selena shouted over his com. "Holy hell, this isn't good."

The welder who'd taken the brunt of the door's explosion squirmed and flailed, the emergency sealer inadequate for re-pressurizing his shredded suit. Globules of foam spun in the smoke and chaos. Shouts and commands and groans and cries of pain came over the com, a cacophony of sound that froze Theo in place, confused and afraid.

Behind him, the survey team clustered by the airlock, waiting for it to cycle open. Misshapen from the foam coating his pressure suit, the injured welder writhed, legs and arms jerking, left behind by the others. He'd die if no one helped him. Theo began to trudge forward, one leg at a time.

Marcus' voice sounded over the com. "Get back here, Theo!"

"I've got to help him. He's going to die."

"So are you if you don't get away from those flames."

"I don't care. He needs my help."

"You're more important than him," Marcus said. "He's

248

nothing but a welder."

Theo ignored Marcus, plunging headfirst into the flames, heat soaking through the protective layers of his suit. He wasn't going to leave the welder behind, no matter what Marcus said.

Above him, Selena detached from the ceiling and dove, catching hold of Theo's wrist. At first he thought she was pulling him away, but she drew beside him, head down, shoving forward into the heat and the smoke.

CHAPTER THIRTY-NINE

"Take his legs, keep him steady," Selena said. Theo grasped the welder's ankles, Selena his wrists, and they moved his weightless body. Bits of debris and flame retardant stuck to their suits as they cut through the smoke, heading for the airlock. The pressure began to equalize between the exchange ship and the umbilical. The flames diminished, no longer fueled by rushing oxygen.

"Is he still alive?" Theo asked.

"Hard to tell," Selena said. "He's in bad shape, that's for sure."

A crack ran in a vertical line across the welder's faceplate. Coated with green foam, Theo couldn't tell if the man's eyes were open. Theo looked over his shoulder to where the beams of the flood lights poured into the hole cut in *Exchange Four*. The darkness on the other side devoured the light, the floods intensity powerless against that much black. An empty nothing—no supplies, no food, a desolation of empty space. Adrenaline from the accident laced his bitter disappointment.

"The ship is empty," he said over the com.

"Maybe," Selena replied.

"It is. I saw inside."

"We won't know for sure until we check."

Did she mean her and Theo or a survey team?

They neared the huddled technicians and welders waiting for the airlock to cycle open. Marcus detached from the group and came to meet them. "Two of the other welders have second-degree burns," Marcus said. "Is this one alive?"

"I don't know," Theo replied.

"I'll take him from here."

"You will?" Theo asked, surprised.

"We're evacuating. I've taken control of the situation. Once we get the injured out of the umbilical the exploration of the exchange ship can move forward." Marcus sounded serene, the intensity that had dominated his every word and action since the exchange ship's arrival gone. Why? What had changed?

"It's empty," Theo said, the words sending cold shivers down his spine. "That's what you wanted to find, isn't it?"

Marcus reached for the injured welder. "We need to get him out of here. He likely won't survive, but we have to try."

"You said that his life didn't matter," Theo said.

"All lives matter," Marcus replied. "Some more than others."

Theo stared at Marcus, wishing that he didn't have a suit on, that he could punch him right in his smug, selfish face. "Like yours?" he said, beyond angry.

"We're both far more valuable to the colony than a welder. That's a simple fact, Theo."

"Why did you want the ship to be empty?" Theo asked.

Marcus tapped the side of his helmet with his gloved pointer finger. "You'll have to figure that out for yourself."

The airlock cycled open. Marcus turned his back on Theo, directing technicians to secure the injured welder and move him into the airlock.

"Hang tight, Theo," Marcus said as the airlock closed. "I'll send someone back for you once the airlock cycles."

"Sure," Theo said. "Once you're safe on the other side."

Theo looked for Selena and found she'd slipped away and now floated near the gaping hole cut in the side of the *Exchange Four*. The edges glowed with heat, but the fire had at last gone out. The worst appeared to be over.

"Selena?" he said over the com.

She didn't answer.

"Hello?"

Nothing.

A loud tone preceded a new, familiar voice. "Cadet Puck?"

"Yes?"

"This is Chief Moorland."

Theo blinked, picturing the Chief in her trim white uniform. "Ma'am!" he said, "Sorry, I didn't recognize—"

"Save it. Listen to me carefully. Cadet Locke informs me that you're in the umbilical waiting for your turn through the airlock and that you're in the company of Selena Samuelson. Is that correct?"

Theo's gaze locked on Selena. Short, brave, intimidating. Marcus thought she was from the rim. Whoever she was, it seemed the Regulatory wanted her badly, all the way up to the Chief herself.

"Theo?"

"Yes, ma'am, I'm here."

"With Selena?"

"Yes—what did she do? Why do you—"

"Go make her speak to me. She's locked me out of her com."

"I don't know if I can make—"

"Tell her that if she ever wants to see Liam again she'd better."

"Liam?"

"Stop wasting time. Go tell her *now*."

"Okay. I'm on my way." Theo clunked to the opening of the exchange ship. The immensity of the space on the other side of the hole seemed to suck at him. Space and more space—he'd never imagined just how large an exchange ship was.

"Something's in there," Selena said, pointing. Hidden in layers of shadow, he could make out several indistinct shapes. Maybe squares or rectangles.

"I can't see them clearly, even with image enhancement. We'll have to go in," Selena said.

"Go in?"

Selena faced him. "I want to see for myself."

"Listen, Moorland contacted me. She wants to talk to you."

"Moorland?"

"She's the Chief of the Regulatory."

"I know who she is."

"She's my commanding officer. My boss. I was okay with helping you avoid those regulator goons, but if she wants to talk to you, you'd probably better do it."

"I 'probably better'?"

"She said that if you wanted to see someone named Liam again, you need to talk to her."

Selena's lips tightened. "She did, huh? Well you can tell her something for me. Tell her she can go screw herself. I don't respond to threats."

"I'm not going to tell her that," Theo said. "Who's Liam anyway? Your boyfriend?"

Selena looked at him like he was stinky fish slime she'd just cleaned from the bottom of her boot.

"Why does Moorland want you?" Theo asked. "What did you do?"

"That's the thing. I didn't do *anything*. But she thinks I did. And she thinks that I can do it again. But I can't."

"What?"

Selena shook her head. "It doesn't matter."

What should he do if she wouldn't talk to Moorland? "Is Liam your dad?" he asked.

He knew from her reaction he'd guessed right. "Maybe you're not completely brain dead."

"Thanks." It was the sort of thing Marcus would say, except from Selena, it had a touch of humor beneath the words. Instead of cutting him, it felt sort of good. He gave her the best smile he could manufacture. She smiled back.

"I'm going in *Exchange Four*," Selena said. "Want to come?"

"What?"

"Let's go see what's in those boxes."

"Moorland said—"

"I don't care what Moorland said. If you want to stay here, be my guest. I'll go by myself."

Moorland's exasperated voice filled his helmet. "Theo? Did you tell her what I said?"

"Yes."

"And?"

"She doesn't want to talk to you. She said she's going into the exchange ship."

"Absolutely not!"

Pulse racing, Moorland's voice shouting in his ear, Selena beckoned to him.

Selena's voice broke in over Moorland's, calm and friendly. "You coming, Theo?"

* * *

Moorland slammed her fist against her console in frustration. The stupidity of the young plagued her like an incurable disease. First Selena and now Cadet Puck—the two of them together, traipsing off into the exchange ship. What the hell did they think they were doing?

"The rapid response team is en route, ma'am. Two teams of Regulators, all in powered pressure suits. ETA two minutes. The injured welders are on their way to the medical bay."

"Excellent. Any luck hacking Selena's com?"

"No, ma'am. She's locked it down to local channels only."

"And Cadet Puck?"

"I've got everything but his local audio, including the video feed from his helmet."

"Good. If they're going to act like imbeciles, at least we can get a few shots of the inside of *Exchange Four*. Put it on the wallscreen."

"Done."

Monochrome imagery showed two beams of light crisscrossing. Feet plodded over the hull, camera jerking, as Theo turned his head one way or another, taking in the vast interior of the ship.

"Empty," Moorland said.

"Not quite. Look there."

"Cargo containers?"

"Exactly."

The imagery changed into a whirl of movement. Moorland's mouth snapped shut as rapid movement blurred the feed before leveling out, cargo containers once more distinct. Three of them, fixed to the interior wall of the ship, the nearest open on one end.

"There!" Moorland said. "Zoom in. Is that …"

"Stephen help us," Blake said, a tremble in her voice.

"Lock it down," Moorland shouted. "Nobody goes in or out of that airlock. I want everyone who's exited the umbilical quarantined."

"Yes, ma'am."

Moorland held her console with both hands, steadying herself as the imagery poured in from Theo's helmet. The feed tightened in on the interior of the nearest cargo container and the horrors inside. Moorland took a deep breath and for the first time in since her childhood, began to pray.

CHAPTER FORTY

Two beams of light swept the interior of *Exchange Four*. Theo walked beside Selena, light moving when he turned his head, crisscrossing Selena's as they took in the vast emptiness surrounding them. He felt as if they were alone in the center of the deepest cave ever discovered, a pair of tiny lights lost in crushing darkness.

"That way," Selena said. Theo nodded, the vertigo he felt when seeing Selena stand upside down in the umbilical intensified by the epic scale of the exchange ship's innards. No down nor up, nothing but an impossibly large cylinder of space, hundreds of meters in length, all of it empty. But not entirely—at the far end of the ship, his light fell on three lonely cargo containers looming in the murk.

"We've got to get closer," Selena said, "and it's a long walk in grav boots."

"Well the sooner we start …"

"I've got a better way." She held up her wrists, displaying the polished silver cuffs.

Theo flinched.

"Calm down—I'm not going to shoot you with them."

Theo eyed the cuffs, nervous. "What then?"

"I'll show you." Selena wrapped an arm round his midsection like a sideways hug. "Hang on tight!"

"What? I don't understand—"

Somehow, quick as a cat, she kicked his feet out from under him. They spiraled into the black. He managed to keep the scream and the vomit inside. The ship spun as they toppled out of a somersault and stabilized into a flight line, rushing at the cargo containers.

Selena's face registered a mix of concentration and happiness, one arm tight around his waist, the other aimed toward the onrushing cargo containers. A burst of thrust jetted from her extended arm. Their course changed, the cuffs creating directional force like the thrusters of a ship.

"Hang on," Selena said. Their momentum shifted, angling down to the cargo containers. Whatever they contained, it wouldn't be enough to resupply the colony. Nowhere close. The *Chimera* would still need a crew. And despite what Selena had said about not being a cadet, Theo had a sneaking suspicion she'd make the roster.

Selena fired a short burst from the cuff, slowing them to no faster than a walk.

"That was fun," Selena said. Not the word Theo would choose, but he nodded, happy to be alive. She grinned at him from behind her faceplate, stern features transformed. She was pretty. Not like Meghan—Selena was tougher looking, sharper featured—but pretty. He realized how much of his body was pressed against hers. As if coming to the same conclusion, Selena pushed him away. They floated down, down, nearer and nearer the cargo containers.

Theo's light caught something floating in the zero gravity. "What was that?""

"What was what?"

"I saw something."

"Where?"

Theo pointed. "Over there. Look, there's another one. See?" Theo tracked the free-floating object with his helmet light.

"Looks like something broke free of the containers. Let's check it out."

They skimmed nearer, a few meters from the ship's hull, momentum bringing them close enough to re-engage their gravity boots. His feet connected to the deck. He scanned the space around him, locating several more pieces of debris. Something about their shape bothered him. His light creased the darkness, traced a path across ship hull, settled on the nearest object.

"Theo!" He snapped his eyes back to Selena. In the corridor, escaping from the Regulators, she'd seemed more annoyed than afraid. Now her face was stricken with dread. The floating object turned toward them. A naked human body. Face shrunken as if from age, mouth a puckered, asterisk-shaped hole.

Behind the body the cargo container's door hung ajar. Inside more naked bodies twirled, each as hideous and deformed as the first. Bodies strapped against the walls of the cargo container, baled together with rope. They looked like the stick figures Liddy drew. Empty eye sockets stared out at them. Hundreds of them. All dead. All subject to the awful effects of traveling through Fractal Space without the protection of hydrostasis.

A hand latched around his wrist. He screamed. The hand tightened, pulling him close. A face peered into his. Not a dead face, but one surrounded by brown hair. The girl's mouth moved but he couldn't hear the words. Couldn't hear anything except the buzzing in his ears, the buzzing that came from the very core of him.

* * *

"Oh my god," Moorland said. She and Duty Officer Blake stared with open mouths at the images relayed from Theo's helmet camera. Staring eye sockets, wasted bodies, warped and wasted by exposure to Fractal Space.

"Ma'am?" Blake asked.

"This doesn't leave command," Moorland said. "Nobody can see this until I'm prepared to make a statement."

Moorland shook her head, weariness weighing heavy against her shoulders, pressing her down into the deck. It took all of her resolve not to slump against the wall. She couldn't let her staff see her show any signs of weakness. They needed her now more than ever. She'd driven the rebuild project forward, organized a fleet of repair ships, fought and scratched with the Economic Office, and formulated the Selection process to find a crew for the *Chimera*. She'd worked the last seven years of her life to try and protect the colony. To preserve hope. To give them all a fighting chance to reach Earth.

But in the numerous scenarios she'd considered, in all the high level conversations among the Stephen's Point elite, she'd never considered that Earth might be so bad off they'd risk terrible deaths aboard a pressurized exchange ship. Horrible, twisted faces. What had compelled them to try something so dangerous? So impossible?

"We've got a problem, ma'am!"

The near panic in Blake's voice yanked her back to full alertness. Moorland scanned the feed on the wallscreen, expecting to see some new horror. Theo and Selena eviscerated by an alien lifeform. The *Hydra* venting oxygen into space. Any implausible disaster now seemed not just possible but inevitable.

"We're not the only ones with access to the stream," Blake said. "It's going ship wide, stream to stream."

"Shut down all communication with Stephen's Point!" Moorland shouted.

The miserable expression on Blake's face told her everything she needed to know. "It's already hit the nets," Blake whispered. "It's grainy, but not *that* grainy."

Moorland's jaw tightened. She stood upright, surveying Blake and the rest of the personnel in command. Good officers. Loyal officers. They would follow her. They would do what had to be done.

"We're going to full quarantine," Moorland said.

Blake paused, hands poised over her workstation.

"You heard me. Full quarantine. We need complete autonomy." *How long until the riots start? How long until different factions go to war?* The colony stood at the edge of a great precipice. Only the promise of the rebuild project prevented them from tumbling over its edge.

"What about the scheduled shuttle from Stephen's Point?" Blake asked. "It's already assumed overtake trajectory."

"Send it back," Moorland said.

Blake keyed the com and shared a short exchange with the shuttle while Moorland paced, mind pulled in fifteen directions at once.

"Ma'am?" Blake called, "The shuttle pilot said that one of their passengers wants to speak to you."

"Do we have weapons lock?" Moorland asked.

"Yes, ma'am."

"Fire a warning shot."

"Ma'am? The passenger who wants to speak to you—it's Duncan."

In the midst of the tension of command, waiting for the world she'd worked her entire life to protect to start grinding itself to pieces, Moorland tracked the blue chevron representing the inbound shuttle as it marched across a tactical display, preparing to overtake the *Hydra*.

Duncan. Here. Now. She took a breath, let it back out.

Nothing would undo the effects of the live feed from *Exchange Four*. She couldn't turn back the tide of fear and desperation about to sweep the colony. But she could still complete her mission. She could still send the *Chimera* and her crew into the void.

"Give them clearance," Moorland said.

Despite her suspicion that the colony would soon descend into anarchy, despite the monstrous dead aboard *Exchange Four*, she still held hope. To have a chance at saving those who survived the brutal days ahead, she'd need all the allies she could get.

More than anything, she would need to wake the *Chimera*.

And to wake her, she would need the girl.

CHAPTER FORTY-ONE

The boy's eyes were just black holes in a skull-like face. Pale skin stretched over his thin bones, his head as bald as an old man's.

Not much older than Liddy, the boy's body twisted in slow motion, completing a macabre pirouette in the zero gravity of Exchange Four. More bodies floated out of the cargo containers strapped to the deck of the cavernous exchange ship, knocked loose by the coupling with the Hydra and the explosion caused by the welding torches used to breach her hull. All the bodies were bald—children, men and women. Bald, deformed, and dead. Except for one.

"A heartbeat," Theo whispered. He could hear it, a faint but steady thumping, coming from somewhere nearby.

He clunked toward the cargo container in his gravity boots. Someone had survived. His pale beam of light cut across jumbles of the dead doing slow cartwheels and backflips, contorted in ways that would be impossible in normal gravity. Some were naked. Some were half-undressed, as if they'd started stripping down for a shower.

Inside the container, straps held even more bodies in place—tied against the walls of the shipping containers. Clothing of all shapes and sizes drifted past. Theo reached out and caught a pink t-shirt with the face of a cat on the front. He kept moving—he could hear the heartbeat clearly now. Whoever it was coming from must be at the very back of the cargo container.

Someone called his name, but he ignored them—he needed to find the heartbeat, to rescue whoever had survived an unprotected trip through fractal space. A hand tugged at his shoulder. He shrugged it off and kept pushing forward. The insistent voice crackled beneath a layer of static inside his helmet. The voice shouted at him. He turned off the com. How could he find the heartbeat with all that yelling distracting him?

His light illuminated the deep shadow of the cargo container's interior. Bodies floated all around him, lifeless fingers reaching for a final connection, a final touch ...

The container was deeper than it appeared from the outside. It was as if he'd entered a long, narrow tunnel. A tunnel without an end. The dead streamed past, all of their faces watching, empty eyes asking questions he could not answer.

A wall rose before him, the back of the container reached at last. He still heard the heartbeat, even louder now, thrumming at a frantic pace. His eyes traveled up the wall. Words were scrawled across it, but he couldn't make them out.

Something tapped his helmet. He held himself motionless, scream swallowed before it could reach his lips. The something tapped his helmet again. Hands gripped it on both sides, turned his head to look at a face. Not a dead face, one hidden behind a faceplate. A dark-haired girl, luminous brown eyes filled with sorrow. Her lips formed words he could not hear but understood nonetheless.

Dead. All Dead. We have to get out of here. Nothing we can do. Have to go. Have to go.

"No," Theo said. "No!"

He had to find the heartbeat. He had to save whoever was still alive in the cargo container. He pulled away, swatting at a pair of pants that drifted their way into his face, shoving, flailing—

His boots broke their magnetic lock. He careened forward, pitching head-over-heels like one of the bodies. He thunked into the ceiling. There, inches from his face, he could read part of a word scrawled in large, sloppy, black letters:

HEL

Help? Hell? Whoever had written the words stopped before they'd finished. Or hadn't been able to finish.

Hands tugged at him, wrapping tight around his ankles. They guided him down and reconnected his feet to the cargo container. The hands forced him to look once more at the face of the girl behind the faceplate. Selena.

Her mouth moved. *They're all gone...dead....*

Theo shuddered, grimacing, lost somewhere between a scream of rage and laughter.

"I can hear a heartbeat!" he shouted into the muting of the glass. "I can hear a heartbeat ...." His voice trailed off as the obvious truth rose to his consciousness: the heartbeat was his own. Slumping against the wall of the cargo container, he squeezed his eyes shut.

He felt himself being pulled backward. Selena draped his weightless body against her shoulder. Horrors floated past them. Dozens of dead men, women and children. Selena extended her arms, aiming the aerocuffs.

They flew away into the silent black.

CHAPTER FORTY-TWO

Selena guided Theo through the ragged hole cut in the side of Exchange Four and into the umbilical connecting them to the Hydra. Rescue workers led them to the airlock. The chemical scent of emergency sealant hung in the air. Free of her helmet, Selena took shallow breaths until the airlock opened to the utility room on the other side.

Theo stumbled out and slumped on a bench. He stared at the ceiling, arms wrapped over his chest. Back in standard gravity, Selena's muscles began to cramp. She kept moving, stripping off her pressure suit, peeling back each fibrous layer, shedding it like old skin. Her clothing clung to her. Hair stuck to her neck in sweaty strands. She wanted to scrub herself clean, then fall into deep, forgetful sleep.

Theo hadn't moved.

"Come on, Theo. Pull yourself together. We're going to be in deep shit with Moorland. We need to be ready for it."

He didn't acknowledge her.

"You've got to get out of that suit."

Silence.

She hobbled to his side. Her legs ached. A dull thumping beat away between her temples. "On second thought, better let me help," she said. Theo didn't resist as her fingers found the release points of his suit. She peeled back layers, pulling them from his motionless limbs. Theo barely looked at her. His eyes stared out from deep eye sockets, made darker by the grime coating his face. She pulled him to his feet and the suit fell around his ankles, revealing the uniformed boy beneath. Thin veins ran through his arms, tight against wiry sinews of muscle.

"No trouble hitting a vein when they prick you," she said. He ignored her attempt at a joke.

"You okay?" she asked, suddenly worried he'd suffered some

hidden injury; internal bleeding or a concussion.

She snapped her fingers in front of his face. "Theo?"

Nothing.

"We're leaving," she said, moving for the door, hoping he would follow. He didn't. Sighing with frustration, Selena charged back, grabbed Theo by the wrist, and dragged him into the airlock.

Dressed in hazard suits, a scrub team met them on the other side. Selena didn't have the energy to resist as they forcibly stripped her down and shoved her into a decontamination chamber. Sonic waves cascaded over her body, making her teeth hum, her inner ears trill. Chemical foam followed. Thick but not unpleasant, more sonic waves washed it free before pulsing streams of water beat against her skin.

Seconds later it was over. Hot air buffeted her body, drying her in seconds.

Naked and embarrassed, Selena covered herself as best she could until a pair of gloved hands shoved a clean set of clothes at her. She pulled on the soft flight suit, cheeks burning, wondering how much the scrub team had seen. She supposed it couldn't be helped, not after being exposed to *Exchange Four*. Better safe than sorry.

Where had they taken Theo? What would happen to him? To her?

The door opened and Chief Moorland stepped through, accompanied by a regulator. Moorland glared at Selena, her brow creased in a determined line. "Can you walk?" Moorland asked.

"Yes."

"Good. Follow me."

CHAPTER FORTY-THREE

Theo sat on the edge of his assigned bed, listening to the faint thump-thump of his heart. Other than singed eyebrows, he'd escaped all injury. All injuries that could be seen with the eyes, tested and measured by machines. Fit for full duty. That's what Doctor Cholewa had marked on Theo's report.

He could leave any time he liked. So why was he just sitting here? What was he waiting for?

The young nurse with curly dark hair popped her head into the room. "You have a visitor," she said with a smile.

She withdrew and Marcus entered the room. He'd changed into a clean uniform and no longer smelled like stale sweat. "Theo," he said.

"Marcus."

"Excellent work in the umbilical. I mean that."

Theo tried to detect Marcus' leader-persona rhetoric in the words, but as far as he could tell, Marcus was being genuine.

"You left that welder to die," Theo said. Not an accusation but a statement of fact.

Marcus shrugged. "I left because it was the most prudent thing to do in the circumstances. There were too many unknowns. It wasn't worth risking all our lives to save his."

"But I did save him," Theo said. "Selena and I saved him."

"Do you want me to congratulate you again?"

Theo looked down at his hands, folded in his lap. He closed his eyes. Saw the empty faces, empty eye sockets. The macabre ballet of the dead in slow motion arabesques. *Don't think about it.* Theo opened his eyes and Marcus came back into focus. There was something strange about the way Marcus was standing, his posture, his slumped shoulders. He looked … defeated? Why? What had Moorland said to him?

"What's wrong with you?" Theo asked. "Did Moorland

bounce you out of the program for being a coward?"

That got a reaction. Marcus moved fast, closing on Theo. He expected a reenactment of their brief fight in the elevator. He was ready. He wanted it. Welcomed it. Maybe it would distract him from the screams of a hundred silenced mouths. He leaned forward, ready to launch himself at Marcus, to meet the attack head-on.

The attack never came.

Marcus stopped beside the bed, his eyes roving around the room, as if counting every square in the patterned ceiling, doing some internal algebra, the purpose of which Theo could not guess. "I came here to tell you something," Marcus said, his voice a low, harsh whisper.

"Yeah?" Theo said. "Are you going to threaten me? You're really good at it."

Marcus eyes wouldn't stop moving, flicking from thing to thing, sometimes alighting on Theo's face for a microsecond before dancing on. "No," Marcus said. "I'm not going to threaten you. I don't need to anymore. We're linked together, me and you. I can't explain it, but it's true. I've always felt it. All the way back to the cave. That's the real reason I didn't kill you, Theo."

"We're not linked," Theo said. "We're nothing alike."

"Maybe that's the point," Marcus said. "We're two halves of the same thing. We both have a weakness in us."

Theo'd never heard Marcus talk about himself like this before. What weakness could Marcus possibly have? Ruthless, strong, malevolent. Those were the words that came to mind when Theo thought of Marcus. Not weak. Never weak.

Then, in a flash, he saw it. The loss of control in the elevator. The hatred in Marcus' eyes. Not for Theo but for the dead man in the cave.

"What did he do to you?" Theo asked.

Marcus shook his head. Swallowed. At long last his eyes settled, his face no longer agitated. His eyes met Theo's. "Everything," he said. "He did everything to me."

Theo looked away, imagining what everything had to include. Pain. Humiliation. Degradation. "I'm sorry," he said.

Marcus stood motionless, a person dispossessed of emotion. He stared into the middle distance. "I'm not sorry. He made me who I am. And I killed him for it. I don't regret it. I'd do it again.

Right now if I had to. I'm never going back to Stephen's Point. I don't care about those people. I never have." Marcus looked at Theo as if waiting for reaction. "I wasn't about to leave him behind so that he could do to someone else what he did to me."

"Some people deserve to die," Theo said, trying the words out for himself. Trying to imagine the hatred behind them. He decided he couldn't.

"This is the first and last time we're going to talk about this," Marcus said.

"Okay," Theo agreed. He looked at Marcus as if for the first time. Not as a threat, but as someone capable of being hurt, being wounded. Dangerous and violent, but for a reason. A reason that Theo knew he would never fully understand. That he was incapable of understanding, even if he tried.

Marcus seemed to become himself once more, broken out his fugue state. "The girl's going to be a problem," he said.

It took Theo a moment to realize what girl Marcus meant. "What makes you say that?"

"She's a loner. She didn't train with us. I don't like her."

"Selena's not so bad," Theo said.

Marcus frowned. "We'll see."

Theo slipped off the edge of the bed and stood beside Marcus.

"We don't need her," Marcus said. "She's just going to get in the way."

Theo nodded in false agreement.

"We need to stick together. I told you my secret so that you'd know that I trust you. Do you trust me?"

The question hung in the air, warring against Theo's better judgement. "I don't know," Theo said.

"You're going to have to," Marcus said. "Because from here on out, we're equals. The colony needs your navigation test scores. They need my leadership. Together we're going to save them."

"I thought you said you didn't care about the colony," Theo said.

Marcus smirked. "I don't. But I want to see Earth. If we can save the colony in the process, so much the better. Now come on— all the other cadets are waiting for you. They want to know what happened in Exchange Four and it's your story to tell. You are the Second Stephen, after all."

He recalled a passage from Ashley's journal, and spoke it

aloud:

"'When we change shifts, Stephen holds the Everything himself for a moment. Sometimes... he groans inside the Sphere, like a man carrying the world on his shoulders. And maybe he is. Our very own Atlas.'"

Again, images from inside the exchange ship filled his mind. The dead child, so much like Liddy. He rubbed his eyes to push the horror away, concentrating on the future. On Earth. On the role he might—would—get to play. "I need to talk to Selena."

"No. You don't. She's not important."

Marcus was wrong. Theo knew it. Something about Selena nagged away at him. The way she held herself. The way she maneuvered in the umbilical and on the Exchange Ship. Her fierceness. The strangeness of the Hydra made Theo feel out of place, but Selena moved as if she'd been born there.

And her last name was Samuelson.

The journal. The girl. The ship.

Something clicked. Selena had to be a relative of Ashley's. A descendant of the original flight crew. He hid his excitement. Marcus didn't need to know. Not yet. Maybe never.

"You can't afford to get distracted by some rimmer girl. You're going to stay focused on waking the *Chimera*. Your hacking skills are the reason I helped you make it through the Selection in the first place."

"Yeah, you were a huge help," Theo said, not hiding his sarcasm. "Like you said. We're equals now. I'll do my part and you'll do yours."

Marcus didn't react, his eyes calm. "Of course, Theo. We're partners. And together, we're going to save the colony."

CHAPTER FORTY-FOUR

Moorland avoided eye contact with Selena as they rode a lift to the inner ring. Selena studied the reflection of the older woman's face in the polished surface of the wall. Calm, cool blue eyes. Silver-blond hair pushed behind her ears, held in place by her head band. An unnatural stiffness in her posture. Wherever Moorland was taking her, she wasn't looking forward to it any more than Selena.

The brisk walk down the corridor left Selena breathless. She'd spent the last cycle running, fighting, fearing. Moorland slowed, ushering her into a small room lined with wallscreens. A table ringed with chairs filled the center.

"Let the record show that Chief Moorland entered at thirteen-hundred hours, thirty-five minutes, accompanied by the detainee, Selena Samuelson." The formality with which Moorland spoke had a greater impact on Selena than the term "detainee."

A female voice sounded from above: "Acknowledged."

"We will now begin the official inquiry into the events leading up to the assault on Regulator Thompson."

Regulator Thompson. She'd fired the aerocuffs into the man's face. Well, what should she have done? Let herself be sent down to the colony? Selena waited for Moorland to speak, fingers lacing and unlacing under the table, eyes downcast.

The older woman read from a handscreen, eyes scanning text. When she looked up, her face was devoid of its usual friendliness. The sharp creases near her eyes suggested intense anger held in check by decades of experience being in command.

"Let's get down to it," Moorland said, voice flat. "Unlike that mockery of a hearing you participated in before you fled the custody of the Regulatory, this proceeding carries the full authority of The Mandate. Do you understand me?"

Selena nodded.

"Please speak your answer for the record."

"Yes, I understand."

"You stand accused, in order of increasing severity, of theft, criminal assault, attempted manslaughter, and espionage. Possible sentences range from fines for theft to the death penalty for espionage."

Selena's body had become an ashen corpse. She spoke in a faint whisper: "I understand."

She fought the impulse to cover her face and instead curled her toes inside her boots and chewed the inside of her mouth until she tasted blood.

"Do you have anything to say?" Moorland asked her.

"No."

"No explanation for your actions?"

"You know why I did what I did." Selena spoke the words without defiance. Moorland did know. Or at least she should.

Moorland sighed. "How am I supposed to help you when you won't let me? I'm the only thing standing between you and the Regulatory. Thompson has two fractured ribs, a punctured lung, and a torn retina. The doctor managed to stop the internal hemorrhaging, but you could have killed him."

"What was I supposed to do? The ombudsman and his puppet arbiter were sending me down to Stephen's Point!"

"You lied, Selena. An obvious lie at that. I gave you every opportunity to tell me the truth." Moorland leaned over the white surface of the conference table, a mix of sadness and disappointment in her eyes. "Why didn't you trust me?"

Selena shifted in her chair. "I don't know."

The creases around Moorland's eyes tightened. "You don't know?"

Selena shrugged, her face as hard and expressionless as a deck plate.

"If you'd stopped to think for even a minute! Instead, you trusted that ... that ... fatuous, lying son-of-a-bitch! And I want to know why. Why didn't you listen to me? Why didn't you let me help you? What did you think you were going to do, anyway? Commandeer a welder? Break your dad out of the hospital?"

Selena stared into her lap. *Yes. Exactly.* How stupid that plan seemed now.

"Look at me!" Moorland shouted.

Selena reluctantly raised her head and stared down the center of the table, keeping Moorland in her peripheral vision.

Moorland stood and pointed at Selena, her face red, voice wavering with rage. "Cut the sullen, wounded teenager act! I've had about as much of that as I can take. Do you realize what's going on right now? Do you have any clue? I've got an exchange ship full of dead bodies attached to the *Hydra*. The colony is falling apart as we speak. They're rioting. Someone transmitted a live feed from inside *Exchange Four* down to Stephen's Point before I could stop them. The colonists are burning the valley, looting food supplies …"

Selena swallowed and risked a shocked glance at Moorland's flushed face. Video from *Exchange Four* had made it off the Hydra? The bodies. The pure horror of it. She could only imagine what that would do to people already pushed to the edge by fear.

"I've got three dozen cadets to train for a rescue mission to Earth—an Earth where something went so wrong that those poor wretches in *Exchange Four* made a suicide jump into fractal space in an unprotected ship. And that's assuming they went willingly."

Moorland glowered, hand shaking as she pointed at Selena's chest. "And in the middle of that, I've got you, Selena Samuelson. Careening through my station using stolen aerocuffs, trashing development labs, hunting for a ship to steal like some bloody, half-crazed pirate! You almost killed an innocent man because of your stupid, selfish loyalty to your drunkard father!"

Selena buried her face in her arms. It was true. All of it. She'd done everything she could to try and help Liam. And in doing so, she'd hurt so many.

"You're loyal," Moorland said, voice quiet. "Unfortunate that you have such a broken man as a father, but it's an honorable trait nonetheless." Selena looked up. Moorland's eyes flickered—a rare moment of vulnerability. "You're tough, loyal, and very, very stupid," she said. "You can't let blind loyalty destroy everything and everyone around you."

Moorland retook her seat. "I've arrested the ombudsman. He's moldering in a cell, probably plotting and planning how he can take over the *Hydra*."

"Arrested?" Selena asked.

"Yes. He's lucky I didn't have him put down. In fact, the only reason I didn't is because we need all the bargaining chips we can get. He's worth something to someone down on Stephen's Point. He's got influence, I can't deny that." Moorland sighed. "Selena, you've got a decision to make. You have to choose to trust someone. I've done everything in my power to give you an opportunity to make something of yourself. Maybe you can't or won't trust me, but you have to trust someone. Eventually. None of us can make it alone."

"I do ... I do trust you. But I wanted Dad to be safe ..." Her voice cracked, and tears welled up in her eyes. "You know about him—you said it yourself. He's a drunk ... but he's the only thing ..." She lost control. Wrapping her face in the crooks of both of her arms, she sobbed her sorrow and anger into the already damp cloth of her shirt.

When she was done, Moorland was standing beside her, face level with her own, eyes clear and blue, her mouth a frown that was both sad and fierce at the same time. She handed Selena a white handkerchief, a gesture so simple and kind that Selena very nearly burst into tears again.

"Listen to me. I know more about you than anyone except your father. I know about what happened to your mother. I know about your spider. I know you're a great pilot and a terrible liar. Most important of all, I know that somehow you managed to form a connection with the *Chimera*. And that's why, right now, in the midst of the biggest crisis the colony has ever faced, I'm sitting here talking to you. Do you understand what I'm saying?"

"What do you mean a connection?"

"Whatever you want to call it—you're the first person I've seen the *Chimera* respond to. The only one in all the years we've worked to rebuild her. We need you, Selena. The colony needs you."

"So does my dad."

"No, Selena. He doesn't."

"That's not fair! You don't get to decide something like that—"

"Yes, Selena, I do. The *Hydra* is on lockdown. I've cut us off from Stephen's Point. While they're down there looting and rioting, we're up here preparing to try and save them. And the only way we can do that is to reach Earth and hope like hell that they're willing and able to help us. Because if they're not, the colony will starve to death in a little less than three-hundred cycles."

Selena's mouth opened. "Three-hundred? I thought we had years' worth of supplies?"

"Not with the rioting. Either we make this work, or we all die. That's the truth, Selena. The only thing you can really do to help your father is to wake the *Chimera* and try to save the colony."

"But—"

"Wait. I want you to see something before you make up your mind."

A wallscreen powered to life. Selena gasped.

Her father's face filled the screen. The right side was swollen and purple, the left concave, his skull compacted, left eye a slit in puffy red skin. His torso had grown so thin he looked no thicker than her.

"Dad!" she called, before realizing it was a vid, not a live feed. When he spoke, his voice came out in a gurgle as if liquid half-filled his throat.

"Hey, sweet pea. They tell me you're getting yourself into all kinds of trouble up—"

Had the video stalled? No. Liam was struggling for air. His chest heaved and he let out a staccato cough before continuing.

"—trouble up there. They asked me to record this for you." He stopped again, his fully open eye roaming aimlessly as he took several raspy breaths. "I'm getting good care. And as you can see, my flying days are over, but they tell me that soon I'll be able to piss without help. So at least I've got that to look forward to."

Selena couldn't help but smile through the mist clouding her vision. Even banged to hell, Liam was cracking jokes.

"Look, kid, I'm not good at this sort of thing. Never liked goodbyes, or even hellos for that matter—"

While he caught his breath, Selena held hers. What did he mean by goodbyes? Supported by a bedframe, IVs running into his arms … surely he wasn't going to die? Was he? A flash of heat surged to her face as she shoved the chair back and stood, staring at the screen, shocked by the intensity of the anger swelling inside her. Anger directed at Liam. At her father. The man she'd done nothing but try to return to since the wreck.

"They want you to help them. Help them with the *Chimera*. As you can see, I've got about as many pipes and tubes connected to me as she does." Liam coughed, sucked for air, feebly wiping at his eyes with the back of his hand.

"I think you should do it. You've got something they need, and that don't surprise me none. You always were special. Always."

Selena couldn't concentrate on his words. The image of her father melted as her tears turned the world to a hazy blur.

"Remember, kiddo. I never did enough to show you. But I love you. Do your best. And make me proud."

The screen went dark.

"Your father is alive because I'm using my authority through The Mandate to supply premier-level care. He will continue to receive all the medical attention he needs, at any expense. But you've got to start helping us. No more faking stupidity. No more lying. No more reckless behavior. I expect you to give me everything you have. Everything. And if you do that, I will vacate the charges against you, and I will do everything in my power to make your father well. That's the deal, and it's the only one on the table."

"What if I can't do it? What if she won't wake up?"

Moorland frowned. "Then it won't matter how well your father is three-hundred cycles from now."

Selena nodded and blew her nose into Moorland's handkerchief. Rubbing at her eyes, she removed the last hints of wetness. A great calm spread through her. A recognition of a truth too immense to be ignored. She'd spent her whole life trying to prove her worth to her father, that she was as tough as any rimmer, as capable as any pilot. That she could outwork anyone. That she mattered. She'd fought and scrapped and picked fights, argued and bargained and sometimes cheated. She wasn't going to apologize for any of it, but things could be different. Moorland was offering her a chance. A chance to matter. A chance to really save her father, along with everyone else in the colony.

Moorland studied her a moment. "We all need you, Selena."

Clear-eyed, Selena nodded her agreement, her sense of calm growing deeper by the moment. "I will wake the *Chimera*," Selena said, her voice firm with determination. "And after I do, we're going to Earth."

THE END

A NOTE FROM THE AUTHOR

Thank You.

Every author sends their work into the world with the hope: that someone will enjoy it. The same is true of this book, the first in the Universe Eventual series. Thank you for the dance, kind reader. Before you slip away into the night, I ask that you take the time to leave a review on Amazon or Goodreads. Three years of writing, revising, and editing went into creating this novel. It will only take you a few minutes to leave a review. Thank you in advance!

To leave a review on Goodreads:
http://bit.ly/Review_Chimera_Goodreads

To leave a review on Amazon:
http://bit.ly/Review_Chimera_Amazon

If you're hungry for more Universe Eventual, you can visit our webpage: www.uebooks.com or check us out on Facebook: www.facebook.com/universeeventual.

Book II, *Helios*, is scheduled for release in the summer of 2015 with Book III due by winter 2015.

AUTHOR BIOS

Who is N.J. Tanger? Three people. Nathan M. Beauchamp, Joshua Russell, and Rachael Tanger.

Writing a book as part of a team presents an obvious dilemma: Whose name will go on the front cover? The easy answer might seem to be "all of them." However, putting three names on a book cover is not only clunky to look at, but makes selling through retailers such as Amazon difficult. Using only one of our names seemed unfair. Instead, we created a new name, pulling first initials from Nathan and Josh and using Rachael's last name.

Josh and Nathan wrote *Chimera*. Rachael gave the book a thorough editing.

Nathan M. Beauchamp:
Nathan started writing stories at nine-years-old and never stopped. From his first grisly tales about carnivorous catfish, mole detectives, and cyborg housecats, his interests have always emphasized the strange. Nathan works in finance so that he can support his habit of putting words together in the hope that someone will read them. His hobbies include reading, photography, arguing for sport, and pondering the eventual heat death of the universe. He has published many short stories and holds an MFA in creative writing from Western State. He lives in Chicago with his wife and two young boys.

You can reach him via e-mail: Nathan@uebooks.com

Joshua Russell:
Joshua started making movies when he was eight years old,

an addiction he's never kicked. His lust for adventure and foolhardy risk have led him on and off of movie sets, through uncharted mountain ranges, to foreign worlds where people speak in strange tongues, and to the seminal co-creation of two human beings. For positive cash flow, Joshua teaches screenwriting at DePaul University. For negative cash flow, he makes independent films, including the upcoming Absolution. The Universe Eventual book series is Joshua's first foray into fiction writing, and he's profoundly happy to be surrounded by writers who are smarter and even better looking than he is.

You can reach him via e-mail: Joshua@uebooks.com

Rachael Tanger:

Rachael has been writing stories since she first learned to hold a pencil. She grew up on a farm in the Midwest but has since lived in large cities, some internationally. She values experiences and is addicted to travel. She has worked in marketing in various capacities, most recently as a freelance consultant for small business. Rachael currently lives in Chicago with her husband and son. This is her first novel.

You can reach her via e-mail: Rachael@uebooks.com

ACKNOWLEDGMENTS

To our long-suffering spouses and children, our friends, and our extended families: words cannot express our gratitude for your love and support. Special thanks to Andrew Broderick, Rebekah Tribble, Natasha Field, Jønny Schult, and Sean Fath for serving as beta readers. You helped shape this story into something worth reading. Yong Yi Lee, our incredibly talented graphic artist, brought Universe Eventual to vivid life and bootstrapped our imaginations. Thanks to Michael Pugh for constant friendship and generous advice. Thanks to Perry Marshall for teaching us how to sell. Thanks to Laura Jennison, Patty Keyuranggul, Erica Henry, and Sarah Turek, faithful members of our writers' group. Your encouragement has meant so much.

Last, no work of fiction is born in a vacuum. Some of the ideas in this story bear similarities to great works of science fiction. Bits of Heinlein's *Starship Troopers*, Orson Scott Card's *Ender's Game*, Asimov's *I, Robot* and Ann McCaffrey's *The Ship Who Sang* have fueled the creation of this novel. To each of these authors and all other storytellers who have shaped our imaginations, we owe an unpayable debt.